DANCE
LIKE NO ONE'S
WATCHING

Other books by Vanessa Jones

Sing Like No One's Listening

THE SHOW MUST GO ON.

DANCE

LIKE NO ONE'S WATCHING

VANESSA JONES

MACMILLAN

First published 2021 by Macmillan Children's Books
an imprint of Pan Macmillan
The Smithson, 6 Briset Street, London EC1M 5NR
EU representative: Macmillan Publishers Ireland Limited,
Mallard Lodge, Lansdowne Village, Dublin 4
Associated companies throughout the world
www.panmacmillan.com

ISBN 978-1-5290-1314-6

1 3 5 7 9 8 6 4 2

A CIP catalogue record for this book is available from the British Library.

Printed and bound by CPI Group (UK) Ltd, Croydon CR0 4YY

For Esther

CHAPTER 1

If my life was a musical right now, it would be that scene at the beginning of *Grease* where Danny and Sandy are frolicking in the waves, chasing each other up and down the sand dunes, laughing and – let's not forget this – *kissing*.

So much kissing.

Fletch and I have been living our best teen-romance lives this summer. And now my head is resting on his lap as we lie on the hill overlooking Crystal Palace Park, the warmth of his thigh under my neck competing with the early evening September sun on my face.

'Should we think about going?' I ask, my eyes still half closed. We're moving all my stuff from my grandmother's house to Alec's flat today, but I wanted to bring Fletch here first, for one last moment of 'us'.

College starts again tomorrow. I'm *ridiculously* excited about going back to Duke's, but it's just been Fletch and me for the whole summer. Everything changes tomorrow: the bubble bursts. Last year, Jade Upton did everything in her power to keep us apart, and it nearly worked. What's to say something like that won't happen this year? The last six weeks have been so good; I don't want anything to change.

'No. Let's stay here forever,' he says.

I laugh. 'You and I both know if we keep Alec waiting that long, he'll be unbearable.' I sit up, shielding my eyes from the sun with my hand. 'At least we've had today. At least you didn't meet *her*.' My grandmother was only too glad to get rid of me when I moved into halls at Duke's Academy of Performing Arts last year. Now that I'm moving in with Alec, I'll never have to see her again.

Fletch props himself up on his elbows and takes off his sunglasses. 'You mean "Auntie"? She doesn't scare me.' My grandmother insists I call her Auntie because she says anything else is "ageing". It's ridiculous, but not worth arguing about.

'I know, but . . . it's been such an amazing summer. I don't want anything to spoil it.' The thought of only having a few precious hours of the holidays left makes my stomach flip over.

Life has been so good since the Summer Showcase. This could all slip through my fingers. What if I can't live up to people's expectations? The end of last year was kind of a big deal for me: after months of not being able to sing, of nearly getting kicked out of college, I finally managed it in spectacular fashion, onstage in the West End with a thousand people watching. Everyone's heard me now. As Kiki has been unhelpfully reminding me all summer, they'll be expecting things this year.

'You're right. It *was* amazing,' he says, reaching up to trace my jaw with his finger, sending feathers down my spine.

'You're not going to get me like that.'

'Wanna bet?'

He leans in and kisses me softly. My resolve disappears as we fall back down on to the grass together.

'Took your time, didn't you?' says Alec, helping me carry a box of sheet music up the stairs.

Alec's your basic pretty, white ballet boy – talented as hell, and knows it too: there's no better dancer at Duke's, nor one with a bigger ego. Or a bigger heart, as far as our friendship's concerned. God knows how I'd have got through last year without him. I glance down at him; his hair's been naturally highlighted from a month of 'summering' (his word) at his mum's chateau in Bordeaux, and his usually creamy skin is now a golden bronze.

'Sorry,' I say, panting slightly. 'Bumped into Auntie.'

Alec rests the box on the banister for a second. 'Whew. How did that go?'

'Oh, you know. As expected.'

'Did you ask her about the video?'

My eyes flicker to Fletch, who's coming up behind us. Thankfully, he doesn't seem to have heard Alec. 'Yeah,' I mutter, jogging Alec into action again with the box. 'I'll tell you about it later.' I'd like to keep the evening drama-free.

Alec seems to understand. 'Is this it?' he says as we reach the top of the stairs, nodding at the stuff we're lugging.

'Two more boxes.'

'Christ, Nettie,' says Alec. 'It's not a mansion, you know.'

It might as well be. After he begged her all year, Alec's mother finally relinquished her swanky London apartment to him. I have *majorly* lucked out. No flat hunting. No more going to my grandmother's house for the holidays. Don't get me wrong, it was fun living in halls with Alec, Kiki and Leon just down the corridor, but I'm really going to enjoy having a shower that's not glacial, and I *definitely* won't miss Jade Upton lording it over the common room like Regina George and generally making my life hell (if she even comes back to Duke's after the humiliation she suffered at the end of last year). Things are looking up.

'Most of it will go under my bed,' I assure him, as we take

the box through to the living room.

'And the rest?'

'I thought maybe it could go in that big cupboard in the hallway? Come on, you owe me.'

Alec cocks his head to one side. 'How, exactly?'

'It's basically down to me that you're even here.'

'All I did was tell Mum how your grandmother treats you—'

'About seventeen times a day for three months.'

'. . . and let her know that she'd be saving you from cruelty and starvation if she let us move into the flat – all of which is true.'

Fletch calls down the hall to us. 'Where shall I put these cases?'

'*Cases?*' Alec looks at me in exasperation. I give him my biggest Orphan Annie grin. 'Oh, for God's sake . . .' He rolls his eyes at me. 'Just put them in the cupboard in the hallway,' he shouts back to Fletch.

Together we heave the last of the stuff up the three flights of stairs. It's a beautiful old building with a wrought-iron Grade II-listed lift, which would be wonderful if it actually worked. Fletch downs a pint of water, kisses me on the cheek, grabs his keys and stretches.

'Off so soon, my love?' says Alec.

'I'm double-parked,' says Fletch. 'Luca'll kill me if I get a ticket.' Fletch usually goes everywhere by motorbike, but today he's borrowed his best friend's car to help me move. 'Be right back.'

'Don't be long,' I say.

'I won't,' Fletch says, kissing me on each eye, working his way down my nose until our mouths meet. God, he's lovely.

There's a deliberate-sounding clatter from the kitchen. We

both jump. Alec appears with a frying pan.

'Oops,' he says.

Grinning, Fletch takes the hint and leaves.

'Subtle,' I say, following Alec back into the kitchen. He points to the mounting pile of washing-up on the draining board.

'I'll wash – you can dry.' He puts some music on, starts doing a dance with the dishcloth (somehow it's sexy?) and throws me a tea towel. 'So first of all, why didn't you tell Fletch about seeing Auntie? He knows about the video, right?'

At the end of last year, I got a mystery envelope through my door at the halls. It contained a video on a memory stick of Mum dancing the part of Odette in *Swan Lake*, except that instead of being graceful and controlled, as you would expect of a prima ballerina, Mum crashes into another dancer before careering off the edge of the stage and falling into the pit. It's full-on drama – audience screaming, ambulance called, show stopped . . .

I've been watching it all summer. It's almost the only connection I have to her life before I came along. And it's throwing up more questions than answers.

There's so much she didn't tell me: how she was best friends with Miss Duke, how she had this amazing career as a dancer, how she left the business abruptly and never went back, and now this video . . . I feel like I barely knew her. How can you live with someone for nearly eighteen years and not know anything about their life?

'I couldn't,' I say. 'Fletch does know about the video – I showed him the day I got it. But at Auntie's, I made him wait in the car. It just seemed like too much of a downer to end our holiday together on. Anyway, you were right. I learned nothing from her.'

'What did she actually say?' asks Alec.

'That it was none of my business. I didn't even collect Mum's stuff – Auntie threw me out before I could get to the loft and grab it.' I'm kind of kicking myself now that I didn't take Fletch in with me – I could've done with the support, and I'd have the boxes too.

'Ah, sorry. I didn't want to be right about that,' says Alec. 'Well, she's not the only person who knew her. There's Michael, Miss Duke – even Miss Moore, if you're feeling brave.' I can't help a little laugh at that last one. One of the ballet teachers at Duke's, Miss Moore, hated Mum and goes out of her way to let me know it. Not exactly my go-to for a cosy chat.

I take a deep breath through my nose. 'I really don't know what to do. Should I even be looking? What if I find out something horrible about her?'

Alec adjusts my fringe and gives me a cute grin. 'Whatever you need to do, I'm here for you,' he says. 'We can search newspaper archives, look at old ballet programmes, talk to people . . . We'll get you the truth. And equally, if you just want to forget all about it and drown your sorrows, I'll be there with a bottle of JD and my Mariah playlist.'

I smile. He just . . . *gets* me. Maybe the drowning-my-sorrows option would be better. It hurts to admit it, but this might just be one area of Mum's life that she didn't want me involved in, and who says I automatically get a free pass to it because I'm her daughter? She must have had her reasons for not telling me. Maybe I have to accept that.

But Mum was all I had. Although I try not to think about it too much, it's horrible feeling like I didn't really know her. Knowing literally nothing about my dad was just something I accepted growing up. I had Mum, and we were everything to each other. But the more I dig, the more I'm realizing there was this secret part of her that I never got to know, and it hurts in a way I've never felt about my dad. I'm like a jigsaw with so many missing pieces that you can't make out what the picture is. Last year was traumatic, dealing with grief and losing my voice. I grew up so much, and now that I'm finding out who *I* am, I need those missing pieces.

But they're all hidden with Mum.

'Thanks,' I say. 'But I'm going to do it – I'll ask them all. Starting with Michael.'

'Whatever you need.' Alec smiles. He reaches for the other end of the tea towel in my hand and uses it to pull me in to a dip. 'So, tell me all about your gorgeous summer with Sir Hunkalot.'

'It was . . . amazing.' I giggle as he spins me out, Fred n' Ginger style, and grab a smooth pearl-grey plate from him that's obviously too posh to bung in the dishwasher. 'We went for walks, lay out in the fields watching the shooting stars, spent days at the beach . . . It was just amazing. His mum and dad were so welcoming, too.'

'And . . . ?' he says.

'And what?'

'Oh, come on. You two have so much drama, I thought there was bound to be something.'

He has a point. The journey to Fletch and me getting together wasn't exactly easy. 'No drama. No fights in the pouring rain. No college mean girls locking me in a cage trying to steal my voice.' I laugh. 'I guess we were too busy having a good time.' My brain floats back to big skies and the feel of his hand in mine.

'Ugh,' he says, rolling his eyes. 'Spare me the gory details.

Actually, what am I talking about? I want to know *all* the details.'

I hesitate. Don't get me wrong, I could shout from our rooftop to the whole of Covent Garden about how my spine tingles when my new boyfriend touches me, how I crave being near him on a minute-by-minute basis. But if I tell Alec, then it doesn't belong to Fletch and me any more. I want to keep it for us.

Fletch sounds the door buzzer, sparing me.

I go to my room to unpack all my stuff while Fletch and Alec go to grab a takeaway. I check my phone to see that Kiki and Leon have been messaging the group chat.

17:53
Kiki:
So?? How did it go at Auntie's?

Leon:
Did you ask her about the video?

I reply quickly.

18:24
Yeah. No joy ☹
She wouldn't tell me
But I know she knows
So frustrating

Leon:

Kiki:
We're here for you.

Thanks, friends ❤
CANNOT WAIT TO SEE YOU TOMO!!!

Leon:
xxx

Kiki:
😍😘😁

I smile. No matter what this year throws at me, with friends as brilliant as these, I can handle anything.

We spend the rest of the evening chilling with a movie. Alec refuses my suggestion of *La La Land* on the basis that he can't stand Ryan Gosling's hands; in the end we settle on *Whiplash*. As the movie starts and I sink into the soft velvet sofa, I look from Fletch to Alec and it suddenly feels like I've lived here a lot longer than a few hours. Like it's *home* – something I haven't felt since before Mum died. Things are going to be good this year.

The credits roll. I thought *we* had it bad in class, but this drumming teacher makes Millicent Moore look like Mary Poppins, and last year she pulled my hair out and burned me with a cigarette in front of my entire ballet class, just to prove a point.

'Wow,' says Fletch. 'That was intense.'

'I mean, I'm with the teacher,' muses Alec. 'Like, you want to be the best, kid? You need to take what's thrown at you.'

'That's because you're institutionalized,' I tell him. 'You're so used to the daily abuse we get at Duke's that you think it's acceptable.'

'Duke's is the best college in the country; it must be doing something right.'

'Yeah, creating a whole new generation of bullies.'

Alec turns to Fletch for support, but Fletch's phone buzzes insistently. As he checks it his smile drops a little. 'Excuse me just one sec . . . *Hello?*' He goes out of the room, closing the door behind him.

Alec shrugs. 'You need to toughen up, Nettie.'

He's right – I do need to toughen up. And I plan to. But surely that means taking less crap from people, not more? His logic's completely warped.

Fletch is on the phone for half an hour. By the time he's finished, Alec is getting ready to go to bed.

'All OK?' says Alec, unusually seriously, as if Fletch just had some bad news. Although, from the look on his face, he might have.

'Yep,' Fletch replies shortly.

Alec looks like he's about to say something else but changes his mind. Instead, he kisses me on the head and breezes out the door.

'Sorry about that,' says Fletch, coming to sit next to me on the sofa. 'It was Michael St. John. He wanted to run through a few things about this year with me.'

'Oh,' I say. Michael's the head of Music at Duke's. He's this amazingly talented and all-round nice guy, and everyone basically adores him. I don't know why he couldn't have done that with Fletch tomorrow, though. Bit odd phoning him at night. 'Everything all right?'

'Yeah, course. Why?'

'I don't know. You look stressed.'

'I'm fine.'

I'm about to snuggle in, when something catches Fletch's attention from the other side of the room. He goes over to the huge windows overlooking Pineapple Dance Studios, where a late-night rehearsal is in full swing.

'What do you think they're rehearsing for?' he says, watching them intently.

I follow him over to the windows to see. The dancers are working on a high-octane fusion of jazz and salsa. 'Isn't that the tall dancer from *Strictly*?' I say, squinting. 'It looks like one of those spin-off tours.'

'You really have to give up your whole life for it, don't you?' he says, watching the lead couple do an impressive death drop. 'Those dancers – it's nearly eleven, and they're still going. And then they'll be on tour soon. Some of them are probably married or with people; others might even have kids. How do they cope with being away?'

'They just manage, I guess,' I say. It's not something I've thought about before. 'Get back when they can. You go where the work is, don't you?'

He doesn't answer for a while, and although his gaze is still directed into the studio, his eyes aren't following the dancers around any more.

'Do you think we'd be OK?' he asks, turning to me. 'If one of us got a tour, I mean.'

Why is he even thinking that? Of *course* we'd be OK. Anyway, that's ages away. He's still got another year at college. And we've only been a couple for, like, three months. Why's

11

he planning our break-up already?

'Yes, I do,' I reply cheerfully, but then I notice his knitted brow. 'Hey, what's brought this on?'

He cups my face in his hands. 'I have to tell you something, Nettie.'

Oh my God.

Why does he look so nervous?

He's going to finish with me.

He's worried about committing so close to graduating.

Urgh, why do I do that? It could be *anything*.

'OK,' I say, all calmity-calm, even though my heart is beating so loudly it could provide the bassline for *Six*. 'What is it?'

'I just –' He pushes my hair back gently, his eyes searching mine. He doesn't say anything for a moment. 'I . . . love you, Nettie.'

It's such a shock that I don't reply. Not that my response needs any thought – I've loved this boy almost a year to the day, ever since we sat opposite each other in the library and wrote the end of a song together and talked about losing people we loved. I knew it, even then. So I should be saying it back, right now. Shouldn't I?

But it just . . . I don't know – it *felt* like he was going to say something else.

'I love you too,' I say finally.

Fletch breathes out and lets his hands drop. This is not how I imagined this scene would play out. Granted, in my head it's probably a little *too* Kelli O'Hara and Matthew Morrison singing 'Say It Somehow' from *The Light in the Piazza*, and I totally get that basing your expectations of romance on musical theatre love songs is only going to end in plummeting disappointment, but seeing Fletch get so stressed working up to saying it and then almost dying of relief afterwards is not where I thought this moment would go. I watch him, waiting for him to speak.

'I wanted to say it weeks ago, but I was scared,' he says finally, like he knows he owes me an explanation. He takes my hands; I notice his are shaking. 'After Danny died, I shut myself off completely. Friends, my family, everyone. The idea of losing you – it terrifies me, Nettie. I'm not saying that to force you to be with me forever or anything – I'm just trying to explain how I feel.'

He doesn't need to. Since I lost Mum, there's been a low-level anxiety prickling at my stomach, pretty much constantly. Mum was the only person I'd ever loved – and she left me. I'm completely powerless to stop that happening again with Fletch, or anyone I get close to. It doesn't surprise me that Fletch feels the same after losing his brother so young.

'You know what?' I say. 'Mum would tell me the grief makes our bond stronger. She'd say we just need to be honest with each other.'

'Danny would tell me to stop being a knob,' says Fletch, and we both laugh. 'I don't know what I was waiting for. I bloody love you, Nettie.'

He tilts my head up, and our lips meet. It's the perfect *I love you* kiss – soft and tender and *definitely* worthy of a musical – *at first*. His arms are around my waist, my hands are clasped behind his neck, the dancers across the road are doing a sultry Argentine tango . . . But after a few seconds, something changes. I can't put my finger on it, except that it feels like Fletch has pulled back. Not physically, but emotionally. Is it even possible to be able to *feel* that in a kiss? I know Cher thinks so, but, like, in real life?

13

Something in the kiss, in the space around us, in the way Fletch is holding me feels like we've gone back in time to that moment before he said he loved me. When I thought he was going to say something else.

When there was doubt in his eyes.

CHAPTER 2

It can't possibly have been two months since I saw Duke's. As we round the corner of Frith Street, I catch my first glimpse of the pale brick building, occupying its space on the corner of Soho Square with self-assurance, calm amidst the camp chaos of Soho. I take a breath. This time last year I had no idea what I was in for. I was a fragment of myself – grieving, voiceless, powerless . . . But today? I mean, don't get me wrong – Duke's is still a daunting place, full of talent and competition and people ready to trample over you in the race to the top, and obviously it would be silly if I *wasn't* shitting myself. But this year there's an inner confidence driving me that I didn't have before.

As we reach the front doors, Alec nips between Fletch and me and throws his arms out to halt us.

'What is it?' I say, almost tripping over.

'I just thought we should take a moment to mark the occasion. You know, enjoying our last seconds of freedom. The moment we walk through those doors, we've signed away our souls to Cecile Duke.'

'*In indelible ink,*' I say, echoing something Alec said last year. I turn to Fletch, but he's staring intently at the plaque on the wall. 'But this year's going to be great. I can feel it.'

'Shall we?' says Alec, offering Fletch and me his elbows to link.

I take his arm and give it a squeeze. Fletch does the same. We take a breath together.

'Let's.'

The noise hits us as soon as we're through the doors. Everywhere I turn there are students singing, laughing and generally throwing themselves around as much as is humanly possible on a Monday morning in mid-September. It's like they're making up for eight weeks without an audience. Just as we start making our way through the crowd, Michael pulls Fletch over from a studio doorway. He shoots me an apologetic smile and disappears.

New people perch on benches against the walls, glancing around nervously. I remember that feeling. I try to smile kindly at a girl in the corner jiggling her legs. She looks away immediately.

'Friendly bunch, these first-years,' says Alec loudly, striding through the front doors and directly through the crowd.

'Alec, don't; she's probably just nervous,' I say.

Alec pulls a snarky face and disappears into the office.

Kiki's stretching against a wall, shouldering her leg way above her head. Her tight auburn curls are shining like polished copper under the rays of sun thrown down from the skylights far above. Her brown skin is dotted with freckles from the summer, and her hazel eyes are glowing. She's your basic goddess.

'Kiki, your body is literally superhuman,' I say. 'And oh my God, your hair.'

She laughs and brings her leg down effortlessly. 'Thanks. Had some highlights. Do you like it?'

'You're the most beautiful person I've ever seen,' I say, hugging her tightly.

'Thank you,' she says with a small smile. 'I feel good.'

I gawk at her. This is a huge change for Kiki; she's *never* acknowledged a compliment about her appearance before. For as long as I've known her, she's viewed her body as something to be improved on, rather like a pirouette or an *arabesque*. The toxicity of this place hasn't helped, insidiously feeding her insecurities, reaffirming what she already thinks. A lot of the girls at Duke's are the same. Miss Duke doesn't care, as long as they look thin. It's institutional, organized body-shaming, cooked up by the teachers, and fed to the students with a side of fear.

But something's shifted since the summer for her. 'You seem . . . different,' I say appreciatively.

'You know what?' she says. 'I *feel* different. Over the summer I had time to really think. I read a lot. Worked out how *I* feel about my body, not just what the industry tells me to feel, or what the teachers say. And you know what I realized? I like myself. Screw them.'

Hearing her say those words makes me so happy. I don't think my smile can get any wider. Kiki raises her eyebrows at me, laughing.

'What?' I say.

'I know that look. You want to hug me again.'

'*So* much.'

'Go on, then,' she says, holding her arms out.

I squeeze her even tighter than before, until I hear her giggle.

'You got strong over the summer,' she jokes, as I release her.

I flex my non-existent muscles. 'Been working out.'

Chortling, she swipes some papers from her bag. 'Here, I got your timetable from the office,' she says. 'Let's see if we've got anything together.' She rips open the envelope and starts scanning through my lessons. 'Let's see . . . Omigod. We've got Dan Coombes for commercial this year. This is amazing!'

'Who's Dan Coombes?' Luca, Fletch's best friend, comes

out of Studio One. He smiles at Kiki's excitement while Kiki continues eulogizing.

'Only the best choreographer in the world, like, ever. He's done all the big pop stars. Kylie, Little Mix . . . I think he even danced with Beyoncé in his early days. We've got him today!'

Alec comes out of the office corridor with an envelope in his hand. 'Kiki!' He throws his arms around her and spins her around. 'Where have you been all my life? I missed you.'

'Hey, Alec,' she says, smiling. 'I missed you, too. Good summer?'

'Babe, dull as dishwater.'

'Doesn't your mum live in a French castle?' she says suspiciously.

'A *very boring* French castle,' he replies, smirking while Kiki hits him on the arm. 'Ouch! Hey, Luca. Omigod, the next time Nettie asks if Fletch can borrow your car, please say no. I can't move in the flat now for vintage clothes.'

'Sorry, Alec.' Luca laughs, as Alec kisses his cheek. Luca hugs Kiki and me. It's good to see him – being with all my friends again has made me realize how long the summer was. Time just flew at Fletch's. 'My taxi services are actually in demand at the moment, so don't worry. Nettie has been one of many happy clients – Seb too, sadly.'

'Where's Seb going?' I say.

'Oh! I thought you knew,' says Luca. 'He's gone to New York on a placement at Juilliard.'

'Wow!'

'Right? Miss Duke's trialling a new scheme with several creative institutes. A few of the third-years are on it. I thought Fletch would have mentioned—'

'Holy shit,' says Alec, cutting him off loudly. 'Leon's decided to stop being frigid.'

'*Alec.*' I give him an exasperated glare. Kiki, Luca and I follow his gaze to the other end of the foyer where Leon's deep in conversation with a tall third-year called Taro. Leon's as smart as ever, his neatly shaved hairline framing his handsome face perfectly. He's wearing a pair of new tortoiseshell glasses that, even from this distance, I can see complement his pretty eyes and smooth dark brown skin, and an outfit that is essentially jeans and a jumper, except that Leon manages to wear it like he's just jumped out of *Esquire*. He and Taro are standing very close to each other, and Leon's laughing at something Taro's saying.

'You need to lay off Leon this year,' Kiki warns Alec.

'Whatever are you talking about?' he says. 'I'm just surprised that Leon's managed to pull quicker than I have, that's all. I'd better watch out; he'll be after my dance crown next.'

'This is *exactly* what I'm talking about,' she says quietly. 'You're always putting him down, Alec. It's exhausting for him.'

'A week sharing a flat with Leon and suddenly you're the expert? I've known him for ten years!' Alec snaps back.

Oh, no. Two minutes into the term, and those two are already at each other's necks. But Kiki's right. Alec is especially competitive when it comes to Leon.

'Just give him a break,' I say to him.

There's clearly a retort on Alec's tongue, but at that moment Miss Paige, the college head secretary, emerges from the office and starts shepherding students into the studio theatre for registration. By the time I look back at Alec, he's staring at something or someone through the door to the office corridor, his face flushed. I crane my neck to see what he's looking at, but

19

I'm too short to glean anything over the sea of heads.

I nudge him. 'OK?'

'Yeah . . .' Alec, transfixed, darts in the opposite direction to everyone else towards the office.

That was weird.

Kiki, Luca and I follow the herd of dancers, actors, musicians and stage management students all fighting to get into the studio. I look around for Fletch, but he's not here. He and Michael must have a lot to talk about.

The doors are flung open and Miss Duke stalks into the room, her dainty dancer's feet covering huge distances with every stride, her sleek dark bob a little greyer at the front than it was last year, or maybe I've forgotten. Her skin is just as pale, and she's wearing her trademark red lipstick. She's dressed in an elegant black suit, red heels, a cream blouse and a huge scarlet necklace. I can see everyone working hard to show their 'best selves' as she passes them: smiling gratefully, lowering their eyes, sucking their stomachs in, hiding their phones. This is a woman who demands perfection. Or at least, her version of perfection.

As she passes me, I don't lower my eyes. Instead, I stare back at her defiantly. Last year I was a wreck, a ball of anxiety with no voice, on the brink of a breakdown and nearly thrown out of college. But this year's different. I've found my voice and I'm not afraid to use it. I have questions about Mum, and Miss Duke has answers. She seems to recognize this, almost like she's been waiting for it, and returns my gaze with a look of grim understanding. Then she moves on, and it's like it never happened.

She comes to a halt at the front of the studio, the students gathered like an audience in the round. It's so quiet I reckon no one's breathing. I'd bet an afternoon in a recording studio with Lin-Manuel Miranda on it.

'Good morning, students,' she says, without smiling. 'I am pleased to welcome the new first-years to Duke's Academy of Performing Arts, the finest establishment dedicated to the arts in the country; the world, even. I need not remind you of the extreme privilege you carry just walking through these doors each day. Never take it for granted.' She pauses for long enough for every student to know that she imagines them utterly ungrateful and unworthy of their place. I see a few wannabe showgirls who've been teetering on their tiptoes sink back to their real height of five foot six and a half, deflated.

'Second- and third-years will tell you there is no coasting at Duke's. Anyone not giving their absolute maximum will be removed with immediate effect –' I imagine a giant hook bursting through the roof of college and winching out unsuspecting students; wouldn't put it past her – 'and I will see to it *personally* that you never work in this business again.

'May I remind you all that you are to be impeccably presented at all times. This includes how you look after your body, notably during holidays and at weekends. The industry does not welcome *fatties*.'

Oh my *God*.

Looking around the room at everyone's faces, they're as shocked as mine. I can't *believe* what I just heard. I mean, the body-shaming is big at Duke's – everyone knows that. But it's always been in an underhand way, often dressed up as health concerns – which isn't any better but at least seemed to recognize that it was wrong and shouldn't be said out loud. Now Miss Duke's put it centre stage, stuck a spotlight on it and given us

21

carte blanche to go along with it. She scans the room like Javert on the lookout for Jean Valjean, her eyes narrowing as they look for a victim. No one breathes; they know what's coming. She's looking for someone to humiliate.

I can't do it. I can't let it happen. I think about my first day last year, when I watched a grown woman crucify a third-year in front of the entire college and I didn't say anything.

A second later I'm leaping out of the crowd and yelling, 'Miss Duke!'

Admittedly it's not the most well-thought-out move. Horrified, I realize I have *no idea* what to say next. Miss Duke turns, ambushed, her stunned face a mirror of my own at what I've just done. Kiki's staring at me, astonished. A couple of people actually *gasp*, like they can't believe it. I can't, either.

'Yes, Nettie?' says Miss Duke, her composure recovered almost immediately, every trace of surprise erased from her face.

What do I say?

The studio door opens behind Miss Duke.

'*Well, Nettie?*' she says, ice in her voice. 'I'm sure we're all on tenterhooks to find out what you've got to say.'

'It's just that, er. . .' Blood floods to my head. Shit, what was I thinking? But everyone's staring at me now, and I have to say *something*.

I've really messed this up.

'Yes?' says Miss Duke.

I look over her shoulder.

'There – there's a film crew behind you, Miss Duke.'

The crowd turns its head to the doorway, where a film crew has mercifully appeared. Miss Duke, clearly ruffled, looks round and, seeing a camera pointing directly at her, smiles instantly with no lingering trace of the previous two minutes on her face. She's pure warmth.

'Ah, Sam – do come in,' she says. 'You beat me to it. Students, I would like you to meet the newest members of Duke's Academy of Performing Arts, from Three Ring TV. They are going to be making a high-profile docu-movie series about our fantastic learning establishment throughout the academic year here at the college. They may ask some of you if you would mind being interviewed. I am confident you will oblige; obviously you will be keen to show Duke's in its best light. Sam, the director –' a freckly white woman with blonde hair and piercing blue eyes in her mid-thirties raises her hand in greeting and flashes a blindingly white smile – 'has asked that unless you are being interviewed, you ignore the cameras so they can get a true representation of what it means to be a student here. So, on that note, I will now pretend you're not here.'

She twinkles at them; they grin back. The man with the camera puts his thumb up. There's a new energy in the room, an invisible pulse of excitement. Still cringing at what I just did, I watch Miss Duke closely as she continues her speech.

'As I was saying, the industry is not an easy place.' I notice she doesn't repeat the end of her previous sentence. She's clearly *not* pretending they're not here. 'What I want to see from *all* of you –' she smiles indulgently at us with a pride I've never seen before, like Mama Rose watching Dainty June perform – 'whichever course you're following, is raw ambition, drive and vitality. Ready for a new challenge. And always remembering your privilege.'

She sweeps out of the room, past the TV crew, who follow her for a parting shot as she clips up the huge spiral staircase in the centre of the foyer.

23

CHAPTER 3

After a gruelling morning, Kiki and I finally catch up with each other on the way down to commercial.

Kiki slips her arm in mine playfully. 'Should we talk about what you nearly did this morning?'

I feel myself blush. 'I just couldn't stand by and watch her humiliate anyone,' I say. 'I knew I'd made a mistake almost as soon as I'd jumped out. But by then, it was kind of too late.'

'I mean, I could sort of see you regretted it the second you'd done it,' she says, smiling. 'I get that Miss Duke's just doing her job in the way she thinks best, preparing us all for a fucked-up industry. But she needs to chill. Honestly, there was a tiny part of me that wanted to see what you'd come up with. Your face, Nettie.' She puts her hand over her eyes, laughing.

'Omigod, I'm so grateful that film crew walked in.'

'Yeah, what about that?' she says. 'Kind of a curveball, right?'

We're interrupted by Fletch walking up the corridor. 'Nettie!' he says urgently.

'Is everything—?' I say, but the rest of my sentence is muffled as he pulls me in for a tight hug.

Kiki laughs and rolls her eyes. 'You guys are a lot for a Monday morning,' she says.

She's right, though – it *is* a lot, even for us. I only saw him a few hours ago.

I notice a little crease in Fletch's forehead. 'You weirded

24

out by the cameras too?' I joke.

'Yeah. Actually, Nettie—'

'Well, I'd forgotten just how good it is in this place.' Alec barges in between us and slings his arms around our shoulders. 'I've had a *superb* morning.'

Fletch goes to talk again but is once more interrupted by Alec.

'And *God*,' he says, dropping his arms from around our necks, 'as if Miss Duke could be any more obvious. We get it – you lost the backing for the new building from Jade Upton's dad after publicly shaming his daughter, and now you've had to find funding elsewhere.' He sighs dramatically. 'I imagine it'll be incredibly tedious for us, but ultimately quite lucrative. I was thinking about bringing out a clothing line, and this will be the perfect way to showcase it.'

'Of course you were,' says Kiki, laughing. 'Sounds interesting, though. Like, the exposure could be good.'

It sounds like one more thing to worry about, if you ask me. But I know I had loads of exposure last year with the clip that went viral, and I don't want to sound ungrateful, so I just smile and nod.

'Are you walking over to the music hall, Fletch?' says Alec. 'I've got voice class.'

'Aren't you in commercial with us?' I say. 'And also, where did you disappear off to this morning?'

Alec shakes his head dismissively like he doesn't know what I'm talking about. 'No idea. And no, I'm not in commercial. Coming, Fletch?'

'I'm due there in a bit,' says Fletch. 'But I was just asking Nettie something.'

'Nettie can't be late for class,' says Alec pointedly. 'Don't want her all stressed and rushing. Especially as apparently *they're filming it*.' He gives Fletch a significant look that I don't understand.

'Just ask me quickly,' I say. 'What was it?'

Fletch glances at Alec. 'It was only that I . . . Mum asked me to ask you if you'd like to come to ours for Christmas. That's all.'

Christmas with my boyfriend? A whole month together? What could be better than that?

'I'd love to!' I say, kissing him. I don't know what was so urgent – it's only September. But it's lovely, all the same. Last year I was in my room alone after a huge fight with my grandmother, crying to Mum's favourite songs. Not a time I'd like to repeat. My brain races ahead, already planning romantic walks around Christmas markets and trips to windy beaches with a flask of hot chocolate. Dancing to cheesy songs, kissing under the mistletoe—

Alec taps Fletch's shoulder impatiently. 'Let's go.'

Fletch kisses me again and before I can say a word, Alec drags him off.

'Well, that was weird,' says Kiki. 'Why was he so desperate to drag Fletch off?'

I was wondering that myself. They've both been a little strange since yesterday. 'I don't know,' I say, watching as they disappear together down the corridor.

Kiki opens the studio door and walks straight to the mirror. I'm less than keen on joining the front row for my first commercial class this year, but the alternative is to move nearer to Jade Upton, who's glowering at me from two rows back with her equally unpleasant BFF, Natasha Bridgewell. I'm not intimidated, if that's what they're hoping, but it makes me angry that they've got the nerve to be so openly hostile after everything that happened at the Summer Showcase. Last year was rough

26

enough, dealing with losing Mum and not being able to sing, and Jade and Natasha went out of their way to make things worse for me. I was hoping they'd let me move on this year, but it appears not. Jade mutters something to Natasha, who snarls nastily at me.

'You OK?' says Kiki, watching Jade and Natasha.

'Yeah. Not gonna let them wrong-foot me on my first day.' Seeing her concerned face, I add, 'Honestly. It's cool.'

Leon spots us and comes over.

'Hi, love,' I say, hugging him.

'Hey. Have you seen Alec? I haven't seen him since boys ballet this morning,' says Leon. 'Or rather, I haven't seen him since *after* ballet when he came out of the shower completely naked and dripping wet, loudly barked at one of the poor frightened first-years to pass him his towel, and proceeded to bollock them all for taking up space on *his personal bench*.'

'Starting as he means to go on,' says Kiki.

Leon nods grimly. 'I left as quickly as I could. But he should be here.'

'He said he had voice class over at the music hall.'

Leon frowns. 'He was excited about having Dan Coombes this morning.'

'Yeah, until he knew you'd be here,' says Kiki.

Leon looks at her in surprise.

'Well, it's obvious, isn't it? Alec hates that you're better at commercial than him, Leon. He can't hack it. I bet a hundred quid he's changed his timetable.'

Leon opens his mouth to reply but is cut off by Dan Coombes breezing in. Short and blond, with fair skin, rosy cheeks, and arms of superhero proportions, he strips off his hoody to reveal a

27

tight racer-back vest and a set of rippling shoulder muscles.

'Er, Leon?' whispers Kiki. 'Your mouth's still open.'

Leon reassembles his face while Dan calls the register. When he gets to Alec's name, someone calls out, 'Timetable change,' and Kiki gives us a significant look.

After a couple of minutes my arms are on fire, my fringe is soaking wet and my usually pale cheeks are the same colour as the inside of a watermelon. I glance at the others, but Kiki looks like she could easily go another half an hour of this arm exercise, and Leon's barely broken into a sweat. I need to up my dance game this year, or I'll get left behind.

Halfway through the session, by which time even the windows look like they're sweating, the door opens and a TV crew enters, led by the blonde woman called Sam who saved me from Miss Duke this morning.

'Ignore us, please,' says Sam. She adjusts her headset. 'Pretend we're not here.'

That's all very well, but every time I turn there's a great furry boom in my face or a camera down by my knees. Seriously, what's with that? They'd be better off focusing on someone who's actually good, like Kiki or Leon, or (much as it pains me to say it) Natasha Bridgewell. I do my best not to embarrass myself, pushing through the pain, kicking higher, working my torso harder, but after a summer of doing nothing more exerting than wandering down to Fletch's kitchen to help myself to cheese, it's painful.

At the end of the class, Sam approaches me. 'The camera likes you,' she says, smiling. She's wearing a khaki shirt and trousers that combined with her blue eyes and freckles gives off strong *Calamity Jane* vibes.

'Oh,' I say, not quite sure how to respond. 'Thanks?'

'It's Nettie, right?' she says, offering me her hand and shaking mine firmly. 'Sam. We'd really like to feature you on our documentary.'

'Um, that's great, but there are much better dancers in here than me.' I point to Kiki. 'That girl over there, for example. She's amazing.'

'But you're a brilliant singer,' Sam shoots back.

Who's she been talking to? 'I—'

'People know you, Nettie,' she continues over me. 'They're going to want your story. How you overcame your vocal problems and became the college's rising star. What's next for the girl who broke the internet?'

I'm never going to escape last year's Summer Showcase, where Jade and Natasha forced me to sing into a microphone under the stage they'd had secretly rigged up while Jade mimed onstage and took all the glory. It backfired when Alec, Leon, Kiki and Fletch exposed them, and I ended up singing in public for the first time in the entire year I'd been at Duke's. I was hoping to put it behind me this year, but somehow it ended up on YouTube and has had millions of views. I've even been recognized a few times around Soho, which is kind of weird.

Now I know why Mum always pretended to be someone else when she got approached. Even around college, the other students seem to just, well . . . *look* at me more. I know for someone who's hoping for a career in theatre it's strange not to want to be the centre of attention all the time, but I also know from being the daughter of Anastasia Delaney-Richardson that attention's not always a good thing.

'I'm not sure I—'

'It'd be great exposure. A good opportunity to showcase your talent.'

'Um, well, can I think about it?' I say.

'Sure.' She brushes a sandy lock of hair out of her eyes. 'But you should know that Miss Duke's already okayed it. In fact, she suggested the idea. Let me know, yeah?'

Well, *whip-crack-away*. She's been here two minutes and already knows how to play the game. How can I refuse Miss Duke?

The skirmish won, Sam grins and leaves. As she passes the studio window, I see her stop to talk to Jade, who's been waiting to ambush her.

'You're going to do it, right?' says Kiki, watching Jade shake her enormous red mane at Sam like Galinda teaching Elphaba how to toss her hair.

'I don't know – should I?'

'Er, *yes*,' says Kiki. 'This could make you, Nettie. I'd kill for that kind of exposure. Think what it would do for your Instagram.'

'I don't think Instagram's going to help me get a job in theatre.' Especially as mine's private.

'Babe, like it or not, it's all about social media these days. You remember Lauren Rose?'

How could I forget her? She was the girl Miss Duke *completely annihilated* on the first day in front of everyone, just for not being perfectly groomed. (I never saw her after that in anything less than a full face and killer heels.) 'Er, yeah,' I say.

'Well, she told me she went for an advert casting to be, like, "friend at the cinema". And they asked her how many followers she had! For an *advert*. Can you believe it? That's what we're up against. And that's why you need to do whatever this Sam tells you.'

'But she's only singled me out because of last year,' I say. 'Not because of my talent.'

'So? You *know* you're talented. Wouldn't it be good for the world to know that you're not just the little girl who needed saving? All anyone thinks they know about you is that you let two girls kidnap you and force you to sing in a cage until your friends rescued you.'

'They were blackmailing me,' I say. 'And it wasn't a cage; it was a vocal booth.'

'Babe, *I* know that. *You* know that. But *they* do not. My point is, there's so much more to you than what people have seen. You can make this work for you, Nettie. Get the exposure on your own terms.' She calls over to Leon, who's stretching out his quads at the barre. 'Leon! Back me up here. Shouldn't Nettie do the documentary?'

Leon releases his leg with a loud exhale of breath. 'Maybe. A great blow for artistic integrity, though, the day Instagram is more of a consideration than talent.' He watches Sam leaving with Jade, then walks over to the door and holds it open.

'So you think I *shouldn't* do it?' I say, as we walk out into the corridor.

'I think you'll be in the documentary whether you like it or not,' he replies, following us through the door. 'We've already had to sign the consent forms. You might as well use it to your advantage.'

'Would *you* do it, though?'

'Ah,' he says. 'Well, that's a bit different. I'm not sure exposure's what I want, right now.'

Kiki looks somewhere between astonished and disgusted. 'But of *course* you want it.'

31

Leon checks there's no one around. 'I'm only out at college,' he says. 'And even then, I'm fairly private. What if the interview makes some reference to my sexuality and my father sees it? Or if something comes out on social media? It only takes one comment . . .'

'OK, fair,' concedes Kiki. 'You have reason to be cautious. But, Nettie, it's different for you. This Sam is handing it to you on a plate. Babe, if you pass up this opportunity, I swear I will die just so that I can haunt you for the rest of your life.'

That word again. *Opportunity*. There's no doubt that in this business it has a lot to do with success. But when I started at Duke's, I was determined not to let my mother's name give me any sort of advantage. Isn't this the same?

At what point does taking an opportunity become an abuse of privilege?

CHAPTER 4

'Oh, Nettie, it's fine. It's not like I've got my cock out.'

Alec's appeared in a monochrome sequinned dress that he found in a vintage store. It's a little tight, to say the least. Fletch and Luca are having a party at their place to mark our first fortnight back at Duke's. They've chosen *Sparkle and Shine* as the theme in Seb's honour now that he's away in New York.

'I'm just not sure it . . . *fits* you?' I say, circling my finger to indicate he should turn slowly.

He obliges, whipping his head round at the last minute like a six-year-old learning to spot. 'Bodycon, babe. And there's not exactly bags of room in yours. Although hot pink sequins are undeniably a winning look for you.'

'Maybe you should take a backup, in case it splits.'

'If it splits, more of me to look at, which is a big yay for everyone. Anyway, I've decided I'm not messing around this year; I'm going for it. *In every aspect of my life.* No backups, no consolation prizes. Second place is for losers. I'm going to look the best, *be* the best, win the Duke's Awards . . .'

'They're not until May!'

'The point is, when they come, I'll be ready for them. I want the world to see I'm a winner, that I've made something of my life.'

I'm not sure how any of this relates to a black-and-white sequinned dress, but the look on Alec's face tells me that he means it. I guess I've felt the same in a smaller way – coming back for second year means a fresh start, a chance to make my mark, to show people I've found my voice – it's natural to have renewed ambition. But there's a vehemence behind Alec's words that's slightly alarming. I know better than to question him when he's in one of these moods, but I've a feeling this won't be the last I hear of it.

'OK,' I say. 'But don't blame me if you end up in a pair of Fletch's old jeans.'

The door's open when we arrive, sounds of music and chatter wafting down the otherwise quiet street. Fletch and Luca are in the crowded kitchen, dutifully putting all the bottles in a corner and trying to tip a huge sack of ice into a bucket without knocking into anyone.

'Hey, you,' I say to Fletch.

Unfortunately, they both turn around. Luca, realizing I'm not talking to him, gives me a good-natured casual wave before going back to the bottles. Fletch squeezes through to meet me while I try to rub out the giant sign on my forehead that says *awkward*. The last time I came to a party here, I got completely wasted and ended up snogging Luca in a game of spin the bottle (before Fletch and I were together, to clarify). We're just friends, and it's all cool now, so I don't know why I'm making it weird.

'You just get more beautiful every time I see you,' says Fletch. 'How is that possible?' He lifts me up and kisses me, and all the awkwardness melts away. It's like nothing else exists for that second except the softness of his lips against mine.

'What's with the blue?' I say, when he puts me back down. He's not wearing anything shiny but seems to have painted

34

a superhero mask over his eyes.

'Michael Stipe,' he says. 'R.E.M.?' Seeing my blank look, he adds, ' "Shiny Happy People"?'

'Oh, right – that's a song, isn't it?' I mean, if it's not in a musical, don't expect me to know it.

'It's a good job I love you.'

Luca comes over. 'Anyone need a drink? Because I'm all over it.' He hands me a vodka and Coke.

'Thanks, Luca.'

Alec, who's been opening a bottle of expensive gin he's brought with him, reaches for some tonic. 'So, how are my boys doing without Seb?' he says to Fletch and Luca. 'Any news?'

'Nope,' says Fletch.

Alec gives him a significant look. 'Or *news in general*. I thought there might b—'

'*No news*,' says Luca, glancing at Fletch as if there definitely *is* news.

'Ooh, Luca, are you sitting on something exciting?' I say.

'Yeah, Luca – if you've got an announcement, *now* would be the time to make it,' says Alec. His eyes flicker back to Fletch, who's watching Luca anxiously.

Luca looks from me to Fletch to Alec. 'No – I . . .' Muttering something about ice, he retreats to the back door.

'Does he actually have an announcement?' I say, half joking, but then I catch another glance between Alec and Fletch. 'What's going on?'

Fletch shrugs. 'Don't know. Drinks?'

'Don't mind if I do – but I'll come with you. God knows you need help pouring a decent shot.' Alec ushers Fletch away. 'Whatever it is, I'm sure he'll tell us when the time is right,' he adds over his shoulder.

Shrugging, I leave them to carry on sorting drinks and go to find the others. Kiki's in the living room, trying to get Leon to dance, only he doesn't seem massively up for it.

'Nettie, will you have a word?' Kiki drops Leon's hands, turning to me in frustration.

'It's *early*, Kiki,' says Leon in protest.

'Isn't the kitchen the dance room usually?' I say.

'I can't get in there; it's too crowded,' she says. She's wearing jeans that she's cleverly customized with shiny fabric paint and a black wet-look crop top. Her hair's covered in little green gems to match her emerald-glitter-painted eyes. 'Ooh, nice dress.'

'Thanks,' I say. 'Charity shop special. You look *gorgeous*, Kiki.'

She smiles. 'Thank you. Fuck Miss Duke; I'm lovely.'

I know she believes it, too. Confidence is literally radiating off of her. It's such a dramatic change from how she was last year, and I know she must have worked really hard over the summer to get here. I'm so happy she's seeing herself the way she really is. She's amazing.

Kiki nudges Leon. 'Taro's just walked in.'

We both follow her gaze, to where Taro Mitsuhashi is leaning against the doorframe, every bit the college hunk with his sweeping dark fringe and cheeky smile.

Leon raises his eyebrows. 'So?'

'So? You like him, don't you?'

'If you mean, have I had one brief conversation in the foyer with him while you lot pointed and stared, then yes.'

'Taro's a really great dancer, for an MT boy,' she says. I love how Kiki always measures people's attractiveness in terms of how good a dancer they are.

36

'Mmm,' says Leon non-committally, but I notice he's still watching Taro, who has spotted us and is making his way over.

'What about you?' I say to Kiki while Leon fiddles with his shirt. 'Anyone here you like? What about that girl from your contemporary class? Over there. Petra, is it?'

'She's going out with Sabrina Pinkett from the stage management course.'

'Well, plenty of other girls here.'

'These things are going to be awful to get out,' Kiki says absently, fluffing up her hair at the back to separate a couple of entangled gems. 'Oh, you know what? I'm too busy for a relationship anyway. Got to focus on my training. Hey, Taro. We were just saying how great Leon looks, weren't we, Nettie?' she says enthusiastically.

I suppress an amused eye-roll as she waggles Leon's rhinestone belt at Taro – the only nod to *Sparkle and Shine* on his whole outfit – which he immediately snatches back, managing impressively to combine smiling at Taro with a warning look at her.

Taro grins and pushes his dark fringe out of his eyes. 'You're a proper sort, Leon.'

Leon laughs just a little too enthusiastically. Kiki elbows me. Not that she needs to. The room temperature just rose by about six degrees.

'Nettie, weren't you about to show me that thing you've got in Fletch's room?' says Kiki.

'What?'

'You know, the Thing?'

'*Oh*, the Thing. Yes.'

'Come on, then.' She giggles, dragging me away.

Shrugging apologetically at Leon, I follow her out to the

hallway. Looking back, I can see Taro laughing while Leon rubs his chin, bemused.

'Subtle,' I say.

'He needs a bit of a gentle nudge sometimes,' says Kiki cheerfully.

We head for the kitchen, where Fletch and Luca have sorted the ice and are now drinking in the corner together, but someone from contemporary waylays us in the hallway and initiates an enthusiastic conversation about the new teacher.

A while later, Alec squeezes past us. Peering into the living room, he freezes for a second, then doubles back on himself.

'You all right, Alec?' says Kiki.

'Yeah . . . just, uh, looking for . . .' He barely makes eye contact, dashing back through to the kitchen without finishing his sentence.

'Who?' Kiki calls after him, but he's gone.

'What's up with him?' I say.

'I think he just saw Leon and Taro,' says Kiki quietly. She nods towards the living-room door at Leon and Taro. They're standing close, talking into each other's mouths and giggling. We watch as they go for what is Definitely Not Their First Kiss of the Evening.

'But they're so good together . . .' I say. Leon hasn't looked this happy for ages. It's lovely to see. Why wouldn't Alec want that for his friend? Unless . . . 'Wait – you mean *Alec likes Taro*?'

'Nah – I just think he can't bear the fact that Leon's hooked up with someone and he hasn't. He's jealous.'

'I never got that vibe last year.'

Kiki looks like she's deciding whether to tell me something. 'Leon said everything was only fine between them last year

38

because Alec was always on top and he never challenged him.'

'He told you that?'

'Yes. He said he's not going to live in Alec's shadow any more. But Alec hates Leon's attention not being completely on him. And since we've been back . . . I don't know. Alec seems . . . different. More intense, right? He'll be annoyed about Taro, for sure. You'll see.'

Kiki generally has a pretty cynical view of Alec, and I understand Leon wanting to assert himself in their relationship, but this seems extreme. Like, yes, Alec can be competitive, but I'm sure he'd be happy for his friend. He probably didn't even notice them.

'Anyway,' says Kiki. 'Big changes for Leon this year.'

'What changes?'

'He made me promise I wouldn't tell anyone. But you'll know, soon enough. And you're gonna love it.'

Around 2 a.m., I'm sitting on the sofa with Kiki and Leon. I'm drunk and sleepy, my hair is plastered to my head from all the dancing, and I've left a trail of sequins everywhere I've been, like I'm in some sort of *Kinky Boots* version of Hansel and Gretel.

'So, *Taro* . . .' says Kiki.

Leon laughs. 'He's cute.'

'He defo seems into you,' she says. 'You guys are going to be such a hot college couple. A definite rival for *Netch*.' She pokes me in the ribs; I swing for her playfully.

'Whoa, hang on a minute,' says Leon. 'We kissed at a party. I don't think we should get the "cute couple" bunting out quite yet.'

'Sorry, I'm just excited.' Kiki grins sheepishly. 'Speaking of

39

Netch – actually – where's Fletch? I haven't seen him all night.'

'I don't know,' I say, suddenly realizing how little I've seen him. 'He was helping Luca for a bit and talking to the muso lot . . . I should probably find him.'

I heave myself off the sofa, head to Fletch's room and knock. 'Yeah?' he says.

When I venture in, I find him sitting on the edge of his bed, swirling whisky round in his mug. He's washed his superhero mask off and there's an open backpack at the foot of the bed.

'I haven't seen you all night,' I say, going over to him. 'Are you OK?'

He doesn't answer me.

'Going somewhere?' I joke, pointing at the backpack.

'I need to tell you something,' he says, standing up abruptly and swaying a little. He's had a lot to drink.

'Um, OK.' A pang of adrenaline hits my stomach. I *knew* there had been something on his mind. I just thought it was third year. Not *us.*

'I got a writing placement,' he says. 'It's an apprenticeship at Chichester's New Works programme. Assisting Oliver and West.'

'*The* Oliver and West?' I say. 'Oh my God, that's amazing!' I'm so proud – he deserves this. But why the build-up?

I go to hug him, but he pulls away.

'It starts on Monday, Nettie,' he says. 'The placement's for six months.'

'*This* Monday? That's a bit short notice, isn't it?' How can they only just be telling him? Have they been waiting for some last-minute funding to offer an intern programme? And who decided Fletch should get it, just like that? These things take months normally.

40

He swallows and takes a breath in. 'I got the offer at the beginning of July.'

July? What?

'Hang on,' I say, confused. 'That was over two months ago.'

'I know. I'm sorry.'

'Why did you wait until now to mention it?'

'I just never found the right time,' he says quietly.

Something inside me explodes.

'How could you have kept that from me?' My voice is shaking with rage. 'Did you think I was going to kick off? Like I'd be so concerned about missing you that I wouldn't be happy for you?'

'No!' he says. 'It's just that everything happened so quickly at the end of last year – suddenly we were together, and then there was that amazing summer . . . I just didn't want to ruin it.'

'So you thought you'd just lie to me?'

'No! I knew very little about it – they'd sent me no details, so it kind of didn't feel real? I just . . . put it out of my mind.' He's speaking more clearly now; the adrenaline must've sobered him up. 'Nettie, I was going to tell you the night before we came back to college. Michael called me with some information about where I'd be staying and I suddenly realized how real it was, how soon. But I just . . . couldn't. Then we came back to Duke's and I told myself I'd tell you, but there never seemed to be the right moment.'

I feel sick. He thinks I'm fragile, that I won't be able to handle long distance, that I'll be pining without him at Duke's. Is that how he sees me? As some whingey, clingy girlfriend who won't let him out of her sight?

'Who else knows?'

He doesn't answer.

'*Who else knows?*'

'Just Luca. And I think I may have told Alec.'

This is ridiculous. 'You "think"?' I say.

'OK, I did tell him,' he says. 'Look, it's coming out all wrong. I just didn't want to hurt you.'

Of *course* Alec was in on it. It seems obvious, now that I think about it.

Everyone thinks they need to wrap me up in cotton wool. What was it Kiki said, about needing to show everyone that I don't need my friends to rescue me? Am I that pathetic? I can just imagine the conversation Fletch and Alec had as they chose to lie to me: *Better not tell Nettie anything bad, she lost her mum, you know, she's a complete emotional fuck-up, what would she have done without us last year?* If Alec knew, why didn't he insist Fletch tell me? I thought our friendship was stronger than that.

Oh my God. That must have been why he's been so weird with Fletch lately.

Something else occurs to me.

'Wait a minute,' I say. 'The day before we went back to Duke's, when you told me you loved me . . . That wasn't what you were going to say, was it?'

He drops his head. 'OK, no. Nettie, I'm sorry.'

'So you used *I love you* to get out of telling me you got a placement?' My ears are pounding now. How could he do that? How could he take something so intimate and meaningful and use it like that, as a substitute for the truth? 'That was a lie?'

'Nettie, I meant it!' he says, looking up at me again, the start of tears in his eyes. He reaches for my hand, but I pull away, stung.

'I don't know how you expect me to believe you. After lying to me all summer.'

42

'Look, I should have told you –' he sighs heavily – 'but please don't think I don't love you. You're everything, Nettie. I fucked up.'

'Yeah, you did,' I say angrily. 'What makes it worse is that I don't even get to be excited and happy for you. This is *huge*, Fletch. *Oliver and West*. It doesn't get much better than that. But all I can think about is the fact that you didn't feel you could share it with me.'

I throw myself down on the bed with my back to him and turn off the light. After a minute, Fletch lies down too, but he doesn't put his arms around me like he usually does.

As I lie there in the dark, my temper subsides but the anger doesn't. I feel betrayed. Fletch must think I'm so delicate to have kept it from me for all that time. Chichester's not even that far, is it – like maybe a couple of hours by train?

I can't even trust that he meant it when he said I love you. Maybe he did, but I'll never know for sure now. He's ruined it, and we can't just cross it out like a discarded line in a script, stick a yellow page in, and write another version.

It's tarnished forever, and neither of us can change that.

CHAPTER 5

At 5.30, I'm wide awake, the shadow of last night still hanging over me. Fletch has rolled over to face the other way and is lying on the edge of the bed. How can someone be literal inches from you but feel so far away?

I can't quite compute what happened last night. Sleep's meant to give you clarity, isn't it? Mum always used to say that things never seemed as bad in the morning, but this feels every bit as hideous as it did three hours ago.

I get up quietly and go into the living room to find Luca, still dressed in his outfit from last night, half watching a documentary about Jonathan Larson on his laptop while he clears up the remains of the party.

'Haven't you been to sleep yet?' I say, rubbing my eyes.

He points to a red wine stain he's in the middle of scrubbing. 'I wanted to get this mess cleared up. The other hardcore dregs of the muso lot left an hour ago – think they went for breakfast – and I didn't think Fletch would need the hassle today, what with . . .' His voice trails off.

'It's OK. He told me.'

Luca stands up. 'I'm sorry I couldn't say anything,' he says. 'It wasn't my thing to tell.'

'I know,' I say. 'I just don't understand why *he* didn't tell me.'

'A conversation we had many times,' replies Luca, getting back down on to his hands and knees to work on the blotch.

'Could you pass me the salt, please? If it helps, I honestly think he was coming from a good place.'

'Protecting his fragile girlfriend?' I say, watching him rubbing salt into the stain, almost like it was my feelings.

He sits up. 'Nettie, he doesn't think that. No one does. The things you've dealt with – losing your mum, then last year at Duke's? As Seb would say, *You're tough as nails – I'm talking Lizzo's acrylics, babe.*' We both laugh a little. 'No, I think *he's* the one he was trying to protect. Fletch doesn't deal with stuff so well. He's completely cut up about leaving you. I've never seen him like this.'

I hadn't thought about it that way. Grief does weird things to you – I should know that. Leaving Luca in the living room, I grab a brush and start sweeping the kitchen. As I go back and forth across the floor, I think about what Luca said, and the anger I was holding on to starts to fall away. Fletch fucked up, but it did come from a good place. This could be the last day I see him for a while, and we're not going to leave things like this.

At around half past nine, when Luca finally takes himself to bed, I go back into Fletch's room expecting to find him asleep, but when I push the door open I'm shocked to find him sitting on the bed almost exactly as I found him last night, except that this time the sun's streaming in and his bags are all packed up and ready to go. If last night seemed like a horrible dream, today is a harsh dose of reality.

'Hey,' says Fletch.

'Hey.'

'I'm so sorry.' He stands up and comes over to me. 'I was a coward. I shouldn't have hidden it from you. It was just the thought of going away – I couldn't deal with it.'

'Did you think we couldn't figure out long distance?' I say. 'Fletch, we fell for each other through a studio wall. Music did that. Our love is literally made of songs – what's stronger than that? Two hours to Chichester is definitely not going to be a problem.'

He smiles. 'I know. But I'm not worried about my feelings fading, or that we'll grow apart. I just . . . don't know how I'm going to stand missing you. It was like, if I didn't say it out loud, I could pretend it wasn't happening.' He pulls on his hair, which is still a mess from sleeping on it but still manages to look sexy. 'I love you, Nettie. I meant it when I said it. I still mean it.'

Suddenly, everything else melts away.

'I love you, too.' I put my arms around his waist and lean my cheek on his chest. He holds my hair, kissing the top of my head over and over. I can feel an ache starting somewhere deep within my ribcage. Like I'm missing him before he's even gone.

'Let's just do this a bit at a time,' he says into my hair.

'Are you home this weekend?'

'I think so. Hopefully,' he adds, almost like a get-out clause. 'But if I'm not, we'll FaceTime, yeah?'

'Yeah,' I say.

'You'll get sick of my face in no time,' he says.

'I'm sick of it already. You should probably go.' We both laugh, but the joke doesn't make me feel better.

He picks up his things. I follow him out to the front door and into the street. He puts the bags into the panniers on his bike and secures the lids. Then he holds my hands, his keys jangling between our fingers.

'I'll call you when I get there.' He leans down and kisses me softly. I want to freeze this moment in time, when it's just me

46

and him and nothing else, and all I have to think about is his lips on mine and the tingle down my spine.

He drops a final kiss on my forehead and swings his leg over the bike.

I wave until he's out of sight, my smile feeling stuck on. Then the tears I've been holding back escape my eyes, and I let them roll down my face, listening to the sound of his bike engine fade until all I can hear is the wind in the trees and the leaves blowing about me.

Alec's cooking an omelette when I get home.

'Ah, Nettie, you're just in time,' he says, grabbing another plate from the cupboard. 'Great party last night.'

'I'm going to bed,' I say, and head back out to my room.

Alec, obviously noticing the chill in my voice, follows me into the hallway. 'He's gone, hasn't he?'

I don't have the energy to make him feel OK about this. I need to be alone, to process what's happened. Before he has a chance to say anything else, I go into my room and close the door behind me.

I know he won't be there yet, but a text is the closest I can get to Fletch right now. I guess I'm going to have to get used to that. Taking a deep, shuddery breath, I get my phone out of my pocket.

09:55

I miss you x

He probably won't see it for at least another hour. I lean against the door, and a desperate loneliness cascades over me. Fletch is gone, and usually Alec would be here, telling jokes to cheer me up, making me laugh, forcing me to watch Cynthia Rhodes videos with him. But I can't get past what he did. Closing my eyes, I sink down to the floor and put my head in my knees, wondering how everything could have changed so quickly.

CHAPTER 6

It's a good thing Duke's is always so intense: keeping busy is what I need right now. Every spare second, my mind wanders to the feeling of Fletch's arms around me, his hand in mine, and I find myself wondering why we wasted so much of our time together not kissing, and dreaming about the next time I'll feel his lips against mine.

I throw myself into college, going to extra classes, practising in empty studios at the end of the day, determined to make my mark, to show everyone that I'm not the same frightened girl I was last year. Alec and I haven't seen a lot of each other since the day after the party. I'm still angry with him for not telling me about Fletch's placement, mainly because he hasn't apologized, but I'm not shocked because apologizing would mean admitting he's wrong. The only thing that is surprising is that he's out of the flat before I am these days. And it's not all parties either – I saw him in the practice rooms the other day. There's this . . . intensity about him that wasn't there last year. I know we can't go on avoiding each other indefinitely, but at the moment I don't know how else to deal with it.

At college, even between classes there's more going on with Three Ring TV filming us at every opportunity. I avoid Sam as much as I can, slipping up the back staircase when I see she's in the foyer, pretending to be on my phone when I pass her in the corridor, and spending more time than I need to over in the music hall, the other Duke's building used mainly for music and drama, where the crew haven't been yet. I know she wants an answer from me about being featured in the programme; I just don't know if I have one yet. Kiki's the opposite: going to extra classes when she knows the cameras will be there, hanging around in the foyer when Sam's doing interviews, doing everything she can to get noticed. I'm pleased to see her going for it. Why can't I feel the same about myself?

After my entire lunchtime alone in the music hall changing room on Friday working through some vocal exercises that my singing teacher Steph set me before the holidays, I make my way upstairs for MT hoping to catch Michael before class. He's top of the list of people I can ask about Mum – not a difficult first choice, seeing as the rest of the list consists of Miss Duke and Millicent Moore, and I'm going to have to work up an obscene amount of courage to talk to either of those two.

But instead of Michael, I find Leon in the otherwise deserted studio, sitting in the corner, reading a book of vocal selections from *Taboo* like it's nothing.

I squidge up next to him on the bench. 'What are you doing here?'

'I've changed to the MT course,' he says casually.

'WHAT?' I shriek, hugging him. 'When did this happen? Why didn't you tell me?'

He smiles. 'It was all quite last minute. Since we've been back, I've been feeling I wanted to change courses. I decided to give myself a shot at it. Michael auditioned me on Wednesday.'

So *that's* what Kiki was talking about at the party when she said there were big changes coming for Leon.

'This is *huge*, Leon! What made you rethink?'

50

Leon looks around to make sure the room is empty. 'OK,' he says finally, giving me such a serious look that I'm actually nervous. 'You might as well know. But please promise me you won't say anything.'

'I promise.'

Leon takes a deep breath, like he's about to take a huge gamble. 'It's . . . Alec.'

'*Alec?*' Oh God, what's he done now?

'It's always been on my mind, whether I made the right choice auditioning for the dancers course,' he says. 'At school, Alec convinced me that it would be better for me –' the posh school they both went to had a vocational ballet school attached; Leon and Alec were both dance scholars – 'but I wonder now if I just did what was expected, or if I just did what Alec wanted me to do.'

'Why would Alec care what course you chose?'

Leon pauses. 'I . . . I can't help wondering if it's because he didn't want me to shine at something he knew he wasn't good at. I often performed in the school musical or sang solos in church. He knew I could sing.'

When I don't answer, he takes a breath and continues.

'I can't explain it, Nettie – except to say that I always feel kind of . . . eclipsed by him. At school, I had other things I was good at – being academic and sporty, which Alec wasn't . . . He didn't care because he had no interest in them. But last year at Duke's, I suddenly felt like I was living in his shadow, and I noticed that Alec liked it that way. And this year he's been even more competitive with me. Haven't you noticed? Like when he dropped out of commercial. He can't bear to be bettered at anything.'

I know Alec can be a little on the arrogant side, but it's always laced with humour, and underneath it all he's kind – really kind. It's hard to believe he'd be that calculating. Maybe he was just worried about getting left behind, or starting out alone when they'd always done everything together. But he does seem strangely agitated this year, like nothing's enough for him. Like he can't settle.

'We came to Duke's as a package,' continues Leon. Students are starting to drift in now, looking over with interest at the new recruit, and he lowers his voice to avoid being overheard. '*Alec and Leon*. But it's never *Leon and Alec*. I just know that all the time we're here, he's never going to stop chipping away at me, undermining my confidence. So, I decided it was time to show everyone I'm not just Alec's cute little sidekick.'

'I mean, you *are* cute.'

He gives a hollow laugh. 'Nettie, cute in this business gets you doing spring-ball-change at some shitty end-of-pier summer season, while Alec's preparing for his opening night at the Royal Opera House.'

I've never heard Leon talk like this before.

'So, I'm making a new start,' he continues. 'Showing everyone I have other talents. I just hope I can do that.'

'Leon, you *are* talented. If Michael likes you enough to admit you late on to the course, that's a pretty solid stamp of approval. Also, I've heard you in the shower. You *are* good.'

Leon smiles. 'Everyone's good in the shower. Even Kiki.'

We laugh. Kiki's not known for her vocals, by her own admission.

Michael St. John sweeps into the studio, a flurry of floral. 'Darlings,' he says to us all, flicking his mop of grey hair out of his eyes. 'I have exciting news. Due to the complex and mysterious schedules of Three Ring TV, and the fact that the first episode of the documentary – which I've been told is called *Triple Threat* (hopefully not the Lina Lamont kind) – will air in the spring, we have had to adapt some of our calendar year. Which means that not only is the Freshers' Ball now officially the Christmas Ball –' various exclamations of outrage ripple through the room – 'but the Easter Musical will now be a dragged-out process taking us up to the summer term, with evening rehearsals, starting in November. You should be aware that this year, *everything* will be filmed. I've been warned it really will slow down rehearsals. We'll be casting . . . Can I have a drumroll? Thanks, Dominic –' Dom, conveniently seated behind the drum kit, obliges – '*Chicago* – I know, how wonderful – next week. Obviously I expect all of you to audition.'

'I love that show,' breathes Leon.

'Me too,' I whisper. But inside I feel heavy. *Chicago*'s so dance-y. I'll never make it through the audition. I'll be like that girl in the yellow leotard in *A Chorus Line* who the director shouts '*Don't dance!*' at in front of everyone.

'Today I want to pair you up,' continues Michael. 'Boy-girl would make sense, for vocal range, but it's not essential. Someone hand out these dots for me – thanks, Lily. I'm looking for connection, above all else.'

Leon looks at me. 'So, would you . . . ?'

'Er, definitely.'

He reaches for my hand. 'The nerves are killing me, and that's only because it's the first time I'll be singing in front of people here. I don't know how you got through last year, with everything you were dealing with.'

53

I don't, either. A whole year without a voice. But since the Summer Showcase, when I 'accidentally' sang in front of eleven hundred people, I've been fine. The fear's gone.

We gather around the piano with everyone else as Michael note-bashes through 'Suddenly Seymour' from *Little Shop of Horrors*. Fletch was always Michael's go-to in the absence of an accompanist. My heart sinks as I wonder what he's doing right now. Making tea? Or helping Oliver and West work out a melody? A small pang of jealousy ripples through me. That used to be *us* writing songs together. I miss it. Then I feel Leon fidgeting next to me and remember where I am. I squeeze his hand.

As we sit down in our pairs, ready to get up and have a go, I whisper to Leon encouragingly, 'You know *Little Shop*, right? Audrey's damaged and into bad guys, and Seymour's desperately in love, but he's never believed he was good enough for her. Should be easy enough to play, do you think?'

Leon murmurs an indistinct, 'Uh-huh.'

The pairs take it in turns to perform. It's thrilling to see the different takes on the same song. But I can feel Leon getting more and more tense as the minutes go by.

'We're nearly out of time, but it's just Nettie to go – am I right?' says Michael St. John. 'With our new recruit, Leon Adigwe. Leon, welcome. I'm so happy you're here.' He smiles at Leon, who tries to give him a thankful grin, but with nerves it comes out as more of a grimace. Poor Leon, having to wait till last. Sometimes I feel like Michael is so theatrical that he can't help putting on a show out of everything, making the new person go last like the principal boy in a panto walk-down.

We walk up to the front. I take Leon's hands. 'Just do you.'

He nods and exhales. The intro starts and Leon takes a breath in to sing. Just then, there's a little creak from the corner behind me, as if someone's come in. Leon's eyes flicker over my shoulder and he looks back to me, panic all over his face. Has Miss Duke come over for a look? Or the TV crew? I pretend to adjust my stance, but really it's to take a tiny peek.

It's not Miss Duke, or Sam.

It's *Alec*.

For a second, I think he's come to support Leon. But then I see the look on his face and I'm convinced it's the same look he has when he's trying to psyche out his competition. Now that Leon's made me aware of Alec's behaviour towards him, it seems so obvious. Am I jumping to the worst conclusion because things are still frosty between us? Or is he trying to psyche Leon out? What's got into him this year? Half my brain silently wills Leon to know that he's talented and wonderful and that he's definitely got this, and the other half is screaming at Alec to get lost.

Leon takes a breath and sings the first few lines still looking at the door, and at first I think he's lost it. But then he tears his gaze away and pours everything into me.

It works. The rest of the class goes wild, clapping and cheering. I smile at him, enjoying the surprise on his face to know his first performance has been such a success.

'I think we can safely say you're where you belong, Leon,' says Michael. 'Wonderful, you two. What a connection. This is what I'm talking about when I say, "Find the truth of the song." It's in there, if you only look.'

I glance back at the doorway, where Alec's smiling at Leon, any signs of competitiveness wiped from his beaming face. As the class dissolves, he makes his way over to us, his sports bag slung over his shoulder, hair still damp from the shower. I can't help but feel suspicious after the way he looked before we started singing, but he seems friendly. I hover in the background, gathering my things with one eye on the pair of them, secretly ready to pounce if Alec so much as puts a toe out of line.

'Congratulations,' Alec says to Leon, putting his arm around Leon's shoulder and patting his back. 'You were made for that part.'

'Right. Underestimated and overlooked.'

'Babe, you know what I mean,' says Alec, smoothing the collar of Leon's shirt. 'I haven't heard you sing since our Year Eleven music gala – do you remember?'

Leon nods with a smile, his eyes down.

'So, this is it, then? Musical theatre for you now?'

'Yes,' Leon says definitively.

'I'm so proud of you. Come here, friend.' Alec pulls Leon in.

Leon, who's much shorter, doesn't quite get his face over Alec's shoulder. He turns it to the side, leans it on Alec's chest and closes his eyes. Maybe Alec did come just to cheer him on – I shouldn't have doubted him. That was a really nice gesture.

'You coming, Nettie?' says Leon.

The studio's empty apart from us and Michael. I promised myself I'd talk to him about Mum today. 'No, you go on ahead,' I say. I see Alec's disappointment as they head off together. Maybe I'm being too harsh on him about Fletch too – I know he wants to talk. And I will. But not now.

Michael's tidying up some sheet music. He looks up as I approach the piano. 'Nettie! Did you forget something?'

'Er, no, actually. I wanted to talk to you. About my mother.'

I'm sure Michael's jaw clenches, but it's gone in an instant, so

56

quickly that I'm not even convinced it was there to begin with. He smiles. 'Sure.'

'I just – someone sent me a video of Mum falling off the stage,' I say as quickly as possible, in case he stops me. 'I just wondered if you knew anything about that.'

'I'm sorry, Nettie. I don't.' His answer comes immediately, almost as if he was going to say that whatever I asked him.

'Oh. Yeah. I thought you probably wouldn't,' I say. 'It was a long shot. But I wondered what other shows she was in – what other ballets? It would be nice to know.'

'It was such a long time ago, Nettie,' he says, back to shuffling his papers now. 'I'd be hard pushed to remember.'

I don't relent. 'I don't know much about her life before I was born. What was she like?'

Michael's hands go still on his music. He exhales quietly through his nose. 'She was lovely, Nettie. A beautiful dancer, a beautiful soul.'

I hesitate before asking the question I need the answer to. 'Why did she stop dancing?'

Michael looks startled, like I've prompted a painful memory. His eyes look suddenly glassy. 'I'm so sorry, angel – it's complicated. Look, I've got to rush over to the other side for a class. I hope you can make peace with what you know about your mother from your lives together – something tells me that's what she'd want you to remember.' He picks up his briefcase and heads out, leaving me more confused than ever.

If I wasn't sure before, Michael's reaction confirms my suspicion: something happened to Mum, something that she was ashamed of. Something bad.

And now that I know that, I can't leave it alone, or make

peace with the little I knew, as Michael said. I have to find out what it was. Even if that means uncovering something painful about her. Even if it's not what I want to hear. Even if . . .

Even if it makes me hate her.

CHAPTER 7

13:10
Fletch:

Hey beautiful

Hey! How's Chich today?

Amazing. Still loving it. Oliver and West are the best. I'm learning so much.

It's been a long two weeks without you, though. How's college today?

Intense! Always a shock after the weekend, lol. I want to audition for Chicago but I'm scared

Of what?

THE DANCING 😱

I've been watching Ann Reinking videos. Trying to channel the spirit of Fosse.

You'll smash it. Keep focused.

Gotta go

I love you

By now, I've stopped looking out for Fletch in the corridors and instead spend my time dodging the seemingly endless cameras. When I head down to ballet with Kiki on Wednesday, dreading seeing the teacher, Millicent Moore (the last time we were in a room together, I told her to go fuck herself, which isn't ideal), Sam's there with two camera operators, a boom and several assistants. Just what I need.

'Nettie!' she says warmly, like we've known each other years and haven't just had one awkward meeting after a dance class. 'This is John – I think you met before – and Dave. And this is my assistant, Anand.' Anand, a shortish guy only just in his twenties with smooth brown skin and slightly scruffy black hair, smiles and gives me a friendly wave. Sam smiles. 'We're going to be getting some footage of this lesson. I had no idea you'd be in it!'

'Bullshit,' coughs Kiki into my ear.

Sam turns to her. 'Wait – you're the girl from the commercial class we visited, aren't you? The amazing dancer.'

'I mean, yeah.' It's a joke, but Kiki means it, which I love.

'We got some great footage of you, too. John, stick to this one. The camera loves her.'

Kiki grins at me excitedly. This is the moment she's been waiting for. We take our places at the barre, trying to ignore the enormous camera lens four feet away, but it's not easy when it's sitting there like a fully grown Audrey II from *Little Shop of Horrors* waiting to pounce.

'Are you going to ask Miss Moore about the video of your mum?' mutters Kiki while the crew deals with a lighting issue on the other side of the room. Kiki's got this theory that Millicent

60

Moore sent me the video, as a kind of revenge for last year, to prove that all the shit she was saying about Mum was true.

'Maybe,' I say grimly, glancing at the cameras. Miss Moore definitely knows stuff. I will ask her. Just not when my knees are shaking and there's a camera in my face documenting it.

Miss Moore sweeps in, her grey hair piled on top of her head in a severe bun, her pale face set in its usual frown from years of anger and dissatisfaction (think Mrs Danvers from *Rebecca* in a leotard, if that's not too much of a stretch). She takes a cursory glance around the class, clocks me and scowls, the lines in her forehead now deep with loathing.

'Antoinette, if you're going to have the audacity to turn up to my classes again, at least make yourself half presentable.' She stalks over to me, reaches behind my head and yanks out my tiny ponytail (my hair's too short for a bun), shoving the hairband into my hands.

Sam, seeing the drama with glee, signals to John to get rolling as quickly as possible. Amazing. Now Miss Moore gets to shame me on TV as well in front of the other students.

We manage to get as far as *allegro* before Miss Moore stalks over to me again. 'Your landing's awful. It needs to be smooth; through the feet, using the *plié*. No wonder your thighs are wobbling five minutes after your feet hit the ground – although that *could* be because *someone's been at the biscuit tin* over the summer?' She smiles, like that makes it OK, and a few girls titter.

Her comments don't hurt me, but Kiki, whose worst fear last year would be a teacher saying something like that to her, raises her eyebrows at me in code for, *You OK?*

I nod, but my blood's boiling. I know it's easy for me to resist the fat-shaming because I'm considered skinny, even in a place

61

like this – there's no doubt it makes life easier for me. But I'm not the only person in the class. I watch Kiki as she goes to pull up the top of her tights, like she used to when she was feeling insecure, but she stops herself and stands up a little straighter. It's the first time this year that I've seen her hard-won self-confidence waver, and seeing her like this makes me want to run over to Miss Moore and rip her hair out.

After the class, I approach Sam in the foyer. 'You're not going to use that, right?'

'Nettie, don't worry. This is all part of life at performing arts college – the tough love from the teachers, the grind – people love that stuff.'

'I'd just rather not be humiliated on TV,' I persist. 'Or have young people seeing someone getting fat-shamed and thinking it's OK.'

'Well, that's very responsible of you. But I think you're being a little over-sensitive.' She winks. 'You'll come out on top, don't worry.' With that, she turns and starts giving Anand some detailed instructions.

Frustrated, I go and join Kiki, who's already halfway up the stairs to the changing room.

'She's using it,' I say glumly.

'I don't think that's necessarily a bad thing,' muses Kiki.

'You're kidding, right?'

'Might it not be a good thing to show the world what goes on here? The body-shaming? The bullying?'

'Hmmn, maybe.' I look at the time. 'Gotta dash. I'm late.'

I leave Kiki behind, grab my sheet music and a sweatshirt from my locker, and head straight across the corridor to the little music room that belongs to Steph Andrews, my vocal coach. She's been away the first few weeks of term, and I've missed her. If it weren't for Steph, I don't think I'd have my voice back. She was brilliant last year, helping me through my vocal (and emotional) problems. Not only is she the kindest, most nurturing person you could ever meet, but full-on fierce, too – alongside her teaching, Steph's still a West End legend. Her voice is *a*-mazing.

I can hear someone playing a beautiful oboe solo next door, but the noise disappears as soon as I close the soundproofed door behind me, grateful that the cameras can't hear or see me in here.

'Hey, Nettie.' She's so tall and elegant, it always makes me feel like an actual four-year-old when I'm next to her. 'Good to see you. Sorry I haven't been here for a couple of weeks. I've been back and forth down to Chichester, at the Festival Theatre. How are you?'

'You were in Chichester?' I say, unable to hide my excitement. 'Fletch is there right now.'

She smiles. 'I saw him, actually. I was auditioning for *Better Spent*.'

The thought of Steph seeing him suddenly makes Fletch feel closer, like he's just around the corner, not miles away. I try not to think about how many times I scroll through our texts, remembering this summer. 'The new Oliver and West show?' I say. 'Did you get it?'

She puts a finger over her lips and gives me the tiniest of nods.

'That's amazing, Steph! Congratulations.'

'It's not common knowledge yet, so please don't share that information,' she says. 'But yes, I'm very excited. It does mean I'll be off quite a bit from February through to the summer, but I'll make sure you're still timetabled with me.'

'Thanks, Steph.'

'Anyway, enough about me. How's the voice?'

'It's fine – no problems.'

'That's great. So, we're on track.' Steph looks through the sheet music I've brought with me. 'What are you going to sing for your audition? You're going for *Chicago*, right?'

I pause. 'I guess.'

'I thought you'd be really excited,' says Steph. 'I had you down for a Roxie.'

'It's just . . .'

She raises her eyebrows. 'The dancing?'

I nod in response. 'There are loads of better dancers than me on the MT course. I don't stand a chance.'

Steph swivels on her piano stool to face me and crosses her legs. 'You're right, there *are* better dancers. But you can work on the steps. The thing you should concentrate on is what you can bring to the role that they can't. Play to your strengths.'

'I guess . . .'

'And anyway,' she continues, 'aren't you friends with three of the best dancers at Duke's? You've literally got free coaching on tap.'

'I hadn't thought of that!' I say.

'So, no more negativity,' she says briskly. 'You won't last long in showbiz with that attitude. Right, what have you chosen to sing?'

'Have you been able to see a bereavement counsellor over the summer?' says Steph as she tidies up the sheet music after our session. I told her I'd go and see someone at the end of last term. So far, I haven't. The holidays were too busy, and since

I've been back at Duke's, I haven't had time. To be honest, the idea isn't massively appealing. I'm not really up for talking about Mum's death with a complete stranger. I just want to talk to people who knew her. But they don't seem to want to talk to me.

'Not yet,' I say vaguely. 'But I will. Speaking of Mum, though, someone sent me an odd video at the end of last term. I wondered if you knew anything about it.'

I show her the clip on my phone. Steph watches, engrossed, as Mum careers straight into a young Millicent Moore, knocking her off pointe. Sadly, she's just as shocked as I was the first time I saw it; I can tell she doesn't know anything.

'Is that—?' Steph stops herself.

'Yup. Millicent Moore.'

'I know you two have had your problems, but maybe you should ask her.'

Not after today's encounter. 'I was hoping you might know something,' I say.

'Nettie, I'm sorry,' she says. 'I was only a kid when your mum was in her heyday. It wasn't really on my radar. I presume you've tried googling?'

'Yep. Nothing.'

'Well, that's odd in itself. But if you're reluctant to talk to Miss Moore, Miss Duke's your best bet.'

The thought of approaching Miss Duke for a cosy chat about the past sends an involuntary shiver up my spine. But Steph has a point – she probably does know why Mum left the business and what happened to make her so secretive about it. Maybe I'll just have to break out my playlist of empowering musical theatre (which is basically 'Seize the Day' from *Newsies*, 'Take Me or

Leave Me' from *Rent* and everything ever sung by Anika Noni Rose), put on my big-girl pants and ask her.

When I come out of my lesson, Luca's leaving the adjacent practice room.

'Oh! Hi, Luca,' I say. 'Was that you playing the oboe?'

'Yeah. Among other things,' he says. 'Michael's interviewing me for assistant MD on *Chicago* and I wanted to make sure I knew all the music parts. Hey – I was thinking about you this morning. It feels really strange in the flat without Fletch, and I can only imagine how you must be missing him. How are you holding up?'

'I'm OK,' I say. 'Actually . . .'

'What is it?'

Since Fletch left two and a half weeks ago, I've been trying to give it Cathy in 'A Summer in Ohio', being ridiculously upbeat whenever we message, telling funny stories about what's been happening at Duke's, saying that us being apart is going to make it *so* amazing when we finally get to see each other. And even when other people ask me how it's going, I reply with something like, 'Yeah, good, thanks,' because it's easier to do that than admit that I'm struggling. But the truth is, it's tough.

'I just miss him, Luca. Like, I sort of feel homesick, even though I haven't gone anywhere. That probably sounds silly.'

'No. It doesn't.' Luca smiles. 'I miss him too, and we're not even a couple. Well, maybe an *Odd Couple*, now that Seb's not around. But you know what I mean.'

I laugh. It's a relief to talk to someone who gets it. 'Yeah,' I say. 'I guess it's going to be weird for a while. I haven't told Fletch I feel like this – I didn't want him to worry.'

'I get it,' says Luca. 'Hey – you know where I am if you ever want to talk.'

I smile gratefully. 'Thanks.'

Fletch would be glad there's someone looking out for me. I just don't want him knowing I need that.

CHAPTER 8

'Hey.'

Fletch's smiling face on my phone is a welcome sight. He was supposed to come and spend a relaxed Sunday with me today, but when I spoke to him last night, he seemed so knackered that I told him to stay put and just chill. He sounded as relieved as I was secretly disappointed.

'Hey. How's the shed?'

He reverses the camera to his feet, which are up on a pouffe. He's staying in a summer house at the end of someone's garden. It's fine – he's got a bathroom and a small kitchen area, but it's still a wooden hut. 'Cosy. I'm going to bed soon, actually. Got auditions all day tomorrow.'

'That reminds me – Steph said she's doing the workshop with you!' I say.

He smiles. 'We're so excited. I'm sorry I couldn't say anything.'

It hadn't occurred to me that he might have told me. 'That's OK – it was her news, and anyway, I bet you're not allowed to say anything about anything at this stage.'

'Yeah. It's weird though – having stuff I can't share with you. I miss you.'

'I miss you, too.'

When I finally get off the phone, I come out of my bedroom to find Alec lingering in the hallway.

'Were you listening to me?' I say.

'I'm sorry,' he says. 'I couldn't help overhearing you telling Fletch that Steph was doing the show with him?'

Oh my God. He's unbelievable. 'Alec, that's private stuff. If I can't even have a conversation without you eavesdropping—'

'When he said he was sorry for not telling you, you told him it was OK because it was Steph's thing to tell,' he presses on. 'Nettie, that's exactly why I didn't tell you about Fletch leaving.'

That's not the same thing. At all. 'We're meant to be friends, Alec.'

'Nettie, it wasn't my place to tell you. I tried to get *him* to tell you; I really did.'

'Apart from on the first day when you *stopped* him from telling me.'

'That was right before you walked into a class where there was a camera crew waiting to ambush you! I overheard Sam talking about it and knew she'd be all over you. Nettie, I was trying to protect you.'

This conversation's way overdue, but now that it's here, I'm not holding back. 'Don't come at me with your morals now. You could have told me.'

He pushes his hair back off his forehead. 'OK. Yes. I could have told you. But what kind of a friend would that make me to Fletch?'

'*I'm* your friend, not Fletch. I don't need you running around trying to protect me from my boyfriend, Alec.'

'He's not just some guy that I've only met twice, Nettie. We do have a relationship.'

I pause. Shouldn't I be pleased that Fletch and Alec get along so well? Am I projecting Leon's version of Alec on to this situation, when in reality, what he did came from a good place – or is Alec just a shitty friend? Everything feels so tied up together, a big confusing knot of emotions and stories and versions of the truth, and it's all being made worse by the ache in my stomach whenever I think about Fletch and the stress of being followed by cameras everywhere I go. And *Mum* – sometimes I think I'm using this quest to know more about her as a way of distracting me from the grief. As soon as one worry leaves my brain, another one's right there ready to go, like a super-keen understudy. I need to step back and separate the strands.

'I just wish you hadn't got involved,' I say.

'Believe me, so do I.'

I get it. Alec was in a difficult situation. But he could have at least told me that I needed to talk to Fletch, and then I could have asked him myself. I'm fed up with everyone thinking I'm this delicate little flower who can't do anything for herself.

'I don't need protecting, Alec.'

'I know,' he says. 'I'm sorry. Please forgive me, Nettie.'

I can see in his eyes that he means it. He takes my hand, and I let him hold it. Friends make mistakes. If I can forgive Fletch, I should forgive Alec. I've got to let go of this now.

'I forgive you,' I say.

Alec kindly spends the rest of the day helping me with my Fosse technique. Kiki keeps sending me handy hints, too.

16:10
Kiki:

So remember what we said: tight centre, no turn out.

70

I'm so scared 😵

You can't afford to be scared. You have to be fabulous. We've been working on the style, and you know you'll kill the singing. Just be confident.

I really want this, Kiki.

I know. And you'll get it. Just hold your nerve.

Easier said than done.

When Alec and I arrive at Duke's on Monday morning, there's a commotion in the foyer. The TV crew seems to have tripled overnight, and now there are at least twelve people setting up monitors and cameras and sound equipment, and another four doing coffee orders and talking to each other on headsets.

'Why are they here?' I stand on tiptoes and crane my neck to see over the crowd. 'And what is this – a documentary or a movie?'

'They've come to film the *Chicago* auditions,' says Alec.

'Are you joking? I don't want the entire world seeing me audition.'

'Why not? I'd have thought it would be a good opportunity to showcase your talent.' He leads me around the edge of the crowd towards the back stairs. 'This is great for you. God knows *I* could do with a bit of exposure.'

'Er, I think you expose yourself enough.' I duck as he goes to swat me. 'Hey – why don't *you* audition? They need dancers.'

He gives me a wry look. 'Two words: *Singing round.*'

Alec actually has a lovely voice, but it's the one thing he's insecure about. Despite his go-for-it, no-second-prizes attitude, I think he's scared. 'It's a shame you won't audition, Alec, because you know full well you'd be beautiful in the show.'

'I can't risk it,' he says, glancing over at one of the cameras. 'I can't afford to show any weakness this year. Not in front of that lot.'

'What's got to you?' I ask him. 'Is it *Triple Threat*?'

He pulls a grim face. 'In a way. Anyway, enough about me. We need to focus on you.'

'I'm terrified, Alec.'

Alec snorts. 'Babe. Just remember everything we've worked on and go in there and knock 'em dead.' And with that, he plants a smacker on my forehead and disappears into his changing room.

Michael pops his head out of the studio theatre, revealing nothing but his huge mop of grey hair and a mint floral silk cravat. 'Darlings, can I have a bit of quiet, please? We're starting now. I'd like Jemima Green first, please . . . Where is she?' Jemima inches her hand up from almost underneath him. 'Ah, there you are. Sorry, darling – I'm used to playing big houses. Ooh, Nettie – I think the crew want to talk to you before you come in. She's here, people.' He waves to Sam, who is talking to a couple of men on the far side of the foyer.

Sam crosses over to me, smiling widely. 'Nettie, would you be able to spare a few minutes to chat?'

I hesitate. 'Are you going to film my audition?'

'Only if you're happy for us to.' Her blue eyes pierce mine. There's something quite compelling about her directness.

'I still haven't decided if I want to be a part of all this.'

72

'OK, how about this?' she says. 'If you don't get the part, we don't show it.'

'Well—'

'Amazing, thank you so much. I'm going to get Anand to set this up now.' She calls him over. 'Nettie's going to do a little pre-audition chat for us,' she says.

Anand smiles at me. The twinkle in his eyes seems genuine, like he's rooting for me, rather than the one in Sam's, which I'm half convinced is all for show. 'Great! Nettie, if you'd like to come over here with me.' He ushers me over to a chair with a massive camera pointing towards it and two oversized plants either side. 'The hot seat. Make yourself comfy. Sam's just going to ask you a few questions.'

'OK, Dave, can we get this rolling, please?' says Sam. Dave does a thumbs-up from behind his camera. 'Thanks. Nettie, which part are you going for today?'

'Um, Roxie, maybe?'

'And who are you hoping will be your leading man?'

'Er . . .' I look quickly at Anand, who shrugs apologetically.

'I mean, didn't you find him last year at Duke's?' continues Sam. 'During the Summer Showcase?'

'What?'

'Fletch. Isn't he your boyfriend now?'

'I—'

The cameras are still rolling, but Sam steps in the way of them. 'So, what we're going to do here, Nettie, is cut to the footage of last term when you sang in the booth for that other girl – Jade, was it? The clip that went viral – you know, when you reclaimed your rightful position centre stage.'

My *rightful position centre stage*?

She doesn't wait for a response. 'We most likely won't see your face at this point, but we'd love to have your comments to run as a VO on the VT.' Seeing my blank look, she adds, 'Voice-over on the videotape.'

'Oh.'

She steps to the side again. 'What was it like to finally find your voice? That life-changing moment.'

'Well, er, I'd found it difficult to sing ever since – since . . .'

'Yes, you lost your voice through grief. Can you tell us about that?'

I don't want to tell her about that. I don't really want to talk to her at all. But the camera's rolling, and she's smiling at me, and my friends think I'd be wasting an opportunity if I didn't. So I put my doubts aside, and try to answer professionally.

'It was hard, but, er . . . I had some brilliant friends supporting me through it,' I say, looking around for my water. My mouth has gone dry.

She nods. 'And what about the girl who betrayed you . . . Jade Upton? You must be arch-enemies now.'

'I . . .' This is bizarre. 'No, we're—'

'We spoke to Jade,' says Sam. 'She says you'll never forgive her for what she did. Do you have anything you want to say to her?'

What is she talking about? What has Jade been blabbing to her? This is spiralling out of control. 'No—'

'I guess you wouldn't want to talk to her, after everything she did.'

'No – I just meant, we haven't spoken about it.'

Sam finally seems to sense my unease. She comes out from behind the camera. 'Hey, Nettie, it's a lot to take in, I know.

Don't worry – it's all weighted in your favour. You'll come off as the good guy.'

'And Jade's OK with that?' I say sceptically.

'Totally on board,' says Sam, winking. She watches a third-year come out of their *Chicago* audition. 'Can we get Nettie in, please?' She waves to Anand, who's hovering politely behind her, over to the studio theatre. I follow him reluctantly.

'Ready, Nettie?' Michael's sitting at a large table with sheets of paper spread across it.

'I . . . Now?' I say, panicking. Since when did Sam control audition schedules?

Michael waits until Anand has left before he speaks. 'Nettie, are you OK? You look a little . . . flappy.' He pushes his chair back and comes to stand next to me, a concerned expression in his eyes.

'Sam wants to pit me against Jade,' I blurt out, watching the door to make sure I'm not overheard. 'Make a storyline out of something that's done and dusted. I don't know what to do.'

Michael sighs through his nose. 'I warned Miss Duke about this.' He pushes his thick mop of hair back. 'There's a fine line between keeping these people happy so we get the right kind of exposure, and not compromising our integrity.' He pats me on the arm and heads back over to his table.

My mind wanders to the interview I just gave while a procession of people and equipment comes through into the studio to set up. Is that what *I'm* doing – compromising my integrity? All that stuff about Fletch and Mum – that was private. Sam had no right to ask me about it. But then, I didn't have to answer. I feel weird, like I've done something shameful, or bad.

'OK, we're ready,' says Sam. 'We're rolling. Just ignore us.'

Not that easy to ignore seven people, two cameras, a boom and a couple of huge square lights pointing at me.

I take my folder over to the piano, scrabbling around to try and find the song at the back. After handing it to the pianist and giving him an idea of tempo, I walk back to the middle of the room, thinking about the last time I stood and sang on this spot. It was at my disastrous attempt to get into Duke's, when I ran out without finishing my song. Second only to Mum dying, it was probably the worst day of my life. Hopefully today I can reset myself. I just need to focus.

But every time I take in a breath, I get a great big flashing image of Jade and Sam, heads together, scheming to manipulate me. I mentally shake them out of my head and try to channel my anger into the song – which is, disastrously, meant to be a comedy. But some of the crew give me thumbs-up signs at the end, so it can't have been that bad.

Michael clears his throat. 'Thank you, Nettie. Dance call is tomorrow.'

I'm through? I thank him and pass around the mass of crew members gathered by the door. Sam pats my shoulder heartily. 'Good one, Nettie. Thank you.' If it had come from anyone else, I wouldn't have minded.

God, I want this so much. If only I didn't have to get through several rounds of dance calls to get it.

22:32
Luca:
How did your audition go?

76

OK, thanks. Did you have your interview for assistant MD?

Yeah. But then the woman in charge told me I had to sing a song?

WTF?

I know. Weird.

To be IN it?

Haha, I know. Must have been my compelling performance as Harry the Horse in Guys and Dolls last year.

SHUT UP YOU WERE EXCELLENT

I'd much rather be doing the music but I don't think I'm going to have much choice

Well, I hope you get it. Music or otherwise!

Thanks. You too.

'What are you laughing at?' says Alec. We're curled up on the sofa watching more Fosse tutorials on YouTube in preparation for my dance call tomorrow.

'Oh, just something Luca said,' I say, putting my phone down. 'They made him sing in his interview today.'

'Luca's messaging you, is he?' says Alec. His eyebrow is raised suggestively.

'What's that supposed to mean?'

'Nothing. Not my fault if you're reading into it.'

'Alec, we're just frien—'

'It's just that Luca happens to be a guy you kissed at a party. *And* he asked you out.'

'So? That was ages ago.'

'How much did he message you over the summer?' says Alec. 'When you were at Fletch's?'

Luca didn't message me at all during the summer holidays. I'm pretty sure that was just because he was off doing his own thing, but I don't want Alec to think he's winning, so I say, 'Loads, actually.'

'Hmmn.'

'Is there something wrong?'

'No. Nothing at all. Anyway, get up. I've got to sort out your rag-doll arms before tomorrow. God knows if I can't be in *Chicago*, then you're the next best thing. My work *will* be seen on that stage.'

Alec *adores* Fosse. He frequently recreates whole sections of 'Take Off with Us' on nights out, to the delight of everyone in the club. And one of his ambitions has always been to work with a first-gen Fosse dancer. The director-choreographer that Michael's brought in for *Chicago* is literally that. What's holding Alec back?

CHAPTER 9

Jade's already in the changing room when Kiki and I arrive early the next morning, wearing a neon-pink-and-yellow two-piece, her red hair piled so high she probably had to duck under the doorframe. Clearly the part of the audition notice that said *Dress only in black* was lost on her.

She jumps when we come in. 'Fucking hell! Is there any need?'

'For being in *our own changing room*?' says Kiki. 'Anyway, what are you doing here?' Jade normally uses the second-floor changing room these days, probably to avoid us.

'Mind your own business,' says Jade.

'*Interesting outfit*,' shoots back Kiki.

Jade looks Kiki up and down. 'Some of us want to stand out.'

Kiki smiles sweetly. 'Some of us rely on our dancing for that.'

I'm about to chime in to ask Jade about her 'arch-villain role' in *Triple Threat* when she pushes roughly past us and walks straight out. Typical that she'd leave me alone on the one time I actually want to talk to her.

Kiki's getting changed into a classic black two-piece. She's customized the neckline to make it look both completely original and very *her*.

'What time's your audition?'

'First thing – with you.'

'I'm so scared, Kiki.'

'Channel your mum,' says Kiki. 'If ever there was a time to be the daughter of a famous ballerina, it's now. If you're struggling, stand just behind me. You can copy me.'

My friends have been so good to me about all of this. Who would deliberately let someone copy them in an audition? I hug Kiki gratefully, pull on my dancewear and heels, stuff a piece of cold toast I've brought from home in my face and dash back down to join the rest of the dancers auditioning for *Chicago*, who are all sprawled out across the foyer, stretching and talking, transforming the dark wood floor into a writhing sea of Lycra. Jade's in a corner, in the splits. Ignoring the two huge cameras that have parked up in the middle of everyone, I make my way over to her.

'Jade?' I keep my voice low in case anyone from Three Ring TV is listening. 'Listen, I'd rather you didn't talk about me in interviews.' As she leans over her front leg, I'm forced to talk to the back of her head. 'Sam said you'd agreed to go along with some bullshit story for the documentary about us having a "thing" and—'

Jade looks up at me like I've just killed her dog. 'Sam told me *you'd* already started it.' She swings her back leg around, forcing me to jump over it like a skipping rope. She stands up, a good ten inches taller than me. 'I graduate this year. I need the exposure.'

'How can you want to be a part of anything like that?'

'My reputation's already in tatters after what happened at the Summer Showcase –' I notice she still doesn't accept any responsibility for this – 'but the fact is, people know who I am now. Sam says she's already had enquiries from potential agents about me, just because they know I'm going to be featured. So, I might as well stick with being "the bitch".'

With that, she walks away. I stare after her in disbelief.

Fuck this. I don't care what she says about me. They can't force me to be in it.

Sam's giving orders to a couple of members of her team when I find her.

'Sam? I wanted to let you know that I don't want to be a part of the documentary.'

'Nettie, has something upset you?' she says. 'Come with me. It's too noisy to talk out here.'

She leads me through to the office, where Miss Paige is sorting through third-year headshots. The walls are covered with student ID sheets and registers and fire safety procedures, and each desk is scattered with 'to do' lists and Post-it notes.

'Pam, would you mind giving us the room for a second?' says Sam.

Shockingly, the usually unmovable Miss Paige gathers her sheets of photographic paper and gets up gracefully, bowing her head to Sam as she quietly leaves the room.

And I thought Miss Duke had power.

'Nettie, I'm sorry if we've done something to make you uncomfortable. Is there anything I can help you with?' Her eyes are full of concern. After a moment, she sighs. 'Look, I'll be honest with you. The reason we got the idea of filming a documentary at Duke's was because of you. I kick myself that we weren't here to catch everything that happened last summer. But we're here now, and – you're going to hate me for saying this – the world wants to hear your story. This could mean big success for you.'

'I just don't think I want success that way,' I say. 'I'd rather get it on my own merit.'

'But this *is* on your own merit!' she says. 'You're the star here. I'm just a filmmaker. What I'm looking for, ultimately, is the truth. Your talent is way more interesting to me than some student drama happening in the corridors.'

'That's not what Jade said.'

Sam smiles. 'OK, maybe that was a step too far. You don't have to make a decision now. We're already involved in casting the college musical, so you'll be filmed anyway. You've signed the consent form, so you can't avoid that. But please tell me you'll at least consider being featured, Nettie.'

'No bullshit stories? Just the stuff that happens at college, not loads about my private life?'

'You have my word.'

'OK, I'll think about it.'

I leave Sam in the office and go off in search of Kiki, who I find over by the studio theatre, doing press-ups.

'Ready?' she says, springing up from the floor in less than a second.

'I think so. Hey, I just spoke to—'

'Remember, it's Fosse, so sit in your hips and don't turn out.' She's not listening; she's in dance mode. 'Turn in, if anything. And isolation means literally that. Keep firm here.' She jabs my abs.

Sam comes over, all white teeth and lip gloss, and I think she's about to badger me again, but she talks to Kiki. 'Hey,' she says.

Kiki takes the hand she's offering and shakes it firmly.

'Thank you so much for agreeing to be featured. Wow – you have amazing eyes,' says Sam. 'What colour would you call them?'

'Hazel, I guess.'

'They really "pop" on camera. Especially with that shade of eyeshadow you're wearing.'

'Thanks,' says Kiki, smiling.

I'm a little more cynical; it's true – Kiki does have beautiful eyes, but I can't help thinking that Sam's using flattery to get Kiki to let her guard down. Nothing she does feels authentic. I nudge Kiki. 'We'd better go. Dance call's about to start,' I say.

'I know what you're going to say,' says Kiki as we head over to Studio One.

'Kiki, I think you *should* go for it. Just be careful, that's all.'

She smiles at me, like she's indulging an overprotective mother. 'I will.'

The cameras have been moved from the foyer to film the audition. I suddenly understand how Alec felt about singing in front of them – this is terrifying. I'm out of my comfort zone, out of my depth, and potentially about to humiliate myself on TV. Oh my God.

'Breathe,' says Kiki.

I try to do as she says, but it's not easy. Not when this is hanging on a knife edge.

Lisa Jacobs strides in. The only thing longer than her legs must surely be the impressive list of Broadway shows she's worked on – I can't believe I'm this close to an *actual legend*. She has dark brown skin, and shiny straight black hair fastened in a ponytail on top of her head, making her seem even taller. Even up, her hair comes down to her waist. She's wearing black tights and a high-neck leotard, and has glossy red lips and a full lash. She bends over into a *penché* to stretch, and I'm not joking when I say it's a full one-eighty. Kiki throws me a silent gasp. We googled her this morning; apparently she's sixty. Goals.

'So we start with a sway,' she says, without introducing herself.

Everyone gets their shit together *immediately*, copying her stance in the mirror. The focus is good for my nerves, and Lisa's so amazing to watch that I'm completely absorbed in what I'm doing.

'My feet are set in granite, and I'm swaying in the breeze,' she says, showing us. 'There's no break in my body. See? Now I place my hands here . . . Give it life, because this is pretty –' she does the position – 'but *this* is better.' She changes something in her posture, I don't even know what, but now it's *living*. And so am I. This woman is a force.

She teaches the routine quickly but in intricate detail, down to where our little fingers are to be placed. I'm not sure if I'm any good, but I feel a deep joy I've never felt before when I've danced. Given who my mother was, it's never made any sense that I've not connected to movement before. Mum always came to watch when I used sing in a local pub and say that it was as if I was 'dancing with my voice'. I'd laugh, but I could never imagine how it felt to be completely taken away by movement in the same way as singing. Dancing was pushing through pain, putting my body in weird shapes and trying to make them feel less weird.

But this is different. Like, it's dance, but it's also something else as well – not quite *acting*, but an attitude, a feeling. Like I'm singing . . . with my body? Is this what Mum felt all the time?

'Step right – it's not so much how you roll through the foot here, but *what you're thinking* as you roll,' says Lisa, demonstrating a walk to the back.

Like, how can walking be that good? I am completely inspired. Everything that comes out of her mouth I want to wrap up and take home with me.

She stops. 'Excuse me – you in the back? In every colour of the rainbow?'

Everyone turns round to see who she's talking to. It's Jade.

'Me?' says Jade.

'Yes, honey. Please go get changed into something appropriate. The dress code was very clear. OK, everyone, get into fours.'

Jade stands there with her mouth open for a second, before turning on her heel and walking out of the studio, her cheeks burning brighter than her neon two-piece. The cameras follow.

Kiki nudges me and gives me an *I knew it* wink.

We split into smaller groups to perform. This is it. I have to nail this. And not even for the cameras. I *need* to work with this woman. I need her in my life. I need this dancing.

'So we've got lots going on,' Lisa says, her New Yorker's voice easily reaching the back of the room. 'We've got arms and we've got heads and now I'm asking you to tilt your pelvis and breathe in a certain way and you're like –' she does a head-exploding thing with her hands – 'but I want you to throw all that away. The only thing you need to remember is that now you have a *secret*. Doesn't matter what. But something we'd all want to know. Dance with that in mind.' She goes and sits behind the table with Michael and two of the dance teachers, ready to mark off who she wants to recall.

When I think about secrets, I can't help but think about Mum's. That won't help – I'm in search of them, not in possession. Looking around, everyone else seems ready, their knowing faces poised for action. I start to panic. But then I spot Sam, staring through her camera at me almost like if she focuses hard enough, she'll see into my mind, and it makes me think of all the things she'd love to know about me. And then suddenly, in this moment, *I get it*. Which is a feeling I've never had about dance before.

Right now, I've got this.

CHAPTER 10

19:10
Fletch:

How'd it go?

Good, I think? Lisa was amazing, so inspired!

Cool. We're up against it here but speak later? X

19:40
Luca:

Heard you nailed it today!

Well, I didn't fall on my arse . . .

😂 😥 How was Lisa?

AMAZING
I want to be her

I met her today, too . . .

How come?

She came into my second interview
and got me doing a few moves

> Are the band going to be dancing lol

> Hope not 😟
> No idea what that was all about
> But I really want to be part of this

> Fingers crossed we both get it! x

> Yeah, fingers crossed! x

'Nettie!' Kiki screams so loudly, I can hear her perfectly through the Friday-night-student-rammed foyer. I push my way through the crowd to her and Leon beside the noticeboard outside the main office.

'It's up! Look!' She points to a piece of paper pinned to the board. It's the cast list for *Chicago*.

My eyes scan down to the role I was hoping for. My heart does its own one-eighty. 'Oh my God, I got Roxie! And Leon, you're Amos!'

'To top it off, I got assistant to Lisa Jacobs,' says Kiki. 'And the part of Liz – what a great end to the week!'

'Kiki, that's amazing! Lisa singling you out and asking you to assist her is the stuff dreams are made of. She's a *god* of dance.' I pick Kiki up and spin her round, both of us laughing hysterically.

'Which one's Liz?' says Leon.

'"Pop"' she says giddily. 'The first one – about the gum? A killer monologue with no singing! Yay, me! You'll have to help me with that, Nettie. Oh my God, this is going to be great,' she adds when I've put her down (not our best landing).

'I can't believe it,' he marvels. 'I barely expected to get in, let alone a part.'

'Well, you shouldn't be so disgustingly talented,' Kiki says cheerfully.

Taro suddenly emerges from the crowd to kiss Leon on the cheek in congratulations. I can tell Leon's looking around to make sure there are no cameras, but they go off together happily, arm in arm. I'm so glad things are turning around for Leon.

'Who else got in?' says Kiki. 'Let's have a look. Velma went to Shaiann Greig.'

'Ooh, she'll be good,' I say.

'Billy Flynn . . . Luca Viscusi? That's odd – he went up for assistant MD, didn't he? Nice, though.'

'Nice for Nettie,' says Alec, who's just appeared behind us.

I look over her shoulder at him. 'Not this again.'

'Well, you're going to be enjoying a *very close relationship* with him onstage. Doesn't Roxie spend a whole number sitting on his lap?'

I barely suppress an eye-roll. Why did I tell him about that kiss last year? Since then, he's refused to believe that there's nothing between us. I open my mouth to reply, but he cuts off my burgeoning retort with a question.

'Where's Leon? I wanted to congratulate him.'

'He went off with Taro,' says Kiki.

It's probably just as well – even a 'well done' from Alec can sound like sarcasm, and I don't think Leon needs that right now.

'Oh,' he says. 'Whatever – I'll catch him later.' He's trying to sound like he doesn't care, but I can tell it's getting to him. Leon's been spending a lot of time with Taro, and I think Alec's feeling left out.

Miss Duke comes out of the office – alone. My last lesson with Steph flashes through my mind. I need to talk to her. I've got to do it now, or I never will. Boosted by the recent casting news, I slip out of Kiki and Alec's grip and join the two of them back together like I'm fixing a circuit.

'OK,' I say. 'Wish me luck.'

'What are you *doing*, Nettie?' splutters Kiki, her eyes darting to Miss Duke.

'Going to find out what happened to Mum.'

'Aren't there easier ways to die?'

'Maybe.' This might be a huge disaster. But at the moment, Miss Duke is the best chance I've got of finding out anything. Outwardly calm (but secretly shitting a brick), I walk over to the office corridor, where she's standing in the doorway, looking out over the crowded foyer. She's only a person. I can do this.

'Miss Duke?' Dammit. My knee's shaking already. I can feel Kiki eyeballing me through the back of my head.

'Antoinette,' she says, unsmiling. I can tell I haven't picked a good time. Still, I'm here now. It's not the moment to waver.

'I want to ask you about my mother,' I blurt out.

'Anastasia? What about her?' Her cheeks go pink under several layers of powder.

'I – just – wanted to know what happened to her.' Even as I say the words, I realize I'm not entirely sure what I'm asking. 'Why she . . . stopped dancing.'

Miss Duke takes a second to consider this. 'I assumed,' she says, 'that it was because she had you.'

'Oh.' Undeterred, I try again. 'I just . . . wondered why she didn't talk about her career. She never even mentioned she knew you. Miss Duke, I got sent this vid—'

'Maybe she didn't think it was worth mentioning,' says Miss Duke over the top of me, glancing over my shoulder as if looking for someone. She gives the tiniest of nods.

I'm not letting her distract me. Scrabbling in my bag for my phone to show her the clip, I press on. 'But you were friends. You said so yourself. Why would she keep that a secret? Unless something happened between you?'

It's a step too far.

She pulls me close to speak into my ear. 'Listen to me, Antoinette.' Though she's whispering, there's an unmistakeable rancour in her voice. 'I am not prepared to discuss a past that has nothing to do with you; airing my dirty laundry in front of the entire world like a fish wife. What happened between your mother and me is *no one else's business.*'

'But—'

She pulls away, smiling. 'And may I say, Antoinette, how proud I am.'

'What?'

'After everything you suffered last year, to overcome your vocal problems and get the leading role in our college musical this year.' Her face is full of pride. Are her eyes glistening? I stare at her, open-mouthed.

Just then, I become aware of something behind me in the foyer. The hairs on the back of my neck stand up, like a warning. I turn slowly.

There's a camera about two feet behind me, aimed over my shoulder at Miss Duke.

I get it now.

She puts a hand on my arm. Its coolness bleeds through my clothes to my skin, an incongruous chill against the warm gesture it's supposed to be. Her grip tightens.

'Thank you, Miss Duke,' I say. 'I'll do my best.' I feel like a robot.

Smiling, she squeezes my arm hard, before retreating into the office. I back away from the doorway, the cold touch of her hand spreading through my body like frostbite. She must have known I'd want to keep my questions about Mum private, which is why she beckoned the camera over. This is so frustrating – I'm at a dead end before I've even started.

Anand peeks out from the office door. 'Nettie?'

'Hey, Anand.'

'Congratulations on Roxie,' he says, smiling.

'Thanks.' I'm still thawing out. 'How's it going for you guys?'

He looks behind him. 'Oh, not too bad . . . Actually, Sam sent me to ask you if you'd thought about what she said.'

'I have thought about it,' I say, 'and I just don't think it's me.' Not after what just happened, anyway. 'Sorry, Anand.' I turn to go.

'Nettie, wait!' he says. 'Look –' he pulls me over to the other side of the foyer – 'I just overheard what you were talking about with Miss Duke. That stuff about your mother.'

'Oh. Right?' I feel kind of weird that he knows about it when I've been trying to keep it to myself. I'd really rather leave Mum out of it all.

'Your mum was a famous dancer, right?'

'Yes.'

'And you want to find out more about her?'

'Yeah – Anand, I don't really—'

'I shouldn't be telling you this,' he says, 'but Sam knows who your mum was. She was on one about it in pre-production, and

91

then, for whatever reason, she changed her mind about including it when we started filming . . . But I just heard her talking about it again with one of the producers. She wants to feature it as a main story.'

And I bet Millicent Moore told her.

'Then I'm definitely not being part of the show,' I say.

'Look, I know Sam,' he whispers. 'If you give her nothing, she'll go out of her way to take everything. She won't stop until your whole life is laid bare. It doesn't matter whether you decide to cooperate with the programme or not. In fact, if you don't give her anything, she'll look for a story elsewhere. And at the moment, it seems like that's going to be . . . your mum.'

Out of the corner of my eye, I see Kiki leaving the building and getting into a sports car that's waiting just outside. As she opens the door, I get a glimpse of Sam smiling up at her. She closes the door and the car speeds off down the road. What the hell, they're suddenly BFFs?

'Nettie?'

'Sorry. I . . . Never mind. Why are you telling me all this?'

'I don't want her taking advantage of you. She . . . does that. You're a nice kid, Nettie.'

'Kid? How old are *you*?'

He pulls his sweater down uncomfortably. 'I'm twenty-one. Look, let me help you. We can keep it from Sam. Just . . . be in the show and let her think she's getting what she wants. That way, she'll leave you alone. I can't change the concept for the show – it's already clear she wants to make you the main feature – but I can try to protect you a little. Nettie, I've seen what she can do to people. Trust me, you don't want to be on the receiving end.'

My own life being invaded is one thing. But having Mum's

life broadcast to millions of people is another, especially when *I* don't even know anything about her. That's too intimate to share. Kiki might have let her guard down, but I won't. As much as I hate it, Anand's right. The only way to keep my privacy is to let Sam think she's getting what she wants.

'OK,' I say. 'I'll do it.'

17:47

CONGRATULATIONS!!!

Luca:

Ahhhhhh, you too ☺

☉ Thanks, I think?

You'll be amazing. So great that we get to work together!

Yeah! Bit weird, though

???

Casting me, I mean!

Not working with you 😆

Like why would they do that?

Not saying this for compliments, but there are so many better people than me. And I really wanted to work on the music side of things.

Not to sound ungrateful but 😕

93

> No, I get what you mean. Like it's your third year, you should be allowed to specialize.

> I feel like it's got something to do with Triple Threat?

> God I hope not

> Maybe ask Anand about it? He seems to be the only guy worth talking to on the crew.

> Yeah. Maybe.

My phone's going off in my bag as I get out of the shower that evening. I know if I leave it ringing, Alec will answer, and who knows what damage that boy could do with it. Shivering, I throw a towel around me and dash back to my room, grabbing the phone out of my bag. It doesn't respond to my slippery hands for a few seconds, so I dry them on the part of the towel that's over my legs, and try again. It's Fletch, on FaceTime.

'CONGRATULATIONS!' he says.

'Hey,' I say, laughing and wiping the water off the screen.

He starts laughing at me.

'What?'

'Nothing,' he says. 'You're just too cute.'

I check myself in the small window at the bottom of the screen and see that my entire fringe is plastered to one side of my forehead. Rolling my eyes, I smooth it back (forwards never goes well when it's wet).

'Well done on getting Roxie – I'm so proud of you.'

'Leon got Amos,' I say excitedly. 'How much fun is that going to be?'

94

'So much fun,' he says. 'I wish I was able to do it with you. Who else got in?'

'From your year? Elizabeth Ferguson got Mamma Morton, Taro's Fred Casely, Luca's Billy Flynn—'

'Luca?' interrupts Fletch.

'Yeah, how great is that?! It's a bit weird, because he went for assistant MD, but kind of cool anyway!'

He pauses. 'I'm just surprised he's not doing the music with Michael.'

'Miss Duke *asked* him to audition, apparently.'

Another pause. 'Well, that's brilliant,' he says finally. 'I'm glad everyone got the parts they wanted. You're amazing.'

'Thanks.'

'I love you,' he says. 'I can't wait to see you.'

'Are you coming home this weekend?' I say. 'I was thinking we could go to Auntie's and pick up some of Mum's stuff.'

He sighs. 'Nettie, I'm not going to be back for a few weeks.'

'Well, can I come and visit you? I could get the train down and—'

'I mean, you could, but the reason I can't get back is because I'll be working all weekend. You'd be on your own the whole time. These writers, they keep weird hours, and I never know when they're going to keep me late. Sometimes we go on past midnight.'

'That's ridiculous,' I say. 'You're an intern!'

'Nettie, remember when we were writing songs together last year?' he says. 'One of us would have an idea, and we'd sit there and work and work on it until we'd got it exactly how we wanted it. Do you remember that feeling when we finally nailed it?'

How could I not? Last year I lived for our writing sessions.

Finishing a song together was the best feeling in the world, and that would have still been true even if I hadn't been in love with my writing partner.

'Of course.'

'Well, this is the same. Honestly, I thought I'd be down here making tea for Oliver and West, but it's not like that. I'm fully involved in their creative process. They listen to my ideas, Nettie – sometimes they even use them. When we work late, it's because we don't want to lose momentum – we need to catch the idea and run with it. It's hard work, but kind of exhilarating.'

I suddenly realize something: if we stay together long term, this is going to be how it is for us. Accepting jobs that take us away from each other, meeting new and interesting people, working obsessively on our own projects. All the things that can make couples drift apart. We've got to find a way to make it work. And I need to start by giving him space to do this.

'I can't wait to hear it,' I say.

'What else is new?' he asks. 'Any college dramas?'

Now it's my turn to pause. As dramas go, the last few weeks have been up there. Jade, Sam, the auditions – it's been non-stop. There were my conversations with Michael and Miss Duke about Mum, and Anand stopping me in the foyer. Mum's boxes are still gathering dust in Auntie's attic and I'm desperate to get them, but at the same time the thought of what I might find fills me with dread. Everything's so confusing right now that I could do with talking it over with someone. But then I remember Alec's comment at the beginning of term, about Fletch and me and the seemingly never-ending drama of last year, and I stop myself. Long distance is hard, and Fletch has got a lot going on. Maybe telling him all my worries isn't going to be helpful when he's away. For this to be anywhere near plain sailing, we've got to keep it simple.

'Nope,' I say. 'Nothing to report.'

CHAPTER 11

8:37 a.m.

Leon:

Morning! So Sam just asked me to be featured in the show . . .

Kiki:

That's great!

Alec:

That's all of us, then 📺

Fame at last lol

Have you decided what to do? I know you were worried.

Leon:

I told Sam I'd think about it.

Alec:

You worried about your dad?

Leon:

🙁

Kiki:

I honestly think it'll be fine Leon

Sam's more interested in your
talent than your personal life

Alec:

I agree, you should go for it

Leon:

Nettie?

Honestly I don't know

But I'm here for you whatever you decide x

I try to drown out Jade's impossible hair-and-make-up demands as I enter the studio for ballet. If the cold early November air hadn't woken me up before I got here, her shrill screeching has done the trick. Cameras are being set up. Coffees are handed out (the *no eating or drinking in the studio* rule seems non-existent if you work for Three Ring TV). Cables are being stuck in a long path around the edge of the studio to avoid being danced on, but people are ignoring the yellow tape and treading on them anyway. *Triple Threat* seems less like a documentary and more like a full-on movie set with every passing day. Sam breezes in with a coffee, smiles winningly at Kiki and me, winks at Jade and sends the crew in various directions as we start the class.

Miss Moore's kind of ignored me for the last few weeks. But I can tell when she marches into the studio this morning that she's out to get someone, and usually that someone is me.

I'm wrong. She doesn't even acknowledge my existence. Which is fine by me – I just wish Sam would stop focusing on me in dance lessons. I might have an interesting backstory, but she'd be far better off getting action shots of the people who actually know what they're doing.

We're doing *jetés* from the corner. When it gets to my turn, I step off with my right leg confidently, but as I go to extend my left, something gets in the way, tripping me up. My right foot goes from underneath me and I land flat on my back with an almighty crash, the sprung floor reverberating loudly. Jade steps over me and performs her *jetés* without so much as a backward glance. I notice there's one camera on her, and another still focused on me. I look over at Sam, but she's deep in conversation. Humiliated and seething, I pick myself up and go to join the back of the line.

Miss Moore glares at me, then disappears out of the studio for a moment, returning with a bowl of water. 'Antoinette, come here,' she says, indicating a spot in the middle of the floor. She hands me the full-to-the-brim bowl, smiling brightly. 'Goodness me. That landing. Like a herd of elephants. No wonder you fell. You will do *sautés* for the rest of the lesson. Without spilling any water.'

I don't quite understand. 'Sorry – you want me to jump?'

'Yes.'

'With this bowl?'

'Exactly. Now get on with it.'

She waits for me to start jumping, before moving on to the next exercise with the rest of the class. Which is difficult, to say the least, because I am right in the middle of them all, jumping up and down and trying not to spill any water. At one point I slosh some over the edge, and Miss Moore points to a cloth

100

on the piano. Horribly aware that Sam's getting all of this on camera, I fetch the cloth and clean up the spillage, my cheeks burning.

After ten minutes of jumping, my legs are like blancmange and I'm spilling more water than I'm keeping in. My face is bright red, now from exertion rather than from embarrassment, and my arms are aching from holding the bowl. At one point I slip over. But I won't let Millicent Moore win, especially not in front of a TV crew. The rest of the students dance around me, working twenty times as hard as usual, terrified of being similarly humiliated. Miss Moore takes no notice, but I know if I stop, she'll be all over me. Jade catches my eye and smiles nastily. Anger surges inside me and I nearly drop the bowl.

Miss Duke's face appears at the window. She takes in the situation and comes to the door immediately.

'Could we pause filming for one second?' she says to Sam, completely unruffled. 'Miss Moore, I'd like a word.'

Miss Moore and Sam both follow her outside. I stop jumping as soon as the door closes behind them, gasping for air and rubbing my quads. Jade slips out of the room while I'm still getting my breath back.

'Oh my God, what a bitch,' says Kiki. 'I can't believe she did that to you.'

'Who – Jade, or Miss Moore?'

'I mean, both.'

'Shhh,' I say. 'If we're quiet we can hear what's going on.'

We creep closer to the door to listen to the muffled conversation.

'I'm well aware that your methods are unorthodox, Millicent,' Miss Duke is saying, 'and I've been willing to turn my back in

101

favour of what they can achieve, as you know, but you cannot conduct your classes like that in front of the crew.'

'I will not compromise my teaching methods for some cheap TV programme,' retorts Miss Moore. (Ear pressed up to the door, Kiki gasps.) 'It's bad enough that you're letting them in at all, Cecile. But you promised us it wouldn't affect our working environment. I won't do it.'

I've never heard anyone speak to Miss Duke like that before. She's surely going to send Miss Moore packing, or give her a bollocking, at least.

But she doesn't.

'Sam, I'm going to have to ask you not to film Miss Moore's classes,' she says. 'And you can't use the footage of today's lesson.'

What Sam says next is unknown because Miss Moore throws open the door (almost smashing Kiki's nose), calls the class together for a hasty reverence, and steams out of the studio, lighting a cigarette as she goes. We pile out behind her, bewildered.

'At least they won't use the shots of you jumping up and down with a bowl in your hands,' offers Kiki, as we trudge up the marble staircase, me clinging on to the banister to take some of the weight off my legs. 'It would almost be comical, if it weren't, you know, actual abuse. And as for Jade . . .' She struggles to find the words. 'What a prick.'

I pause. 'I think Sam put her up to it.'

'Sam wouldn't do that,' she says.

'But the cameras were all ready to go on me.'

'It was your turn! You're being paranoid.'

I think having the director tell me she wants to create a narrative where Jade's basically after me, and then finding myself

102

the subject of a close-up while Jade kicks my leg from underneath me is more a case of putting two and two together than paranoia. 'I just wonder if Sam's a bit intent on stirring up this feud between Jade and me,' I say. 'Like, she seems a bit . . . ruthless?'

Kiki frowns. 'If you mean she's a successful woman in what is essentially a man's world, and in order to become this, she's had to play hardball occasionally, then yes, I guess she can be a little tough. But I think you're worrying unnecessarily.'

'I'm just anxious about this whole *Triple Threat* thing. We really have no control over how we're portrayed. And Sam . . .'

Kiki smiles and puts her hand on my arm. 'She's cool, Nettie – you know, the more I get to know her, the more inspiring I find her. You'd like her. Next time we hang out, you should come.'

There's not a world in which I'd want to spend time with Sam, but I also want to show my friend I'm making an effort. 'OK,' I say, giving her what I hope is a convincing smile.

A week later, I get a surprise but welcome message from Fletch.

08:30
Fletch:

Got the weekend off! ☺
See you at mine on Friday?

OMIGOD! YES! ❤
4 days . . .
Can't stop thinking about you
I love you

18:30

I love you too

Friday takes a long time to arrive. Kiki wakes me up early with some welcome news.

06:45
Kiki:

Did you hear??? Miss Moore's gone on Sabbatical!!!

WHAT? WHY?

Obviously something to do with Triple Threat

Looks like I can't ask her about Mum now . . .
But also no humiliation, so 😕

Right? 😄 Hey – Sam, Anand and the rest of the crew are going to BKB tonight. You coming?

Oh no, I can't, sorry Kiki

I thought you said you'd be up for it 😕

Fletch is back this weekend. I haven't seen him for weeks and I just want to spend every possible second with him

Ahhhh, you pair of cuties
Next time?

104

Promise ❤

13:10

Just reminding you I won't be
home tonight. Flat to yourself ☺

Alec:

Great. Everyone's deserting me.

??

Kiki's going out with Sam, Leon's gone to Taro's, and
now you're leaving me. And it's only going to get worse
when Chicago rehearsals start. I'll be a Fosse widow.

How about Fletch and I come back tomorrow?
We can all spend the day together!

Can't Saturday, I'm out.

My stomach's filled with so many butterflies as I smooth down
my fringe on Fletch's doorstep that I feel like I'm living Eliza's
'Helpless' moment from *Hamilton*. Being apart's making it feel
like we've only just got together – like it's all still exciting and
new and unknown. I guess that's one upside of long distance.

I press the doorbell to the ground-floor flat. To my surprise,
Luca answers.

'Hey, Nettie. Fletch isn't back yet. Tea?'

'Uh, sure. Thanks, Luca.'

My phone rings and I pop it on speaker as I follow him through the flat. 'Hey, beautiful.'

I glow at the sound of Fletch's voice. 'Hey, you.'

'Are you at mine yet?'

'Yes! What time are you back?'

'That's why I was calling,' he says. 'They've asked me to stay late. The orchestrator's only just arrived. I'll get on the road as soon as I can, but at the moment it looks as though I won't be leaving until eight.'

My heart sinks. I take him off loudspeaker and nip back into the hall. 'Are you sure you want to drive home that late? It's cold, and you'll be tired. Maybe you should stay down tonight.' I hope he can't hear the disappointment in my voice.

'Nettie, this week's been hard,' he says. His voice sounds heavy. 'The thought of getting home to you is the only thing keeping me going. I'll text you when I'm leaving. I'll be there as soon as I can. I love you.'

He hangs up.

I go back into the kitchen where Luca hands me a tea. He sees my downcast face. 'Hey, don't worry, Nettie. Fletch won't be long. In the meantime, are you hungry?'

This cheers me up a little. 'What are you thinking?'

'Linguine.'

I can't say yes fast enough.

Luca makes and serves dinner. It's delicious. I feel a bit strange eating in Fletch's house without him, but I'm too hungry to wait.

'So, *Chicago* should be fun,' Luca says, handing me some black pepper. 'Now that I've got over being in it and not on the music side. Shame it's going to be such a drawn-out process. Could do with getting it all over and done with so that I can concentrate on my thesis.'

'Yeah, we're rehearsing for *ages*. Thanks to Three Ring TV.' I roll my eyes and shake my head briskly.

'You're not a fan?' says Luca.

'They just won't leave me alone,' I say. 'Like, I'm not *that* interesting.'

He laughs. 'Yeah – they seem to hang around you a lot. Meant to ask – did I see them filming you talking to Miss Duke a couple weeks ago? What was that about?'

It's like this unwritten rule at college that you only talk to Miss Duke if you're in trouble or about to get a West End contract – there's no in-between.

'One minute she was bollocking me. The next, she'd called the cameras over and was telling me how proud she was, talking about last year and my voice, all misty-eyed.' When he looks at me, confused, I add, 'She didn't want to answer personal questions.'

'That's intense,' says Luca. 'What were you asking her?'

'I just wanted to know why Mum stopped dancing. What happened. They were friends, years ago. Miss Duke kind of hinted that they fell out.'

'Wait, what? How did they know each other?'

My first instinct is just to brush it off, change the subject, but then an image flashes through my mind of the picture I found on my first day of college last year – a photo of Mum and Miss Duke laughing together, arm in arm – and the pang that goes through my chest reminds me not only how desperate I am to find out what happened, or how frustrating it is that no one will tell me the truth, but how much I need to talk about this with someone. The last few weeks have been taken up by *Chicago* and *Triple Threat* – for everyone, not just me – there hasn't been space to talk. And Fletch hasn't exactly been around.

I go and get my phone from my bag to show Luca the video. There's a message from Fletch. It looks as if he wrote it in a hurry.

18:45
Fletch:
Sorry still waiting
Call u soon

19:30
OK. I love you x

Luca and I finish clearing up together while I fill him in on everything I know so far. We end up collapsed on the sofa. It's one of those big L-shaped ones you kind of get lost in and can't get out of easily, in dark green corduroy. The flat is generally quite shabby, but they've made it their own, with quirky throws and cushions, rock band tour posters and a huge red sequinned lampshade in the centre of the ceiling that Seb left behind. Luca's drum kit sits in the corner in front of a brown-and-beige condemned gas fire, and an electric-blue rug hides a threadbare carpet.

'Let's see it, then,' Luca says, pointing to my phone.

After locating the clip, my finger hovers over the play button. Is it weird that I'm sitting here so comfortably with him, as friends, after what happened last year? But it kind of feels . . . fine? We're both here for Fletch in the end.

I hit play and show Luca the video. He looks stunned.

'Wait – was that one of the ballet teachers?' he says.

'Yes – Millicent Moore,' I say. 'Did you see the look she gave Mum when she knocked her over? She's furious. But the girl behind Millicent – watch it again.' I play the beginning of the video and keep my finger on the girl just off Millicent's shoulder. As Mum comes careering towards them and collides with Millicent, it's hard to make out, but the girl behind definitely rolls her eyes.

'She looks pissed off,' says Luca.

'Don't you think if it was a one-off, she'd be shocked? She looks like she's seen it all before. And if you watch all the *corps de ballet* girls, their body language looks kind of nervous, like they're watching out for Mum, waiting for her to trip up.'

Luca rubs his neck. 'You think it was a regular thing?'

'I just wonder if Mum had a – a problem,' I say.

'Did she drink much?' says Luca. 'Before she . . . When you lived with her? Like growing up, I mean.'

People don't want to say the word 'died' in case it upsets me. It's nice of them, but I'm well practised at hearing it. It's kind of worse when they avoid it.

'Never.'

'You think she'd have told you,' says Luca. 'When you were old enough to understand, I mean.'

'She never did.' I take a pink-and-yellow *Never Mind the Bollocks* cushion out from behind my back and put it on the armrest. 'It's killing me, wishing I'd had these conversations with her when she was still alive.'

'What about your granny?' says Luca. 'Couldn't you ask her?'

I almost laugh at his use of the word 'granny'. Not the image you'd conjure up for my grandmother. 'I'm not going anywhere near her if I can help it. Annoying though – there's a couple of boxes of Mum's stuff there I could do with picking up . . .' The thought sends equal thrills of fear and hope through me. I need to stop putting it off and go and get them.

'Well, if you ever need help, I'm always here,' says Luca.

'Thanks.' I'm thinking back to my last encounter with my grandmother and kicking myself for not taking more with me. Why didn't I just grab Mum's stuff and go? My grandmother could be chucking it all out right now. I wouldn't put it past her.

Luca, sensing the conversation is over, changes the subject. 'So, what are we watching? Your choice,' he says, tossing me the remote.

I wake up with my mouth open and dribble running down the side of my chin on to Luca's shoulder, who's fallen asleep too. Fletch's bike helmet is in the corner of the room, next to his jacket and gloves. Yawning, I wander out to the kitchen, where I find him waiting for the kettle to boil.

'Hi,' I say, rubbing my eye.

He turns around and smiles. 'Hi, sleepy.' He puts his hand out and pulls me in as I take it, wrapping me up in his arms. He's cold from the ride home, and I shiver involuntarily.

'Why didn't you wake me up?' I say.

'You looked so peaceful.'

That wasn't how this was supposed to go, that Fletch would find me dribbling all over his best friend.

'Was I asleep on—?'

'Luca's shoulder, yes.'

The kettle clicks off; Fletch pulls away to go and make a cup

110

of tea. Like, I get that he's probably thirsty after his journey, but it feels abrupt.

He's making a lot out of busying himself with the tea, which makes me think he's not happy. It's fair enough. I guess I'd be cross if I found him asleep on some random girl from the show in Chichester. But, I mean, Luca isn't some random guy. I wipe my chin. 'Well, you had a lucky escape. Luca's sweater's basically made of drool now.' It's not my best material, but hopefully it'll lighten the mood. 'It's nothing, you know that, right?'

'Of course.' Fletch sighs, turns around and takes my face in his hands. He kisses me. 'Nettie, you don't have to worry. I trust you.'

Which is lovely. But it's almost like he had to have a word with himself to say it.

We talk into the night. He holds me close, like he can't get enough of me – as if he's building up reserves for when he has to leave again. I don't remember what time we fell asleep, but I know we were wrapped around each other.

After a leisurely Saturday morning in Camden, we spend the rest of the weekend mooching around a mixture of vintage shops, listening to music back at mine, and having a Sunday roast with Alec. It's perfect. So perfect that I don't mention my worries about Mum or *Triple Threat* or any of the other hundred things on my mind. I don't want to spoil it.

When Sunday evening arrives, I walk him down to his bike, which is parked a few roads away from the flat. I've got that ache in my stomach that I used to get as a kid the night before school, but this time it's got nothing to do with Monday mornings and everything to do with not seeing my boyfriend for a month.

'Well, this was amazing,' he says, taking my face in his hands and kissing me.

'Call me when you get there. I love you.' *And I'll miss you so much it actually physically hurts.* Is what I don't say.

He knows anyway. I feel his arms wrap around me, his lips on the top of my head. We stay there for a couple of minutes. Then he puts his helmet on, swings his rucksack over his shoulders and heads off towards the river on his bike.

I know I should be all driven and hard and into my career and not moping around after my boyfriend, and I'm trying to be all of these things, but it's much harder to be apart from him than I thought it would be. I'm not being ungrateful – I love it at Duke's, and I know thousands of people would bite my arm off to swap places with me, but right now I wish I was on the back of Fletch's bike, arms around his waist, swerving round corners, riding somewhere that no one could find us.

CHAPTER 12

The group chat's never been busier as we gear up to our first *Chicago* session.

11:37
Leon:
Rehearsals start tomorrow . . .

AGH. Fosse session at mine later?

Leon:
Sure!

Alec:
Can I come? I AM a Fosse Queeeeeeen . . .

Leon is typing . . .

I mean you live here

Alec:
😄

Lisa flew back in today.
I saw her heading out with Michael.

Can't wait to get started with her . . .

But also v v scared

Leon is typing . . .

Alec:

She's going to love you.

You've been working so hard on this.
You've got no worries.

♥

12:30

Kiki:

I can't, sorry. Meeting Sam.

Leon messages me privately a little later.

13:10

Actually, Nettie, I'm really sorry, but if Alec's going
to be there, I'd rather not come to yours later. I
just don't need it right before we start rehearsals.

I'm sorry – I know you're trying to keep your distance.
I thought he'd have known I meant you and Kiki.

Wanna come to mine? Kiki can join us later that way.

Perfect x

114

07:30

Thanks for last night. You and Kiki have helped me so much already. How are you feeling about today?

Leon:
NERVOUS
You?

SAME

It's been a long time coming. Taro and I were saying that it'll be a relief to get started!

How IS Taro?

Still cute ☺

Leon and I walk over to the music hall together after college on our way to our first *Chicago* rehearsal. The November rain is making it feel as if winter has come early. It's less than four weeks until we break for Christmas. How is that possible?

Less than four weeks until the Christmas holidays means less than three weeks until the newly-named Christmas Ball, and I *can't wait*. I've already planned what I'm wearing. Seriously, I've been crossing off the days on my calendar. True, he's been kind of hard to get hold of the last couple of weeks, but the next time I'll see Fletch will be at a ball. What could be more perfect?

Leon adjusts his umbrella to cover both of us. 'What if Michael realizes he's made a mistake casting me and asks me to leave in front of everyone?' he says, out of nowhere.

'That's not going to happen, Leon. Michael's not silly. He wouldn't have given you the part if he didn't think you could do it.' I take his arm. 'You're brilliant. Just do what you do, and you'll be more than enough.'

He squeezes my elbow. 'Thanks.'

Michael's rounding up stage blocks and chairs as Leon and I file in with the rest of the cast. We rarely use this studio – it's still laid out like a music hall auditorium, with a raised area and a pit and a small stage over the far end that makes it an awkward space to work in. Old-fashioned sconces on the wall are the only lights, and the floor is mostly covered with a threadbare carpet. I love it – like Fletch once said, it just *feels* like theatre in here. If you put your ear to the wall, you can almost hear the whispers of hundreds of performers from centuries of showbiz.

Obviously the cameras are here. Michael waits until he gets the thumbs-up from Sam before addressing the cast. It's like no one can breathe without her permission. Even just thinking about how Miss Duke overhauled the entire college performance schedule for her on day one is mind-blowing.

'Welcome, everyone.' Michael looks around the dimly lit studio, taking us all in. 'The competition was stiff this year. In a bold move, the musical will be staged here, in this beautiful room, taking it back to its original purpose, which was to house theatrical performance. Yes, the process is a little . . . dragged out this year –' he glances over at Sam – 'but being able to rehearse here should eliminate the need for a long tech week . . . Do I hear sighs of relief? I'd like to hand you over to Lisa Jacobs, who not only is a *Broadway legend*, but a Fosse veteran, having worked with the man himself on several productions. Lisa, it's an honour.'

116

Everyone applauds. I catch myself grinning at her in delight like a four-year-old at a panto. I can't wait to start learning from her.

Lisa puts her hands up to stop the clapping. 'Thank you, Michael. And what a pleasure it is to be working with *you* again.' She turns to us. 'We're going to start with class at every rehearsal. It will help you to form the shapes that you're going to need for this production – shapes that may feel alien to you for a while. Go with it. It'll happen.'

We spread out and start work, studying Lisa in the mirrors Michael's had installed all the way down one side of the music hall. Lisa sets us up with an exercise and then walks among us, correcting technique and encouraging us. At one point I catch Luca's eye in the reflection; he grins sheepishly. As someone playing a non-dancing role, I don't think he was expecting to have to do a full-on class. It's weird seeing him dance – almost like watching him discover the ends of his limbs for the first time. To be fair, he's doing it with gusto. And in jeans.

'What's your name, honey?' says Lisa, as she passes him, unable to hide a smile as she watches him roll his hips the other way from everyone else. 'You're adorable.'

'It's Luca,' he says, wiping a trickle of sweat off his forehead. 'Am I . . . doing it wrong?'

'Wrong and strong, Luca. Wrong and strong.' She winks and carries on up the line.

I stifle a giggle.

Class finishes at around seven, followed by an hour's vocal call, after which Michael gives us a break. Leon goes to make a cup of tea with Kiki. In the absence of anyone to talk to, I go to the mirror and try to refine some of the moves we learned in class.

'Hey, you want to sit back in that.' Lisa's behind me, doing the same move except a ton better. 'Like this, in your hips.'

I try her suggestion. It works. 'Thank you!' I say in delight. (I fall short of, *You're-amazing-I-love-you-please-like-me*, but it's dangerously close to happening.)

'You know, I think there's potential here,' she says, addressing my body rather than my face. 'Why don't we schedule some extra rehearsals? Just you and me.'

My heart stops. 'Omigod, that would be amazing. Thank you.'

'Pleasure.' She points to Luca over by the coffee station. 'I think that guy could do with some help, too.' She calls him over. 'What do you say? A few extra dance sessions? I wasn't counting on my Billy Flynn doing too much movement, but . . .' Her eyes drift over to where Sam and the crew are milling about.

'Uh, sure,' says Luca, smiling. 'Anything to help.'

Lisa smiles at him and goes to speak to Michael.

Luca talks to my reflection in the mirror. 'With all this dance training, maybe I'll give Alec a run for his money by the end of *Chicago*. We could do a dance-off.'

'I'd be here for that,' I say. 'But it would only be fair to make Alec play six instruments as well.'

He grins. 'Hey, I was thinking about your mum. Have you had any more thoughts about where to start searching?'

'Oh.' I don't know what to say. It's taken me by surprise, hearing him talk about it in the middle of rehearsals. Looking behind me to make sure there's no one from the crew lurking nearby, I grab Luca's hand and take him out to the corridor. 'I had a look online and found nothing. How could she have been that well known but so elusive?'

'I don't know,' he says. 'It's odd. Maybe you should get the boxes of her stuff from your grandmother's? I'd happily run you over to get them.'

I pause. 'That's so kind of you, but I couldn't poss—'

'Seriously, Nettie. I don't mind.'

'I . . .' Should I accept his offer? I do want to get my hands on the boxes, but equally, it feels daunting, and I kind of wanted to do that with Fletch. Also, I can't help thinking Fletch seemed – well, not *annoyed*, exactly, but a bit uncomfortable about my spending time with Luca? But he's not here, and Luca's been really kind, and . . . Jeez, why am I even having this conversation with myself? Luca's a friend, there's *nothing* between us, and if I start avoiding him, then I'm *making* a thing of it. And I'm meant to be going for it this year, not sitting around waiting for things to happen to me.

'Thanks, Luca. That would be really helpful.'

20:45
It went well tonight!
Only four weeks, then we get a whole month together!
ALSO THE BALL BEFORE THAT 😊

Fletch:
Glad it went well still at work will call later x

22:03
You were great tonight. I could tell Lisa was really impressed with you.

Leon:

Thanks. It felt OK?

It was more than OK. Taro said you were brilliant too . . . 😊

😏

Hey, guess what?

?

Luca and I get to have extra coaching with Lisa!

I'm so happy

I love her

Yeah, she's awesome. That's great, Nettie. You'll be a Fosse pro in no time.

DANCING IS LIFE

'Extra rehearsals with Luca, huh?' Alec peers over my shoulder from behind the sofa.

I flip my phone screen side down and bat him away. 'Stop doing that! Like, personal space.'

He ignores me. 'That'll be nice. You and Luca, cosying up while I'm stuck here like some sort of loner—'

'We will not be *cosying up*. Ugh, Alec, stop making out like Luca and I are—'

'Making out?' Alec's smirking is at unendurable levels.

'Just stop, OK? It's annoying. And stop reading my messages, too. You're always doing it, especially when I'm talking to Leon.'

Alec's cheeks flush. 'No, I'm not.'

'Yes, *you are*. If you want to know how he got on tonight, just ask him.'

For once, Alec has nothing to say. He mutters something under his breath like 'as if', and slinks back off to the kitchen.

CHAPTER 13

Luca's waiting down at the Aldwych in the only parking space in the whole of London on the first Sunday of December. After a hectic fortnight, we've finally managed to find a day to go and pick up my stuff from Auntie's. I get in and we set off over the river.

My phone rings. It's Fletch. 'Hey.'

'Hi, Nettie,' he says. 'Sorry I didn't call yesterday. It got late. How are you doing?'

'Good. How's it going?'

'Great, but they've just asked me if I can work next Saturday. I'm really sorry. I can't say no, not when the entire team has committed to staying the extra day. It'll only be the daytime.'

I have to physically stop myself from sighing. 'It's fine.' It's not at all fine; we'd arranged to spend the day together before going to the ball. But I try to sound upbeat because I don't want him to feel guilty.

'Are you sure?'

I take a breath. 'Yes. Completely. We knew it was going to be like this. You'll make it in time for the evening, won't you?'

'Wouldn't miss the chance to take my girl to the ball,' he says. 'I love you.'

'I love you, too. Take a left here.'

'What?' says Fletch. 'Are you in the car?'

'Oh, Luca's taking me back to Auntie's to get Mum's stuff,' I say.

122

He doesn't say anything for a second.

'I'd have done that,' he says eventually.

I suddenly feel bad. Of course Fletch would want to help me.

'I know,' I say, trying to sound understanding but also hoping to disguise the awkwardness of our conversation from Luca, who can probably hear every word. When Fletch doesn't answer, I add, 'I was just scared she'd get rid of it if I didn't go soon.'

'Nettie, I'm sorry,' says Fletch, after a couple of seconds. 'I feel like I haven't been there for you.'

'It's fine – I know you're busy.' I gesture right to Luca, who gets into the filter lane.

'I'm really glad Luca's there to help you,' he says, and there's a surprising warmth in his voice. 'Makes me feel better about being stuck down here.'

Luca takes a wrong turn and I gesture for him to go back. 'Fletch, I'd better go. I'll call you later.'

'Oh, OK. Good luck.'

'Thanks.' I hang up.

'Fletch OK?' Luca's obviously pretending not to have heard out of politeness.

'They seem to want a lot from him. I think he's feeling it.'

'He doesn't mind that I'm helping you with this, does he?' says Luca, his voice mirroring the anxiety I already feel.

'Honestly, I don't think it's you, specifically. He's just sad that he can't be here. I think he just feels a bit left out.'

We arrive outside the house. Luca spends a few minutes trying to get into a tiny parking space while I get my keys out of my bag and prepare for battle. A year ago, I wouldn't have even come. But I feel different this year – like I've grown, like I'm finally ready to take back control of my life. I've found my voice, and I'm not going to let anyone silence me.

I knock on the door. Best not to surprise her.

As luck would have it, there's no answer. There's no one in as far as I can tell, so as Luca joins me, I unlock the door and we head inside.

He looks up at the chandelier hanging from the high ceiling. 'Wow. Your gran's posh.'

'I know. It's weird, isn't it?'

We shrug off our coats and toss them over a kitchen chair so we can lug the boxes down the stairs unrestricted, and I lead him up to the attic. It's a proper working room with a bed and a sofa, only it looks like someone's just moved in due to the seven or eight boxes piled up at one end. That's all that's left of her, along with the memories inside my head. Funny – it's not much, but it's also everything.

My throat's tight. 'Can we get them all in the car?' I say quietly.

Luca sizes up the boxes. 'Yeah, I reckon.'

We start carrying the boxes down to the front door, and after the final lot has been brought down, Luca begins to load the car while I head back to the kitchen to collect our coats.

I look in the fridge, just for a laugh (although there's actually nothing funny about it). As usual, it's almost completely empty, apart from a small amount of salad in the drawer at the bottom, a tiny bottle of skimmed milk and a few slices of ham from the Sydenham deli. There's no bread in the bread bin, just a packet of Ryvita. When I was living here and she was trying to force her regime on to me, I despised and resented her. Now that I've had some distance, I can see her for what she is: a lonely old lady, damaged by her years in ballet. I can only imagine what it must have been like for Mum growing up with her.

'Nettie?' Luca's voice echoes from down the hall. 'Er, you might want to come here.'

'No need, Antoinette.'

I turn around to find my grandmother standing in the doorway of the kitchen, still wearing her hat and coat.

'Auntie.'

'You can't take those boxes.' She marches past me and closes the fridge door. 'They were Anastasia's.'

'Exactly. And now they're mine.'

Luca's appeared in the doorway now, looking awkward. 'Everything OK?'

I nod. Silently, he retreats back into the corridor.

'I don't know why you're so insistent on digging up matters that don't concern you, Antoinette.'

The familiar rage bubbles up, starting in my stomach and travelling up to the top of my head where it explodes like a volcano. 'What is it with all of you? Miss Duke won't talk to me, and neither will Michael. What are you hiding? She was *my* mum. I have a right to know.'

'If your mother didn't tell you these things, it seems quite self-explanatory that she didn't want you to know.'

Her comment hits me straight in the chest. I hurry past her out of the room, gesturing to Luca, who's hovering by the front door, to run.

Auntie follows me. 'You're not taking those boxes, Antoinette. Come back!'

We fly down the path and scramble into the car. Luca throws the last box on to my lap, starts the ignition and drives. 'Whew,' he gasps, checking his mirror as we speed down the hill. 'That was a close one!'

After the initial shock, Luca and I laugh and laugh, almost all the way home, I think out of relief more than anything. When we arrive back at the flat it takes us a few trips to get all the boxes up the stairs and into the living room. After the last one, I hug him.

'Thanks. I don't think I could have faced her on my own.'

He waggles his phone at me. 'No worries. I'm here if you need me – Oh, hey.'

Alec has surfaced from his room. His face still has bed creases down one side; it's clear he's been asleep all day.

'I thought you were out,' I say in surprise.

'No,' Alec replies bitterly. 'I've been lying in my *own bed* on Sunday afternoon, *alone*. The shame of it.'

Luca opens the front door. 'I gotta head – let me know if you find anything.' He hugs me.

'Will do,' I say. I turn my head to catch Alec behind me making obscene gestures with his mouth. I give him the finger as Luca leaves.

Alec follows me through to the living room and balks at the sight of Mum's boxes. 'Holy fucking Bernadette Peters, Nettie. What's all this?'

'Mum's stuff.'

He smiles slyly. 'Well! Luca's turning out to be quite the prince, isn't he? Helping his damsel in distress.'

'Alec, you're starting to annoy me.'

'Nettie, the mess in here's *starting to annoy me*.' Alec mimics my tone so well that I laugh in spite of myself.

'I'll put it all away when I've finished looking through it.' I

126

look at the pile and suddenly feel overwhelmed. What if this is it – the moment I've been waiting for, the information I crave? And what if – what if I can't handle it?

Alec puts an arm around me. 'You're not doing this alone. I'm calling in the cavalry.' He pulls out his phone.

'Oh, don't bother them,' I say. 'Kiki's been so busy lately. And Leon's probably with Taro . . .' What I really mean is that Leon's been reluctant to spend any time with Alec lately while he asserts himself and takes ownership of his new direction. So I feel uncomfortable asking him over.

'Are you kidding?' says Alec, overly enthusiastic, even for him. 'They're your best friends. Of course they'd want to be here for this. Plus – rummaging through years of unseen documents to uncover the truth about a mysterious star of the ballet world? What could be more fun than that?'

By the time Kiki and Leon arrive, Alec's whipped up a load of macaroni cheese and a huge salad. We get them up to speed while we eat.

'Seconds, Leon?' says Alec.

Leon shakes his head. 'It was lovely, but I'm so full. I had a late breakfast.' His eyes flit to Kiki, whose mouth tilts upwards in a tiny smile.

I'm not the only one to notice.

'Er, what's that supposed to mean?' demands Alec.

'Nothing.'

'Yes it does. A "late breakfast" means just that – but a "*late breakfast*" accompanied by a smirk means something else. Oh my God, Leon – did you have sex last night?'

Leon smiles. 'Actually, Taro stayed over.'

Alec looks genuinely shocked.

Kiki's grinning along like she's watching someone watch her favourite bit in a movie. 'It's not the first time, either,' she blurts out. 'Sorry, Leon.'

'That's OK.' He laughs, rolling his eyes at her. 'Kiki's basically planning our wedding.'

'You never said anything,' said Alec. 'I had no idea you two were an item.'

'Oh, we're not,' said Leon. 'It's just a casual thing.'

'Ah well, I suppose you'll be keen to practise, now that you've actually done it. Get yourself up to Taro's level, as it were.'

Why does he always have to spoil things? No wonder Leon's been avoiding him if this is how he treats him. Kiki and I both open our mouths to bollock Alec, but surprisingly, Leon gets there first.

'Oh don't worry. He'd say I've already done that.'

The best thing about the comeback is that Leon's not at all bothered – the opposite, in fact. Alec's clearly ruffled. Kiki and I catch each other's eye. It's good to see the dynamics changing.

Kiki stands up. 'Shall we clear up? It's getting late.'

'Yes,' says Leon. 'Are you ready, Nettie?' He takes my hand, and I suddenly do feel ready. It's the first time we've all been together since the party, and I'm grateful that Leon put aside his own stuff to be here for me. Maybe we can all start getting back to how we used to be last year, when it was us four against the world. But us four against my mum's boxes is a good start.

Everyone grabs a box and starts digging. I find a bunch of Duke's photos. Mum's in most of them, sometimes alone, smiling or in a ballet pose, sometimes with friends.

'Wow,' says Leon. 'Apart from the long hair, it could be you.'

128

'Well, and the *arabesque*,' adds Alec. 'Nettie's not known for her lines – a fact of which I've reminded her on more than one occasion.' He pokes me in the ribs, and for once, I'm grateful for the piss-take. Despite everything, he always knows how to make me feel lighter.

'Where do you think this one was taken?' I ask, pointing to a group shot taken midway through a routine.

Alec squints at the background. 'It looks like King's.'

'King's?'

'Duke's has only been called that since Miss Duke took over,' he says. 'Before that, the school was split in two. Drama and music at the music hall; dance at the studios in Bermondsey. They're not there now – I think they were condemned. Miss Duke managed to get some makeshift premises closer to the music hall for a few years until she acquired the new building. Then she merged the lot and started the up MT and stage managers courses.'

'How do you know all that?' I say.

'Babe, *everyone* knows that,' he says.

Kiki and Leon nod in agreement.

'Oh,' I say, surprised that there's all this secret history to Duke's that I've never heard of. 'I thought it must have been taken at college, but I don't know exactly when she was there.'

We continue searching through the boxes for several minutes, until I find something that almost makes my heart stop. It's a letter, addressed to Mum.

My dearest Ana,

Thank you for your letters. I cherish each and every one. It feels like such a long time since we were together.

129

Congratulations! I cried when I heard your happy news. I'm so glad you're embracing this baby for the miracle it is.

Jerry sends his love. Ana, we're together! After all that time being friends – I can't believe it. I think he might be the one. I think it may be time to share my love with the world. 'I'm ready now,' to quote a man we both love.

I'm so glad you're getting better. The view from the gardens in the photograph you sent looks absolutely stunning. May your stay be short but nourishing.

Do let me know when I can come and visit you.

Until then, my love

xxxxx

'Who's it from?' says Alec, when I show him. 'They haven't signed it.'

'I don't know.' I reread the letter.

'It sounds like maybe she was in hospital?' says Leon.

'Or . . .' Something connects in my brain. The video. The comments from Millicent Moore last year about Mum drinking and sleeping her way to the top. The fact that I never saw Mum take so much as a sip of alcohol. 'Rehab.'

No one answers, but I can tell it makes sense to them, too.

Kiki holds up the letter. 'Who do you think it's from?'

'Well, I thought it was a boyfriend or something,' I say, 'but then they talk about Jerry, so it must be a woman.'

'Er, excuse me?' Alec demands. 'Gay people did exist then, you know.'

'Omigod! I didn't even think of that! Sorry, Alec. You might be right – listen: *I think it may be time to share my love with the world – "I'm ready now"* – it could be a man. Like, coming out, or something?'

'Yes, maybe,' he agrees.

I sigh. 'Well, now it could be anyone.'

An hour later, after finding mainly bills and a few photos of Mum dancing that make Alec shriek with joy ('Dear God, those feet!'), Leon comes across a small bunch of letters, held together with a green elastic band.

'Nettie, I think these might be worth a look.' He waves one he's extracted from the pile. 'Doesn't say who it's from, but I think it's the same handwriting as the one you showed us.'

I take the letter from him and read it aloud.

My darling Ana,

Hope this week has been a little better. I can't tell you how proud of you I am for tackling this head on.

I was sad to read your latest reply. You say, quite vehemently, that you 'will never forgive her'. Do you not think there's forgiveness to be had on both sides? It would be devastating for it all to come to an end, after everything you've been through together.

Will you let me confront her? Ask her if it's true? What if this is all just miscommunication? If I can help salvage your friendship at all, I will. You've been close for too long just to give up on it.

Love from Jerry, too. We can't wait for you to be out. I miss your smiling face.

All my love to you x

'Seriously, who writes a letter and doesn't sign it?' I say. I'm almost tempted to rip it up.

'Someone you're so close to that you don't feel the need to bother,' says Alec, squeezing my shoulders.

'Who do you think she won't forgive?' says Kiki.

Long before my brain's even connected the dots, my body has put two and two together, and I have to fight to keep the letter from shaking in my hands. But before I can vocalize my suspicions, Leon's on to another letter.

'There's more here,' he says, having now untied the entire bundle of letters and scanned at least half of them. 'Read this one, Nettie.'

My dearest A,

Well, I did it, just as you said. I confronted her. Her first response was to ask me why you didn't just ask her yourself, said it was between you and her, that she'd rather not air her dirty laundry with the whole theatre world. She thought you were too afraid to speak to her. She was angry, Ana – there's no dressing it up.

When I pressed her, she didn't deny it. She just said, 'Well, didn't I have good reason?' But I don't think it was her, Ana. I just don't think she'd stoop so low as to betray you like that.

When I told her where you were, she seemed to soften. She said, and I quote, 'I'm glad she's dealing with things, but until she takes responsibility for her actions, I can't make peace with her'.

How is it going? Please reply as soon as you can. I can't stop thinking about you.
Yours,

B xxx

Air her dirty laundry – I've heard that phrase before. There's only one person it could be. My heart's racing now as I grab the letter from Leon and read through it again.

I look up. The others are all staring, enthralled.

'The person she won't forgive . . .' says Leon.

'You think?' says Alec.

'Uh-huh,' agrees Kiki.

'Cecile Duke,' I say. 'It has to be. What do you think about the sender?'

'At least you've got an initial,' says Kiki. 'Can you think of anyone your mum knew whose name began with "B"?'

I shake my head. 'I've no idea who she was friends with back then. I knew her friends from her book club and the mums from primary school she was close to, but that's it.'

The other letters are vague, more conversational. There's one more that mentions the person we think could be Miss Duke, but only to say that 'B' has told her about Mum's pregnancy, and that she had a *'funny look in her eyes'*. It's bizarre. There's so much I never knew about.

'Must've been quite serious for them never to speak again.' Alec looks at the last letter. 'Anything else in there, Leon?'

'I don't know. Help me, will you, Alec? It's heavy. Feels promising.'

Leon and Alec take the box over to the sofas.

'Nettie, look,' says Kiki, sitting down next to me and putting her feet up on the sofa. 'It's a load of congratulations cards from when you were born! There might be something here.'

'*To Ana, so happy for you and your bundle of joy, much love, Sadie and Jonathon*,' Alec reads aloud. 'Know them?'

'No.'

'How about Ling? Matt and Sean? Debbie?'

'Nope, none of them.'

'Ooh, here's another letter!' says Kiki, jumping up off the sofa. She passes it over to me – it's written on expensive cream notepaper.

Dear Ana,
Congratulations on the birth of little Antoinette. A fitting name. I am very happy for you.

I hope this joyful new beginning can help us put the past behind us. I am ready. Let me know when you are.

Love,
Cecile x

'So, your mum did something to upset Miss Duke, and Miss Duke in turn betrayed her?' says Kiki. 'Then Cecile tried to make peace, but they never spoke again? It's like a soap.'

'*Allegedly* betrayed her,' says Leon. '"B" thinks that she wouldn't have, remember?'

I lie back against the cushions. What could Mum have done that was so bad? And what was Miss Duke's revenge? It all sounds so . . . sordid.

'We'll get to the bottom of it, Nettie,' says Alec.

He walks behind the sofa and rubs my head. I'm more confused than ever – finding these letters has opened up as many questions as it has answered – but knowing my best friends are here for me makes all the difference in the world. I couldn't have opened those boxes without them.

As the conversation drifts to other things, I watch a couple in the studio opposite being coached for their 'first dance'. They just look so in love, the way he's holding her, the way she's looking at him, that it makes me ache for Fletch. I should have told him everything about Mum. He's away, sure – and I wanted to keep things simple, but this is *part* of me. If I keep it from him, it's only going to put a wedge between us.

I text him.

18:48

Found out some intriguing stuff about Mum . . .

Missed you today x

He doesn't reply, but I can see he's read the messages. I know he's busy, but would a kiss be too much effort, or a '*cool, speak later*'?

I'm trying really hard to stay positive, but I feel like he hasn't got time for me any more.

Fletch finally calls at ten past midnight.

'Sorry, Nettie. The producers came in and didn't like half of it, so we're doing rewrites. They've already binned two songs that I thought were brilliant. Then they wanted to take us all out for dinner, which was awkward because the writers were pissed off about the songs being cut.'

'Sounds intense.'

'It was – I mean, it's amazing being here, don't get me wrong – but sometimes it's hard to sit there and watch them throw away weeks of work.'

'Mmn. I bet.' A message from Luca pops up while I'm talking. I've been screenshotting all the letters to him for the last hour. I put Fletch on loudspeaker so that I can see what Luca's said.

00:10
Luca:

> I think we need to find out
> who 'B' is. That's our best bet.

'I just . . .' Fletch trails off. 'Hey, you still there? I didn't wake you up, did I?'

'No, not at all. I was watching TV.'

00:10

> I just don't know where to start.

136

'You OK, Nettie?'

'Yeah, fine.'

> I reckon it's someone she worked with. Narrows it down a bit. We need to find out what shows your mum was in and look through the cast lists to see if there's anyone with that initial.

'You sound a bit distracted.'

I realize I'm not really listening to him. 'Sorry. Long day.'

'Ah,' he says. 'I forgot you went to Auntie's today. How did it go?'

Finally, he's actually remembered. 'Well, Luca and I managed to get most of the boxes out of the loft, but then she came home and tried to stop us, so we had to leg it. But I found out loads of stuff about Mum,' I say.

'Luca met your grandmother?' says Fletch.

'Er, yeah – is that a problem?'

'I just . . . thought you didn't like people meeting her,' he says. 'I had to wait in the car when I took you there.'

I can't believe what I'm hearing. What I really need to talk about is the letters. But somehow we're having a conversation about Fletch feeling hurt that Luca got to meet my grandmother and he didn't?

'She just happened to come home while we were there,' I say. 'It's not a big deal.'

We carry on talking for a couple of minutes, but it's stilted and awkward, and I'm too cross to go into any more detail. Eventually, I hang up, promising to call him tomorrow.

I lie in bed, feeling wired, and angry that I didn't even get to tell him about everything we found out today. Why is Fletch making this about him? What does he expect me to do – sit indoors doing nothing until he's back from his adventure? It's hard, being apart. Things get misconstrued, moments misread . . .

We're just missing each other. It's the ball in a week. Fletch is coming back, and I get to rewrite last year's horrible memories with amazing new ones. And then there's Christmas – we get to spend that together, too. It can't come a moment too soon.

I sit up and reach for the bundle of Mum's letters. Maybe Luca's right – if we find 'B', it's a start, at least. I wish I'd had a chance to talk about it with Fletch, instead of getting irritated with him. As I read through the letters for the seventieth time, the same two questions come back to me, over and over again.

Why all the secrets and lies? What did Mum have to hide?

I keep imagining angry conversations between us, where I accuse her of keeping things from me; she breaks down, and eventually tells me everything.

That's the trouble with dead people. They take all their secrets with them.

CHAPTER 14

'Is something wrong with that?' I say to Kiki on Wednesday evening at the music hall. We've brought food from home to eat in the changing room before rehearsals. She's left the whole of her sandwich.

'No – I've eaten the filling,' she replies.

'Why would you just eat the filling?'

'Leon made it for me this morning, but I thought I should lay off the bread, what with the ball this weekend. It's not a myth, you know, that the camera adds ten pounds. Sam says it's true.'

Well, this is new. Kiki's been so completely anti weight-talk that hearing her speak like this again is strange. And worrying.

I choose my words carefully. 'That's a . . . weird thing for Sam to be talking about.'

'She's just doing her job.' Kiki sounds defensive. 'It's better that I know these things. Sam says as little as four or five pounds will make a huge difference to how I'm perceived onscreen.'

'I thought you weren't buying into that bullshit any more,' I say.

'Isn't it possible not to buy into it but still acknowledge that it exists?' she says. 'Sam agrees it's bullshit, but as she says: like it or not, it's how the industry works.'

Sam's getting to her. What astounds me is how quickly she seems to have done it.

'Babe, you shouldn't be trying to lose weight just because Sam's—' I start.

139

'Says the thinnest person in the room. I'm sorry, Nettie, but this has nothing to do with you. Like, I get where you're coming from, but maybe if you were under constant pressure to stay slim, you'd be a bit more understanding. I don't hate other people's bodies. I don't even hate my own body – I just need it to work for me right now, and that means making it a little smaller. You might feel differently if you weren't already a size four.'

'I just meant—'

'Do you realize what it costs me to stay this size?' Kiki continues. 'If I ate what you ate, I'd be three stone heavier. No one would employ me. I just want to dance, Nettie. And sitting there in your Brandy Melville jeans with your enormous tub of cheesy pasta doesn't exactly qualify you to criticize.'

As her words settle, the realization hits me. Kiki's always been hugely affected by the fat-shaming that goes on at Duke's. Expecting her to be suddenly cured of her insecurities just because she had one good summer is crap of me. How could she be, when the obsession with skinny runs through the very brickwork of this place, insidiously shaming, subtly whispering negativity until everyone's bought into it? Her body is her business, not mine. I feel like a shit friend.

'I'm sorry,' I say. 'I didn't think. Sorry, Kiki. I just meant that Sam shouldn't be telling you what to do with your body.'

'She's looking out for me,' says Kiki. 'The business is superficial and judgemental. She completely gets how I feel.'

I don't think Sam *does* get how Kiki really feels, or she wouldn't be having conversations like that with her. But I already feel bad enough about the comment *I* just made, and I don't want to upset Kiki any more than I already have. I hug her tightly, hoping she knows how sorry I am, and get my things ready for the rehearsal.

140

'OK, everyone. Take five.' Lisa smiles. 'Good work, everybody.'

Shaiann and the dancers relax, panting. They've just finished 'Cell Block Tango'. Kiki's magnificent, starting it all off with her murderous speech. She was worried about the acting, but Lisa's made it so dance-heavy that Kiki's been able to treat it like a piece of choreography, which has helped her to relax into the role.

We're all heading to our various corners of the room when Michael calls us back. 'Can I have everyone's attention for a sec? Thank you. Just to remind you that because the third-years are needed to rehearse the little concert they're putting on at the Christmas Ball, this is our last *Chicago* rehearsal until after the party.'

I'd forgotten about that. It'll be nice to have some time off, to be honest. Four hours of rehearsals after a full day at college is exhausting, especially when Sam insists we run numbers again and again so that she can get them from a million angles. It makes for slow progress.

Kiki and Lisa go off into the corner to go through some choreography together, and Luca takes the opportunity to join me.

'Hey,' he says. 'What's new?'

'Not a lot. Bit tired.'

'Fletch OK?'

'Yeah, I think so,' I say. He looks at me quizzically. 'Haven't spoken to him for a couple of days,' I add. 'They've had the orchestrators in, so it's busy. We've messaged a couple of times, but . . .' What I don't add is that I've messaged him lots, but he only replies briefly and usually at midnight. I've kind of got used to the disappointment.

'Oh – yeah, I guess that would be full on,' says Luca. 'Well, cheer up – it's the ball this weekend. He's still coming, right?'

'Yes,' I say, and my mood lifts instantly. The thought of the Christmas Ball and seeing Fletch is keeping me going right now. Last year at the Freshers' Ball, Jade threw two glasses of red wine all over the yellow dress of Mum's that I was wearing, and in what was admittedly a bit of a Cinderella move, I ran home early and spent the evening crying into a bowl of stain remover. This year, I'm going to spend the evening dancing with my friends and kissing my boyfriend. I can't wait. So what if Fletch is a little preoccupied this week? Saturday night's going to make up for it.

'Hey – any joy with the letters?' Luca says.

I look over my shoulder. Sam's nowhere nearby. 'No. I did check the library, but "B" isn't much to go on. There was a Jerry who danced at the Royal Opera House – but there's nothing to link him to Mum, and we don't know who wrote the letter. It's a bit of a dead end.'

'There must be a way,' says Luca. 'I'll keep thinking about it.'

I smile at him gratefully. 'Thanks,' I say. 'You're a really good friend.'

Luca goes to refill his water bottle while I head outside for a couple of minutes of fresh air. On the way I pass Leon and Taro talking at the bottom of the stairs. Taro's leaning against the wall next to a poster for a cabaret evening with *West End Star Sissy Flynn*. Leon's kind of nestled under his arm. They look pretty cosy.

'Ooh, I love Sissy Flynn,' I say, tapping the poster. 'We should go to that.'

'We were just saying it's weird,' says Taro, 'not having rehearsals next week. I'll kind of miss everyone.'

142

'Can't wait for the concert,' I say.

'Yeah, should be good.' He leans in and kisses Leon smoochily. Leon joins in for a second before pulling away awkwardly – I'm not sure if it's for my benefit or because he's worried about lurking cameras.

'Anyway,' says Taro. 'Gotta go over something with Michael.' Another smooch. This time I rummage in my bag for something very important and also non-existent so that Leon doesn't feel awkward. 'See ya.' Grinning, Taro goes back upstairs.

'Are you and Taro doing a ball-thing together?' I say. Leon raises a quizzical brow. 'You know . . . going as a couple—'

'Er, no.' He pinches my arm. 'He just said he'd catch up with me there.'

'You're spending more time together these days . . . and you seem happy.'

Leon thinks about this for a moment. 'We are. I might have a chat with him at the ball . . . that we could be exclusive? Do you think it's too soon?'

'Leon, you've been seeing him for nearly three months. It's perfectly reasonable.'

'What if Taro doesn't want that? I've always been very careful to keep it casual so far. What if that's how he likes it? What if that's how *I* like it?'

I laugh. 'You might want to work that part out before you talk to him.'

Leon sighs. 'Ugh. This whole relationship thing is so complicated. No wonder Alec never goes on more than two dates with anyone. Much less hassle.'

'I thought we were talking about Taro.'

He pauses. 'We are. I just meant that maybe my life would be simpler if I was more like Alec.' The thought visibly brings him down. I can't help noticing with Leon how every conversation eventually comes back to Alec. He's so happy with Taro, and really making his mark in MT and the college musical, but it's like he can't enjoy any of it because there's this whole Alec thing hanging over him. I wish they'd just sort it out. Hugging him, I grab my coat from the changing room and head outside.

I check my phone to see, unsurprisingly, zero messages from my boyfriend, but weirdly a load from Alec.

19:10
Alec:

How are rehearsals?

I miss youuuuu

When are you home?

I start tapping in an answer.

20:11

Not sure. Going to the pub
with everyone after rehearsals x

The rest of the rehearsal is actually pretty fun. Luca and I get to do our first scene together, which wasn't at all awkward, as Alec had been suggesting it would be. In my head I do a smug little *'ha ha, told you so'* at him. Sam turns up with a camera just as Luca's saying his line about how he'll manipulate Roxie's story for the press, show them what they want to see, which seems . . . well timed.

We have to do the scene over and over because it's underscored.

144

When we finally nail it, Michael cheers. 'By Jove, I think they've got it.'

I throw myself on Luca in mock relief, and everyone laughs. It's so good to end on a high after the slog of this morning.

When we come out into the cold street later, Alec's waiting across the road.

'Alec! What are you doing here? It's freezing.'

'I just wanted to see you,' he says through chattering teeth. He's obviously been there a while. 'Thought I'd come along to the pub.'

I go to check Leon's response, but he's gone ahead with Taro. 'Come on, then,' I say. 'We need to get you warm.'

It goes surprisingly well, actually. Alec makes an effort to be really supportive of Leon, asking him how it's going, wanting to hear all about the show, not taking over the conversation. Leon's at ease for once. It's good to see them getting on at last. We don't see much of Kiki because she's over at the bar with Sam and Anand for most of the evening, but she looks over and smiles at me a couple of times, and I know she's glad I came.

When Alec and I are leaving, I go over to say goodbye to Kiki, who's just with Anand now. Sam's further down the bar with her back to us, but I notice she's replaying a file of what she's captured this evening. I have a peek while Alec and Kiki are saying their goodbyes. The camera's focused entirely on me during that last dance number we did. It's a little . . . intense. I'm also surprised to see the hug I just gave Luca at such a close angle on the little screen – just our faces and nothing else. It sort of looks cinematic, like she's slowed it down?

As soon as I'm outside, I quiz Alec. 'Did you see it? On Sam's screen?'

'Yes, I saw it,' he says grimly.

'What do you think?'

He takes a second to collect his thoughts, like he's working out how to phrase it. 'I think,' he says, 'that you're going to be more of a star than you realize.'

CHAPTER 15

On the Saturday morning of the ball, we all go to Alec's posh beauty salon, where he's generously paid for us all to have treatments, and now we're having lunch in Covent Garden (his treat again). It's really kind of him, and with the huge effort he's been making with Leon ever since we all went through Mum's letters together, it sort of feels like things are starting to be normal again – the four of us all together, hanging out. Tonight's going to be amazing. The boy I was secretly in love with last year is now my boyfriend, and we're going to the ball together. And to top things off, an enormous burger's just arrived with my name on it.

Alec steals a chip.

'Oi!'

'What? Your dress'll be uncomfortable if you eat all those. It's boned, remember.'

'I'm not putting it on for another six hours. I think I'm good.'

'If I ate a burger like that, I wouldn't get into my dress for about three days,' says Kiki. She scrapes some of the dressing off her tiny salad irritably. 'For fuck's sake. What part of "on the side" do they not understand?'

My heart hurts for her, but I keep quiet. She's been on a diet all week. I know that because on Monday I saw a piece of paper sticking out of her bag with an eating plan printed on it. Sam's email address was at the top of the page.

Leon moves his drink to accommodate the enormous plate

147

of calamari being set down in front of him. 'I've heard they're filming tonight.'

'There's no way I'm drinking until they've left,' says Alec. 'Miss Duke's normally long gone before all the debauchery starts. Can you imagine her face, when it's broadcast? All the shenanigans?'

'It'd almost be worth it, just for that,' says Leon, his eyes gleaming. 'Alec Van Damm: dishevelled, shamed, ruined . . .'

'It'll never happen,' says Alec. 'I'm too fabulous, *and you don't even know it.*'

Ordinarily this would have provoked an eye-roll, but today, Leon laughs. I wonder if he's happy because he's going to have 'the talk' with Taro later.

'Remember that thing you said you were going to do tonight?' I say to Leon, hoping he'll know what I'm talking about. 'Are you going to do it?'

Leon looks at Kiki and me with a smile. 'Yes.'

'What thing?' demands Alec.

'Leon said he'd help me with something,' I say vaguely. 'For . . . *Chicago.*'

Alec looks at me suspiciously but settles for pinching another of my chips. He ducks out of the way as I go to swat him. 'What? I'm still hungry.'

'You're another one,' says Kiki. 'Huge bowl of curry, half Nettie's chips and still thin as a rake. It's not fair.'

'I just want to say for the record,' says Alec, 'that we all think you're completely gorgeous, Kiki.'

'Yeah, and we love you,' I say.

'You're beautiful, friend,' says Leon.

'Thanks, guys,' she says, laughing. 'I mean, I *am* hot.'

If she'd said that to me two months ago, I'd have believed her.

I'm just not sure if *she* believes it any more.

We head back to ours to get ready for the ball, and by seven, we're all ready. It's got to be said: the boys scrub up well. I'm so used to them in tights and trackies that it's a shock to see them in DJs. I'm wearing a vintage emerald-green beaded dress, strapless and kind of flowing – another of Mum's – that suits my pale skin nicely (Alec's finally stopped trying to get me to have spray tans). Kiki's is the complete opposite – peach bodycon with cleavage and cut-outs. She looks beautiful.

'Omigod, Kiki – why are you so stunning?' I say, tripping over my gown to run and give her a hug. 'Oops.'

The four of us head up to Soho together. People watch us curiously. One guy even gets his phone out and starts filming.

'They think we're going to a premiere,' says Alec. He turns around to the guy with the phone and waves.

This is hilarious. They've put a red carpet down Frith Street and halfway round Soho Square. Lights sparkle from within. I imagine dancing with Fletch, his arms around my waist, my hands on the nape of his neck, looking into each other's eyes like nothing else exists (except the conveniently placed string quartet in the corner and the thousands of glittering fairy lights above us, of course). Tonight is going to be literally something out of a movie. We're going to have a perfect evening, and then tomorrow I'm going to tell Fletch all the stuff I've discovered about Mum. We're going to get back to how we were in the summer, before everything got so complicated.

Flashing bulbs catch my eye to the left, and I turn to see two men with long-lens cameras taking photos of Kiki.

'Hey, gorgeous – what's your name? Fancy posing for us?'

Alec takes over. 'What's this in aid of?'

'*Hello*, *OK!*, *Heat* mag . . . Raising the profile of the college. Got a tip-off from someone at Three Ring TV.' He checks his phone quickly, before stuffing it in his shirt pocket.

'OK, let's do it,' says Alec. He gestures to us to line up with him on the red carpet. 'Smile!'

The two guys snap away furiously.

'So you've got Alec Van Damm, Leon Adigwe, Nettie Delaney-Richardson and Kiki Steadman,' says Alec smoothly. 'We're all starring in the Three Ring doc, so it'd be in your interest to use us.'

'Alec—' I begin.

He shushes me.

'*Nettie?*' says the pap. His eyes light up.

'Er, yeah,' I say, confused.

'Amazing. Got told to look out for you. Can I get a couple of you on your own?'

Before I have a chance to reply, I hear someone yelling behind us in a high-pitched screech to the other photographer.

'What do you mean, "No, you're all right"?'

It's Jade Upton, dressed in what looks like a ballroom dance costume, half orange, half white, feathers *everywhere*. 'Do you know who I am?'

'No one knows who you are, love,' says the photographer, who has lit up a cigarette and couldn't look less interested.

'Shit, who does that?' whispers Kiki in horror, looking down at Jade's feet. She's wearing one white shoe and one orange shoe.

'Someone who's been told to by Sam, I imagine,' says Alec. 'Seriously, there can be no other reason for that aesthetic.'

My phone rings. 'Gotta get this, sorry,' I say. Glad to escape the circus, I cross the road over to the square.

150

'Hi,' says Fletch. It sounds like he's trying not to be overheard. 'Listen, I'm really sorry, but I'm not going to make it tonight.'

'What?' My heart almost stops. The one thing I've been looking forward to for weeks, and now it's not even going to happen.

'I'm so sorry, Nettie.'

He doesn't sound sorry, more like he's in a rush to get off the phone to me.

I take a breath before I reply. 'Why not?'

'David wants a recording of the show as it stands so far, and there have been lots of changes that we haven't been able to get down as we go. We've got to record the new songs.'

'Who's David?'

'He's the director.'

'Oh. Do you have to do it *now*?'

'Yes,' he says shortly. 'Nettie, you don't say no to people like David Hirst. Anyway, they've got the entire cast and band here – do you think I can just waltz on over and say, *"Hey, guys, I know I'm just an intern, but my girlfriend wants me at a party. Can I shoot off"*?'

He's never spoken to me like this before.

'OK,' I say, stung. 'There's no need to be sarcastic.'

He blows out air like he's trying to exhale stress. 'Nettie . . . it's hard to explain the kind of pressure we're under here.' Before I can reply, he's talking to someone else. 'Yes, of course – I'll get the strings in now.' He lowers his voice again. 'I'm sorry, Nettie. I've got to go.' He hangs up without waiting for me to answer.

The wind picks up through the square, whistling through the iron railings. Reeling from his words, I make my way back across the road, shivering in my dress, angry and embarrassed. He made me feel clingy and immature. It's like, I get it, Fletch? You're working out there working with professionals, and I'm just a silly second-year at college. I've got no idea what it's like in the real world. I'm too busy worrying about parties.

I go into Duke's, ignoring the fairy lights that ten minutes ago probably would have looked magical and romantic but now just seem tacky and shit, to find Sam beside an enormous Christmas tree, talking to Alec, Leon and Kiki. Seeing my thunderous face, Alec raises a concerned eyebrow, but I quickly shake my head.

'Gorgeous dress,' Sam says as I approach.

'Oh. Thanks.'

'Actually, now that you're here, Nettie, would you four be able to come and chat to us quickly? It'll only take a moment.'

Before I can reply, she's leading us through the entrance hall. My eyes start to blur with tears. I can't do this. I peel off and head upstairs to the changing room.

I switch the lights on and flump down on a bench. Hot tears form on the inside corner of my eye, and I grab a tissue to blot them. Sitting on a bench alone in the changing room angry-crying was not how I envisioned tonight would go. I *know* the job's stressful, that Fletch is up against it, that a lot's expected of him. I *know* all those things. But just then he acted like I was an annoying kid sister. What did he think I was going to say? '*Oh well, never mind, Fletch. I couldn't really care less whether you're here or not. I'm too grown-up and cool. Have a lovely time and see you soon.*'

It's not just tonight. Over the last couple of weeks, it really feels as if he's pulled back. He's so wrapped up in this new exciting world that he hasn't got the head space for me. For us. I feel like he's leaving me behind.

Alec pops his head around the door. 'Everyone decent?'

'You're good.'

He comes and sits next to me, puts both his arms around my neck and nestles his face in my hair. 'He's not coming, is he?' he says quietly. I shake my head miserably. Alec strokes my hair. 'This was always going to be hard. Long distance isn't easy. Even Meghan and Harry have the "two-week rule".'

'I really miss him, Alec.'

'I know,' he says. He stands up. 'But this is helping no one. Come on. There's a party downstairs waiting for that beautiful dress to arrive.'

I can't help but smile.

Alec wipes a tear from my cheek, takes my hand and leads me downstairs into the blindingly lit Studio Three. Sam's crew is set up in one corner, the camera and lighting operators ready to go. She smiles warmly at us.

'Hi, guys. Just stand there. I'll do you all together. Rolling.'

I drop Alec's hand. For a moment, I think about turning around and walking straight back out again, how good it would feel to be that dramatic, but then I remember how my boyfriend thinks I'm a huge baby who can't cope with grown-up matters, and it gives me a new energy – a sort of fighting spirit. He's let me down, but I'm not going to let anyone know I'm hurt. Least of all him. When Fletch watches the programme, he'll see me having an amazing time. *Without* him. I take a breath and go to join Alec, Kiki and Leon against a backdrop covered in the Duke's logo and various sponsors, like the kind they have at award ceremonies.

Sam's removing an earpiece. 'So, your second ball,' she says, off camera. 'What are you hoping to achieve this year at Duke's?'

153

Alec looks like he's about to launch into a soliloquy, but Leon beats him to it. 'Well, I've just transferred from the dancers course to the musical theatre course,' he says, 'so this year's a whole new adventure for me.'

'How are you finding that?' says Sam.

'Actually, it's incredible,' he says, smiling. 'I got one of the leads in the college musical.'

This is fantastic – I've never heard him big himself up before. I watch Alec shift his weight impatiently, and I know he's thinking of a way to steer the conversation back to where he's centre stage.

'And what about you, Nettie?' she says. 'How are you looking forward to this year?'

'I guess . . .' I don't know what to say. Something that sounds exciting and independent and grown-up but also carefree and breezy. 'I'm . . .' It's no good. My mind's still outside in the square. Tears of frustration form and I blink angrily.

Kiki comes to the rescue. 'You were saying you were looking to build on last year?' She flashes me a look.

'Oh! Er, yeah. Like, study hard, raise my standards. Just like everyone else.' It's not the answer I was hoping for, but to be honest, I'm doing well not to be crying. I smile at her gratefully.

'Tonight you're at a ball,' says Sam. 'Will you be able to let your hair down?'

'We all love a party,' says Kiki, speaking over my 'erm'. Oddly, Sam ignores her. Kiki notices too, and glances at her nervously.

'Duke's looks like a fairy-tale castle tonight,' says Sam, directing her comment more pointedly to me. 'Are you looking for the perfect fairy-tale evening? Romance?'

'I—'

'It must be hard, with your boyfriend away. Are things still good between you?'

Oh God, why did she have to ask? How am I going to talk about this without dissolving into a pile of tears on the floor? I swallow and try to smile. 'Of course.'

'Where is he tonight?'

I glance at Alec, who does the minutest shake of his head.

'He's . . . on his way,' I say, beaming excitedly, when what I really want to do is push the cameras over and storm out like a diva. 'Can't wait to see him.' I'll just have to make sure I'm away from Sam later when he clearly hasn't turned up. When I'm quietly weeping into my drink in the corner. 'Sorry, you'll have to excuse me a second.'

I head back out into the foyer and leave the others to wrap things up with Sam. At least I'm away from the cameras – but, honestly? Being at a glitzy party on my own isn't exactly ideal right now, either.

'Nettie!' I'm relieved to hear Anand calling me over from the Christmas tree. He's talking to a couple of people I don't recognize. Two of them head off to get drinks as I approach.

'Hey, Anand. How's it going?'

'Great. Nettie, this is Benjamin Wells, of Wells Brignall. You must have heard of them – big talent agency in Covent Garden. Benjamin, Nettie.'

Benjamin smiles cordially. 'Hello, Nettie. I was just telling Anand that we're very interested in representing you when you leave Duke's. You must come and see us nearer the time.'

'Oh,' I say, surprised. 'I will. Thanks. But don't you need to see me in a showcase or something?'

'No need. We may do an interview as a formality, but the

155

offer's there. And from what I hear, you'll be performing at the Duke's Awards finals? Excuse me – I must catch Sam before the show.' He offers his hand for me to shake (which I do) and makes his way up the marble staircase.

'That was weird,' I say to Anand. 'How would he know if I'm performing at the finals? *I* don't even know that.' My stomach lurches at the thought of the college-wide competition that's seen by almost the entire industry.

'He was determined to speak to you,' says Anand, shrugging. 'Nettie, this is amazing! Wells Brignall are one of the biggest agencies around. My flatmate Jay works in the literary department, and he says that mega-famous people are in and out of there all day.'

'I know they're big, but why are they interested in me?'

'Sam's agent is with them. Jay thinks he's probably seen some of the *Triple Threat* rushes.'

'Oh.' Not for my talent, then. 'They want me because I'm going to be on TV.'

Anand kind of shrugs. 'Does it matter?'

'Er, kind of?'

He sighs. 'Nettie, as someone who had no connections, no family in the TV industry, no "in" to get this job, let me give you some advice. If I'd had a chance like you've just been given, I wouldn't be complaining. You'd be crazy not to go for a meeting with them.' He looks at his watch. 'Got to run.'

He jogs off into Studio Four. The message that I keep getting from everyone – not just Anand – is that I'm lucky to have all these opportunities and I should be taking them. Maybe he's right. But on the other hand, wouldn't that just be propping up a corrupted system? I'm so confused right now. I wish Fletch was here.

'Hey.'

Luca's behind me, looking smart in his DJ. I smile in spite of myself.

'Hey, Luca.'

'Has Fletch arrived yet?' he says, bending down to kiss my cheek.

He's shaved off his stubble and his face feels smooth against mine. It must jog a memory because without permission, my brain flashes back to our drunken spin-the-bottle kiss last year. Agh. Why am I doing that? Behind Luca, I see John and Sam coming out of Studio Three, still rolling, the camera pointing directly at us. I shut down the memory immediately and focus on answering the question Luca's just asked me. *About my boyfriend.*

'He can't make it now,' I say. 'He's got to work.'

'Oh,' he says. 'That's a shame. Sorry, Nettie.' He goes to put his arm around my shoulders, but because I feel weird about what just happened in my head, I sort of subtly shrink away towards the tree, getting a bauble stuck in my hair.

'Hey – I was thinking about the, erm . . . *letters.*' Luca helps me untangle myself while checking to see if anyone's listening. 'I thought "B" might have trained at Duke's with your mum. So I went to the office to ask if they had a list of alumni. I went through every year from the late Eighties to early Nineties, and I found her. She graduated in 1989. There were thirty students in her year, but only one had a name beginning with *B*.'

'Who was it?'

'A boy called Brahms Jones-Carter. Anyway, I looked him up. He's been living in the States since 1992. So it's . . . unlikely. Our best bet is her career, I think. Find out who she danced with.'

'Oh. Well, it's kind of you to look. Thanks, Luca.'

157

Michael's beckoning Luca over from the studio theatre.

'I'd better scoot – I'm on percussion.'

He leaves me by the Christmas tree. Another dead end with Mum – God, this is all so disappointing, almost like there's someone out there actively stopping me from finding anything out.

I catch up with Kiki, Leon and Alec a little later back in Studio Three, where the raised seating is already filling up. The front four rows are packed with casting directors, agents and creatives, with a conspicuous space left in the middle of the front row reserved for Miss Duke. I'm surprised there isn't a spotlight shining on it.

We squeeze on to the end of a row next to some excited first-years – it's a tight fit.

'Mind the frock,' I say, pulling my skirt out from under Alec's bum.

'Well, you should've saved me a better space!'

'Move up.' Leon nudges Alec fiercely.

'Ow!'

'Yeah, Alec, stop manspreading,' hisses Kiki. She still seems upset.

'Hey, Kiki, are you OK?' I whisper.

'Sam was angry that I'd cut you off,' she says. 'I thought I was helping you out.'

'You were! I really appreciated it.'

'Well, Sam didn't. Sometimes I think she's only friends with me to get closer to you.'

'Kiki—'

I'm cut off by Cecile Duke making her entrance, but take Kiki's hand and give it a squeeze. A hush falls over the audience like a spell as Miss Duke takes her seat. She's wearing a long-sleeved cream satin dress, high heels and a mask of warmth and kindness. What's behind it, I wonder? Mum knew.

The third-years come on to the stage, led by a girl called Landi, who's on the stick. She smiles at the audience, who applaud while she takes her place in front of the band. This time last year, I was watching Fletch conduct the show, trying to hide my racing heart from Alec. Now he's my boyfriend. Which would be lovely if he was actually here.

Luca takes his place with the rest of the band upstage. His eyes scan the crowd and settle on me with a wink. I smile back. Fletch has always admired how Luca can pick up any instrument and be a total genius on it, and he's right – Luca kills the percussion (and randomly plays a really high trumpet part at one point) as the third-years perform several numbers from *My Fair Lady* and *Camelot*, followed by the finale from *Candide*.

At the end of the show, Miss Duke rises from her seat and turns to face the audience, smiling until the applause dies down. 'Welcome, industry friends,' she says into a mic that Michael St. John has just produced from nowhere. 'Thank you for joining us at what is transpiring to be one of the most prestigious evenings in the entertainment industry's calendar.'

Alec leans in. 'She's going to tell people that until it's true.'

I glance at him sideways. 'What?'

'It's always been a big evening for us,' he breathes, 'but Miss Duke is turning it into something bigger than the BAFTAs. Film crews, paps . . .'

Yes. Miss Duke's doing *exactly* that. Or maybe Sam is.

'I'd like to extend a special thank-you to the team at Three Ring TV for joining the Duke's family,' she continues. 'I know

I speak on the students' behalf when I say that it has been exhilarating to welcome you into our daily lives here at Duke's. Your presence gives us fresh life, renewed ambition. With you at our side, we go forward into the world stronger. Thank you.' She smiles as the room breaks into applause.

'To our new students, I would like to take the opportunity to congratulate you. It is no mean feat, securing a place at Duke's. Across all our courses this year, we had to process around ninety-six thousand hopefuls applying for a place. Ninety-six thousand. *Ninety-six thousand.*'

'If she says it again, I reckon Lin-Manuel Miranda's going to pop up and offer her a part in *In the Heights*,' whispers Alec.

'I'm sure our industry friends will agree that there is no training ground like it –' Miss Duke scans the front three rows of the audience, daring anyone to disagree – 'a place to find the best talent, the greatest work ethic, the biggest drive.

'Students, enjoy tonight. Be sure to introduce yourselves to these wonderful industry people – they will be the next to nurture your talent, to see you along your way in the entertainment business. Have fun, everyone, make friends and Merry Christmas.' She hands to mic to Michael, who kisses her on both cheeks.

A low murmur becomes excited chatter as people head back to the party.

'Right, let's get wrecked,' says Alec, scooping up four glasses of champagne. 'Miss Duke'll be gone soon. We need to get started.'

'What about the cameras?' says Leon.

'They're set up in Studios Three and Six right now.' Alec looks up the central staircase. 'And one at the top, there. We can stick together and avoid them until they've gone.'

I don't much feel like drinking. All my plans have gone to

shit. I smile at Alec, and take the champagne he's offered me, but I don't drink. What I really want to do is go home.

Predictably, Alec is the first to disappear to a different part of the party. Kiki heads over to Sam and the crew not long after. Leon and Taro find a table in the corner of the foyer and are deep in conversation in minutes. Maybe Leon's having 'the talk'. I don't want to encroach, so I go and listen to Luca and some of the third-year musos playing jazz versions of musical theatre songs upstairs in Studio Four. The tables are decorated with lanterns, each containing a flickering candle – you know, the kind of place that would be *perfect* to be with your boyfriend.

As I watch Luca play, I wonder what I was thinking downstairs. Maybe I was just confused and angry about Fletch not being there, and then Luca turned up all handsome and talented and complication-free and my brain went straight to snogging? That's reasonable, right? He's a nice boy who I just happen to have kissed, not someone I'm crushing on. I need to give myself a break. Yeah, OK – Luca and I are spending more time together, and we really bounce off each other at rehearsals, and he's attractive and talented . . . but we're *friends*. I can appreciate all of those things but still know where to draw the line, right?

'Watching your boyfriend?'

'Awww, so sweet.'

Lucinda and Florinda – aka Jade and Natasha – have crept up behind me, a mass of hair and feathers like *Strictly* on acid. A bad trip.

I don't turn around. 'I'm not in the mood.'

'Was Princess Nettie feeling lonely while her real boyfriend was away?' says Jade nastily.

'Can't bear not to have *all* the attention *all* of the time,' Natasha adds, sitting down next to me and fingering my sleeve. 'Nice dress, Nettie – although . . .'

'What are you doing?' I say, shrugging her off violently.

'I was just thinking about that beautiful yellow gown you wore last year,' she says, smirking. 'Much nicer than this pathetic effort.' Says the girl in neon marabou.

'Such a shame it got spoilt,' says Jade. 'If I remember correctly, there was some kind of silly little accident involving wine . . .' She holds her glass dangerously over me.

This is ridiculous. I don't even know what's going on. Last year Jade was under the false impression that she and Fletch were about to become an item and was furious that I'd been talking to him all night. What's her excuse this year?

'What – you're gonna do it again?' I say. 'Go on, then.'

As I stand up to face her and Natasha, I realize they're wearing mics. Not only that, but there's a camera pointing directly at us through the studio doorway. Suddenly it all makes sense.

'Just leave me the fuck alone.' I push past them (and the camera) and go downstairs. This is turning out to be the worst night.

I plonk myself at the champagne bar in the foyer and take a glass from the waiter, who has carefully plucked it from the beautiful tower he's zealously tending to. All of this is *so* amazing – like what party has a *champagne bar*, for God's sake? – and I can't even appreciate any of it because I'm so angry. At Jade, at Sam, at Fletch . . .

The night before we started back at Duke's, Fletch asked me if we'd be OK if one of us went away. I answered yes without even considering that it might be difficult. I thought that being in

162

love with each other would be enough, that it was our protection against all those external things that split couples up – growing up, growing apart, having separate lives . . . But now? The minute we burst our bubble, things got hard. It shouldn't have to be like this.

I spot Alec on the other side of the foyer, flirting outrageously with a handsome guy who I think works for one of the big casting directors, India Lovejoy. From what I can tell, he's doing all his best moves, but the guy just smiles politely and excuses himself. I watch as Alec furiously drains his drink and reaches for another. He downs that, and then, swaying slightly, heads over to where Leon and Taro are talking.

I should intervene, shouldn't I? But Alec's been so great lately, I'm sure he wouldn't do anything to damage the progress he's made with Leon. But his tongue does loosen when he's drunk. Oh, you know what? I'm not getting involved. I've got enough of my own shit going on. Avoiding them, I go back up to Studio Four, where the jazz has finished but some of third-year musicians are still playing, joined by some second-years on strings.

'Nettie!' Luca calls me from over by the bar. 'Where did you go? They're about to start a reel.'

He points over to where the musicians have gathered. A third-year is lifted on to a chair and shouts to the fifty-strong crowd. 'OK, everyone – find your partners and get into groups of four. We're going full-out *Pride and Prejudice* tonight, and I want everyone to end up with their Mr Darcy.'

'Shall we dance? I won't embarrass you, I promise.' Luca smiles at me.

'I'm not really in the mood for dancing, Luca.'

'Yeah, but listen! First one sounds like a polka. Perfect for bad moods.'

The band does sound ridiculously jolly. It would be silly to stand in the corner. 'Oh, go on, then,' I say with my first real smile of the evening. I let Luca lead me to the middle of the room.

One couple at a time gallops down a centre aisle. It's quite energetic, and I'm sure the only thing in the room shinier than my face right now is the disco ball suspended from the ceiling. Just then, Kiki appears, dragging Leon in by his tie. In an uncharacteristic fit of aplomb, he sweeps her into his arms and carries her on to the dance floor. She giggles and throws her head back. Wow, I guess the talk with Taro went well, and Alec must have behaved. I beam at them and wave.

Luca and I take our turn, laughing as the rest of the dancers clap us down the aisle in time to the music. He was right – it was perfect for my bad mood.

'You're good!' I shout, as he takes my arm and skips around me.

'Turns out I'm better suited to galloping than Fosse,' he yells with a wink.

Watching him dance across the floor so full-out-with-feeling, honestly I'm laughing so much that it's hard to get air. It's such a riot that we miss hands at one point and my bracelet breaks and falls on the floor.

'Oh no!' I say. 'This was Mum's.' I stop to pick it up.

'Let me see if I can fix it,' says Luca. I hand the bracelet to him. 'Yeah, it's just the clasp. I can do that at home for you.'

'Thanks, Luca.' Last year Mum's dress got ruined; this year her bracelet's broken. It's hard not to see that as a sign.

'Watch out.' Luca pulls me out of the way of the next couple.

We go back to dancing and I try not to feel sad about ruining yet another thing of Mum's at a Duke's ball. The next reel is much slower, and couples are required to weave in and out of each other elegantly, returning to their original partners. Luca smiles his cutely awkward half-smile at me.

'I'll probably step on your foot,' he says.

'*Wrong and Strong*,' I say, smiling. 'It's OK.'

The violin starts up and we walk around each other, our hands pressed together. Luca's about to say something but is cut off by a familiar voice.

'Excuse me – do you mind if I cut in?'

I turn to see Fletch standing behind Luca, smiling at me, his brown eyes twinkling. He's still wearing his leather jacket and jeans, looking every bit the James Dean in a roomful of suits. The turmoil of the last three hours melts away; our argument fades. As I smile back at him, it's like the rest of the room has disappeared.

Luca steps back, patting Fletch on the back with a grin. We circle each other, sparks flying as our palms touch.

'I thought you weren't coming.'

He laces his fingers through mine, sending a thrill down my spine. 'And miss being here with you?'

'How did you get away?'

'I just . . . told them. Turns out they're just humans, like us. We got most of it down before I left.'

'I can't believe you're here.' We're dancing much closer than is proper for a Georgian reel. I can feel the heat from his body.

'Sorry about how I look,' he murmurs. 'I'll go and get changed in a minute. I just wanted to see you as soon as possible.'

165

'You're perfect just as you are,' I whisper.

We've stopped dancing now, our faces almost touching, our breathing synchronized.

'Only when I'm with you,' he says, and as his lips touch mine, I forget about everything else.

CHAPTER 16

Fletch looks so cute when he's sleeping. Sometimes, when he's lying on his front, arms relaxed over his head and his face a little squashed on to the pillow, the temptation is real to get my phone out and start snapping. I wonder if he's staying for the whole day. We didn't talk last night; we both knew there was stuff we needed to say but didn't want to spoil the moment. Now it feels like the moment's passed.

It's only eight o'clock. I can't go into the living room. Kiki and Leon stayed over last night and they won't appreciate being woken up. Maybe I could sneak past them, grab a juice and get back to bed without disturbing them.

As I slip through the nearly closed door (it's old, and creaks if you open it past about thirty degrees), I notice that the living room is empty. That's weird. Fletch and I left the ball before the others last night, but Kiki had a key for her and Leon.

I grab my phone from the table and start flicking through it while I put the kettle on. I've got so many messages, the first from Leon at about midnight.

00:03
Leon:

> I'm not coming back now.
> Going home. Call me when you're awake x

Why would he go home? All his stuff's here. Maybe Taro went back to the flat with him?

Alec's messaged me on Snapchat about sixty-seven times. There are several photos of him pouting with various drinks in his hand and a slew of messages starting at about 2.30 a.m.

02:36
Alec:

Not coming home tonight babe wink wink

Can't find Kiki

Can you tell her she can have my room

It's ok, found her

What the hell happened? With a bad feeling in the pit of my stomach, I call Leon.

He answers straight away. 'Hello?'

'Hey. I thought you were staying here?'

'It's – it's complicated. I'm outside, actually. Can you come down? And bring Kiki?'

Fletch is still asleep. I want to creep back to bed and snuggle back down in the nook of his shoulder. But something in Leon's voice worries me. I don't even know if he had the talk with Taro last night, but something's wrong. If I don't at least go down and make sure he's OK, I can't keep calling myself his friend.

'Er, sure.' Hastily, I scribble a note for Fletch explaining where I am and leave it on the pillow, quietly throw some trainers on and knock on Alec's door.

Kiki's just finished getting dressed. 'He called me.' She looks as worried as I feel.

Together, we slip downstairs. Leon's sitting on the steps of

168

Pineapple. His eyes are unusually puffy. We run over to him.

'Are you OK?' I say. Leon's usually so level-headed, and as he shakes his head, I realize I've never seen him like this before. What could have happened that was so bad?

'I need to talk to you both.'

'OK,' says Kiki. 'We're here for you.'

Oh my God, I feel nervous for him, and I don't even know what it's about. We sit either side of him and each take one of his hands, which are cold and shaking.

He takes a deep breath. 'Right. So Taro and I were having a great time last night – but I wanted to give him a little space to be with the third-years, it being their last ball and all that, before I tried to talk to him about our relationship. Then, Kiki, you dragged me upstairs to dance, remember?'

'Yes,' says Kiki, her eyes fixed on his anxiously.

'Well, I thought I'd just catch up with him later. How long were we up there? An hour?'

'I think it was more like two,' she says. 'Way after Nettie and Fletch left.'

'Right?' he says. 'So when I came back downstairs, he wasn't there. Obviously – It's not like I expected him to be there waiting patiently or anything. I'm not Alec. But it was so loud and busy, and full-on with all the industry people, that the thought of going into the crowd to look for him kind of filled me with dread. I just needed five minutes on my own, to recharge.' He takes in another deep breath. 'So I went up to the library. It was piled high with all the crap from every room they wanted to hide for the Duke's party, like a big *Les Mis* barricade at the far end of the room, you know?'

Always appreciative of a musical theatre reference, I nod

enthusiastically, wondering where any story can possibly be going that finishes in a deserted college library. 'Just to clarify – you were in the library in the dark?' I say. 'It's kind of eerie up there at the best of times.'

'It was completely dark,' he says. 'The only light was from the lamps in the square. I went round the pile of tables and boxes to the window. Then the door opened and I heard . . . something. I peered through a gap in the barricade and saw Taro.'

'Taro?' says Kiki. 'What was he doing up there?'

Leon takes a shaky breath in. 'He was with Alec.'

I nearly choke on the cold December air. 'With *Alec*?'

'Yup.'

'Were they . . . ?'

'*Of course they were,*' he says bitterly. 'And I was trapped beyond the fucking barricade. I had to stay there until they'd left.'

We're both stunned to silence. I never thought Alec would stoop that low. After a moment I say, 'I'm really sorry, Leon. I don't know what to say. Alec's got a lot to answer for.'

Kiki nods angrily. 'He knew you were into Taro.'

'Do you know what, Kiki? I like Taro – he's cute and we have a nice time – but I'm not sure I'm *really* into him. I know I was going to have the "boyfriend chat", but I wasn't a hundred per cent sure. Alec didn't know that, though, when he slept with him.'

I'm furious with Alec. He knew *exactly* what he was doing. What is going on with him? Not just last night, but generally lately? I take Leon's hand. 'Have you . . . heard from Taro?'

'I messaged him. While I was in the library. Said I thought it was getting too intense and that we should cool things off. I didn't want to lose face. He just said, "OK, cool" – I mean, later, obviously, not while he was shagging my best friend.' He lets out a hollow-sounding laugh. 'I suppose at least I didn't try to have the talk with him. That would have been *really* humiliating. God, what a mess.'

Leon insists he doesn't want to come up, so Kiki and I hug him goodbye. He heads off down to Covent Garden, after arranging to meet Kiki there later, once she's grabbed all her things from the flat.

'What a fucking shitshow,' says Kiki.

'I'm so angry with Alec, I don't even know where to begin, to be honest,' I say.

Alec appears round the corner, dressed in an Arsenal hoody and joggers. Not his.

'Hi, chickens,' he says. 'Early class?' He slings a carrier bag full of clothes on to the steps of Pineapple.

'Where have you been?' demands Kiki, even though her voice says she knows full well where he's been.

'Out, *Mum*,' says Alec.

'Do you mean *at Taro's*?' I say.

Alec sighs, like he's been waiting for this. 'I'm not going to apologize for being horny,' he says. 'We're both free agents.'

'But you knew Taro was seeing Leon!' I say.

'They're not exclusive,' replies Alec. 'Taro told me that last night. Anyway, Leon finished it with him.'

I know for a fact that Leon didn't message Taro until *after* he'd seen them together, but obviously I can't say anything that will give this away. Ugh. I can't believe the nerve of him.

While I'm formulating the right words, Kiki basically explodes. 'And what about Leon? The fact that your best friend has been seeing this guy for nearly three months? It didn't occur to you that maybe – *just maybe* – you shouldn't be going there? Did you check how he felt about the whole thing?'

'I did,' said Alec. 'Last week. I asked Leon if it was the big L.O.V.E. He told me not to be so ridiculous, that it was just a bit of fun. Basically gave me the green light.'

'You think that's a green light?' says Kiki irately. 'You're disgusting. I'm going after Leon.' She storms into the flat.

Alec looks at me like he's expecting me to back him up. I mean, what the actual hell?

'Alec, I don't know why we're having to explain this to you, but you don't just sleep with someone who's involved with your friend, however casual they may make it seem,' I say angrily. 'You betrayed him.'

He genuinely seems taken aback by my reaction. 'I think that's a little strong—'

'Leon was about to ask Taro to be his boyfriend,' I say, cutting off whatever bullshit he was about to come out with.

Alec shrugs. 'That's not what he told me last week.'

'So? You've known him for ten years, Alec!' I yell, causing the studio receptionist to look up in alarm from the foyer. 'Surely *even you* must know that Leon doesn't always broadcast his feelings? How can you be so insensitive?'

Kiki comes back out of the flat. She calls across the road to me, 'I'll message you later. Let you know how he is.' She gives Alec a dirty look worthy of all three Heathers and heads off down to Covent Garden.

Alec seizes the opportunity to slink inside. I'm freezing, but I don't want to spend a second longer in his company, so I linger on the steps for a moment.

I'm just about to go when Luca runs around the corner,

dressed in joggers and a hoody with a set of headphones slung around his neck. 'Hey.'

'What are you doing here?' I say.

'I mean, you're the one on the steps of Pineapple in your pyjamas . . . Anyway, I fixed your bracelet. Thought I'd combine returning it to you with a run,' he says. 'You OK?' he adds, seeing my thunderous face.

'Yeah, I – just . . . Alec.' I try to smile. 'We just had a huge fight.'

'And you took it outside? Must've been bad.' Seeing from my face that it's too soon to joke, he adds, 'You know, last night after you'd gone, he was out of control. I mean, we were all drunk, but Alec took it to another level.'

'Doesn't surprise me. That's kind of what we were fighting about.'

'Anything I can help with?' he says.

'Not really – but thanks.'

Neither of us speaks for a moment.

'Did you . . . say you had my bracelet?'

'Oh! Yes.' He puts his hand in his pocket and pulls out my bracelet. 'Here. I mended the catch so that it won't slip off again.' His hand feels warm against mine as he lays the bracelet in my palm.

I turn it over in my fingers. 'Thank you – how did you do it? It's been dodgy for years.'

'I just tightened it up here –' he lifts it up by the clasp to show me – 'so that when it's closed, it stays closed.'

'That's so kind of you, Luca,' I say, hugging him. 'Thanks again. It means a lot.'

'No worries,' he says, grinning. 'Anyway, have a good day.' He

173

puts his headphones on and starts running. 'Laters,' he calls over his shoulder before disappearing round the corner of Shelton Street.

I look down at the bracelet in my palm. It was really so sweet of him to fix it.

I turn to cross the road. Fletch is standing in the doorway.

'Hey.'

'Oh my God,' I say, running over to him. 'How long have you been there?'

'Sorry,' he says. He seems agitated, and his eyes won't meet mine. 'I wondered where you were.'

'Oh. Is everything . . . OK?' I say.

'Yeah, fine,' he says. He looks at my hoody/pyjama shorts/trainers combo. 'You must be cold.'

'Yeah, I am.' I don't move. 'Is there . . . a problem?'

'No – I just thought you were meeting Leon. Not Luca. Maybe I read the note wrong. It's fine. Coffee?'

Fletch is smiling brightly, but it's obviously not 'fine'. He's being careful with his words, but it's clear what he thinks.

'I *did* see Leon. I was just about to come back in when Luca dropped by to give me back my bracelet, which fell off last night when we were dancing. Which we were doing *as friends* because my boyfriend had told me that he was too busy at work with the grown-ups to come to a silly college ball with me.'

Neither of us speaks for a minute.

'Can I say something?' he says finally.

I kind of shrug-nod.

'I'm sorry.'

I look up at him, my eyes full of hurt and disbelief. 'You didn't seriously think—'

'No! I just . . .' He rubs his face, like he's trying to get himself together. 'It's lonely down in Chichester. Like, I lie awake thinking about the next time I'll get to see you, what you're doing, and then the next day I'm exhausted and stressed. And then I take it out on you, which is horrible. I know I'm doing it, but I can't seem to stop myself.'

'You're the one who never replies to messages, or asks me how my day was, or even notices when we haven't spoken for a whole day,' I say, shivering in the cold air. 'If anything, *I'm* the one who should be insecure.'

'I know, I *know*.' He pulls at his hair. 'I'm sorry. I guess my brain was making up stuff about you and Luca because deep down I think that's what I deserve. I don't really think it. I'm truly sorry, Nettie. Please forgive me. *Please*.' He reaches into his pocket. 'Listen – I got you something. I was going to give it to you at the ball, but – well . . .' He pulls out a small box.

I literally don't know what to think about anything. He's giving me presents when things literally couldn't be weirder between us? Confused, I take the box and open it. Inside is a heart-shaped silver locket with a moonstone in the middle, surrounded by flowers. It's gorgeous. But why has he picked now to give it to me, seconds after a fight?

'It's vintage,' he says eagerly. 'French – they think it's Victorian. Or like, the French version of Victorian.'

'I don't know what to say.' I mean, literally. Like, how am I supposed to respond to this after what he just said to me?

'Look inside.' He opens the clasp for me and the locket clicks open. There's no picture inside, but he's had it engraved. It's the first song we ever sang together.

As the song lyrics come back to me, my mind floats back to that moment. I remember how special it was, how those words just seemed to 'fit' us. How much I loved him, even then.

'Thank you,' I say.

He taps my heart. 'Just so I'm here, even if I'm not actually *here*.'

Something doesn't quite sit.

'What do you mean?' I say, pulling away.

He seems surprised at my reaction. 'Nothing – I just wanted you to know that I'm committed to you and that . . . I'm always thinking about you. Is that . . . wrong?'

'It's just that . . . two minutes ago you were pretty much accusing me of cheating on you with your best friend, and now you're presenting me with a necklace and saying that it's to represent how you're always *here* –' I tap my chest harshly – 'and I can't help feeling you're . . .'

'What?'

'Claiming ownership of me or something?'

He looks shocked. 'Nettie, that's not what this is.'

'What is it, then?'

'It was just something to let you know how much I love you! I had it all planned – I was going to give it to you before the ball. It's got nothing to do with Luca.'

'Or the fact that you don't trust me.' My voice breaks; I put my head in my hands.

'I *do* trust you, Nettie.' There's a slightly panicky note to his voice, an urgency. He tries to pull my hand down from my face, but I resist. 'Listen, don't wear it if you feel like that – although that wasn't my intention at all. But I'd still like you to have it.'

I look up. 'So now I *shouldn't* wear it?' What is he even saying?

He hits his forehead with frustration. 'Oh God, I'm doing this all wrong! This isn't how it was meant to go. *Please* believe me. I've been planning it for ages. Alec was helping me.'

I want so badly to believe him. But he's not doing himself any favours.

'I told him I wanted to get you a locket, and from then on, he kind of asked to be involved in the process. When I say "asked", I mean "demanded".' Fletch half smiles hopefully. 'He tried to convince me to get "Netch" engraved in it, but I decided against it.'

I manage a small smile at his little joke in spite of myself. 'That does sound like him, even if he's currently the worst person in the world.'

Fletch takes my hands. 'Listen, Nettie, I'm going to do better from now on. Stop letting things get to me. Stop being short with you on the phone and not replying to your messages. Stop being jealous. Will you give me another chance?'

I think back to last night and how happy I was to see him, how perfect the rest of our evening was. Everyone makes mistakes sometimes. 'OK, Fletch. But you have to try.'

'I will – I promise.' He takes my hand and kisses it several times. I can feel him shaking with relief. 'And we're going to have the best Christmas ever. I can't wait to be with you. Nettie, I love you so much.'

A small crowd of early morning dancers has gathered inside the front window of Pineapple across the road. They're watching with interest. As Fletch puts his arms around me, one of them applauds. I think they're enthralled by the *Moulin Rouge* levels of drama unfolding in the street.

'Come on,' I say. 'Let's go inside.'

Fletch leaves just after 6 p.m. I'm on the sofa watching Alex Newell videos on YouTube when Alec returns home with numerous shopping bags, having been out most of the day. Typical. Devastates his best friend, gets called on it, and then does a spot of retail therapy to cheer himself up. Job done. He takes his shoes off and comes and sits next to me. I turn away pointedly.

'I've messaged Leon,' he says. 'Said sorry.'

I'm not sure what that means – like, a quick *soz mate* text isn't going to cut it. I fold my arms and move further away from him.

'Nettie, please don't be angry with me,' he says, trying to unfold them by taking my hand out of the crook of my elbow and holding on to it.

I jerk my arm out of reach. 'I don't know what the fuck's got into you lately. All this with Taro – it's just another way of competing.'

'I'm not competing—'

'Lay off Leon!' I shout, turning back to him with fury coursing through my veins. 'If you value his friendship at all, you'll stay away from Taro. And if you value mine, you'll start being less of a complete twat to Leon.'

I get up, storm to my room and slam the door, leaving Alec speechless for once in his life.

I can't compute it all. This time yesterday, I was the happiest I've been in a long time: I was hanging out with my best mates; Leon and Alec were back on track; Fletch was taking me to a ball; and I felt excited about the future. Now suddenly I feel like the rug's been pulled from under me.

It's not just the fight that's bothering me, or Alec's behaviour. Something has shifted. Between Fletch and me, and my friends, too. Kiki spends most of her free time with Sam, Leon's rightly been avoiding Alec because of the way he always treats everything as a competition, and Alec's out of control. I wish we could go back to how it was before the summer, when Fletch and I had just got together and everyone was happy to be finishing first year. When we'd all stay up in the common room talking and listening to music together until the sun came up. When I was ridiculously happy to get my voice back and I'd thought second year was going to be easy. When I thought I'd be able to find out what happened to Mum.

Things haven't panned out as I'd hoped. My boyfriend is away, the group is drifting apart, and I feel like I'm never going to fully know what happened to Mum. It sounds dramatic, but right now, I just feel kind of . . . alone.

CHAPTER 17

10:41
Luca:

Hey. How's it going?

You know, the usual. Missing Fletch a bit.

At least you get to see him in three days!

I CAN'T WAIT
You OK?

Yeah, good, thanks. Can you spare
twenty minutes after rehearsals tonight?

Aren't we meant to be going for
end-of-term drinks with the cast?

Got something I need to show you.
I promise it won't take long.

OK. See you later x

Lisa schedules an intensive Fosse workshop with Luca and me
for an hour before everyone else is called. God, she must think

we're really bad. I arrive early to discover her and Sam arguing in the corner. Taking care not to be seen, I hover outside the studio entrance to listen.

'I don't understand why you made me cast a musician in this role and then want to force all this dancing on to him,' Lisa's saying. 'There were plenty of people who could've played Billy.'

'I saw potential in Luca and needed him at the heart of the story,' says Sam. 'Lisa, you're amazing. If anyone can get this out of him, it's you.'

Lisa replies, but I don't hear what she says. It sounds like Luca's suspicion was right – Sam *was* the one who got him cast. But *why*? I wait a few more seconds before going in, which is just as well because Sam comes marching out of the room and nearly knocks me over. I duck my head down and go into the studio to join Lisa, who's keen to start.

'Nettie, your dancing's improving,' Lisa says after fifteen minutes of isolation technique. 'I'm getting some great work from you. I know from talking to Michael that dance isn't really your thing?'

'Um, no. Not really.' I glance at Kiki, who's there to assist Lisa. She smiles encouragingly at me.

'Well, Fosse is definitely your thing,' says Lisa. My insides melt with delirious happiness at her words. 'And all the small stuff, the style, you're really there. But I want to add a *pas de deux* between Roxie and Billy Flynn, and if we're gonna do that, we have to nail your technique. Let's just jam for a while. Follow me.'

She starts moving, very little at first. I copy her in the mirror.

She smiles at my reflection. 'That's it, honey – now just loosen it up.'

The movements become easier as I familiarize my body with them, until I feel a sense of freedom I've never felt before. Something releases, and I suddenly feel closer to Mum, like I've started to understand some of who she was, how she must have felt when she was dancing. It's not a sad feeling – quite the opposite – I feel connected to her in a way I never have before, like she's here with me. This is amazing. If I never find out a single thing more about her, then I have this. Forever.

Lisa looks over to the door. 'Oh hey, Luca . . . Come join. Those hips need work – am I right?'

Luca walks in, grinning sheepishly.

'You look strong, so that's good,' continues Lisa. 'We're practising lifts today. I've got a couple from "Take Off with Us" – google it –' (don't need to; already watched it a gazillion times, plus Alec's many incarnations of it) – 'and "Bye Bye Blackbird".'

We work hard to nail the lifts. Lisa throws in some schmoozing for Luca to practise his hips. It's a way of travelling with a lot of wrist circling, shoulder rolling and hip fluidity – unset, but very specific in style. Lisa describes it as 'oil on water'. She gets us to schmooze together, which looks very sexy but is in fact a huge slog. I'm learning that it takes a lot of internal effort to make something look so easy – that what people see is never the full picture.

Lisa puts it into words perfectly. 'Your outer body, the moving image we're seeing, is the swan gliding on water. It's beautiful, it's fluid, it's serene. Inside should be a struggle. You're conflicted, you're working hard, you're tense. Inside you're the swan's legs fighting the current.'

'I think my outer body and inner body have been switched,' says Luca.

I giggle.

'You're getting there.' Lisa laughs. 'Baby steps.'

We work for an hour. Towards the end of the session, I notice Sam has slid in with a handheld and is filming us dancing. Lately my anxiety's been sky high about how she's going to portray me. The first episode airs soon, and at the moment, we're all just getting on as best we can, living our lives. Soon everyone will be living them with us. But which version will they see?

Sam collars me as Lisa breaks us. 'Nettie. Great footage today.' She taps her camera with a knowing wink. 'This documentary is going to make you a star.'

'I'm not sure I want to be a st—' I begin.

'No? Then why are you at Duke's?'

The reply stops in my mouth. Why *am* I at Duke's? To sing, to act, to do musical theatre . . . But Sam's right – it's kind of hard to do that anonymously. I've never really thought about the other side of it. There are West End performers out there at the moment, instagramming their every move, updating their stories in order to increase their followers, get the bigger parts, further their careers . . . Will I get left behind?

But trading invasion of privacy for – what, exactly? Fame? Success? – isn't what I wanted.

'I'm here to train, Sam,' I say. 'Not to be famous. I didn't ask for any of this.'

'I totally get it.' Sam lowers her voice. 'It's just a shame you didn't read that little piece of paper you signed at the beginning of the year more carefully. You can't go back on that now – well, not unless you want to be sued, right?' Her lips play in a little smile. 'And when Three Ring TV decides to sue? Well – *you can imagine*.' She gives a knowing little laugh, but there's something menacing behind it.

Kiki comes into the studio. 'Hey, Nettie! Guess what?' She sees my nonplussed face and Sam's smiling one. 'Everything . . . OK?' she says tentatively.

'Yep! I'll talk to you later, Nettie,' says Sam, calmly taking the door from Kiki and stepping through it. She turns back. 'Nice top, Kiki.'

'I tie-dyed it myself,' says Kiki, staring at us.

'You should wear it more often. It's really flattering.'

Flattering? Ugh, she's just the worst.

Kiki waits until the door closes behind Sam before she speaks. 'What was that all about?'

'I honestly don't know,' I say. 'But I think she just threatened to sue me if I backed out.'

'Well, to be fair, you did sign a consent form,' says Kiki.

I suppress a surge of anger. Why does she always take Sam's side? 'What was it you were going to tell me?' I say, changing the subject.

'Oh, yeah!' says Kiki, oblivious. 'I got an email from someone at See Me Now – you know, the online fashion company – saying they'd seen my photo in *Grazia* and looked me up on Instagram. They're interested in doing a clothing collaboration! Apparently there's loads of buzz around *Triple Threat* and they want to get in on it. Nettie, I can't believe it – I've always dreamed of my own dancewear line!'

'That's brilliant, Kiki.' The anger melts away as I hug my friend. I'm so pleased this is working out for her. It's just a shame I can't get as excited for myself. 'So, what will you have to do?'

'I don't know yet – I'm meeting someone called Michelle next week. We're going to sketch some designs together, talk through what we want from the collection. Nettie, the money's really good! Means I can stop worrying for a bit.'

'That's great!' I say.

As the rest of the cast trickles in, I sit in the corner with my head in my score, trying to focus on Kiki's good news but invariably slipping back into thoughts about my conversation with Sam. Over the little music notes, Anand's warning floats back to me almost like a melody:

If you give her nothing, she'll go out of her way to take everything . . .

I can't shake the look on her face just now when she joked about suing me . . . It doesn't matter how many times Kiki says Sam's fine, I just don't buy it. If I was doubting Sam's integrity before, now I'm certain: she's definitely not to be trusted. In fact, I'd go further than that.

She's dangerous.

'OK, everyone, well done. We're ahead of schedule, but I don't want to lose momentum over Christmas, so make sure you keep working on those harmonies.' Michael starts playing exit music on the piano. I'm exhausted; since the Christmas Ball and all its drama I've been living off the raw energy of nerves and anticipation. But on Saturday I finally get to see Fletch.

'And practise that schmoozing,' calls Lisa, circling her wrists at us. 'I want you all looking like Fosse dancers by January.'

She'll be lucky. My hips are killing me.

We all start to pack up. A few people linger in the corner, working on their shoulder rolls and walks (who knew walking could be so difficult?). I haul my bag over my shoulder.

'Ready?' I say to Luca, opening the door.

'Yep. You're gonna love this.'

I have to admit, ever since I got the text from Luca, I've been intrigued what it is he has to show me. We don't walk far, just to Shaftesbury Avenue. He stops outside a small shopfront covered in adverts for West End shows.

'Here.'

'The Theatre Cafe?'

He smiles. 'You'll see.'

He leads me inside. It's really cute how they've done it out, with the box-office sign behind the counter, *Theatre Cafe* written in lights across the bricks at the back, and the walls pretty much fully papered with show posters. Full on MT *geek chic*. Obviously I love it.

He grins. 'I wanted to show you something.' He moves aside to reveal a framed poster on the wall behind him. It's an advert for *An American in Paris*, an oldish production by the look of it.

'I'm sorry. I don't understand.'

'No – *really* look.'

I see an anticipatory smile spread across his face as I turn to search the poster, like he's waiting for me to open a birthday present he's spent hours choosing. I half smile back, wishing he'd stop being so cryptic and just tell me.

Then I see it.

Starring Anastasia Delaney-Richardson and Peter Russell

'Oh my God!' I squeal. 'It's Mum!'

Luca laughs at my excitement. 'I came in here the other day with some friends from home,' he says. 'I couldn't believe it when I saw it.'

'I didn't even know she was in this show,' I say.

'It's the one about the ballerina and the artist, right?' says Luca. 'Now we've got one more show we know she worked on. It's a start, Nettie.'

'This is really helpful,' I say.

Luca smiles ruefully. 'Unfortunately, no "B"s in the cast. I looked on Wikipedia.'

'None at all?'

'No. Michael was Musical Director, though.'

Only problem is, Michael clearly doesn't want to talk about it. I wish there was some way of getting the info out of him. 'Was Mum in the article?'

'You'd have thought so, but when I researched *An American in Paris*, this is what happened.' He shows me on his phone. The show comes up with a Wikipedia entry. Luca scrolls down to the section entitled 'Productions'. 'Look – cast list.'

'She's not there.'

Luca nods. 'And considering this poster says, "Starring Anastasia Delaney-Richardson", you'd think she would be. It was a big deal – David Hirst directed it, for God's sake.'

The director's name, David Hirst, rings a bell but I can't think why. 'Look up Oklahoma, Copenhagen,' I say. It was the show Mum was in with Miss Duke.

Luca types it into his phone. 'Same,' he says. 'Her name's not there. You know, I tried just looking her up, too.' He stirs some sugar into his coffee. 'Wikipedia says her page has been removed. I just thought there was nothing to begin with. Why would it be removed?' A little thought pecks at me, like one of Cinderella's birds from *Into the Woods*. Mum? She hid a lot from me, after all. Who's to say she didn't go one step further?

Neither of us speaks for a moment. Then it hits me. 'There are other places like this – you know, the Nell, the corridors at theatres – that have old show memorabilia on the walls. I bet we could find her there. Or even the person who wrote the letters.'

'You're right. We should definitely be looking in those places. Let's do it in the New Year. If we haven't got weekend rehearsals.'

'That would be great. Maybe we could—'

My phone rings. The sight of Fletch's name makes my stomach do a little somersault.

'Hi, my love.'

'Hey, Fletch!'

'Three more days,' he says excitedly. 'What time do you want me to pick you up on Saturday?'

'Can you come early?' I say. 'I'll be ready.'

'Nettie, getting to spend Christmas with you is kind of all I can think about right now. I'll be camping outside your doorstep.'

My insides glow at the thought of seeing him.

'How's it going?' I say.

'We've got David in tomorrow. He's coming to check us out. Everyone's stressed.'

'Wait – it's David Hirst, right?' I say.

Luca, who up until now has been doing that thing of trying to seem like he's not listening to my conversation even though I'm right next to him, looks up sharply.

'Yeah, why?' asks Fletch.

'I – it's just the second time his name's come up today, that's all . . .' I trail off.

Luca's frantically mouthing, *Get Fletch to find out!* at me, and I'm momentarily distracted. Is now the time to be filling him

188

in? I was going to do it over Christmas, when we've actually got some breathing space.

Fuck it. I need to know. 'Could you do something for me?'

'Name it.'

'Could you ask David Hirst if he knew my mum?'

There's a pause. 'That's a strange request.'

'I've just seen a poster of a show that Mum was in, at the Theatre Cafe. David Hirst's name was on it, too – he directed it.'

'You're at the Theatre Cafe?'

'Yeah – just popped in here.'

'On your own? You absolute nerd,' he says, laughing.

'Oh, no – um, Luca just dragged me in here to show me the poster.'

'You're with Luca?'

'Yes.'

He pauses, like maybe he's expecting an explanation. Determined not to give one, I keep silent.

'Well, that's cool,' he says finally, and he sounds like he's trying to mean it. 'I'll definitely ask David about your mum. Listen, I've got to go. Can't wait for Saturday.'

We say goodbye, and I go to join Luca, who's hovering at the door.

'Come on,' he says. 'Leon's saved us a table.'

It's been a long day, and I'm tired. But when we arrive at the pub, all cosy and inviting and Christmassy, I soon relax. Kiki and Leon are on good form, and Luca and I tell them what we just found.

'Amazing,' says Kiki. 'Have you googled Peter Russell?'

'Ooh, no – I'll do it now,' I say. Disappointingly there's not a

189

lot: only that he retired from theatre fifteen years ago and lives in the Cotswolds.

'Maybe he had an agent?' says Leon. 'You could try that?'

'Yeah, maybe. Well, it's a start, at least,' I say.

'It's brilliant,' says Kiki. 'Luca, you're a legend.'

'Yes,' I say, smiling at him. 'You kind of are.'

Fletch picks me up on Saturday morning. I've been waiting for this moment all term. He turns up on his bike with a huge smile and some hand warmers for me for the journey, and Wednesday's slight awkwardness is forgotten.

His parents, Bob and Rosemary, are waiting at the farmhouse door when we arrive, waving. The house is old, and shabby in places, as if they've lived there so long that all the jobs like painting and fixing need doing again and they haven't got round to them. It's homely. There's a wide gravel driveway leading to a pond in front of the house where we park.

Rosemary bounds over and pulls Fletch into a tight hug. 'How was your journey?' She releases him to look at his face, as if checking he's been looking after himself. He smiles at her. Seeing me emerge cautiously from around the pond, she takes my hand and draws me into an equally tight embrace. 'Nettie. So lovely to see you again. How have you been?'

'Good, thanks,' I say. It feels nice to be hugged by a mum.

'Let's get those bags,' says Bob, taking our luggage out of the panniers on the back of the bike.

'I've mulled some wine,' announces Rosemary.

'Mum's pulling out all the stops because you're here,' mutters Fletch in my ear.

It's just good to be wanted, to be honest.

Christmas is amazing. They've got all these family traditions (I mean, Mum and I had a few, but they were *basic* compared to this lot), like making mince pies together, which is pretty darn cute; decorating the big tree outside; going to choose a turkey (I duck out of this one – choosing food while it's still alive is a bit too much for this city girl); and having something mulling on the stove at all times. It's perfect.

10:51

MERRY CHRISTMAS!!!

Kiki:

Happy Christmas!

Alec:

Joyeux Noel, babes

How's everyone's holiday?

Kiki:

Good. Going running later to work off the choc. Mum's idea. Once a dancer, and all that 😊

Alec:

Kiki, it's Christmas, give yourself a break

Kiki:

We're back on film in two weeks. Can't do that.

Alec:
Fuck that, have some cheese

ALEC . . .
Do what makes you happy, Kiki. But also you're perfect and we love you x

Kiki:
Thanks, love x

Gotta keep at it though, especially with the collection coming out, been working on that loads btw!

OMG pics, please!!
So excited for you!

Alec:
What collection??

Kiki:
Got a clothing line collab with See Me Now!

Alec:
What? When did this happen?!

Kiki is typing . . .

Alec:
Well, I'm starting on the champagne now. Gotta go. Love you all x

Leon left the group

192

I message Leon to make sure he's OK.

11:09

> Hey, love. Happy Christmas! All OK?
> I notice you left the group chat.

All good here. Just can't deal
with Alec. Miss you, though.

> Are you still not speaking?

I might, if he apologizes.

> He told me he HAD apologized!

'I'm sorry you're upset' more like it.

> ❤ How's your Christmas going?

Dad's only been back for two days, so
I haven't had to see much of him this year.
It's been nice being with Mum, though.

> That's good.

How's yours?

> I've had such a good time! Can't believe half the
> holiday's gone already. Call me if you need me, yeah?

193

11:27
Alec:

Leon left because of me, right?

Basically

🙁 What can I do
to win him back?

You could start by apologizing properly?
Maybe stop seeing him as something to 'win'?
And don't even bother getting all competitive
with Kiki about her dancewear line.
This is really special for her
Don't ruin it

I wasn't going to!

Well maybe be a little more encouraging, then.

On New Year's Eve, I'm lying on a beanbag in Fletch's treehouse under an enormous blanket, looking up at the stars through the skylight. This time last year, I was crying into a Malibu and Coke with Alec. It's funny how things change. How you can be so miserable and lost one minute and so happy the next. When Mum died, I thought I'd never smile again. It

194

still catches me, the grief – and when it does, it's just as close and as painful, but it's less often now. I get a chance to breathe in between the hits.

Being here with Fletch and his family has been really healing, not just for me but for us both – a chance to just 'be'. Things were getting a little *Stop the World – I Want to Get Off*: hectic, stressful and dizzyingly confusing. Now we've had time to breathe. Together. Fletch has opened up about the stress of his placement, and I've shared everything I've discovered about Mum. He was quite upset that so much had happened that he hadn't been around for, and I think he found it hard to hear how much Luca had been doing to help me, but he took it well and promised to be there for me in the future. I promised not to keep stuff from him, too. We're going to start over again; everything's going to be better this year.

'You OK?' says Fletch. He's got one arm around me, the other nursing a mulled wine.

'Yes.' I watch a plane fly over, brighter than the stars, passing across the window like a large comet. 'Thank you for having me to stay.'

'I can't imagine you not being here,' he says. 'Mum's elated. I think she secretly always wanted a girl. You two get on well, don't you?'

'Well, she's basically you in Mum form, so it's not hard,' I say. 'You even look the same. Apart from inheriting your dad's scruffy hair, you're exactly like her.'

'Are you calling my hair messy?' He looks down at me, feigning indignation.

'It's hot,' I say. 'Besides, all the best MDs have messy hair. It's a prerequisite.'

'Do they also have the most beautiful girl tucked up next to them?' he says.

'Smooth.'

'I'm known for my eloquent chat-up lines.'

As we lie there together, my phone beeps. Fletch sits up to refill our mugs from a flask next to the beanbag; I take a look.

23:15
Luca:

> Happy New Year! This is the year you find out about your mum 💪

'Who's that?' says Fletch, handing me my cup.

As he reclines next to me and puts out his arm for me to snuggle into him, I make a split decision.

'Oh . . . just Alec,' I say.

CHAPTER 18

Three weeks into the spring term, and I'm already beginning to feel more frazzled than Peggy Sawyer after her 24-hour-long tap-dance rehearsal. Fletch is working late every night and all weekend, he's hardly ever able to speak, and when we do manage to talk, I can tell he's really trying not to sound distracted and stressed. Christmas seems a distant memory. At Duke's, we've had assessments, and rehearsals for *Chicago* are getting intense. Lisa's had Luca and me in dance calls at every opportunity, and my brain feels like a saucepan that keeps boiling over, full of dance moves with strange names like 'boiled eggs', 'blackbird', 'Sophie Tucker' and 'the mess around'. My hips ache, and Luca's hurt his knee. He's never danced so much in his life.

All anyone talks about is *Triple Threat*. The first episode airs in a couple of weeks, and the corridors are filled with gossip about what may or may not be shown. Everywhere I go there's a camera lying in wait, almost like Sam's got hold of my timetable and is stalking me. Every rehearsal call with Luca, she's there, and since we're in most nights, it's pretty much constant. I don't see her following the rest of the cast like that. It's like she's watching for me to slip up, waiting to pounce like Scar the minute she smells drama.

On top of everything else, the Duke's Awards, a whole-college competition with the finals held in a West End theatre, is looming, and I've got no idea what to sing for it.

Everything suddenly seems stressful.

Steph doesn't exactly seem her usual chilled self, either.

'Sorry I'm late,' she says, after I've been waiting in her little room for twenty minutes. 'Train from Chichester was delayed. I'm on the back foot today.'

'How's it going?'

She sighs. 'Well, you must know from Fletch that the tension has ramped up.'

'Yeah, kinda. What's going on?'

'It's this possible West End transfer.' Steph unpacks a load of sheet music from her bag. 'They want us to do loads of promotion "just in case" it goes to town. Press calls, gala performances, stuff that's nothing to do with the show in Chichester and won't help to sell it locally . . . We don't even know if we'll be *in* the show if it transfers. They often recast.' She looks tired. 'I just didn't sign up for this.'

'That sucks,' I say.

She smiles. 'You take the job because you love the work. But the longer I stay in the business, the more I realize that my narrative, both onstage and off, is being controlled by other people. Sorry, Nettie. You don't want to hear this. You're about to go out and take on the world.'

Seeing Steph so disheartened makes me realize what a hard time Fletch must be having. 'I just wish I could help.'

Steph flips through the sheet music until she finds the song we're working on today. It's 'Astonishing' from *Little Women*. 'You can help,' she says, 'by starting out in your career without taking shit from anyone. It's harder than it looks.'

As the term goes on, it's clear that Alec still hasn't got the message that we're all angry with him. He's got thicker skin than Gaston these days. I finally get through to him over text one afternoon in February.

14:01
Alec:

Babe, are you walking home tonight?
Wanna pop to the shops with me?

Sorry. Got class with Lisa. Then I'm practising my song for the Duke's Awards. Luca offered to play for me.

That's not until May!

Yeah, but I'm busy. Want to be prepared

Ugh, I'm so abandoned
Saw this really cute top I wanted to buy Leon. What do you think?

Honestly? I think Leon would rather you just treated him like a proper friend than try to buy his friendship back.

I've tried. He's not interested.

You'll have to try harder, Alec. And maybe when you do, everyone will want to hang out with you again.

21:10
Leon:

Alec called me.

And????

He apologized. Properly.

How do you feel about that?

idk – I believe that he IS sorry, but I don't trust that he wouldn't do it again. So the jury's out, I guess.

It's a start, though – right?

Yes. It's a start.

'Guess what?' says Kiki excitedly as we're walking over to the music hall for rehearsals. It's nearly March now, the winter chill's gone from the air and the evenings are starting to get lighter. 'I told Sam about the collection. She's going to include it in *Triple Threat*! Show some of my designs, film me at work with the team. She was really fired up about it. Nettie, this could be *huge* for me.'

I've seen some of Kiki's drawings. They're beautiful. But – 'Kiki, that's amazing,' I say, hugging her. 'Just – are you sure having Sam involved is a good thing?'

'Why wouldn't it be? It'll only help sell my collection.'

'Yeah, it's just—'

Anand calls up the stairs, saving me from a potential argument.

'Hey, Nettie. Got a sec?' He looks nervous as he approaches.

'Er, sure.' I turn to Kiki. 'I'll see you in a bit.'

'OK.' She looks as if she wants to stay, but it's clear Anand is hoping for privacy. 'See you later.'

'It's taken a while to access my usual source –' his eyes dart around shiftily, making me wonder who or what his 'usual source' is, and he lowers his voice – 'but I did get a chance to go through some old newspaper archives, and I found this.' He hands me a printout of an old article, dated September 1999. It's a review of *Funny Face* at the Prince Edward Theatre.

Funny Face *Review: Delaney-Richardson channels*
Hepburn in Reworked Musical

Your only recollection of this pseudo-sophisticated musical
may be the 1957 film of the same name, starring an
almost over-the-hill Fred Astaire and a young Audrey
Hepburn. This revival of Funny Face, *directed by David*
Hirst at the Prince Edward Theatre, retains much of the
film's original charm, whilst tidying up some of the more
feminist elements the original script failed to bring out
convincingly.

Anastasia Delaney-Richardson and Peter Russell are
reunited after their hugely successful An American in
Paris *in 1997, and audiences will not be disappointed*
to see the sparks flying as usual. These two have such
chemistry that it's been hinted they might indeed be a couple,
although frustratingly the mystery that surrounds Delaney-
Richardson's private life continues.

After the recent controversies, aficionados will be glad

201

to see her back on form, with a delightful performance of
vulnerable-but-assured Jo Stockton, the bookshop assistant
who becomes a fashion icon. Notable moments include Jo's
bohemian dance in a Parisian nightclub, and the tenderly
sung 'How Long Has This Been Going On?' Delaney-
Richardson, much like Hepburn, shines most when she
dances, and although her singing is sweet enough, it's
the ethereal quality in her movement that continues to
hypnotize crowds.

Peter Russell delivers his usual 'song-and-dance man'
charm, and national treasure Imogen Barker is unsurprisingly
sublime as fearsome magazine editor Maggie Prescott.

Funny Face *is in preview until 3rd October.*

'Is it . . . helpful?' asks Anand.

'Yes – hugely,' I say. 'Thank you.'

I read over the bit about Mum again. What does it mean – the 'mystery' around Mum's private life? And what controversies? She sounds like some sort of Nineties 'it girl'. This is so frustrating.

'Are you OK?' says Anand tentatively, jolting me out of my daydream.

'Yeah . . . I – where did you get this, Anand?'

He looks over his shoulder. 'I went on Sam's laptop. She's got subscriptions to all the archives. I only had a second, though, so sorry there's not more.'

'Oh my God. Surely that's dangerous?' The thought of Sam discovering Anand going through her computer is enough to make me shiver.

'Yes. It is.'

'Then why do it? It's really kind of you to help me like this, but it's not worth it. You could lose your job.'

He takes a deep breath. 'I know. I just . . . This job's not everything I thought it would be. Some of the things Sam does are morally dubious. And sometimes I wonder if she's . . . Well, let's just say I hate being a part of it. But what can I do? My flatmate Jay says I should just quit, but it was so difficult to get my foot in the door, and chances like working for Three Ring TV don't come along often. When I found out where Sam was going with your story, I knew I could at least try to keep your family out of it. What she's done is bad enough . . .' He trails off, like he's just misspoken.

'Bad enough *how*?' I say, my mind leaping to Trunchbull levels of villainy.

He lowers his voice so much that I have to get close to hear what he's saying. 'Listen, I can't change what Sam's already done, but . . . maybe try to stay away from Luca when the cameras are rolling.'

What?

'Wait—'

Anand looks really stressed now. 'I shouldn't have told you! Please don't tell anyone we spoke.'

I'm too shocked to even think about asking for more information. 'I won't.'

He goes into the office shaking his head, and I head home.

How can I stay away from Luca? We see each other every day. What could Sam possibly say about us? With a horrible jolt, I remember the footage I watched over Sam's shoulder in the pub. At the time, I couldn't work out why she'd gone in so close and slowed it down. Now I'm wondering if she was trying to make it look . . .

No. Surely even Sam wouldn't stoop that low. Would she?

Saturday 3 March
To: Nettie D–R, Luca Viscusi
From: Michael St. John

Hello, my darlings,
I was wondering if you might be able to help me with
something. I've got to get some bits of set and costume from
the Duke's store tomorrow, and I might need a couple of extra
pairs of hands to help me lift stuff. Nettie, I could use your eye,
too – a little costume scouting needed! I know it's short notice,
but would you both mind terribly?
Yours,
Michael

There's barely been time to process what Anand told me yesterday, or nearly told me. Now this email from Michael, basically asking me to spend *more* time with Luca. This is a disaster. I should just say I can't go.

But seriously – how bad could it be? Sam can only film what's there, and what's there is Luca and me, working well together, being friends. I can't stop living my life because of Sam's agenda. Pushing aside my anxiety, I reply to Michael and Luca to say that I'm in, and send Fletch another text letting him know what I'm doing.

On Sunday morning, after a tube, a bus and a chilly walk up a deserted residential street, I see Luca outside what looks like the small warehouse where Michael's said he'll meet us.

'Cold?' he says, looking at my jiggling knees.

'Freezing.'

He leans down and kisses me on the cheek. Despite my decision not to let what Anand said affect me, I immediately look around, paranoid that Sam's lurking in a doorway with a lens pointing at us. Luca doesn't seem to notice – I mean, why would he?

'You OK?' he says.

Should I tell him about Anand's warning? Or will that just make things weird between us?

'Er, yeah – just chilly,' I say.

Michael parks up in his Mini. He gets out and sets about sliding the metal doors of the warehouse open with many wrenching and grinding sounds. 'Hello, lovelies. I just need to hit the lights . . .' His free hand fumbles around on a wall to the right of the door. 'Here we go.'

I step inside and look around. Strange and wonderful objects protrude from every shelf. A costume cow's head stares at me from on top of a table. Shelves are piled high with baskets and ropes, silver urns, gramophones, a genie's lamp . . . I spot what looks like a giant Audrey II behind a silver tree in the corner. There are benches and chairs of all shapes and styles, and about thirty old-fashioned leather suitcases balanced precariously on top of each other. At the very top of the pile sits a pair of striped stockinged legs that someone has artfully crossed, complete with ruby slippers.

'OK, Nettie, while Luca and I find this butcher's block, would you mind going up and seeing if you can find some hats? I'm looking for bowlers and fedoras. Two black beaded tutus. Oh, and if you can find the fans— I'm not sure if they'll be classed as props or costumes, though.'

I give him a nod and head off.

At the top of the metal stairs, I'm greeted by an enormous loft space, cool and quiet, filled with row upon row of meticulously categorized costume rails. The fans are leaning up against the far wall, along with some feather backpacks, which look like they'd be painful to wear. I find a load of hats and balance them against the fans. As I sift through a rail of inside-out ballet costumes, looking for the tutus, it occurs to me that Mum might have worn any of them. The thought makes me ache with missing her and brings a lump to my throat.

Just then, my phone rings. I grab it out of my pocket. 'Hi, Fletch.' I can hear my own voice struggling under the weight of the emotion.

'Hey. Are you OK? You sound upset.'

'Yeah – sorry. Just having a moment about Mum, that's all. I'm fine.'

'I wish I was there to hug you.' Sometimes, his timing is absolutely perfect. Just when I think I'm about to be swallowed whole by grief, he's there for me.

'I wish you were, too.' I shiver. God, it's cold in here. 'How's it going? I didn't hear back from you last night.'

'Yeah, sorry – it was a late one. Finishing off one of the songs for David Hirst to hear today. He can get quite shouty,' he says. 'They're all still hoping it'll get past workshop stage at Chich, and David'll take it to the West End – he's still leaving everyone in suspense about that. Where did you say you were?'

'At the Duke's store looking for props. I'm helping Michael find a desk and some fans.'

'Well, I hope he's got something bigger than the Mini with him,' says Fletch, chuckling.

'We think we'll get it in Luca's.'

'Luca's there?'

'Yes – I messaged you last night? Maybe if you actually read your texts . . .' The line's gone silent. 'Fletch?'

'Sorry. My bad. Tell me how rehearsals are.'

I hesitate. 'Good – though the extra dance lessons we're doing with Lisa are starting to take their toll.'

'The extra lessons with Luca?'

'Yeah, I'm sure I mentioned?' I say impatiently.

He's quiet again. Then he says, 'Why do you always get defensive about Luca?'

My mood plummets. 'Because you're making me!' I say. 'You're making me feel like I can't even say hi to him in a corridor, Fletch. You're the one making it into a thing, not me. We're friends. He's your *best friend*. You're being ridiculous.'

'I'm –' He goes to speak but stops himself. 'It's just . . .' He tries again. 'Sometimes I get the feeling he's . . . into you.'

'Fletch, that's absurd.' My eyes start to blur a little with angry tears. 'And even if he was, *which he's definitely not*, do you think I'd cheat on you?'

'No, of course not, but—'

'Nettie?' Michael's voice shocks me, echoing through the store.

'Look, I've got to go,' I say to Fletch. 'We'll talk about this later.'

I hang up without waiting for a reply. If Fletch is so insecure that he can't handle my friendship with Luca, maybe we shouldn't be together. I'm so angry with him. Why is he making this so hard? And if this is how he's acting now, what's he going to be like when *Triple Threat* comes out next week? Blinking my eyes dry, I shout to Michael that I'm still searching, and I keep looking for the black tutus, which I find about a minute later. I head back down to find Michael and Luca struggling to navigate the prop obstacle course with an old oak desk.

'Trouble is,' says Michael as I join them, panting a little, 'this store hasn't been cleaned or organized since we moved buildings. All the old office stuff is still stashed here. Student files, timetables . . . It should've been chucked out years ago. Even this old desk of Miss Duke's! Nettie, be a love and move that basket of flowers for me. Thanks.'

Between the three of us, we manage to clear the way and drag the desk to the entrance. Luca and Michael go off to grab some bistro chairs while I start pulling out the desk drawer to get it ready for loading. Surprised at the weight, I drop it with a far-too-loud crash.

'Everything all right there, Nettie?' Michael calls.

'Yeah, sorry! I'm on it.'

The drawer, weirdly, is full of stuff. *Was* full, I should say. Now the contents are strewn everywhere: papers and keys and pens and odds and ends, spilt out all over the floor. I scrabble around, trying to pick everything up and stuff it back in before I'm discovered. As I put the first few things back, I notice a brown envelope poking out from the corner, stuck under the drawer floor. I pull at the thin hardboard, and it comes out completely, revealing a stack of papers and photographs. They can't have got in there by accident – it must be a false bottom?

I start to sift through them. There's an old rental agreement – it looks like it's for some studios somewhere – Miss Duke's signature at the bottom in fountain pen ink; a picture of a pale man with dark hair, all bouffant at the front, wearing a rust-brown jacket with green-and-blue mosaic patterns woven into it (clearly very Nineties); and a sealed A4 manila envelope, which says:

208

I don't waste a second before ripping it open.

The envelope's full of photos: some of Miss Duke as a young woman. I can see her with the dark-haired man in several pictures (one looks like a first-night party, a group shot of what looks like a cast line-up, all grinning at the camera in their rehearsal clothes; they're both in there). There's a brilliant one of Michael, still with the same unruly mop of hair, only it's jet black instead of light grey. And a few taken from the outside of the music hall . . .

And another photo. It's dated 06.06.99 03:02 in red digital writing across the bottom right-hand corner. There's a man asleep in bed, facing away from the camera, naked. The patterned jacket from the first photo lies in the foreground, draped over the end of the bed. Behind it, next to the man, lies a woman, asleep on her back, her naked breasts visible where the covers have slipped down, her long dark hair sprawled across the pillow.

It's my mother.

'Where have you been?' Alec demands, coming out of his bedroom in only his boxers.

Since he slept with Taro I've been frosty with Alec, but he seems infuriatingly determined not to recognize it. Like, why does he get to demand to know where I've been?

'I found this,' I say, thrusting the bunch of photos at him unceremoniously.

'Miss Duke without greys – amazing,' he says, sifting through. 'Why have you brought me these?'

'Who's that guy with the jacket?' I demand, without explanation.

He looks at him more closely. 'I'm not sure. Why?'

I take the *other* photo out of my pocket.

'Ooh, what's this – the big reveal?' he says in mock-excitement, taking the photo. 'Wait – Anastasia?'

I nod.

'Oh my God.' He clutches the wall for effect, but I can tell he's actually shocked.

'I *know*.'

'I . . . I need to google something.' He starts scrolling furiously through his phone.

By the time I get a proper look at his screen, there are several photos of a sixty-something-year-old guy across the top, receding grey hair, fashionable in an older man kind of way. It reads:

Nick Prescott is a theatre and fashion photographer.
Notable works include photography for the Royal Ballet,
Vogue, Bazaar, Tatler *and* The Face *magazine.*

Alec scrolls down, although too quickly for me to read over his shoulder, then clicks on 'Images' at the top of the page. There are loads of photos of this guy – he seems to get around. Society events, fashion evenings, gossip column photographs. Alec whizzes through them but doesn't seem to find what he's looking for. Finally he goes back to the search bar at the top and types in 'Nick Prescott young' then clamps the phone to his chest before I get a chance to see.

'What is it?'

'Oh my God, Nettie . . .' Alec looks shocked. 'I . . . I think we know why your mum fell out with Miss Duke. I was right – this guy in the photo *is* Nick Prescott.'

'Who's that?' I say.

'Well, he's a photographer,' replies Alec. 'But at the time the photo was taken, he was Cecile Duke's husband.'

CHAPTER 19

It's 6 March, the dreaded day. Kiki and Leon have come over to watch the first airing of *Triple Threat*. Luca couldn't come – he has a big assignment due in tomorrow. I'm secretly relieved. Anand's warning has been turning over in my mind, Sam couldn't *actually* make out Luca and I were together. It would be lying . . . right?

Alec has ceremoniously put out a velvet curtain on the floor in place of a red carpet and dressed himself in a DJ. Thankfully Kiki and Leon have turned up in joggers and sweatshirts, so I don't feel too bad for being in my pyjamas.

Leon took some persuading to be here. Things seem . . . OK between him and Alec since Alec apologized. I'm glad to see Alec making an effort tonight, too.

'Top-up, Leon?' he says, offering the bottle of fizz. 'I bought your favourite.'

Kiki and I exchange a look. These rich boys and their wine.

'Er, thanks.' Leon seems surprised, but pleased. He gives Alec a small smile, and doesn't even protest when Alec sits next to him.

The documentary opens with a queue, clearly staged, outside the main building. The camera follows it all the way down Frith Street, round the corner to Bateman Street and back up Greek Street to Soho Square. A narrator tells us that thousands of hopefuls audition to be at Duke's every year.

'That's not how they run the auditions,' says Alec indignantly.

212

'Everyone has an allotted day. There's no queue.'

The first ten minutes show clips of class, interviews with Miss Duke and a couple of the teachers, and a general day at college. But it does it with this kind of intensity that I've never noticed in real life. The hunger to succeed, the competition, the need to thrive . . . Is that how Sam sees it? My first instinct is to dismiss it all as TV bullshit, but maybe it isn't. Maybe it just doesn't feel that way because we're all used to it. Even though we don't talk about it all the time, we're all pretty driven. Kiki's all about pushing herself to the limit. And Alec this year has gone beyond anything I've seen of him before, to the detriment of all of us.

The programme looks more like a movie than a documentary, with dance numbers like pop videos, shot from all angles and highly edited (I notice Jade comes across well with this technique). Kiki, Leon and Alec all have featured moments. Leon's interviewed about changing courses. There's a small but beautiful clip of him singing.

'Leon, you sound great,' says Alec.

Leon smiles but doesn't say anything. I know they're a long way off healing, but this at least feels like a step in the right direction.

The next part shows Kiki and Alec dancing. Alec's more than satisfied with his footage, but Kiki wrinkles her nose in disgust.

'Oh my God, is that how I look?' she says.

'You look . . . *amazing*,' Leon says.

There's an interview with Kiki where she discusses her collaboration with See Me Now. Then she talks about her body issues and tells Sam that she's going on a healthy-eating kick. I almost have to put my sock in my mouth to stop myself from commenting. I know it's her life, her choice, but the difference

213

between her in September and her now is huge. She was so happy, so positive at the beginning of the first term back. Now she just seems anxious and stressed – well, at least during the limited time I get to see her, when she's not with Sam or in rehearsals.

They show Jade auditioning for a dancer's role in *Chicago* and talk to her about last year. She doesn't hold back, going into full detail about how she blackmailed me to sing for her and how she liked Fletch, but he was interested in me all along and broke her heart. They then show the footage of the Summer Showcase while Jade tells viewers that we're basically sworn enemies. My eyes are rooted to the screen, but I can sense everyone looking at me to gauge my reaction, and I can feel it's making me go the reddest I've ever gone in my life – my cheeks feel even more flushed than that time last year when Miss Duke singled me out in a group of third-years to sing.

'Ugh, I just seem so . . . basic,' I say. 'Was I really that pathetic?'

'Babe, you were grieving, you'd been living with a woman who mentally abused you, you'd lost your voice, *and* the college bitch was making your life hell,' says Alec, putting his arm around my shoulder. 'You're literally made of steel to have come through all of that.'

I lean into him. Even if the world thinks I'm a nervous wreck, at least my friends know the real me.

The documentary then shows my audition for *Chicago* and runs the interview where Sam asks me about Fletch. If that wasn't embarrassing enough, there are clips of all my friends talking about how wonderful I am (I had no idea they were even asked about me) and some random shots of Luca watching me sing . . . I'm starting to understand what Anand was warning me about as I watch more footage of Luca and me laughing in a corner. My stomach starts to squirm uncomfortably when I realize that Fletch could be watching. I've been angry with him for his reaction to our friendship, but after watching this, I wouldn't blame him.

Then the documentary gets to the part at the Christmas Ball. Anxious, I get up to go, but Alec pulls me down.

'Nettie, there's like one minute left. You're not going anywhere.'

So I sit through the interviews, the awful Jade-and-Natasha scene, and finally the reel. There's a moment where Luca looks like he wants to tell me something but is interrupted by Fletch cutting in. I watch through my fingers as we kiss. Omigod, this is excruciating.

The camera zooms in on Luca. I watch incredulously as the camera closes in on his face, which looks completely gutted as he sees us kissing. Then he rushes out of the room, head down, eyes on the floor.

The credits start rolling.

Everyone looks at me.

Fuck.

Fuck.

'An evening with Antoinette Delaney-Richardson,' says Alec. 'She's here all week.'

I bury my face in my hands. 'What am I going to do?' I say. My cheeks flush hot again, and I can feel a stress rash appearing on my neck.

'I think the first thing you should do is stay calm,' says Leon. 'Everyone knows it's been heavily edited. We were all there, remember?'

'There's nothing going on between Luca and me,' I say.

'They made it look more like Luca has a crush on you,' says Kiki, 'which . . . seems fair.'

'See – even you're buying into it!' I say. 'They could have used footage from literally any moment. Surely you can see that?'

'You can't deny he's always been a tiny bit into you,' says Kiki tentatively.

'There's no way Luca would go after Nettie,' Leon says to Kiki. 'Fletch is like a brother to him.' He holds my hand; I squeeze it gratefully. 'Right, Alec?'

Alec's not listening. He's staring at the credits like he's seen a ghost.

'Are you OK?' says Kiki, waving in front of his face.

He comes out of his trance. 'Sorry. Just looking for our names. Leon's right,' he says, snapping back into action. 'If we can all see that the footage has been put together, then I'm sure Fletch can.'

I'm momentarily distracted by what he said about the credits, but it's just a load of line producers and the financial department and people we don't know. 'Fletch already has a thing about Luca and me. We had a fight about it on Sunday. I should never have agreed to be part of it. Sam's gone too far.'

'She's not exactly going to be like, "*The students have breakfast, do some classes, and go home*," is she?' says Kiki. 'She's looking for the drama, and whether you like it or not, Nettie, you *are* the drama. It's not like she's making you look *bad*, exactly . . .'

Leon puts his arm around me. 'At least Jade's not making up rumours about you like she was last year.'

'*Yet*,' I say. And to be honest, it feels like a crap consolation prize. 'Well, you guys all looked amazing anyway.'

*

We talk into the night, and I try to distract myself by focusing on my friends' brilliant performances. But when I eventually head to bed for the evening, there's only one thing on my mind.

What on earth am I going to say to Fletch?

I can't imagine what he must be feeling right now – I just hope he'll understand. I'll have to make myself as boring as possible from now on and stay away from Luca. There's nothing else I can do; I've got no say in how they portray me, no control over my own story. It sucks, actually.

I can't help remembering the close-up of Luca's face as he watched Fletch and me kissing. Desperately, I wrack my brains trying to think of what happened at the reel. Was he standing up against that wall at any other point? I can't remember. Could Sam have taken random footage of him deep in thought and made it look as if he was watching us? Or was Fletch right to be concerned? *Does* Luca have feelings for me?

Maybe Fletch didn't even see it. He's so mega busy, he probably forgot.

I message him.

23:39

Hey x

Fletch:
Hey, you

How's it going?

Good, thanks. Steph's amazing, isn't she?

The BEST 😎

What have you been up to tonight?

Working?

Or like at home chilling with TV or whatever

Working!
I don't really remember what chilling is.

You'll be home soon. Three more weeks ❤

Yeah. About that . . .
Nettie, I'm so sorry but they've
asked me to extend my internship.

Oh no! How long for?

Another two months.

What about your degree?

I've got an extension on my dissertation. And
I can use a lot of the work I'm doing here, so
it won't be too bad. I'm sorry – I know this is
going to make things hard for us.

We can make it work. I'm just glad you told me.

Thanks for being so understanding.
I'm missing you so much, Nettie.

But what if we don't get through it? Another two months? I don't think we'll survive it. Not after the trash I've just watched on telly tonight. This is completely gutting – we were on the home straight. Now the finish line's been moved and a shit load of emotional hurdles put up. I don't know how to deal with this.

One thing I'm certain of, though. He hasn't seen it. Yet.

'Nettie!'

Luca's calling me from the other end of the foyer at lunchtime the next day. I've managed to avoid him so far, but we still have hours and hours of rehearsals together – staying completely clear of him will be impossible. We'll have to face it at some point.

Everyone turns to look at him, including two members of the crew. Great.

I pretend not to hear, but he calls me again.

'Nettie, I just wanted a word!'

I turn around. '*OK, but can we do it outside?*' I mouth, beckoning him as I push open the front doors.

He seems to cotton on and follows me outside. 'Oh, right. Sure. Listen . . .' He looks around to check we're alone. 'Did you watch *Triple Threat*?'

'Um, yeah.'

'You know it's all bollocks, don't you?' he says.

'Yeah, kind of what I thought.' I hope he can't see the relief on my face.

'I mean it, Nettie. I don't want it to be weird between us. So

219

I went to Michael, and he suggested I talked to Sam if I'm not happy.'

'Don't be surprised if she goes back on her word,' I say. 'She's completely untrustworthy.'

'What about Fletch?' says Luca uncertainly.

'Fletch won't care. He knows how it is with these TV programmes.' I try to sound confident, but my stomach squirms nastily. When did everything get so complicated?

CHAPTER 20

'Well done. I think we're getting there,' Lisa says, as we finish cooling down after Wednesday night's session. We are now into early April, and this whole process has been less 'college musical' and more 'intensive training', but I can see the improvement in my dancing. It's been amazing to learn from Lisa; I totally get why Michael introduced her as a 'Fosse veteran'. She's an actual legend. And if I thought Kiki was amazing before, since she's been working with Lisa, she's reached new heights of incredible. She's going to be tremendous in the show.

'A reminder that you're to be at the Prince Edward Theatre on Sunday for the publicity shoot,' Lisa continues, 'and also that you may be asked to be photographed in your own clothes as well as your costume.'

Michael and Leon come down from upstairs, where they've been working on 'Mr Cellophane' together. Not that Leon needs any more work on it – he's got a real flare for comedy that no one could have predicted; his characterization of Amos is both hilarious and moving.

As we leave, Sam stops him. 'A quick word, Leon?'

Luca and Kiki and I leave them to it. Looking back, I raise my eyebrows at him to check he's OK. He nods quickly in response. I hope it's not something awful, but you never know where *Triple Threat*'s concerned. Maybe it's an interview about tonight's rehearsal. He was on fire just now.

Since the programme aired, everything's been really strange. People come up to us on the street, or they take photos on their phones from a distance. Magazines want to interview us. And now we're doing a huge photoshoot. I've tried not to watch the show, but at the same time I need to keep tabs on what Sam's saying about me, so I dip in and out and leave the room when it gets too cringey. As expected, Sam hasn't kept her word about not making a story of me and Luca and is still making it look as if we're in love with each other. Luca's outraged but I'm not at all surprised. I still don't know if Fletch has watched it; it's like this big elephant in the room between us.

Luca and Alec have been going through all Mum's stuff again with me, combing it for anything we might have missed the first time around. I've checked pockets of her old clothes, anywhere she might have left something, but so far we've come up with nothing. Luca's been trying to contact Peter Russell's old agent, but it seems he was already old school in the Nineties and is now ancient (I think Luca had to post a letter in the end because he's got no online presence). It's really kind of them both to help. Alec's definitely making an effort to be a better friend to all of us, which I can see in the fact that Leon's cautiously letting him in a little more.

Three Ring TV have deemed the music hall too shabby for their shoot, so we're decamping to the Prince Edward Theatre on Sunday. They're photographing all the featured students on *Triple Threat* – actors, dancers, MT students and stage managers, as well as the cast of *Chicago*. Alec's beside himself that he gets to come – he's made it abundantly clear that he feels out of the loop because he's not in the college musical. Maybe if he wasn't such an arse, we'd loop him in a bit more.

My phone rings on Sunday morning. I'm kind of awake, but I was lounging around in my bed, putting off getting up. It's Fletch.

'Hey, you,' I say.

'Hey, beautiful. Where are you?'

It's good to hear his voice. 'Er, just watching TV.'

'No, you're not.'

'What?'

'Get out of bed and come to the living-room window.'

I do as he says, shivering.

Fletch is outside, on his bike, his helmet dangling in one hand, smiling up at me. I scream and bolt out of the front door, down the stairs and out into the street in my shorts and vest. He laughs at me as I tiptoe over the cobbles with bare feet. When I reach the kerb, I fling my arms around his neck and he lifts me on to his lap.

'I didn't know you were coming back this weekend,' I say. I put my hands on his face; it's pink and cold from the ride.

'You'll freeze out here,' he says. 'Get in and put the kettle on. I'll go and park in the square.'

Kissing him, I hop off the bike and run back up to the flat. Then I peg it to the shower, wash my hair, shave my legs and get out again in one minute and thirty seconds. I blast my hair with the hairdryer, bung some lip balm and mascara on, and quickly fasten the locket he gave me around my neck. Then I scramble out to the kitchen and clear the mound of plates that I've let pile up, knowing that Alec wasn't going to surface until later.

Fletch comes in through the open door, just as I put my feet up on the sofa and grab one of Alec's magazines. So tidy, so nonchalant, me.

'*Loverboy*?' says Fletch.

I turn the magazine round to look at the front.

'It's very interesting reading,' I say.

'You were panic tidying.'

'Me? Never.'

He comes and lies next to me on the sofa. I drape his arm around me and lay my head on his chest. My whole back aches with missing him, or being with him – I'm not sure which.

'I wish we could just stay like this,' I say. 'Forever.'

Fletch looks down at me. 'What about snacks?'

He knows me too well. 'OK, with snack breaks.'

'Talking of snacks,' says Fletch, 'do you want to go and get breakfast somewhere?'

'Yes,' I say. 'Oh, wait.'

'What?'

'I've got a photoshoot at the Prince Edward. For *Triple Threat*.'

'Ooh, get you. Well, can I come?'

'Of course!'

'I want to be involved in any way I can. Hey, I watched *Triple Threat* last night.'

It's pretty surprising he left it this long to watch the first episode. I wonder if he's being *entirely* honest with me about when he watched it. He never mentioned seeing it, and I was always reluctant to ask him, for obvious reasons . . . But he's done it now. I wait with bated breath . . .

'You were beautiful.'

'Oh – thanks.' I wait for him to say something else, but he doesn't, so I fill the silence with explanations that I hope don't sound like excuses. 'Sam's really over-edited it. Like, made up narratives out of nothing.'

'Yeah – I thought that, too.' He knows what I'm talking about. But neither of us actually wants to say it.

I sit up next to him and rest my head on his shoulder. 'I'm going to stay away from the cameras as much as possible from now on.'

'Nettie, you shouldn't worry about that. Just keep being normal. Who cares what some TV exec thinks is good telly? As long as we know what's real and what isn't . . .'

'And we do, don't we?'

He strokes my hair. 'Yes.' There's a hint of an apology in his voice. He kisses me, his hand on my cheek now, like it's cradling a precious thing. 'I love you, Nettie. That's all that matters.'

I'm almost shaking with relief. The more of *Triple Threat* that's been aired, the worse the storyline has got, and I'd convinced myself that as soon as Fletch watched it, we'd be over. Sam's edited it so cleverly that I can't imagine a single person out there who wouldn't get the impression that Luca and I were an item. Well, fuck her. Even she can't stand in the way of Fletch and me.

'I love you too,' I say, and kiss him back.

'Well, who knew photoshoots would be so *boring*?' complains Alec.

To be fair, we've been hanging around for two hours waiting to be called. They spent the first hour looking for a missing skull to photograph with one of the actors (*I know, original*). Now they're messing around with stage lighting while Kiki does various poses as we watch her on the monitor in the foyer. She's wearing a prototype of one of her designs, a baby pink and blue ensemble. I'm standing by a merchandise stall with Fletch, who's got his head down, busy checking 'very important' documents on

225

his phone. It's not exactly the romantic day I'd hoped for when he turned up this morning.

Alec's sitting a few feet away with Leon – they are playing a game on Leon's phone together. Taro comes up the stairs.

'You're up next, Alec,' he says, glancing nervously down at Leon.

After everything that happened at the ball, he's lucky Leon's still speaking to him. It's not just Alec who behaved badly. I know they weren't official, but to sleep with his best friend without even having a conversation with Leon is a pretty shitty move.

'Thanks.' Alec doesn't make eye contact with Taro. I've noticed he avoids Taro at college these days – I guess it's awkward. He jumps up off the floor, whacks his legs up a couple of times in place of a warm-up, and goes down to the stalls. Taro follows him down the stairs with a strange look in his eyes. What does he expect?

Luca's been at the other end of the foyer talking to some of the students from the actors course, but now he comes over to where Fletch and I are standing.

'Hey, mate,' says Fletch.

'Hey – it's great to see you,' replies Luca. I watch nervously as they hug. 'How's it going?'

'Oh, you know –' Fletch rolls his eyes – 'more changes. Everyone stressed. Two more months of it . . . I never realized how much pressure there was.'

'I thought you just wrote it and then took it to someone,' says Luca. 'Then it was kind of plain sailing.'

'Yeah, me too,' says Fletch. 'I think if you're already successful as a writing team and someone commissions you, it really turns the heat up. They're being paid to deliver.'

'I'd rather just work at home in my bedroom,' says Luca.

226

Fletch laughs. This is good. All fine so far.

Just then, one of the front-of-house staff, who's been watching us for several minutes, bounds over. He's a young white guy with ginger hair. 'Hey, I know you,' he says. 'You're the girl from *Triple Threat*, right?'

'Er, yeah, that's me.' This is weird.

He claps his hands. 'Oh my God, you're *Nettie*! I'm Liam. I love you! You sang the solo in the show last year, too, right? I've seen the clip. When those girls kidnapped you and forced you to sing for them? That was like a total Cinderella moment. Was it real?'

'All real,' I say. 'That part, anyway.' I glance at Fletch and Luca.

'Sometimes I imagine it's me,' says Liam. 'I've recreated "the moment" so many times in my bedroom. At first, I'm, like, really shy when that hot boy drags me on to the stage – like, so nervous. Then the principal comes onstage, I sing the song *amazingly*, and everyone loves me, and the other hot guy kisses me – Oh . . . is that you?' He points at Fletch next to me.

Fletch grins awkwardly. 'Er, yeah.'

'And now you two. . .' He flits his finger between Luca and me.

'No!' we reply in unison.

'Oh, it was just that on *Triple Threat*—'

'Yeah, we know. All made up,' says Luca. 'Not by us,' he adds, looking at Fletch worriedly.

Fletch seems to be taking it surprisingly well – on the outside, anyway.

Liam shrugs, like he doesn't care if it's real or not. 'So can I get a picture?'

227

'Er, sure,' I say.

'Amazing.' He pulls me in clumsily. 'Thanks.' He immediately applies a filter and puts it on Instagram. 'Can't tag you, though. I think your account's private – I've tried following you before.'

'Yeah – I just . . . didn't want the hassle.'

Liam waits for a second as if deciding what to do, then spontaneously hugs me and heads down the stairs. I stare after him, partly because what just happened was so bizarre, and partly because that way I don't have to look at Fletch or Luca.

Fletch's phone rings. 'Sorry, I've got to take this. It's the boss . . . Hello? Hi, Jules—' He walks over to the entrance.

Luca sighs through his nose. 'Well, that was . . .'

'Interesting,' I finish. 'Come on, let's go and watch Kiki.'

We go through to the dress circle. The theatre's an art deco palace of red and gold, grand and vast, each level edged with scalloped lighting that trims each tier like seashells clinging to a cliffside. It's stunning. Looking down, I can only imagine what it feels like to perform here. Kiki's onstage in a tilt, looking stunning in her pastel two-piece, her leg lifted over one-eighty, her body on the side. People are moving lights around her as a photographer prepares to shoot.

Sam pauses everyone while she takes Kiki aside to say something. Whatever it is causes Kiki to run offstage and return a minute later wearing an old Nike set she's had for ages. That's a shame – her original outfit was gorgeous and it was part of her collection – it would have been great publicity for the range. Maybe it didn't work with the lights or something.

They finish shortly after that. Alec leaps around the stage while the photographer snaps him mid-jump. He looks disappointed when, ten minutes later, Sam declares that she's got what she needs.

Anand pops his head through the curtain at the back. 'Nettie, Luca! You're up.'

Luca rolls his eyes as Anand disappears.

'What was that for?' I ask as we head up the stairs to go backstage.

'Just . . . not keen, that's all.'

'He's lovely!'

Luca snorts. 'He works for Sam. I don't trust him.'

Bemused by Luca's comments, I follow him to the stage. Anand's always been really kind to me. What's made Luca react to him like that? Does he know something I don't?

We do the lifts. Some of them aren't fully there yet and we collapse, laughing. Fletch slips in at the back of the theatre stalls. He stands there completely still, watching us work together. The auditorium's too dark to see his face. I wish I knew what he was thinking right now. Is he proud? Or . . .

After several more lifts and a couple of poses that can only be described as clinches, Sam lets us go. I jump off the stage and head up the aisle to Fletch. He's clutching a handful of his hair, which is never a good thing.

'Fletch—'

'Nettie, I'm really sorry, but they've called me back.'

'You're going now?'

'They need me,' he says. His face looks conflicted, impatient to go but reluctant at the same time.

I try stalling him. 'Can you at least wait and grab some food before you go? We've nearly finished.'

'I'll eat when I'm back in Chich. I'm so sorry.' He puts his hand on my shoulder. As a gesture it feels final, like both an apology and an end to the conversation all in one.

Luca joins us at the back of the stalls.

'Nice moves,' says Fletch. He smiles awkwardly, like he's trying really hard to be supportive.

'Thanks.' Luca grins. 'Not really what I expected for my third year as a music student.'

'It's not really what any of us expected.' Fletch's smile drops for a second.

No one speaks.

'Oh,' says Fletch. 'I forgot to say – I asked David if he knew your mum, Nettie. He said he didn't.'

'That's weird,' I say. 'Did he say anything else?'

'No,' says Fletch. 'He moved on to another subject. I couldn't quiz him about it. He's quite a ferocious man.'

Luca frowns. 'But they worked together. Twice.'

'I thought it was just the one show?' says Fletch.

'*Funny Face*, too,' I say. 'We found out a couple of weeks ago.'

'Right,' says Fletch, and I feel like the slow nod he gives us is at my use of the word 'we'.

'But why would he lie?' says Luca. 'He has no reason to.'

'Is it possible you're mistaken, and they didn't work together?' says Fletch.

'They definitely knew each other.' I can't hide my irritation. Why is he taking the word of a random old guy over his girlfriend?

'Maybe he just didn't remember her,' says Fletch, clearly also irritated.

'No,' says Luca. 'She was the star. He'd remember her. You need to ask him again.'

'I'm not pestering David Hirst with questions he's already given me the answer to.' Fletch's voice is raised now, and a nearby front-of-house worker looks at him, alarmed. 'It's not like college, Luca. Everyone's not there to attend to your every whim. David Hirst is a world-renowned director with a vision and a very busy schedule and I can't just go up to him saying I'm not satisfied with what he told me.'

Luca looks shocked. 'All right, mate. I'm sorry – I was just saying—'

'Well, don't,' snaps Fletch. 'You don't understand.' His tone is so sharp that neither Luca nor I know how to respond. Fletch's face softens. 'Look, I'm sorry, OK? It's really hard going down there, and I just wanted to come back and spend the day with my girlfriend. I feel like I never get away from them. I'm sorry I took it out on you.' He puts his hands up in admittance, and Luca nods.

'Can't you tell them you need a break?' I say, putting my hand on his shoulder.

'They really like what I'm doing, how I'm helping,' says Fletch. 'They said that if it goes to town next year, they'd like me to come and be assistant MD. I can't pass up an opportunity like that, Nettie – I just can't. People would kill for that kind of position straight out of college. Listen, I'll call you when I get there.' He pulls me in for a hug.

'When will I see you again?'

'If I can't get back before, I'll be at the Duke's Awards. I wouldn't miss seeing you sing for anything.'

'I might not even get to the finals.'

He kisses my nose. 'You're amazing. Of course you will.'

'Drive safely,' I say. 'I love you.'

'I love you, too. See you, guys.' He hugs Luca briefly, gives me one last kiss, and disappears through a curtain at the back.

'You OK?' says Luca.

231

We sit down together on the back row.

'Yeah – it's just really hard to watch him go through such a tough time. I hope he gets a break soon . . .'

Five minutes later, another call goes out for us, this time for us to get into costume. Luca and I go our separate ways to get changed. We can't use backstage because the cast of the current show are using all the rooms, so they've set up the girls dressing room in a reception room on the ground floor called 'The Julie Andrews Room'. Similar in décor to the bar, it's where the producers bring the VIPs to schmooze.

Kiki's already in there, getting changed into her *Chicago* costume.

'Hey,' she says.

'Hey – great tilt earlier,' I say. 'Why did Sam get you to change?'

Kiki's face clouds over. 'She said it would be better to keep the actual clothes a secret until the line launches. Make more of an impact when it finally drops, which should line up with the season finale of *Triple Threat*.'

'Oh.' I can sort of see that it makes sense, but it seems like Sam's missing a trick. Why not get people interested early?

I'm about to say as much when my attention's grabbed by the walls, which are lined with photographs, mostly of celebrities from decades past meeting various cast members of shows. My heart quickening, I cross the room to scan them. Kiki, realizing what I'm doing, comes to join me. A couple of minutes pass while we both search.

Then I see something that makes my heart come up into my throat.

Among the many photos of Julie Andrews, there's a photo

232

of Mum. It could be me in that picture, except for the fact that she's got her long hair scraped back in a bun. She's dressed in a white ballgown, in front of a group of cast members and crew, all smiling at someone opposite. That 'someone' is Princess Margaret, who is shaking hands with Mum, mid-conversation. The caption underneath reads:

HRH Princess Margaret meets Anastasia Delaney-Richardson

'You're really like her,' says Kiki.

'I guess I am,' I say. It's strange, the echo of Mum that follows me everywhere. I see it in Michael's eyes sometimes when he talks to me, or when I'm performing. Like this nostalgia about who Mum was, mixed in with . . . I don't know – pride in me, at what I've overcome? There's a similar recognition from Miss Duke, and Miss Moore, although it's mostly hatred on her part. It's frustrating to be on the receiving end of it without really knowing the person they're remembering.

'When do you think it's from?' says Kiki.

'Mum's wearing a 1950s wedding dress, so it's probably from when she did *Funny Face*.'

Kiki drapes her arms around my shoulders and gives them a squeeze. I take two pictures on my phone, one of the group and a close-up of Mum. It hurts to think that the girl in the picture would become my mum and I don't know anything about her.

Later in my room, I study the photos on my phone. Who else is there? I zoom in. Princess Margaret, but I'm pretty sure Mum didn't know her. I don't recognize the other cast members, apart from Peter Russell, who's grinning on Mum's right, and one

233

other man on her left, also smiling and chatting with Princess Margaret . . .

I type 'David Hirst' into Google Images. Several pictures come up of a balding elderly man with a posh-looking mouth, turned down at the edges like he's sneering at the camera. Going back to the original photo, the man here is younger, slimmer, less lined, has more hair – but it's definitely him. It's David Hirst. I *knew* it. I knew he was lying when he told Fletch he'd never met her. But why?

Then I spot something else. Zooming in on Mum's left hand (the one that isn't shaking hands with the Princess), I can see that it's next to David Hirst's hand. Although it's difficult to see through the top layer of Mum's net skirt, what I *can* make out is that the backs of their hands are touching, and David's forefinger is entwined loosely around Mum's. Maybe that was accidental? I turn the photo sideways, trying to get a better view. They're all crowded together – maybe their hands just happened to be touching.

But then I look again at how his finger's curled around hers. So intimate. And not fully holding hands, which would've been a public gesture of affection. There's no denying it – it's the body language of two people who are shagging.

Which would be fine, except that I know from just googling him that David Hirst has been married to Lucinda Hartley for the last forty years, which means they were together when this photo was taken. What was Mum doing with all these married men? Was she OK? It's like she was out of control. And her eyes in this picture . . .

My fingers are shaking as I type in something else. Seeing the words appear in the search box shocks me, despite them coming from my own head.

234

As usual, nothing. Mostly stuff about the Russian princess, missing the words 'drug problem'. I scroll down to the second page. Underneath 'Some results may have been removed due to data protection in Europe' is a headline from *The Times* along with the first few words of the article.

Star Collapses Onstage – Are Drink and Drugs to Blame?

An unnamed source informs us that Anastasia Delaney-Richardson's future hangs in the balance as the company seeks to distance itself after last night, when ambulances were called during La Fille Mal Gardée . . .

Holding my breath, I click the link.

Oops, this page cannot be found.

What?

I try again. Still nothing. Someone's taken it down. Who would do that? And who is the 'unnamed source'?

Something clicks into place. The letters from 'B', the mention in them of a betrayal, the photo of Mum with Miss Duke's husband, and now this article . . . They all add up to one undeniable fact: Miss Duke must have spoken to the papers.

She ended Mum's career.

CHAPTER 21

Triple Threat is ruining my life. Ratings are through the roof, and all anyone seems to care about is the supposed love triangle between me, Fletch and Luca. I now can't go *anywhere* without someone pointing a phone at me, calling my name or coming up to me and asking for a selfie. One guy in Soho last week shouted at me across the road, 'Oi! When you gonna let Luca into your pants?' Alec, who was with me at the time, went over and threatened to punch him until Leon managed to talk him down. I'm sure at least four people filmed it. The whole thing's a mess.

I'm heading up Wardour Street with Kiki after *Chicago* rehearsals. We're exhausted. Lisa, concerned that too much of our rehearsal time is taken up with performing stuff over and over for Sam, has had us in all over Easter to catch up. I don't blame her – we're approaching mid-April and we still haven't finished setting everything – but it's taking its toll on our bodies.

'Hey!'

We turn around and see a group of schoolgirls in the doorway of a shop. Two of them have their phones out and are filming us.

One of them squeals. 'It *is* them!'

'Excuse me, are you the girls from *Triple Threat*?' says another. Kiki smiles. 'Er, yeah.'

'Omigod, we love you! Kiki, you're, like, the best dancer in the world. And Nettie, your singing is LIFE! Can we have a selfie?'

'I guess?' Kiki looks at me, and I shrug.

They huddle around, one of them with her phone held out, and we smile for the camera.

'Gonna tag you in my story,' says the girl with the camera.

'You're so beautiful,' adds another to Kiki. 'Like, I want to be you.'

'Thanks,' says Kiki, bewildered but clearly pleased.

We promise to like their photo on Instagram, and they head into the shop, giggling excitedly. Both of us are slightly weirded out.

'Well, that was strange,' I say.

'Cool, though.' Kiki looks back towards the shop, smiling. 'That's the first time I've been recognized. It felt nice! Everyone's so talented at Duke's, it's almost like no one's talented. Your reward is just *being* there. No one ever says well done, or tells me I'm good, or says I look pretty.'

'I tell you you're amazing, and incredibly beautiful,' I say. 'All the time.'

'I know,' she says, smiling. 'I meant the teachers, though. I was talking to Sam about the Duke's Awards, how I feel like I need to win just to keep my head above water, get noticed. How I feel the pressure to look a certain way. How I'll never be enough. Sam says it's a bullshit industry, but if I want to be part of it, I've got to play the game. Go that extra mile, keep the weight down. Look the best.'

Sam says, Sam says. 'Kiki, you're more than enough. You're *everything.*'

'But I'm not skinny. Not *skinny*-skinny. And that's what the industry wants. It wants shoulder bones, perfect cleavage, tiny ribcage, minuscule waist, arse like a firm peach, and a thigh gap you could park a truck in. It wants smooth, glossy hair. It wants

237

big lips, small noses, high cheekbones. It wants white girls, Nettie, and even when it does let women of colour and Black women in, it judges our bodies on white standards. It wants us all homogenized: the same shape, colour, height and weight until we all look like one person. It doesn't care about the thousands of hours of ballet, or the exams, or the sweat, or the tears. It only cares that we fit the mould. Like, maybe when I'm a world-famous dancer, I'll be able to shake things up, say what I think, but right now I'm at the bottom of the pile. And from down here, I've no other option. I've got to play the game.'

I hate that Kiki feels so shit, but Sam's advice, while completely toxic, actually has a twisted logic behind it. Kiki and I are starting out, right at the bottom; we can't go tearing the industry up from its roots.

But maybe that's exactly what we should be doing.

All anyone can talk about at rehearsals lately is the Duke's Awards. *What are you singing? What are you wearing? What monologue have you chosen?* Everyone's desperate to get to the finals, which are held every year at a West End theatre and are watched by the whole of the theatrical glitterati. This year there's the added pressure (or benefit, depending on how you look at it) of the *Triple Threat* cameras. Everything we do is basically a self-tape for the entire industry.

Leon and I are just discussing what he should sing for the first round, when Taro comes over. Leon visibly tenses but smiles politely.

'Don't tell me – the Duke's Awards?' Taro says.

'What else?' I say. 'What are you singing, Taro?'

He shakes his hair off his face. 'I dunno. I was going to do

"If I Can't Love Her" from *Beauty and the Beast*, but Alec said it was basic.'

'*Basic?*' I say. 'It's a beautiful song.'

'Alec said that?' says Leon at the same time.

'Yeah, that's what I told him,' says Taro, answering my question, which was louder than Leon's. 'I think I'll do it anyway.' He drifts off casually to the coffee station, leaving Leon and me open mouthed.

'Why has Alec got any input in what Taro's singing, anyway?' says Leon.

'I don't know. I didn't think they were even speaking.'

When Leon looks at me doubtfully, I add, 'Alec always said the ball was a one-off. He hasn't mentioned Taro, or stayed out all night, and Taro hasn't been to our flat. I don't think he'd do that to you, Leon, not after everything that's happened.'

'Yeah,' says Leon, but his face tells me he's thinking something different.

The next two weeks go in a blur of extra lessons with Lisa, who's intent on turning me into Ann Reinking before opening night, and panicked lessons with Steph, practising for the Duke's Awards. She seems as stressed out as Fletch. If this is what creating a new musical is like, I think I'd rather not, thanks. Just bung me in *Mamma Mia!* and I'll be happy. Actually, what am I saying – I'd be happy with *any* job.

Fletch and I have barely spoken these last two weeks. When we do talk, he barely asks me anything about *Chicago*, or my weekend plans. How can he expect me to share stuff with him if he shows no interest in my life? There's been no mention of *Triple Threat*, either – I don't even know if he's seen any more episodes. That kind of hurts, too. Which I *know* doesn't make any sense when I'm also dreading him seeing it, but it's, like, your girlfriend's on TV every week and is now randomly quite well known. Surely that's a big enough deal for you to watch it, or at least acknowledge it, even if it does end in us fighting?

Luca's as determined as I am not to let things get weird between us, but we're definitely still censoring our behaviour in front of the cameras. Every time we run 'Razzle Dazzle', I cringe at the way Sam swoops in on us.

Lisa's not impressed. 'Come on, you guys. This *pas de deux* shouldn't even be in the show –' she glares over at Sam – 'so it has to be impeccable to work. You two just don't have the chemistry you used to. I need more authenticity. More sexual tension.'

More sexual tension? Oh my God.

Michael's becoming increasingly bothered by the scheduling changes *Triple Threat* has caused. As we pack up after the sitzprobe, I overhear him arguing with Sam in a low voice.

'I just don't see why *Chicago* has to be the week after the Duke's Awards.'

'I've told you, Michael. We're building towards the season finale.'

'The students are exhausted, Sam. They worked all through Easter to give you material, and these awards are a big deal. I don't think having them the week before *Chicago* is good for focus.'

'You knew it was going to be like this from the off. Miss Duke agreed to hand all scheduling over to me.'

Luca, who's also eavesdropping, raises his eyebrows at me. 'Come on, I'll walk you home,' he says.

As we walk down Wardour Street, I check my messages.

This morning I sent Fletch a picture Kiki took of me dancing in rehearsals. Without being too vain, I was quite pleased with it – I can see how much my dancing's improved with all these classes with Lisa. Fletch saw the photo more than twelve hours ago but still hasn't replied. I know he's busy, but would it have killed him to send a heart or a kiss? I'm always asking how it's going down there, cheering him on when he gets down, and being supportive. Why can't he do the same?

'Hey, well done tonight,' Luca says, stopping for a moment. 'Your dancing was looking really great in "Me and My Baby". I can tell how hard you've worked.' His shiny dark hair whips across his face in the wind, and he puts a hand up to push it back.

Why is Luca saying everything I want my boyfriend to say? It's almost a shame we don't have feelings for each other. Things would be undeniably less complicated.

I smile. 'Thanks, Luca. You were pretty good yourself.'

'I mean, that's kind, but we both know I'm miscast in this role. If it weren't for all the fun we've had, I'd be having major regrets.'

'It *has* been fun, despite all the hard work . . . I don't think I've ever seen you laugh as much as when I flung myself backwards to sit on your lap at the start of the number, but you'd gone to talk to Leon.'

He grins. 'I *was* sorry, but it was too funny. Your surprised face was what got me. And the fact that you were on the floor.'

We both chuckle at the memory. Almost like clockwork, someone wolf-whistles from the other side of the road. I step back automatically. Luca bristles.

'Seriously, people need to do one,' he says.

We walk back through St James's and Piccadilly, less chatty

241

than we normally would be. It takes us both a while to shake off what just happened. When we arrive at Langley Street, Luca doesn't hug me like he normally does; we just part ways with an awkward wave. I can't deal with this any more.

When I get home, Alec's waiting with a wooden spoon in his hand, wearing a new pinny with a life-size photo of Shirley MacLaine on the front.

'Where have you been? Out with your other boyfriend?'

'Alec, I'm not in the mood,' I say.

For once, he takes the hint. 'What's up?'

'Urgh, nothing,' I say. I try to slink off to my room, but he pulls me back.

'It's Luca, right?'

'Someone just wolf-whistled at us on the street.'

'Nettie, if you're worried about your feelings for Luca—'

'I'm not!'

'Hey, there's nothing wrong with finding people attractive. There's no rule that just because you have a boyfriend, you must suddenly start pretending you don't fancy anyone else. It would be weird if you didn't.'

'That's not it.'

'Well, what is it, then?'

'It's the programme. It's made everything weird between us. We don't want Sam to film us together, so we avoid each other when the cameras are on, but then it feels like we're censoring our behaviour, which makes me feel guilty, even though there's nothing between us.'

'Maybe you should stop spending time with Luca. Fletch is clearly jealous, and—'

242

'Fletch is being an arse about it, actually,' I snap.

'Well, look at it from his point of view. There's *Triple Threat* and all the unfathomably unreasonable things being shown on there – plus he's away and you're having a fabulous time with his best friend. You can't really blame him, can you?'

'Have you been talking to him?' I say sharply.

'No! Not about that, anyway. Nettie, I wouldn't do that – not behind your back. But he's my friend too, and I don't think you can underestimate how tough he's finding things right now.'

'What am I supposed to do – stay in bed crying? Quit *Chicago*?'

'Of course not. Just remember that Fletch is having a really hard time, too, so if there are things you can do to make everything smoother sailing, do them.'

Smooth sailing? If only. This year's been nothing but drama since we started. I wish I could go back and do it all again, make everything right. But real life doesn't work like that, does it? It's not a preview. Every day of real life at Duke's is like opening night: no second chances. But throw *Triple Threat* into the mix, and suddenly I don't know what's real and what's part of the show any more.

CHAPTER 22

07:36

Where are you?

Alec:
Went in early to rehearse.

You're keen!

DUKE'S AWARDS TODAY
I HAVE to win this, Nettie.

May's arrived, and with it comes a load of stress: our performance of *Chicago*, and the Duke's Awards. Last year, I entered the Duke's Awards as a singer-songwriter with Fletch, but because of my disastrous vocal situation couldn't actually sing the song, so Jade ended up duetting with him. I was devastated.

This year I'm singing 'The History of Wrong Guys' from *Kinky Boots* for my first round entry, and I intend not to fuck it up. The first round of each category – classical dance, jazz dance, acting, singing, songwriting, composition, choreography – takes place in the studio theatre. Students, teachers and even Miss Paige and the office staff come to watch. No classes. No rehearsals, either. Michael's seething. Honestly, I'm nervous about the time off, too. I was just beginning to feel happy with what I was doing, and now we're stopping right before we open.

Kiki's got two pieces in the competition: her commercial solo and a contemporary group dance that she's choreographed. She's been worrying about her costume all week because Sam told her that the sequinned two-piece she was wearing 'wasn't very flattering' on camera. Kiki was hurt, I think – especially as the outfit was from her collection and she was hoping to showcase it. She ended up changing her costume at the last minute. I literally don't even know why she insists on being friends with Sam.

Sequins or no sequins, she smashes her jazz dance. There's no way she won't get through to the finals. *And* win it. No one else comes even close with their performance.

When Jade gets up to dance, Sam busies the cameras with at least five different shots, and Jade has to do the dance several times until they get what they need. It makes me angry that Kiki, who so clearly deserves it, got a tenth of the time they're spending on Jade.

'I don't get it,' says Kiki, who's come from backstage to watch. 'She's not even good.'

'That's why they need all the shots,' says Alec, who's already killed his dance in the morning and is enjoying the luxury of not having to stress about it any more (unlike Leon and me, who are both still sitting there stiffly in our smart clothes, waiting for the singing round). 'Close-ups, lots of different angles. Standard pop-video stuff. People won't be able to get a clear view. It'll look good; they'll believe what they're told. Don't be surprised if she gets through.'

Leon is *brilliant* in the singing round. He emerges from the wings, looking gorgeous, and gives a performance of 'What Would I Do?' from *Falsettos* that's beautifully understated and

245

deeply emotional. There's a pause as he finishes the song where you could hear a hairpin fall to the floor. Then the audience erupts. I'm so happy for Leon; he deserves this recognition.

Alec sniffs next to me. I glance at him, about to comment about how amazing Leon is, but seeing him, the words stick in my throat.

Alec is *sobbing*.

Not just a couple of token tears. He's ugly-crying. His chest is heaving shakily and his nose is running. Like, I get it, Leon's performance was emosh and I'm feeling it, too, but Alec . . . *doesn't* cry. I've never seen one tear exit his face.

'Do you . . . want a tissue?'

He nods, wiping his cheeks with the back of his hand. I reach into my bag for one and pass it to him. He blows his nose loudly.

'Are you . . . OK?' I say.

He gulps. 'He's – That was . . .'

Alec can't seem to find the words. It's strange to see him like this. The song's about deep, loving friendship. Maybe he feels bad about the way he's treated Leon. Or is he just sad their relationship isn't quite back to where it was? It's an odd, out-of-character reaction. Maybe it's . . . guilt? Recently, I've been watching Alec's behaviour around Taro. He goes out of his way to avoid him. I think he can't handle what he did.

There's no time to discuss it. The girls round is next and I have to go. Leon's performance and Alec's bizarre reaction still lingering in my brain, I go to get myself ready backstage, feeling a little battered.

Kiki's in early the next morning to deliver the news to us all.

246

07:50

Kiki:
Hey, have you seen the board?

Alec:
We're still at the flat! Tell me TELL ME

Kiki:
We're all through!

Yay!!!

Alec:
FINALS, BABY!

Phew 😄

Would have been embarrassing
for them if I hadn't got through

Kiki:
Could you just for once not be a bighead pls, Alec?

Alec:
Jokes

Well done Leon for your first singing final!

Leon:
Thanks! And you, Nettie!

Kiki:

Oh yeah, I forgot you didn't sing last year. That seems like another lifetime.

It REALLY does.

After the break for the Duke's Awards first round, Michael and Lisa get straight back into rehearsing *Chicago* before everything stops again for the finals next week. Tonight it's obvious we've lost ground and the general mood is . . . panicky. We've only got just over a week until the show and it's clear we've lost momentum. And another problem is that with all the stop-starting because of the cameras, we've never run the show from start to finish. We're trying it tonight and I'm scared.

'So, we're kind of back to where we were,' says Lisa at the end of the run. 'We can't afford to lose ground again.' She gives Sam a sneer of disapproval.

We pack up and leave the studio, as do the TV crew – except Anand, who hovers in the corner nervously. 'Nettie – can I have a quick word?'

Luca, who's heading out, looks over suspiciously.

'Sure – is it quick?' I say, looking for Leon to ask him a question about our scene. But he's already left.

'Sam's asked me to ask you if you'd mind changing your song choice for the Duke's Awards finals. I know it's a pain – sorry.'

A pain? I've been working on 'You Matter to Me' from *Waitress* for weeks. Also – I was hoping Fletch would know I was singing it for him. He said he'd be there to watch me.

'What does she want me to sing?' I say, sighing. 'And I'm assuming she's telling me, not asking?'

'Well, yeah.' Anand looks nervous. 'It's . . . "Dead Mom" from *Beetlejuice*.'

Oh my God. You couldn't make it up. I let out a hollow laugh. 'Is she doing this just to spite me?'

'I honestly don't understand how her brain works,' says Anand, letting out a slow breath. He looks really sad. In fact, he's been looking increasingly low these last few weeks.

'Anand, are you OK?'

'I just – she gets to me sometimes. And then I get angry at myself for not speaking up or being braver.'

'You can't blame yourself for that. Sam's intimidating.'

'It's not just her. I'm the same in every area of my life. Afraid of acting. Like . . .'

'Go on.'

'Well, there's this person I'm in love with, but I'm too scared to tell him.'

'It's not your flatmate Jay by any chance, is it?'

Anand looks taken aback. 'How did you know?'

I smile. 'You mention him a lot. So why can't you tell him?'

'I don't even know if he's into guys. Sometimes I think he likes me, but then I'm not sure.'

I give him a smile. 'Well, there's only one way to find out.'

Anand smiles awkwardly back. 'Yeah.' He goes to leave but then stops, like he's psyching himself up to do something. He pulls me close. 'Listen, I found something out,' he whispers. 'About . . . Well, I just need to confirm it's true, but when I do . . .' He trails off, almost like he's too scared to say anything.

'Yeah . . . ?'

'. . . It'll be huge.'

The way he's looking at me right now, I'm almost certain it's got something to do with Sam.

I go downstairs to catch up with Leon, wondering what Anand's found out about Sam. Maybe she's been bullying the people who work for her . . . Or doing dodgy business deals, I don't know – Ugh. I balk at myself. I'm kind of done thinking about bloody Sam. I pop in some earphones, blast 'Whataya Want from Me' from *& Juliet* and head for the main doors.

When I push them open, I'm surprised to come face to face with Alec, Taro and Leon.

They look . . . tense. Like something's going down.

Fuck.

I pull out my earphones.

'Nettie!' says Alec, looking shocked. He starts saying something about coincidences as Leon swiftly shakes his head. Taro looks confused.

'What's going on?' I say tentatively, but I think I already know. 'I—'

'I just caught Alec and Taro together,' says Leon, his voice shaking. 'Apparently they've been seeing each other this whole time.' He wipes the start of angry tears away from his eyes.

I turn to Alec in disgust. 'After you *swore* you wouldn't see Taro? What the fuck, Alec?'

Taro pipes up. 'I swear to God, Leon, I had no idea Alec was keeping this from you.'

'Then why didn't *you* tell anyone?' I say accusingly. Taro's spent over five months working with us. Would he not have thought to mention it?

'It was only a casual thing!' says Taro. 'It just . . . never

250

came up. I swear I wasn't hiding it.'

It all makes sense now. That moment when Taro said he'd been discussing what to sing for the Duke's Awards with Alec – he obviously assumed we knew they were seeing each other. Alec was very rarely in the same place as Taro because he was trying to hide it. But Taro had no idea.

'I never meant to let it continue,' says Alec. 'Leon, I realized last week watching you sing that I'd been a terrible friend to you for years. I came here today to end it with Taro!'

'What?' says Taro.

'I'm . . . sorry,' says Alec. 'I haven't been thinking straight all year. I shouldn't have slept with you in the first place, Taro. And I should never have let it carry on.'

'Amazing,' says Taro. 'You're a fucking twat, Alec – you know that?' He picks up his bag and sets off towards Old Compton Street. Part of me feels sorry for him, but a bigger part feels vindicated on Leon's behalf.

'You're a blatant liar,' says Leon, letting rip now that Taro's left. 'You weren't coming to end it. Since when have you ever worried about other people's feelings?'

'Leon, I'm sor—' starts Alec, but Leon doesn't let him finish.

'You're sorry you got caught,' he says harshly. 'This is so fucked up, Alec! You don't do that to friends.'

'You were finished with Taro! If you weren't, I'd never have hooked up with him in the first place!' says Alec, but unfortunately for him, the comment has unwittingly set off both mine and Leon's bullshit radar.

'I SAW YOU!' yells Leon, oblivious to the people hurriedly crossing the road to avoid us on the narrow pavement. 'I was in the library when you and Taro came in. The *reason* I sent Taro the message saying I just wanted to be friends was because I already knew you two were hooking up. I was there, Alec.'

'You were . . . *there*?'

'I was just getting in the right headspace to talk to Taro about us being exclusive, and there was my supposed best friend – shagging him!'

Alec scoffs. 'We haven't been *best friends* since you came back from the summer and decided you didn't want to know me.'

Leon throws his arms up. 'Yeah, and do you know why? More and more, our friendship has been less about being there for each other to get through some tough times, and more about you constantly competing with me. And this year you seem to think I only exist to feed your ego, to make you feel better about yourself. Why do you think I changed courses? *To get away from you, Alec.*'

'Leon—'

'No – I'm done with it. I'm done with you.'

'You're . . . *done*?'

'Yep,' says Leon, growing visibly less heavy by the second, like literal tons are being lifted off his shoulders. 'Why stay in a friendship that makes me the worst version of myself?' He puts his jacket on. 'Ever since we started at Duke's you've treated me like crap. Put me down continually with your little digs, made me run around after you, sought out every opportunity to get people to compare us. And this year it's been ridiculous. I'm disappointed in myself for ever letting you treat me like that. And I've realized that I'm disgusted with you.'

Alec looks shocked. 'Leon, I *was* ending things with Taro! I *do* care! Come on, we can't just forget everything we've been through. At sch—'

'School was awful,' says Leon. 'What you went through was

252

terrible, and I'm glad I was there to help you through it. But we're not there any more. You need to work through your trauma. You can't use it as an excuse to hurt people.' He starts to walk off towards Oxford Street. 'You know what, Alec?' he adds, turning back to us. 'If even once you'd asked me to talk, been honest with me, I'd have given you my blessing. But instead, you abused my trust. It's over.'

Alec watches him go, his mouth slightly open, like he's on the verge of calling after him. But he doesn't. As soon as Leon's turned the corner, Alec slumps against the wall, head in his hands.

'I should go,' I say. I don't want to spend any more time with Alec than I have to. Not when I'm still shaking with anger.

Alec nods, his eyes still closed.

'I'll see you back at the flat,' I say coldly.

He opens his eyes, and there's a look of anguish in them I've never seen before.

'Nettie, what am I going to do?'

I take a deep breath to steady my voice. 'You're going to make it right. You're going to work hard to earn Leon's trust back. And if you can't do that, then you're going to take responsibility for once in your life and accept that you lost a dear friendship because *you* fucked it up.'

Later that evening, I'm still thinking about Leon. I know Kiki's with him, so he's got support tonight, but I wish I could be there to hold his hand right now. He must have felt so hurt to find out about Alec and Taro like that. If Alec had just been upfront with him at the start, all of this could have been avoided.

It makes me think about my own relationship. Things haven't

exactly been great on the communication front with Fletch. If we're going to make it through to the end of this internship, we need to talk. We've both made mistakes: Fletch in lying about the placement; and me keeping stuff about Mum secret from him and trusting Luca instead. And it's not just Fletch who's been jealous; I've totally been guilty of that, too. I've resented *Better Spent* every time it's taken Fletch away from me, and if I'm honest with myself, I've probably made him feel guilty for it.

We can talk about it this weekend when he's back; move forward together. I love him, and I'm not ready to give up on this.

CHAPTER 23

I can't believe I get to see you tonight!

Fletch:

I know! I can't wait.

Ticket's in your name, just collect
it at the box office, 7.30 p.m. start.

I think that's the fourth time
you've told me that 😄

Just making sure you don't miss it!

I'm nervous

You're going to be great x

Leon, Kiki and I sign in at the Novello stage door early, the chosen venue for tonight's Duke's Awards finals. Alec went in earlier.

I've hardly seen him since Leon walked away from their friendship earlier in the week. They're being civil with each other – Leon is determined not to make things awkward for Kiki

255

and me (Kiki's too angry with Alec to be bothered about feeling awkward, but I literally have to live with him) – but I think the thought of having to face Leon on such an important night was just too much for Alec.

'Got any guests watching?' asks the guy in the little booth.

We're allowed two guests each. Leon doesn't have anyone watching, Kiki's got her mum and youngest brother, and I've got Fletch. I'm desperate to see him.

Kiki and I make our way up to the second-year girls dressing room, which is three floors up. We set up in a far corner of the room in front of the mirrors.

'How are you feeling?' I ask as I watch her unroll a small towel and place her make-up neatly on it.

She smiles nervously. 'Jittery.'

'You're going to be amazing,' I say to her reflection, resting my head on her shoulder.

'Thank you,' she says. Her phone buzzes. 'Oh, sorry – it's Michelle. I've got to take this. Hello?' She leaves the room.

I get my phone out to text Fletch.

18:30

> Still nervous. It's getting worse. What if I can't do it?

Fletch:

> You're going to be fine. Just breathe.

> It feels huge, singing onstage in front of everyone.

256

You did it last year in the summer showcase, you can do it again.

But I had you with me last time.

I'll be here this time. Just watching, not singing. I love you.

Kiki's gone for ages. When the half's called, I spend time going through my song in the top-floor toilet, away from everyone. For Sam to ask me to sing a song about a character who's grieving her dead mother is so twisted it's unreal. I go through it and through it and through it, hoping that the repetition will desensitize me from the painful lyrics. I know when I get on the stage, with the audience and the cameras and the pressure, it's going to be emotional. I'm not sure I can do this.

As I'm heading back down to the dressing room after the fifteen's called, I hear crying. I run along the corridor to the stairs to see Kiki sitting in a ball at the bottom of the first flight, sobbing. I run down to her.

'Kiki! What is it?'

She looks up, her eyes swollen and her face wet. 'It's the collaboration,' she says. 'They've pulled out.' She bursts into fresh sobs.

I get down on the floor with her and put my arms around her tightly. 'But why? The collection launches next week.'

'I don't know,' she says. 'Michelle just said that they felt it wasn't working and they had to pull it. She said it "just wasn't up to scratch". Like, why couldn't they have said earlier if it wasn't

257

what they wanted? They seemed so pleased with me.'

All that work she's put in. All the anticipation and excitement. Gone, just like that. 'Oh God, Kiki. That's awful. I'm so sorry. I—'

'Kiki, my love! What's wrong?'

Sam's approaching us with Dave and a camera in tow. For fuck's sake, it's like she can smell the drama.

'It's not really the time, Sam—' I start.

'It's OK, Nettie,' says Kiki. She relays to Sam what she just told me. Sam seems as shocked as I am, and I notice that for once she's not insisting that Dave films it.

'This is fucking outrageous,' says Sam. 'I'm getting in touch with the company. They've no right to treat you like this.' She gets her phone out to make the call.

'No!' says Kiki, straightening up. 'Please don't do that, Sam.'

'But they can't get away with this,' says Sam. 'I'm really angry – obviously for you, Kiki – but also because this has completely fucked up our storyline. We were going to do a big reveal of your clothing line next week, really make a thing of it. Let me call them.'

'I appreciate it, Sam, but I think it'll make it worse right now,' Kiki says in a small voice.

Sam thinks for a moment. 'Maybe you're right. There's a better way of dealing with it. Would you be prepared to tell us about it on camera?'

'But . . . I've got to get ready,' Kiki says, sniffing. 'I'm a mess. And people will see I've been crying . . .'

'Even better,' says Sam. 'Raw emotion. Let people see how this crappy company have treated you. I can get the show delayed, Kiki. It's important people know the truth.'

258

I look at Kiki. She's in a state. There's no way she'll agree to it. 'OK,' she says. 'I'll do it.'

Half an hour later, still reeling from her news, I sneak down to the wings to watch Kiki. She's beautiful in her dance, despite the shock she's just suffered; she whips and turns and suspends and releases with such grace and energy that I realize I've been holding my breath for the whole performance. When she comes offstage, I hug her tightly; she clings to me like a lost child and breaks down again. My heart aches for her.

The other finalists are good, apart from Jade, who smashes around downstage like a wrecking ball with limbs; no precision or line or stage presence. Kiki's the clear winner, no doubt about it. Hopefully she will – it'll make up for what just happened a little.

Alec is *stunning* in the boys classical round. The gruelling regime he's put himself through this year has paid off. There's a first-year boy from White Lodge who's also brilliant, but aside from that, no one comes close. I'd love to see Alec and Kiki do a *pas de deux* together one day. They'd probably kill each other in rehearsals, but I bet it would be breathtaking.

The boys singing round is next. Kiki and I hang around to watch. Luca accompanies a third-year boy on the piano with a song he wrote for him called 'All About Us'. It's about friendship – clearly his friendship with Fletch, which has been hugely affected by Fletch's reaction to *Triple Threat* – I know Luca's cut up about it. Watching him play, I feel so proud of my friend, so in awe of his talent, and so angry that he's been dragged into all this drama. They were always going to come for me, but if I'd known what Sam was going to do to Luca, I'd have protected him more.

259

Shortly after, Leon comes on to sing his song. I knew he was nervous about tonight, but he walks on with a poise and confidence that I've never seen before. As he begins his song, I can see that something's released in Leon, like he seems somehow freer, less inhibited. As much as the break-up of their friendship saddens me, I get how much Leon needed it, and with Alec's competitiveness no longer there to drag him down, he's *flying*.

He smiles shyly as the audience erupts with raucous applause. I sneak a look from behind the curtain to see the first five rows on their feet. It can't be students; they're not allowed. Squinting, I recognize India Lovejoy, the casting director, and a couple of musical directors among those standing. Actual industry people on their feet. I'm so delighted for Leon; he deserves it.

As the girls round starts, my nerves are electrified; I scan the audience roughly where I think Fletch should be sitting, but it's too dark and I can't see him. How must it feel for him right now, watching the last awards at his time at Duke's, knowing he should have been part of them? Is he sad? Or has he moved on?

I want him to be proud of me so badly it actually makes my stomach hurt. This song is going to be so difficult for me. I need to know he's there, supporting me, loving me.

Wow. *All* the emotions. I need to calm down. Or go method and try to channel it. '*Think of Meryl Streeeeeep*,' or something.

I meet Leon on the backstage crossover as I go over to stage left. There's only a second to congratulate him as we pass; we'll do all that later. Right now, I need to focus.

My name is announced; I step out on to the stage knowing that the whole college, half the industry, and – later – several million people will be watching. My left knee's trembling. It's a hangover from last year, when I couldn't sing at all without completely going to pieces – my body seems programmed to react that way now. But I can't let it win this time. Steph's watching from the third row; she nods her head slowly and puts her fingertips together. Kiki and Leon are in the wings – I can just make out the shape of their heads in the darkness. Alec's on the other side . . . Where's Fletch sitting? Will I make it through? All these thoughts are whizzing around my brain at once, shouting to be heard. For extra added fun, there's a camera pointing at me from the front row. My cheek twitches. Mum's face flashes before my eyes as I wait for the intro, and I feel overwhelmed.

I can't do this.

I can't sing this song about her, right here in front of all these people. Oh, God.

Sam gives me an encouraging thumbs-up from downstage left.

It's the gift I need. Not because I'm suddenly instilled with a newly blossoming confidence I didn't have a second ago, but because it makes me so *angry* that I forget to be nervous. Was that what she was hoping – to get me to break down mid-song? Well, fuck her. The fear and grief drain, like a plug's been pulled, and are replaced with something more like fire. Don't assume you know how I'm feeling, Sam. And don't pretend to be my friend.

I don't remember much about my performance, apart from the fact that it's the end now and I feel good. Kiki and Leon are mouthing '*Smashed it!*' in the wings, and the audience seems to have liked it. I see Miss Duke slow clapping, like she's all proud and moved, but I can't take that as an indication of how good I was because Sam probably told her to do it. But there is one thing I am certain of: Sam wanted me out of control, in tears. She

261

wanted all those moments from last year that she missed, when I was grieving for Mum and couldn't sing. She tried to manipulate me by making me sing something she knew would be difficult. But unfortunately for her, I killed it. I took back control, and for a minute up there, it felt amazing.

After everyone has performed, we all gather onstage in a line to wait for the results. I notice Leon is shaking next to me and I grip his hand in solidarity as the curtain goes up.

The dancing is announced first. Alec smiles politely when his name is called out as runner-up, but I can tell the way his cheek is pulsing that he's livid at losing out to a first-year fresh out of White Lodge. Ordinarily, I'd have been disappointed for him, and I am to some extent. He was amazing. But I also feel like maybe it'll do him some good. Karma's a bitch.

When it comes to the boys singing round, I grip Leon's hand tighter. Surely he knows what's coming.

'And the winner is . . . Leon Adigwe!'

He freezes. I release his hand and give him a nudge. 'Leon! Step forward!'

He does, looking up into the light like he can't believe what's happened to him. I watch his silhouette, like a cut-out against the dazzle of light beyond him, join the front line with the other winners, and feel so happy that he's had this recognition of his gorgeous talent.

Then girls jazz is announced. I look at Kiki, and I can see that even though she's probably picking apart her performance, she knows that she deserves this. Maybe this win will be the thing to give her back her confidence after the knock she's just suffered.

'Jade Upton!'

262

No.

There's actually a gasp from the audience as Jade's name is called out. Kiki flashes Sam the quickest of looks as Jade steps forward looking every bit like she knew all along that she was going to win. Surely Kiki can see what's going on here? Anger wells up inside me and suddenly I've got an urge to run to the front, grab the mic off the stand and tell everyone that it's all a fix. No one deserved to win more than Kiki. She's diligent, dedicated and so, *so* talented. How *dare* Sam do this to her?

I'm so busy thinking about Kiki that I'm not listening to the judges and I miss the next thing they say. Poppy McAllister steps forward, smiling to be runner-up.

And then my name is called.

I did it. I've *won*.

A cheer goes up, and I tiptoe to the front, hardly daring to believe it.

But only for a moment. As I take my bow, everything suddenly feels fake. Sam thinks I make good telly. It's clear Jade's victory was a fix – what's to say Sam didn't have a hand in *me* winning? Is this whole thing just a charade now? Leon smiles and takes my hand as I return to the line and take my place next to him. I scan the audience, hoping for a glimpse of Fletch. Just to feel his arms around me would be everything right now. Something real, not this circus I'm starring in. To know that we're still good, that he's proud of me. To know that he still loves me. But my desperately searching eyes can't find him . . .

After the results, backstage is chaos. People dash everywhere, congratulating each other. Alec hangs back, hiding from the cameras. I hug Leon but then quickly lose him to a crowd of adoring fellow students. I leave him to his newfound fame and follow Kiki as she heads up to our room.

'Well done, babe. You were brilliant.' She's halfway up the first flight of stairs, already pulling off her costume straps and tucking them under her arms.

'You too,' I say. 'How do you . . . feel about Jade?'

I notice she speeds up slightly. 'She must have been better than me.'

'Are you kidding? She wasn't even close.'

'Well, she won.'

'Yeah. About that.'

Kiki stops so abruptly that I almost crash into the back of her. 'If you're going to use this as a way of dragging Sam, forget it. Honestly? She probably *did* suggest Jade should win, and I'm sure Miss Duke went for the idea, providing they could make Jade look good onscreen. That's just how show business is, Nettie. And, no, I'm not going to ask her about it. It's her business. The exposure I'm getting from the TV show is enough for me, and I don't want to jeopardize that, especially when Sam was so good earlier about letting me get my side of the story over with the clothing line, which she didn't have to do. People will see my dancing on next week's show. They can make up their own minds.'

I take a moment to let it sink in. It's Kiki's moment that got stolen, not mine. I guess it's up to her how she reacts.

'Look, I get it,' I say eventually, extending a placatory hand to Kiki's arm. Kiki smiles. 'I just don't like it. You're the winner I choose.' I take her hand, and her strap dislodges from under her arm. We both giggle.

She puts it back in her armpit. 'Thanks, babe. You're mine, too. Forever.'

264

The after-show party's in full swing front of house by the time I get back down. Fletch hasn't messaged me, and he wasn't at stage door. Not that I expected gushing adoration, but he did just watch me win a competition. A 'well done' might have been nice. All night I've been desperate to see him, and now I can't find him. A little put out, I get myself a drink and sit down at the stalls bar on my own, trying to channel Patti LuPone in any of her *Company* incarnations but feeling more like the party loner.

Fletch and Alec appear together from the empty auditorium. I slide off the barstool (not at all like Patti) and walk over to them, ignoring Alec as much as I can.

'I couldn't find you,' I say to Fletch. 'Where've you been?'

He doesn't hug me like he usually does. 'I've—'

'I just found him, talking to Michael about how amazing you were,' Alec says.

'I wasn't sure if you'd made it,' I say again to Fletch, turning my back on Alec. Why won't he get the message? I don't want to talk to him.

Fletch opens his mouth, but Alec jumps in again. 'Got here just in time to see you perform. Didn't you, Fletch?'

'Nettie, you were amazing,' Fletch finally says, kissing me, although I notice his eyes flicker to Alec, who shrugs and walks out. 'God, I've missed you.'

He cups my face in his hands, as if trying to block out everything else, and kisses me again. It's like the stress and angst of the last few weeks disappears, and we're just us again. Like this is how it *really* is between us, and everything else was just a bad dream.

I realize how much I've missed him.

265

A couple of hours later, Alec's downing the gin and tonics alone on a barstool at the stalls bar like Mary in *Merrily We Roll Along*, Kiki's dancing with Leon, and Fletch and I are snuggled in the corner together.

'Kiki was amazing, wasn't she?' I say to Fletch, watching her party with Leon. Fletch gently pulls my face back to his, like he wants all my attention. It's cute.

'*You're* amazing,' he says, and kisses me.

'But don't you think she should have won?' I say, backing away so that I can see his face properly. 'It was definitely a fix.'

He's not biting. 'I think you're beautiful, is what I think.'

He kisses me again, and this time I don't pull away. It's the perfect end to the evening. I know that Fletch and I have got things to work through, but tonight is proof that we're still worth fighting for. We're going to get through this.

I put my forehead against his. 'Thank you for coming tonight. Knowing you were watching made me feel braver.'

He doesn't reply; he kisses me instead. For a second I'm distracted by the softness of his lips and the feel of his arms around me. Then I try again.

'Fletch, I'm sorry I haven't involved you in all the stuff about Mum as much as I could. I was trying to keep everything simple because you were so busy and stressed, but I should've been more honest about it. As long as we're truthful with each other, even if we're miles away and stressed and missing each other, we're going to be fine.'

'Exactly.' He holds me closer. 'I'm going to do better from now on,' he murmurs. 'Nettie, you're everything to me, and I'm not going to let you down again.' His lips brush mine, and I feel like I never want to let him go.

Jade bursts through the door at midnight like Maleficent, looking a little worse for wear.

'Hi,' she says. She's smiling, but it's coming over as a snarl. 'Well, isn't this *nice*?'

Why do I get the feeling this has something to do with me?

Jade staggers over to us, grabbing Leon's shoulder on the way for support. She reaches the bar, puts her hand out to lean on it and misses, making her stumble on to the floor. Fletch offers his hand to her, which she takes.

'My prince,' she says.

'Erm, do you need some water, Jade?' says Fletch warily.

'Oh, Fletch. Always so caring. Shame it's wasted on *that*.' She looks pointedly at me. 'I'm surprised you're still talking to him, after he missed your little song.'

I stare at her, a little foggy from the booze myself. 'What?'

Alec steps in. 'Shut up, Jade.'

'You're cute.' Jade smiles at him spitefully. 'I heard you guys talking after the show.' Alec swallows. She turns to me, her eyes flashing maliciously. 'He was *so* cut up about missing your performance. Didn't know *how* he was going to tell you. Alec came to the rescue, though – didn't you, sweetie?'

'You're vile,' says Alec to Jade. 'Just fucking get out of here.' He glances at Fletch, who's speechless.

'Gladly,' she says happily. She reaches across and ruffles Fletch's hair. 'Shame. We could have been so good together.' And with that, Jade sweeps out.

I look at Fletch in confusion.

'What's she talking about? You saw me sing, didn't you?'

'I—' Fletch puts his hand through his hair and grabs at it. 'I'm sorry, Nettie. I missed you.'

'What?'

His eyes shift to Alec briefly, before settling back on me. 'I watched a recording of you on Alec's phone. I meant what I said about you being amazing – even on the small screen, I could tell that.'

Everyone's staring at us now. I can't get this straight in my head.

'But you said – You told me you were there.'

'I'm sorry – I didn't want to unnerve you by saying I was running late. But then the A3 was closed, and I got diverted, and it was wet . . . I'm sorry. I should have been there.'

He's missing the point here. 'It's not that, Fletch,' I say, stung. 'You lied to me. Again.'

I pick up my bag and reach for my coat on a nearby barstool, and Alec goes to stop me. 'Don't you fucking dare say a word, Alec. You've done enough. Get out of my way.'

He freezes. I've never spoken to him that way. I push past him and start to move.

'Where are you going?' says Fletch, standing up as I try to button up my coat with shaking fingers.

'Home, Fletch.'

'But you're meant to be coming back to mine.'

'Well, you'll just have to pretend I did. Shouldn't be hard – you're good at making stuff up.' I turn and leave the theatre bar, ignoring the cameras that have appeared out of nowhere.

I feel utterly betrayed.

This is the second time Fletch has lied and hidden something

268

from me – and with *Alec*, too. How could he say he'd watched me, when he hadn't? He *knew* how angry I was after he'd lied about the placement in Chichester. He promised he wouldn't do that again, but here we are again. And there I was, saying sorry for not being upfront about the stuff with Mum while he was literally *lying to my face*. If Jade hadn't overheard them, they'd both *still* be lying to me. I wouldn't expect any less of Jade – but my *boyfriend*? What the fuck is with him?

I march up Tavistock Street, the wind pushing hot tears back to my temples. My phone buzzes with a notification.

00:17
Kiki:
Are you OK, babe?

I reply to let her know I'm headed home and that I need some space. But when I get to the flat, I discover that I don't have my keys to get in, only my key to Fletch's flat. For fuck's sake, what do I do now? Going back to the theatre isn't an option. Even if I could find Kiki or Leon without bumping into Fletch or Alec, I'm not ruining what's left of their night by asking to stay at theirs.

00:29
Missed calls log:
Fletch (7)

00:29
Fletch:
I'm sorry, Nettie.

269

I'm too angry to accept his apology.

00:30
Fletch:
I didn't want to disappoint you again.

Ugh, I'll have to go back to Fletch's. Hide in Seb's old room – I don't know. This is a disaster.

00:31
Fletch:
I fucked up. I'm sorry.

I put on Do Not Disturb and order an Uber, which arrives almost immediately. The driver can see me crying in the back, but he doesn't say anything. He's probably seen loads of drunk girls sobbing their way home. Fletch calls me nine more times. Why won't he just leave me alone?

I'm such a pathetic teary mess that I don't even notice the lights on in the flat.

On the doorstep, I fumble with the keys and let myself in.

'Nettie!' Luca's in the living room, sitting on the sofa calmly with a cup of tea, everything about him a complete contrast to the chaos I've just left. He's such a welcome, warming presence that I'm able to calm down a little in the doorway.

He stands up. 'What are you doing here? Are you . . . OK?' he adds, staring with concern at my face.

I catch a glimpse of my mascara-stained cheeks in the mirror. My teeth still chattering from the cold (and the adrenaline), I rub under my eyes outward towards my hairline and sink down into the sofa. 'I had a fight with Fletch. Why aren't you at the party?'

'Didn't feel like it,' he says with a shrug. 'Whole thing seemed like a circus tonight.'

'Yeah – with Kiki losing out to Jade? I couldn't believe that.'

'Miss Duke made a big mistake letting the cameras in. Sam's fucked with everything . . . Kettle's still hot. I'll make you a tea. Here.' He grabs a blanket from the back of the sofa and throws it around my shoulders.

I clutch it gladly, realizing how cold I am. 'Thanks.' I get up and follow him out to the kitchen to wait while he makes the tea. Then we sit down at the table together.

'Want to talk about it?' he says.

I give him a grateful smile. 'Fletch didn't make it in time to watch me,' I say. 'But that's not the problem. The problem is that he and Alec concocted some story and lied to me. If Jade hadn't taken great delight in telling me that she'd overheard them scheming, I'd still be none the wiser.'

'Oh. Yeah. I get why you'd be upset,' says Luca, nodding, his eyes full of concern. 'I mean, I think it comes from a good place, but that was a bad choice on Fletch's part.'

'It's not just that,' I say, feeling warm new tears pile on top of the cold ones clinging to my eyelashes. 'We haven't been good for weeks. I know he's trying to hide it, but Fletch is really bothered about . . .' I trail off.

'What?' asks Luca.

I pause. 'You.' Maybe I drank more at the party than I thought.

'About me?' he says. He puts his head in his hands. 'It's *Triple Threat*, isn't it?'

'Yes,' I say. 'He's been wrestling with his own . . . jealousy for a while, and I tried to be understanding because I know he feels

271

isolated down there in Chichester. But since *Triple Threat* aired, he's literally just stopped mentioning anything that involves you. Nothing about *Chicago* rehearsals or Mum. I think he believes it.'

'He's not phoned me for ages,' says Luca. 'Occasionally, he'll reply on our flat's group chat, but only if it's something about bills or whatever. I thought I was imagining it at first. But then I started to worry that he hated me. What do we do about it, though?'

'Nothing!' I say. 'You and I are *friends*, Luca. We shouldn't feel we have to apologize for that. Fletch needs to grow the fuck up. If he wasn't so bothered in the first place about our relationship, or if he'd *actually bothered to speak to me about it*, he'd have known that *Triple Threat* was all bollocks and that it was all made up. I'm angry with him for believing it. And I'm furious with Sam for making something out of nothing.'

Luca is beginning to look agitated. 'Yeah,' he says, into the steam of his tea.

I let out a breath. 'Just talking to you about this, I already feel so much better . . .'

Luca fiddles with the handle of his mug. 'Actually, I need to talk to you about something . . . Can I?' he says. He looks worried, like I'm going to react badly to whatever it is. I suddenly feel nervous. What could be that awful?

'Go ahead. Although I'm a hot mess right now, so I'm not sure I'll be much help . . .'

He swallows. '*Triple Threat*. And us. I should've told you this, Nettie, and I want you to hear me out before you say anything . . .'

'OK . . .' I go cold and pull my cup of tea closer.

Luca clears his throat nervously, like he's about to conduct a seminar. 'I haven't been honest with you. You said that Sam

272

made something out of nothing. Well, she didn't.' He swallows, looking at me guiltily.

'What do you mean?' I say cautiously. A hundred reasons whir around my brain. Was Fletch right? *Does* Luca have a crush on me? This is the last thing I need after tonight's drama. 'Luca, I—'

'Please, I need to finish this. So, right at the beginning of term – the first week, I think – I was talking to Anand in the common room. No cameras, just us. He said you and I would be spending a lot of time together this year. I asked him what he was on about, and he said they knew about Fletch's placement, and that Sam had said that you and I would most likely be heavily involved in *Triple Threat*, and in the college musical. At the time I was hoping for assistant MD, remember? And then he asked if that would be awkward, with Fletch being my best mate and all that. And Nettie . . . I told him about us at the party last year. I told him I'd asked you out, and that I used to have feelings for you. Which I *a hundred per cent don't any more* and haven't for a year. I'm so sorry – if I'd known he would tell Sam, I'd have never—'

'You think *Anand* told Sam?'

'How else would she have known?'

Everything implodes. *Anand?* I thought I could trust him. He was helping me out, wasn't he? Agreeing not to tell Sam about Mum; bringing me the *Funny Face* review . . . It makes sense – there are some things on the documentary that I've literally no idea how she could have known. He must have been feeding information back to Sam this whole time. How could I not have seen it? I feel like I've been punched in the stomach.

'Oh my God.' I'm shocked to my core. I can't believe he would do that. 'Honestly, Luca, the way Sam was portraying us, I was beginning to wonder if you *did* have feelings for me. I even

273

started questioning my own behaviour.'

'I don't blame you. There were times watching myself back that I thought, *Did I really do that?* Like at the ball, when it looked like I was sad about Fletch cutting in. But when I thought about it, Sam must have taken that from earlier, when we were waiting to dance – when I was watching the other dancers' footwork and worrying that I wouldn't pick it up!'

We both laugh for a moment at the weight that's been lifted off our shoulders.

'It's awful that she even made *us* doubt ourselves,' I say eventually. 'Luca, your friendship means a lot to me. We need to not let this affect us.'

'You're right. Hey, come here, friend.'

He stands up and holds his arms out. I get up and go around the table to him. I feel my body physically relax as we hug each other. I'm still reeling from the shock about Anand, but knowing that Luca and I are on the same page and that we've got each other's backs makes me feel like I can deal with it.

'Well, this is awkward.'

Fletch is in the doorway, undoing the top button of his leathers with one hand and holding his bike helmet in the other, the wind blasting through the open door behind him.

'Mate—' says Luca, letting go of me. But he doesn't do it in a hurry, like he's guilty of something. He just lets go.

'Don't be all over my girlfriend and then call me "mate", *mate*,' says Fletch.

It's so shocking that he would speak to Luca in that way that for a second I'm too winded to speak.

Eventually I find my voice. 'Fletch—'

'Is this why you've been so helpful, Luca?' Fletch doesn't even look at me. 'So that you can hit on her while I'm away? *"Don't worry, Fletch. I'll make sure she's all right."* This your way of doing that?'

Jesus Christ. I know Fletch has struggled with seeing us together, but this is beyond anything. Is this what he really thought the whole time? That we were secretly together? Or that Luca was waiting to steal me?

That's it. I've had enough.

'Fletch, listen!' I say angrily. 'Luca has *never* come on to me! Not even once.'

'Nettie, everyone knows he's always had a thing for you,' shoots back Fletch, still staring at Luca.

'Fletch, one drunken snog during a game of spin the bottle doesn't equal a lifetime crush,' says Luca heatedly.

'You asked her out!' yells Fletch.

'Yeah, and as soon as I knew you two liked each other, I backed off! Our relationship's completely platonic, Fletch. The idea of getting off with my best friend's girlfriend is actually disgusting to me. I'm really fucking disappointed that you think I'd do something like that.'

'And what gives you the right to storm in here and start making accusations?' I say, my voice raised. 'Especially after your behaviour tonight.'

'Do you know how many messages I've had since that fucking programme started?' says Fletch. 'Not just from people at college, but from total strangers, telling me that my *girlfriend* is definitely cheating on me, or that I'm a shit boyfriend and you should be with Luca!'

'And you *believed* them?' I say. 'Have you listened to anything I've said about Sam?'

275

Fletch's face reddens. 'It's not just that. It's all the time you two have spent hanging out.'

Luca, who is still remarkably calm, looks at me. 'We're literally playing opposite each other – we *have* to spend time together. It's not like I *chose* to be in *Chicago*!'

Fletch snorts. 'Oh, so you were rehearsing at the Theatre Cafe?'

'Oh my God, *really*?' I say.

'I was helping her find out about her mum,' says Luca. 'Which she tried involving you in, but from what I hear, you weren't that interested! Nettie's had a lot to deal with. Not just with her mum – *Triple Threat*, Alec and Leon, Kiki . . . If you hadn't been so busy worrying about me and her, you'd know about all of that.'

'*Right, of course*,' says Fletch. 'This is the bit where you tell me you know her much better than I do, that I don't deserve her.'

'No one's saying that, Fletch. You're my best friend – I would never come between you and Nettie. Look – I'm going to leave you two to talk. This isn't about me.'

And with that, Luca grabs his coat and keys and leaves before Fletch has a chance to stop him.

I throw my hands up. 'Fucking hell, Fletch. He's a *friend*. You don't begrudge me the time I get with Alec, or Kiki.'

There's a pause.

'No,' he says. 'But—'

'So, that's it,' I say, my throat hot and sore. 'You don't trust me.'

'I *know* he's got feelings for you!'

'He DOESN'T. For the thousandth time, Fletch – we're JUST FRIENDS!'

'And all this stuff with your mum – why have I found out everything since Christmas from Alec? Why are you telling Luca things you're not telling me?!'

'It's not like you've actually taken an interest in any aspect of my life for months. So don't give me that bullshit. And I get it, you're under pressure from all angles down there. It's stressful. I've tried to be understanding, Fletch. But it's been stressful here too, and you've put me last every single time. I've asked very little of you the whole time you've been down in Chichester – and the one time I was disappointed that you didn't show and actually *told* you how I was feeling, you snapped at me and made me feel like a baby. That really hurt, Fletch. So excuse me if I didn't want to share anything else with you. You've made it blatantly clear that you think I'm too emotionally fragile.'

He doesn't speak; he just stares at me. But the wheels are turning too fast now and I can't stop.

'What are we even doing together? Luca and Leon and Kiki and *even Alec* have been there for me when you were away, and I was just fine. You, on the other hand . . .' My hands slide up to the locket around my neck. 'That's all *this* ever was – a way of tagging me. Well, I don't want it any more.' Before I even realize what I'm doing, I've undone it and thrust it into his hand.

'So, what are you saying, Nettie? That you're finishing with me?'

'I'm saying I'm really fucking angry with you. It didn't have to be like this, Fletch.'

He just looks at me for a moment, almost as if he's just realized something.

'You're right,' he says.

Then he puts his helmet back on and walks out into the hall. It's not until I hear the front door slam that I realize he's actually gone.

CHAPTER 24

I don't know whether I ended it with my boyfriend, or he ended it with me. Either way, we haven't been in contact for four days, and I sure as hell won't be the first one to message. My mood ranges from deep, burning anger to lacerating hurt and rejection, with a fog of nothing in between, like all my senses have been switched off. How could something so amazing have gone, just like that? Did it mean nothing to him?

I can't sleep, either. But it's not just thoughts of Fletch keeping me awake; it's Mum. When I do manage to fall sleep, she's in my dreams. Sometimes she's the Mum I remember; other times she's younger, smiling and laughing with a faceless dark-haired man. When I run to her, they both disappear, and I wake up sweating, my heart racing like I've just seen a ghost. I need her now more than ever. Where is she? Who *was* she?

In the early hours of Thursday morning, after a particularly vivid nightmare, there's a soft knock at my door.

'Nettie, are you OK?'

The door gently opens. Alec has turned on the hall light, but I can make out his silhouetted form against the brightness behind him. It's the first time we've spoken since the Duke's Awards.

'Yeah, I – bad dream.' I sit up in bed and wipe the sweat from above my lip.

'You were shouting. I was worried.'

'Oh. Well, I'm fine.'

Alec pauses in the doorway, like he's not sure what to do. Then he edges into the room and leans against the wall next to the door. 'Nettie, I'm truly sorry for what I did,' he says. 'I was just trying to protect you. God, I've fucked up royally this year.'

'It's not even the worst thing you've done this year,' I say. 'But I thought we'd been through this, Alec: I don't need protecting. I need a friend who tells me the truth.'

'I know,' he says. 'I'm sorry. And I'm sorry I ruined things between you and Fletch.'

'You didn't ruin things for us,' I say. 'We did that all by ourselves.' My throat suddenly feels swollen again and I burst into tears. As I sob, the image of Mum and the faceless man flashes up on the inside of my eyelids. God, I'm a mess.

Alec gets on the bed and puts his arms around me. 'It's OK not to be OK with this, Nettie. You don't have to hold it together all the time.'

'How can I be like this at college when there's a TV crew following me everywhere I go?' I say. I accept the tissue he's handed me from the bedside table and blow my nose loudly. 'Sam's, like, obsessed with me, or something. I can't give her any more ammunition.'

'Are things OK between you and Luca?' asks Alec.

'Actually, yeah. Ironically, we'd just had a talk about how we absolutely do *not* have feelings for each other, and then Fletch came in and saw us hugging and got completely the wrong end of the stick and . . .'

'Wow,' says Alec. 'I bet Sam would be gutted to know she missed that one.'

I punch him in the ribs.

'Sorry,' he says. 'Too soon.'

279

'I'm having trouble holding it together at college all day and then at rehearsals,' I say. 'And now I keep dreaming about Mum as well. I can't go on like this.'

'*The show must go on* . . .' says Alec, with not even a trace of his usual irony. Then he looks down at me. 'Promise me this: when it's just us, here in the flat, I want you to cry, shout, scream – maybe only scream when Mrs Jeffries downstairs is out – and live your hurt, however you need to express it. I'll be here for you if you need me, or I'll fuck off to my room if you want to be alone. I wouldn't blame you. But let this be the one place you can be your authentic self.'

I feel a rush of gratitude. In Alec saying this, in giving me a space where I can just 'be', without having to pretend or bottle stuff up, and knowing that he's got me, it's reminded me why we're friends. He's done some shitty things this year, but he does care. I hug him tightly; he strokes my hair.

'Thank you,' I whisper.

We sit there in the dark room together, arms around each other, until our breathing is in synch. Then I sit up straighter, breaking the hug. 'What are you going to do about your own life?' I say. 'There's no point being so kind to me if you're still going to be a fuck-awful friend to Leon. What you did to him is the sort of thing I'd expect from *Jade Upton*, not my oldest friend.'

'*I know, I know.*' He covers his face with his hands. 'Why did I do it?'

'Why *did* you do it?'

He drops his hands and looks at me seriously. 'Nettie, I've thought of nothing else since it happened. Leon's right – I *have* made everything into a competition, and I've been using

280

Leon as a punchbag for my own insecurities. It's complicated, our relationship – it's all tied up in what happened at school, and . . . There's – there's been something bothering me all year. Something happened in September – and it's made me do things I'd never normally do, act out of character . . .'

'What happened in September?'

He draws a slow breath. 'I saw someone at college – someone from my past.'

'Who? And what were they doing at Duke's?'

'His name's . . . Josh,' says Alec, and I can tell it costs him to say it aloud. 'He's on the post-production team for *Triple Threat* – he was here for a meeting on the first day.'

'Was he one of the boys who . . . ?' I can't finish the sentence. Alec was subjected to horrifying abuse and bullying at school, a trauma he's always brushed under the carpet but one that I know affects him deeply.

'No,' says Alec. 'But he was friends with them. Still is, from what I gather. Seeing him just . . . I don't know . . . fucked me up. I kept thinking that he'd be watching me and reporting back to Piers and the others, that they'd all be laughing at me, and . . .' He breaks off.

'And you needed to show them that you'd left them all behind?' I offer.

Now it's Alec who's crying. 'Kind of – I can't explain it, Nettie. I just went into overdrive. I thought if I could be the best, win everything, *have* everything, they'd see how successful I was and . . . I don't even know *what* I thought they'd do . . . None of it makes sense now that I'm saying it . . . Like I could prove that I'm not just some loser from school, make them all sorry or something. But it made me angry, competitive. I hurt people I love. And all because I was reacting to . . .'

'Trauma,' I say gently, putting my arms around him. My heart aches for him.

Alec puts his head on my chest and sobs. 'I know. I'm – I'm going to get help, see a therapist. Work through all the stuff I went through at school. And I'm . . . going to try and make things right with Leon, even if he doesn't forgive me. I'm going to make up for what I did.'

At the end of a really shit week, this is a tiny flicker of light. Alec has needed to deal with this stuff for so long. I'm suddenly too choked up to speak, but I rest my head on top of his to let him know all the things I can't say right now.

'Wanna talk about it?'

I'm tired. After my talk with Alec last night I didn't go back to sleep for ages. We're onstage in the music hall teching the show, and I've been sitting in silence on Luca's lap for seven minutes, waiting for the LX technician to plot the lights for 'We Both Reached for the Gun'. My thoughts have, as usual, fallen into a Fletch spiral.

I blow out slowly. 'Why hasn't he texted me? I just don't get it.'

'Have you contacted him?'

'No. But he's the one in the wrong.'

The LX girl pipes up from the back. 'Nettie, can you go into your next position, please?'

Sighing again, I slump over so that my body's hanging down over my legs and my head's upside down. Luca gasps as one of my sit bones digs into his quads.

'Sorry!'

'That's OK,' he says, adjusting his leg position. 'That's better. Maybe Fletch just needs time to process what happened. Honestly? Knowing Fletch, I think he's probably feeling like a douche.'

'He behaved like one. And *he* had the audacity to walk out on *me*? What the actual fuck?' I'm trying to strike a balance between being loud enough for Luca to hear me from my upside-down position, but not loud enough for anyone else to hear. Fortunately, Sam's not in this morning. I bet she'd love this.

'I'd offer to call him, but I don't think it would go down too well,' says Luca.

'That's another thing: aren't *you* furious with him? He basically accused you of getting off with me behind his back.'

I feel Luca sighing. 'I mean, yes, but I've had time to think about it. Watching *Triple Threat*, it really made it look like you and I were a thing. If I'd been in Fletch's position, I'd have believed it.'

'He should've trusted us—'

'Nettie, Sam had our friends doubting us, and *they were there*. She even had *us* doubting us. If she can do that, what must it be like for someone watching it out of context?'

'Next position, please,' calls the LX girl.

I resurface and go into an extreme reach forward with Luca holding my waist.

'OK, fine, but Fletch was still jealous before *Triple Threat* even came out.'

'True. But he was trying to keep a lid on it. He knew he was being unreasonable.'

I'm surprised Luca's jumping to Fletch's defence after everything that happened last weekend. Luca might be able to forgive him, but I can't. Not yet. And anyway, there's nothing to forgive if he hasn't even apologized, is there?

An hour later Leon and I are standing together in our light, waiting for our next instructions. Leon covers his mic.

'I think Sam's going to out me,' he blurts out.

'What? How does she even know?'

Leon shushes me, panicked. 'She asked me if I'd do an interview,' he whispers. 'A while ago. She said it would be a lovely end to the show if I shared it with the world, inspire loads of young gay people. I don't know how she discovered I'm not fully out at home. Someone must've told her.'

My blood runs cold. 'Oh my God, Leon. What are you going to do?'

'I don't know. Originally I said no, and she seemed to accept it, but this week she's been putting the pressure on again. Insinuated that if I don't agree she'll probably reveal it anyway. Isn't it best to do it on my own terms, where I'm in control of what's being said?'

'No. She can't do this,' I whisper, covering my own mic with both hands. 'It's blackmail. We need to tell Miss Duke.'

'No!' says Leon. 'Nettie, I haven't told anyone yet. Just leave it. There's a chance she won't do it. I'll just have to take the risk.'

This is horrific. I have to help Leon. I have to find a way to stop Sam. But with only two days left, time's running out. What am I going to do?

At lunchtime, I'm heading out to grab the sandwich I left on the kitchen counter, when Anand literally jumps out of Michael's office.

'Nettie. Can I talk to you?'

'I'm not interested, Anand.' I pick up the pace and walk past him.

He runs after me. 'Please, Nettie.'

'So you can worm stuff out of me and then feed it back to Sam?'

'What?'

'I know it was you, Anand. You told Sam that Luca and I had history. And I bet Leon's new storyline had something to do with you as well. I can't believe I trusted you.'

'Nettie, I didn't tell her! I swear I didn't.'

I stop so abruptly that Anand actually overtakes me and has to take a step back.

'No?' I say. 'Then how did she know?'

'I . . .' He looks around suddenly, as if he's expecting Sam to jump out at us. 'I can't . . . Omigod, this is a mess. Nettie, you have to believe me.' His expression is desperate, pleading. Despite what Luca told me, I want to trust him.

But I'm done with secrets. I'm done with lies. Anand may be telling the truth, but he's still hiding something. There's so much going on right now what with splitting up with my boyfriend and the performance of my life in just two days that I don't have the energy to engage with this.

'I'm sorry, Anand. I can't do this right now.'

Kiki comes up to me after lunch while I'm running over some of my dance steps on the stage. I keep thinking about Leon. I thought *my* problems were bad. What's he going to do?

'Remember, you need to feel like you're holding boiled eggs,' she reminds me, demonstrating the move. I copy her obediently.

'Looks amazing in here, doesn't it?' she says, looking out into the audience. It's the first time the music hall's ever been used for a show at Duke's, and the studio's been converted back into an auditorium.

'Mmmn-hmmn.' I'm trying to focus on the movement, but I keep going back to Leon. There's so much going on right now that it's hard to concentrate. What if I lose it onstage and forget I'm meant to be holding boiled eggs and start galumphing around like I've got a grapefruit in each hand? 'Hey – Kiki? I need to talk to you. It's about Leon.'

'Sure,' she says. 'What's up? But you'll have to be quick – there's a whole college meeting in a minute.'

I quickly fill her in on everything Leon told me this morning. Kiki stares at me in horror.

'Oh my God, Nettie.' She's almost crying.

'You . . . believe me, then?'

She bites her lip. 'I've been doubting Sam for a while now. Something just hasn't been adding up. And the last couple of episodes? I know you haven't been watching but they're so far from the truth that it's unreal. Remember when I was upset about my contract being terminated backstage at the Duke's Awards? Like, she *really* went to town on that – made me seem really pathetic. I felt embarrassed watching myself. And then she kind of made out that I'd danced badly because of it, and that was why I didn't win. She barely showed any footage of me dancing. After promising she would.' She takes my hand. 'Nettie, I'm sorry I took Sam's side so much. I really thought she was a friend.'

'She had us all fooled,' I say. I mean, I kind of had her sussed early on, but I can totally see how she had everyone sucked in. 'What are we going to do about Leon?'

286

'I don't know,' says Kiki. 'But I'm damned if I'm going to let her get away with this.'

People start to pile in: cameras, crew, students and, of course, Sam. She grins at Kiki and me from the other side of the studio. Kiki looks like she's going to be sick.

Miss Duke arrives last, bringing with her a swathe of silence as usual.

'Good afternoon,' she says. 'As you know, the last episode of *Triple Threat* is going to focus largely on the opening night of *Chicago*. Sam has requested –' here she pauses to smile, but I can tell she's livid at being dictated to – 'that the episode is a live finale. Yes – to those of you wondering – the show will go out live on Saturday, combined with backstage footage and live interviews. It will be no mean feat.'

What are they trying to do to us? As if it wasn't stressful enough knowing the performance was being filmed, it's now going to go out *live*? I'm not sure how much more I can take right now. Why has Miss Duke agreed to this? How many of her own powers did she sign away to Sam at the beginning of the year?

'In addition to this,' she continues, 'Sam has negotiated with the producers of the annual West End fundraising gala *A Night of a Thousand Stars* to feature some of the Duke's students in its programme the very same night. This is unprecedented, and a great honour.' A murmur goes through the room. 'So, without further ado, may I congratulate our chosen ambassadors: Antoinette Delaney-Richardson, Luca Viscusi and Alec Van Damm.'

A ripple of applause echoes around the old music hall. A camera's light flickers in my retinas. I've been chosen to perform in a gala? On the *same day* as *Chicago*? On *live TV*? How's that going to work? I glance at Luca. He looks back at me in horror.

My eyes flick to Alec, who ordinarily would be smiling gregariously and enjoying the limelight he so clearly feels he deserves. But he's not doing that. He's looking intently at someone on the other side of the room. I follow his gaze and see Leon at the other end of it.

'Miss Duke?' Alec says loudly.

Everyone who's not already looking at him turns around.

'I wanted to say something.'

'Yes, Alec?' she says, surprised but, as ever, unruffled.

'I'm sorry, but I don't think I can do the gala,' he says.

Someone stifles a gasp near me.

Miss Duke puts one hand in the pocket of her creamy-beige trouser suit. 'Why not, may I ask?'

I can feel the danger; everyone can.

'I've hurt my ankle,' he says. 'The, er . . . physio told me to stay off it for two weeks.'

This is odd – Alec hasn't mentioned his ankle. What's he playing at?

Miss Duke seems satisfied. 'I'm sorry to hear that,' she says. 'We will have to choose someone else.' She's about to move on when Alec speaks up again.

'Miss Duke?'

She almost sighs in frustration. 'Yes, Alec?'

'I'd like to nominate Leon Adigwe to take my place.'

'I'm sorry?'

'He's an amazing dancer. And he's proven this year that he's a brilliant actor and singer, too. I just . . . I wanted to say that he'd be my choice.'

288

There's something so utterly brazen, so cocksure, so . . . *Alec* about all of this. And yet . . . it's a lovely gesture. Leon rolls his eyes, but I can tell he's touched.

Miss Duke studies Alec hard. 'Ordinarily, I wouldn't expect a student to make decisions for me,' she says sternly. We watch her like the playing cards eyeing the Queen of Hearts, wondering which way she'll go, whose head will roll. 'But on this occasion, Alec, I think you're right. Leon, the job's yours.'

More applause, as Sam glares at Miss Duke in rage, presumably for daring to go against her plans, and Leon, looking a tad bemused, steps forward in acknowledgement.

Later, after everyone has gone, Leon comes over to Alec and me.

'I'm sorry,' says Alec, before Leon has a chance to say anything. 'I'm sorry I did it in front of everyone – it was naff. But I was so surprised to be chosen, and the truth is, you deserve it more than I do. The world needs to see you. I'm not doing this to be manipulative, or to try to get you to forgive me. I don't deserve your friendship, Leon. But I hope you can see how sorry I am, and that I am in awe of your talent.'

Leon doesn't say anything for a second, and I honestly have no idea how this is going to go. I imagine at least five scenarios: in one, Leon embraces Alec crying; and in another, he punches him in the face.

Then Leon speaks. 'I can see it, Alec. Thank you.'

He doesn't embrace him crying, or even extend a hand, but he does give Alec a small smile.

Maybe this is the start of a new friendship between them.

The dress rehearsal opens on Friday night to a small invited audience and four cameras. I dance. I dance and sing and smile and turn and kick. I fight with Velma, flirt with Mama, jostle with Billy Flynn. I'm like a weird fake version of myself. You'd never know that I'm broken inside because the boy I love has left me. When I take my bow at the end, I pretend I'm pleased and grateful, when really I'm empty and lost. I'm not playing a role. I'm playing someone who's not heartbroken who's playing a role. Luckily for me, *Chicago* is a cynical piece of theatre, deliberately superficial and laced with dark humour, and Roxie's part of it all. I'm not sure I'd have such an easy time playing Fantine.

Sam watches the dress from the stage-right wing tonight. From my position onstage during 'Razzle Dazzle', I can see her lost in thought as she watches Luca and me and the dancers put on a show of putting on a show. The song's about fooling the audience. Giving them the truth you want them to see, rather than the reality. I wonder if the parallels have dawned on her.

When the rehearsal's done, I stay onstage after everyone's left and perch myself on the edge of the apron, looking out into the empty audience. I just need a moment to breathe. We open tomorrow, and Fletch won't be here to see me. As much as I'm angry with him, I miss him so much it makes my insides hurt. Where did we go so wrong? My eyes prickle uncomfortably; I press the corners of them with my thumb.

'Nettie?'

Sam's standing at the far end of the auditorium. She must have gone out and come back in.

'Hi, Sam. I don't really feel like talking on camera right now.'

'I get it. I wasn't going to ask you to. I just came to say well done. You were fantastic in the dress rehearsal.'

'Um, thanks.'

'Listen – I'm sorry about all the attention you've been getting from *Triple Threat*.'

'"What?"'

She walks over to where I am sitting on the stage, my legs dangling over the edge. 'All the public speculation about you and Luca.'

She has no idea what it's like to be filmed everywhere I go, or have people shouting at me across the street. To have to avoid social media because of all the trolling. And now she comes to me with this half-baked, glib apology?

'What you did was wrong, Sam. You're not sorry.'

She shifts her weight. 'Nettie, I was just showing what I could see. You might not want to admit it, but you and Luca have chemistry. There's nothing in *Triple Threat* that wasn't there in real life.'

'Yes, *there was*,' I say. 'You edited it to make it look as if Luca and I had feelings for each other, when the truth is, we were always just friends. Well, you got what you wanted. Everyone believed it.'

'This documentary is going to change your life, Nettie,' says Sam. 'You've got absolute star quality – it's obvious the second you step on to the screen. It's the one thing that drew me to the project, and I wanted to honour that with how the documentary represented you. The Luca thing was just to create plot. With Fletch gone, we needed a romantic element to the story. A sort of will-they-won't-they. It's what kept people hooked. But ultimately, they'll forget about that. What they'll remember is you.'

'I don't care about being remembered. I care about not being misrepresented.'

'Boys come and go. Star quality lasts forever.' She turns to go. 'Like it or not, *Triple Threat* has made you,' she says over her shoulder. 'You'll thank me one day.'

'I won't thank you!' I call after her. 'You're messing with people's lives, Sam.' The old walls of the music hall carry my voice all the way to the back of the auditorium.

She doesn't look back. Frustrated, I get up and head backstage. How are you meant to deal with someone like that, who just won't listen? I wish I'd never agreed to take part in the damn documentary. It's wrecked all our lives. Alec, haunted by old trauma, letting his competitiveness almost destroy a friendship; Leon, hurt and confused and threatened; Kiki, losing all her self-confidence and feeling let down by someone she trusted; and me and Fletch, ruined over something that wasn't even real to begin with. I hate her, and I hate what she's done. And the worst thing is, I'm powerless to do anything about it.

My phone beeps. It's a message from a number I don't know.

22:20

Meet me in Soho Square.
In ten minutes. It's about Sam.

What the hell?

By the time I get upstairs to the studio we're using as a dressing room, everyone's gone. I quickly take off my costume and get dressed but leave my lashes and make-up on. Should I go? A horrible thought occurs to me that it's some sort of trick. Maybe I'll get there and Sam'll be there waiting to film something humiliating that she's set up.

But something tells me it's not that. I grab my jacket and bag and head outside.

I decide to approach the square from the other side, avoiding the entrance she'll be expecting me from. It means walking all the way round to Greek Street, but I'm not chancing it. When I arrive, I stop in my tracks.

It's Alec, Kiki and Leon.

With *Jade*.

I run over to them. 'What's going on?'

'You know as much as we do,' says Alec. 'I had no idea the rest of you were coming.'

'Jade ambushed us one by one,' said Leon. 'Me, as I was leaving the music hall. Kiki, the same. And Alec's been here a while.'

'An hour, to be precise,' says Alec impatiently. 'Right, Jade. Tell us what it is so that we can all go home and carry on despising you from a distance.'

Jade takes a breath. 'It's Sam.'

'What about her?'

'She's been . . . doing something. Something bad.'

Her words are a shock, but at the same time they don't surprise me. My heart pounding, I look around the circle, its energy charged, the others on tenterhooks.

'What's she been doing?' I say. 'Besides telling lies about us all on national TV?'

'It's *how* she's been doing it,' says Jade. 'She's been recording us without our knowledge. Secret microphones in the dressing rooms, even some of the corridors – wherever she thinks she can get away with it. That's where she's been getting all her information.'

My stomach plummets. I think back to the conversations I had with Kiki in the changing room about Fletch. The time

I cried on Alec's shoulder at the Christmas Ball. Suddenly it all makes sense. Of *course* that was how she knew. She couldn't use that footage – doing so would have given it away – but she used it to construct a narrative that she could manipulate. And there I was blaming Anand. I feel sick.

'Oh my God,' I say. This is horrible. All the stuff Sam could've heard. Personal, private things. Things she had no right hearing.

'Wait – how do you know all this?' says Leon sharply.

Jade pauses. 'I – I helped her put them there,' she says. While we stare at her open mouthed, she adds, 'I regret that now. I'm sorry.'

I don't know what's the bigger shock: knowing that Jade had a hand in it all or hearing her apologize. Probably the latter.

'You've known *all year*,' says Kiki, her eyes blazing. 'Why tell us now? Don't tell me you've seen the error of your ways after all this time. The show first aired months ago. You could see what it was doing to us all.'

'It's backfired,' says Leon cynically, watching Jade closely. 'Something's gone wrong for her. Hasn't it, Jade?'

She tosses her hair back. 'Well . . . kind of. Yeah. I thought I was in control, that if I cooperated with Sam, she'd make me look better, give me more exposure. I was happy to play the villain if it got me known. And then, she set up a meeting for me with a big agency – Wells Brignall? I went along, thinking it was in the bag, especially as she'd got the crew to film the interview. And they refused me. It was a set-up. You saw it, right?'

I've been deliberately avoiding the show, but Leon nods grimly. 'She told them to refuse you?'

'Yeah. And every other agent I've applied to has knocked me back. It's Sam's doing – I know it is.'

294

'Why would she do that?' says Alec.

'Because it makes good television,' says Leon wryly. 'Presumably she got some of the other rejections on camera, too, Jade?'

'She filmed my first couple of phone calls, but then I refused,' says Jade. 'She didn't care – she'd got what she wanted.'

'An end to her story,' I say. I think back to my first meeting with Sam when I flagged up that I was unhappy to be pitted up against Jade. What was it she said to me? *Don't worry – it's all weighted in your favour. You'll come off as the good guy.* Ironically, in a fucked-up way, I did. But look what I lost in return.

'*Fuck*,' Kiki says suddenly. We all stare at her. 'You don't think that's what she did with me?'

Leon smacks his forehead. 'Of course – it has to be. She was there as soon as you'd finished the call, wasn't she, Kiki?'

'Within minutes,' says Kiki. She looks like she's going to be sick. 'And remember how she persuaded me to talk to camera about it, Nettie? Like, she was pretty insistent. Made up some bollocks about revenge, and then put it out on TV that I was too much of an emotional wreck to dance well.' Kiki's breathing is deep and measured, as she tries to keep her emotions under control, but I can see the rage rising.

'Leaving the door open for me to win,' says Jade. 'I wondered how she'd managed to do that. Kiki was way better than me.' We all stare at her. 'I'm not proud of myself, OK?' she adds in a mumble.

'So what do we do about it?' says Alec impatiently. 'Remove the microphones? Confront her about Kiki?'

'We can't,' says Leon. 'If we do that, she'll know we're on to her, and goodness knows what she'll do to us. There's still the live episode to go, remember? We can't risk it, not when all our futures potentially hang on this god-awful show.'

'So what, then?' says Kiki, livid. 'We *have* to stop her. Prove what she did to me. Make it known she's been listening to us. But unless we catch her in action, none of us can do anything about it.'

Something clicks into place.

'No,' I say. '*We* can't. But I know someone who can.'

CHAPTER 25

It'll be a miracle if this all works out.

The morning of the feature-length live finale of *Triple Threat*, I don't go straight to college. Instead, I get my costume and make-up ready for the gala, to drop it off at the Piccadilly Theatre en route to college. We've got a whole day of rehearsing camera angles and timings at the music hall. After that, Miss Duke is letting Luca, Leon and me out at five to run back over to the theatre for a quick soundcheck and tech for the gala. That's all we get. Then it's back to the music hall for the opening night of *Chicago*, which will be filmed, live, both onstage and off, and straight back to perform in the gala, with the TV crew in tow. I'm furious that Miss Duke has bowed to pressure from Sam and allowed it all to happen. She's many things, but I never thought she was a sell-out.

There's so much going on in my head right now, but I've got to put it all aside for one more day and just focus on the small matter of having two live-broadcast shows to perform in. I just hope I don't fuck it up.

The guy at the Piccadilly Theatre stage door lets me go and find my dressing room, which is three floors up. I've got my own room for the gala – I can't believe it. My name's on the door and everything. I take a picture on my phone. My first thought is to send it to Fletch, but then it hits me like a train: I can't. Swallowing my feelings, I dump my stuff and head back to the music hall. Today I just have to focus.

The *Chicago* camera rehearsal is slow and dull, especially after having done a dress run last night, which was so fast and tight. Sam is business as usual – just as sunny as she usually is with me, like we didn't have a massive row last night, like she hasn't just fucked up all of our lives. Part of me wishes I could just throw the whole thing back in her face, refuse to do the live finale, but I know I've just got to stick this out for one more day and hope that what we've planned works out.

At five, Luca, Leon and I are excused and head to the theatre for tonight's gala soundcheck. We're ushered straight on to the stage (where everything, embarrassingly, is paused for us like we're some sort of A-listers), given radio mics, told who we'll be following, walked through our blocking, and given a quick run-through.

Luca watches me staring at the floor as I get my mic adjusted. 'Nettie, are you OK?'

'Hmmn?'

'You seem . . . distracted.'

I glance at Leon, who obviously knows exactly why I'm distracted. I'd tell Luca, but there's not time to go into it properly, and I know he's stressed about the live later. 'Yeah, I'm fine. Today's just . . . a lot, you know?'

Luca nods. 'Tell me about it. I'm sticking to writing as soon as I leave Duke's.'

'Nettie!' a voice calls from the back of the stalls.

Shielding my eyes from the light, I can just make out Steph working her way down the aisle to the stage.

'Hey, Steph!' I say. I wait as she walks up the treads on stage right and then go over to hug her tightly. 'I had no idea you were performing here tonight.'

'Didn't Fletch tell you?' she says, surprised. 'David Hirst got *Better Spent* a spot in the gala as promo, and Fletch was going to accompany me on the guitar. Saves them money using an intern – you know what these producers are like – and he'd helped to write a lot of it, so he seemed like the obvious choice. But, you know, since his accident we—'

'Accident?' I say, my heart almost stopping. 'What *accident*?'

Leon and Luca look as shocked as I am. Steph seems surprised at our reactions.

'You didn't know?' she says, confused. 'Fletch had a motorbike accident last weekend in London. He's been in hospital ever since. Cracked ribs, concussion, broke his leg, too, I think. He's going to be fine,' she adds, seeing the alarm on my face. 'I think he was having an operation on his wrist today. But obviously, it's put him out of action for a few weeks. I thought you'd know.'

'Fletch and I broke up,' I say quietly. 'Last week. I haven't heard from him since.'

'Oh, Nettie, I'm so sorry,' she says. 'I'm going to the hospital tomorrow to visit him, while I'm still up here. He's at Lewisham. You're welcome to come?'

The thought of Fletch injured, in hospital, makes me want to drop everything and run all the way to him. Suddenly our fight seems small and insignificant. I have to go to him. I have to see him. But . . .

'I'm not sure he'd be happy to see me,' I say. 'But thanks anyway, Steph.'

Steph is called back to the sound desk, so she hugs me again and heads back down the treads. Luca and Leon look at me.

'Oh my God,' I say.

'I know,' says Leon.

'I can't believe it.' Luca puts his head in his hands.

'Why didn't he tell me?' I say. 'Or any of us?'

Leon holds my hand, the shock etched on his face as clearly as it must be on mine. 'You know what Fletch is like. He probably didn't want us worrying.'

Oh God, I hope that's true. Suddenly everything else I'm feeling is swamped in a desperate need to see Fletch. We can't leave things like this, without talking. I need him to know how I feel. I need him to know that I love him.

We take off our mics and hand them back to the sound number two. As we walk up the stairs to the stage door, all I can think is that I have to see Fletch. I *have* to. Maybe I could go tonight, after the show? But what if he won't see me?

'Give me a sec,' I say to the others. Then I run back into the building, suddenly dark after being out in the bright daylight again. I head to the auditorium and up to the sound desk, where the sound number one is on the desk, fiddling with several volume levers.

'Excuse me?' I say.

He turns around. 'Hi, darling. You all right?'

'Yeah. I was hoping I could send you a different track for my song tonight,' I say. 'I sent the wrong one earlier.'

This had better work.

Leon, Luca and I walk back to the music hall in silence, just in time to find Miss Duke, mid-speech, riling everyone up into a state of greater anxiety than they were already in about tonight's performance.

300

'I am sure I need not remind you that there is a lot riding on the success of tonight,' she's saying. 'As rehearsed, the sections Sam wants to focus on will be filmed in here, the studio theatre, during the first performance of *Chicago*, with interviews taking place backstage. When Sam leaves for the Piccadilly Theatre with those of you who are lucky enough to have been chosen for the gala –' she locks eyes with me for a second – 'Anand will be heading up the production side of things here.'

Miss Duke continues. 'At Duke's we are used to live performance. We are a theatre family, after all. But in half an hour, over *three million* people will be tuned in to watch you. No second chances. No making up for it in tomorrow's performance. No second or third takes. You have only now, this moment. Show the world why you're here, why you were chosen. Show them why you're at Duke's.'

Sam takes the floor. 'The most important thing from our point of view,' she says, 'is for you to ignore the cameras. Obviously be aware of them, especially the dolly cams, but other than that, act as if we're not here.'

I sneak another peak at Kiki, whose eyes are fixed on Sam as always, except that now, instead of their usual adoration, they look cold.

We go and get ready backstage. I quickly write a message to Alec, Kiki and Leon on our group chat.

18:02
CHANGE OF PLAN!

Kiki looks at me in the mirror in alarm but doesn't say anything. Instead, she texts straight back.

301

Kiki:
WTF??

Alec:
Nettie, don't do this to us.

Will explain, but first I need to have a clear and loud conversation right now with Kiki in the changing rooms. You have to trust me.

Leon:
OK x

Kiki:

Alec:

Kiki looks terrified. It's fair enough – acting isn't her strong point, and I've basically just asked her to star in an impromptu improv scene with me.

'I've decided not to do the finale of the concert,' I say loudly.

'Oh, really?' says Kiki nervously, wisely plumping for a safe answer that gives me the chance to explain without actually having to add anything much herself. 'Why not?'

'Because Fletch is in Lewisham Hospital,' I say.

*

When the five's called, Kiki and I head downstairs together holding hands. Kiki crosses the stage to be with Shaiann and the rest of the dancers; I stay in the stage-right wing and try to centre myself, switch off all the noise, and focus.

This is the moment I've been building up to all year. All the hard work, the tears, the drama – it's all coming together now, in this moment. And millions of people are watching, judging. I start to panic. What if I fall flat? What if – What if I . . . let Mum down? An overwhelming anxiety starts creeping over me. I suddenly feel cold.

Lisa appears next to me in the dark. 'You're gonna be great.'

I turn to face her. She holds my shoulders and looks down at me kindly.

'A lot to live up to, huh?'

My eyes are blurred. I nod, smiling through the tears.

'You know, I did class with your mother once,' she says. 'A fundraiser for ACT UP on Broadway. All the famous dancers showed up. She was fantastic – so beautiful to watch.'

'But I'm not like her,' I say. Fresh panic surges and I can feel my throat start to tighten like it did last year. Oh God, not now. Not after all this time.

'No, you're not at all like her,' agrees Lisa. '*Nor do you have to be*. Yeah, she was . . . ballet. But you – you're scrappy and ballsy and razor sharp. You're *Fosse*.'

Something releases at her words. She's right – I don't have to be Mum. I just need to be *me*. And this work, this choreography? Well, right from day one, I knew inside that I could do it. I *felt* it.

'You've put in the work,' says Lisa. 'Now just *enjoy* it. Remember, imperfection can be beautiful. You've got this.' She gives my shoulders an encouraging squeeze and goes through the pass door to watch the show.

Shaiann's started singing 'All That Jazz'. I go and find Taro for our entrance together. After everything that's happened this year, I just need to celebrate this moment, lose myself in it. As I make my entrance, Lisa's words echo in my mind and I forget about everything else – Mum, the cameras and Sam – I just concentrate on letting the movement flow, enjoying how it feels.

It works: I'm *dancing*.

Alec's in the front row, and I see him give me a little nod as I finish singing 'Roxie', as if to tell me I'm fabulous and he approves. But I don't need it – I can already feel it. Something's finally connected.

Kiki's stunning. She dances everyone else off the stage. Leon's also brilliant as Amos; honestly, he's the true meaning of the phrase 'triple threat'. He really can do it all. Luca's looking confident, but as our added dance break in 'Razzle Dazzle' starts, I see the tiniest spark of fear in his eyes, presumably at the thought of the lifts. I give him a wink with my upstage eye as we go for it, and before I know it, I'm way over his head, flying high above the audience and the band and all the performers as he carries me round the stage. Part of me wishes Mum was here to see this, but another part of me can feel she already is.

In what seems like seconds, the show's over. We all take our final bows and the curtain drops. Raucous chatter breaks out as the cast congratulate each other.

'You did it!' cries Kiki, launching herself at me.

'*You* did it!' I joke, hugging her back.

There's no time to linger. Luca, Leon and I are ushered offstage and told to immediately make our way over to the gala.

We sprint over to the Piccadilly Theatre, where Dave is waiting with a camera at stage door. We run past him and up the stairs to our dressing rooms. I push my door open, dump everything on the floor and grab my dress, which I wriggle into and run back down the three flights of stairs, flinging my bag at the stage door keeper and asking as politely as I can while running if she wouldn't mind looking after it. Someone's there to meet me at stage level, which is good because I can't remember where I'm going. A sound number two puts a radio mic on me, shoving the pack down the back of my dress without a waistband.

'Will it stay?' he says through the torch in his mouth.

I nod, unceremoniously hitching up my dress to tuck the mic pack into my pants. Wow. My first professional gig and dignity's already gone out the window.

The intro starts, and I walk onstage, with no idea if the sound guy will actually play the track I sent him, or (thinking about it now, which is admittedly a little late in the day) if I can even remember the words. Oh my God, actually, I *can't* remember the words. Shit.

I can just make out some of the faces in the dark, waiting for me to sing, expectant. My mind goes back to the first time Fletch and I met, when he played his song for me in the library – the one I helped him finish about losing someone you love. That wonderful moment when we first connected. When I knew I loved him. Without even thinking, my lips form the shapes of the first few lines, and before I know it, I'm singing *our song*. I don't even have to act; the emotions are all there.

What have we both been doing – this strange dance around each other? If both of us had just been honest in the first place – about everything – none of this would have happened.

Fletch wouldn't have been jealous; I wouldn't have been angry and resentful. In all the drama, the miscommunication, we forgot the most important thing: that what we had was precious, and we should have done everything we could to protect it. I was so bent on making it perfect that I forgot perfection doesn't exist – as Lisa says, there's beauty in imperfection. What we had wasn't perfect, but it *was* beautiful. I know all of this as I sing; I just hope he knows it, too.

The audience lets out a roar as I finish. I smile gratefully, but there's only one reaction I care about right now. The lights dim, and I run straight off the stage, bung my mic at the sound number two, and pelt up the stairs to stage door, grabbing my phone on the way. The Uber's outside waiting; I throw myself in, almost ripping my dress in the process. As the driver speeds off towards South London, I check my phone. There are messages from Kiki and Alec.

21:30
Kiki:

Stage One activated ;)

Alec:

Stage Two complete ;))

Presumably Leon's about to go onstage at the gala. I hope he's OK with all of this – it's a lot to lump on him on a day like today. I'm so lucky to have such good friends.

We pull up outside Lewisham Hospital, and I jump out of the car and head straight to reception, but there's an enormous queue. Visiting hours will be over soon, and there's no way they'll let a random girl in a ballgown in after kicking-out time. There's nothing else for it – I'm just going to have to find him myself.

The hospital layout is a little confusing. There's a board telling visitors where all the different wards are, but where will Fletch be? Steph said he was having an operation today. Orthopaedics? I run through A&E to the yellow zone and call out to a passing nurse.

'Excuse me, I'm looking for my . . . brother. He had surgery on his wrist today.'

Without stopping, she calls back over her shoulder, 'Straight ahead, through two sets of doors, then left. Ask at Ward Ten.'

'Thank you!' I shout.

As I run, my ankle half goes underneath me and I cry out in pain but manage to keep running. At this rate, *I'll* be needing a bed in orthopaedics.

I push through the first set of doors and head down a long corridor, through another set of doors at the end, turn left and—

Sam's there, pointing her handheld at me.

'Smile,' she says. 'You're live.'

CHAPTER 26

I stare at her.

'Tell us how you're feeling right now,' she says, pointing to the little red light on her camera to indicate that whatever I say will be heard immediately by three million people. She knows I can't do anything; she's relying on that little red dot to keep me under control. She thinks she's trapped me.

Which is why this is going to be so brilliant.

'How did you know I was here?' I say calmly.

'Magic of telly,' she says. 'But exciting events tonight. Maybe you can fill us in on what happened. Why did you make the decision to sing a different song at the gala? Was it your love for—'

Just then, Kiki and Anand burst through the double doors and run towards us.

'Nettie!' Kiki shouts.

'You made it!' I'm so relieved, I almost forget that Sam's still pointing her camera at us.

Sam stares at us. I can tell she's trying to work out what's going on.

'We broke into your laptop, Sam,' says Anand. 'We found out what you've been doing.'

Sam turns her camera off immediately. 'OK, cut back to Duke's,' she says into a wire attached to her earpiece. 'I don't care who – just cut back!'

'We know you've been recording us in the changing rooms, Sam,' says Kiki breathlessly. 'That's how you've known what's been going on. Listening to us through hidden microphones.'

'Yes,' says Anand. 'Backstage at *Chicago*, too.'

'This is ridiculous,' splutters Sam.

'You've been doing it all year,' Anand pushes on. 'I thought I was paranoid at first. But then I began to notice a pattern. So I looked on your computer and found hundreds of audio files.'

'You had no right to go through my files,' says Sam. 'They're private!'

'I feel sick to my stomach that I ever trusted you,' says Kiki. She turns to me. 'That's not all we found. It's as we suspected – there was also a string of aggressive emails to See Me Now, threatening them if they didn't terminate my contract.'

Sam smiles dangerously at her. 'Can you blame me? I had to give you some sort of story. Otherwise you were just . . . hardworking. Bland. It's a shame, Kiki. So much potential. Wasted on this pointless tattling. I'd have thought you'd be grateful after that lovely little story I gave you. People went wild for it last week. Everyone loves a cryer.'

Kiki looks like she's about to punch Sam in the face. 'You're revolting,' she says.

'You know what else we just found on the laptop, Nettie?' Anand says, watching Sam with utter disgust. 'The video of your mum falling off the stage.'

'Wait,' I say, rounding on Sam. '*You* sent me that?' I'm shaken to my core. It was her all along? The fury inside me is at bursting point now.

'Just a little teaser,' says Sam with a pleased smile. 'Things needed spicing up before we started filming. But I didn't need the dead-mother storyline in the end. You created enough drama without that.'

Even after everything she's done, I'm still shocked at this new level of depravity. Sam was controlling me even before I met her? How could she do that? I almost feel bad for ever suspecting Millicent Moore. Almost.

'We've got evidence, Sam,' says Anand. 'Three Ring's going to be very interested to know how one of their biggest documentary makers gets her stories. You'll be investigated and likely prosecuted.'

'They won't do that,' says Sam. 'Who broke into my laptop unauthorized? You've made it easy, Anand. What was the last thing I got before I turned off the camera just now? Your admission of guilt. I'll tell the bosses that you planted the files. Who's going to take your word over mine?'

'Of *course* you're relying on your power to keep it all secret,' says Kiki. 'Because Anand and Nettie and me, we're young and at the bottom of the pile – no one ever believes us. People like you – the ones in control – forget that you're only in control because the rest of us allow you to be. I mean, I thought hard about whether to come here, because exposing you is pretty fucking dangerous for me. I'll probably get expelled and never work again.'

Kiki reaches for my hand, like it'll give her courage. 'When you're training for something you want so badly, you're completely at the mercy of the people in charge. One wrong move could destroy your whole life.' She takes a breath. 'So you do everything that's asked of you, you take all the shit that comes with the training – the comments about how you look, the criticism – because that's the industry, right? Isn't that what you were always telling me? *The camera adds ten pounds, Kiki. You're*

310

looking great, Kiki. Keep working on those designs, Kiki. But I'm not talking about the industry, or the fact that the whole time you were criticizing it but telling me to "play the game", you were propping up its bullshit by feeding the world lies about us all. I'm not talking about your attempts to keep me down, those little digs to make me insecure so that I wouldn't question you. And I'm not here to talk about our so-called "friendship". I'm here to talk about the fact that you came into Duke's and spied on us. That's exploitation.'

'Wait till Miss Duke hears about this,' I say. Although – honestly? – I've been worrying about this part of the plan. What if Miss Duke had any knowledge about what Sam was doing and either turned her back to it or enabled her? That would be beyond disgusting. Would she go that far?

'Wait no longer.' Miss Duke steps around the corner, followed closely by Leon, who bravely volunteered for the task of bringing her in on the plan. She's completely unruffled, as if it's the most naturally occurring thing for her to be at Lewisham Hospital on a Saturday night.

'Cecile,' says Sam smoothly, her face a mask of calm. 'What are you doing here?'

'I came to see how my students were,' she replies, taking off her gloves and handing them to Anand, who takes them without a word. 'But I see you're looking after them.'

I catch Leon's eye. 'You told her, right?'

'Oh, he told me,' answers Miss Duke, her eyes flashing. 'In fact, we've been watching it unfold on our way over. Leon introduced me to the Three Ring app,' she says, holding up her phone. 'Wonderful invention.'

'What do you mean, "watching"?' says Sam.

'You've been live since they interrupted you, my dear,' says Miss Duke calmly, like Miss Marple revealing to the killer how they were found out. 'They cleverly arranged for the live footage to be transferred to that marvellous little device on Anand's shirt.' She points to Anand's chest, where there's clearly a tiny camera attached that no one's noticed in all the drama. 'So at least – how many people was it again, Leon?'

'Three million,' says Leon, smiling.

Miss Duke turns back to Sam. 'After a brief word with Leon and the crew, it was the obvious thing to do. It seems your employees all resent you, Sam, because each and every one of them happily agreed to the plan.'

'You're bluffing,' says Sam. She holds her wire up to her mouth. 'Dave? Have you heard this bullshit they're spouting?' Her eyes widen in shock as she hears his answer. 'I don't believe it. I don't fucking believe this.' She rips out the earpiece and rounds on me, her face contorted with anger. 'Your hypocrisy astounds me, Nettie. This show has elevated you to beyond anything you could have hoped for in this industry – even a famous dead mother can only carry you so far. You were willing to play along when it suited you just fine. You owe me your career.'

'I don't owe you anything,' I say in disgust. 'All you did was spread lies about me and Luca. You shattered Kiki's dream and threatened another of my best friends. You destroyed my relationship with the boy I love. You manipulated people with the promise of successful careers and abused your power. This show has never been anything but bullshit! The only thing that was ever real about it was the talent of these wonderful people. And you even tried to manipulate that. If there's one thing I hope people watching *Triple Threat* take away from it, it's that

312

nothing's as it seems. There's always been a story, an angle – and the truth was hidden, trapped behind your smoke and mirrors. You're disgusting.'

Anand circles his fingers and whispers the word '*Credits*' into a hidden earpiece.

This is bizarre.

Miss Duke takes the baton. 'I know what the industry is, Sam. I understand what makes it go round, those little transactions and compromises everyone has to make. And believe me, *I* – more than anyone – have seen what it can do to people, how it chews them up and spits them out.' She glances at me, and I realize she's talking about Mum. 'My job is to prepare my students for that industry. Sometimes that involves being harsh with them – especially the girls. Showbusiness is hard, and I have to make sure they are tough enough to handle it. But equally, I expect the industry to respect my girls, and *all* women. You have betrayed us. You have cheapened our industry. Now be gone.'

Sam flings her earpiece on the ground and storms off towards the exit. She's disappeared through the double doors before you can say 'Razzle Dazzle'.

Anand fiddles with his camera and looks at us awkwardly. 'Erm . . . cut?' he says.

Miss Duke takes her gloves back from him. 'We'll discuss tonight's events in the morning, I think. Kiki and Leon, whilst I can't "officially" approve of your actions, I do appreciate the fact that you saved the college. Thank you. Now, if you'll excuse me, I have a few phone calls to make.' She turns and walks calmly down the corridor.

We stare after her.

'Oh my God,' I say. 'Did that all just go out live on TV? Seriously?'

'Basically,' says Kiki.

'Stage three complete,' says Leon with a wink.

Just stage four to go, the part I've been hoping will go to plan most of all. Right on cue, Alec steps out of a room at the far end of the corridor, waiting like the top turn until last to make his entrance. The levels of drama in this corridor tonight are almost farcical.

'Alec!' I run up to him, not sure if my heart's still hammering from what's just happened, or for what's about to happen.

'Nettie,' he says. 'He's in here.' He's holding the door open for me.

This is the moment I've been waiting for, but now that it's here, I'm not sure my nerves can take it. Silently, I hug Alec and enter the room.

Fletch is sitting up in bed. His face is swollen, and one eye is only just able to open, although his bruises have the purple-yellow hues of having had a few days to heal. His right arm is in a cast, and so is his leg.

I gasp. 'Oh my God, Fletch!'

'I know – this hospital gown does nothing for me,' he says.

His eye that isn't hurt twinkles at me. I want that twinkle to mean that everything's OK between us, that he still loves me. I want to run over to him and stroke his hair and put my face close to his. I want to kiss him so badly. But I just stand there, rooted to the spot, trying not to cry, unsure what to say. Neither of us speaks for a moment.

'I'm sorry,' we both say eventually at the same time, and then laugh.

'Why didn't you tell me?' I ask.

He exhales. 'I knew you had a hard week coming up and I didn't want to stress you out even more. You had *Chicago* going on, *Triple Threat* and apparently a gala performance to worry about. And also . . . I thought you wouldn't want to hear from me. I behaved pretty terribly.' His voice breaks. 'Nettie, I'm ashamed of what I said to you. To you both. I'm truly so sorry.' He's shaking.

I go over and kneel next to the bed; gingerly I take his hand. His fingers feel strangely soft as he threads them through mine, and looking at his other hand, bruised and in a cast, I remember with a pang that he won't be able to play for a while. I press his fingertips to my lips, and he closes his eyes.

I almost don't have the courage to ask him. 'Did you see . . . ?'

'I saw you. Nettie, you sang our song so beautifully.' He adjusts his weight in the bed; the action makes his face cloud over for a second. 'It's more than I deserve. I know I was an arsehole about you and Luca. I never really thought there was anything going on between you. But by then, I'd already started being a jerk and it was too late to back out. So I stomped off into the night like a complete knob, when what I should have done was explain how I was feeling and not let you think I was blaming you. I'd already been feeling like a shitbag boyfriend and had started worrying that you'd realize how rubbish I was and leave me. It's like Sam could see my darkest fears and exploited them with that stuff about you and Luca.'

'You're not alone in that,' I say.

'I know. Alec and I have been riveted tonight,' he says. 'Are you OK? Everything she put you through – I wasn't there for you, Nettie. I'm sorry.'

'I'm sorry, too. I should have told you how I was feeling and looped you into everything. But I was trying to hang on to what little was left of our perfect bubble from this summer. And I'm too stubborn.'

'*I* was stubborn,' he says with a grin.

'Maybe a little,' I say, smiling.

'I'd put my arms up, but . . .' He nods at his cast.

I stand up, lean over him as slowly and as carefully as I can and brush his lips softly with mine.

'I love you so much,' he whispers.

'I love you, too.'

He puts his hand up to stroke my cheek. The effort makes him wince and I pull back, alarmed, but he smiles and kisses me again – warm and tender and slightly tickly because of the way I'm hovering, trying not to hurt his face.

And in that one kiss, both of us manage to say everything we need to say to each other. It's everything a make-up kiss should be.

Something occurs to me. 'Where did you go that night?' I ask Fletch. 'Was that when the accident happened?'

'I went to your grandmother's,' he says.

'What? Why?'

'When I asked you if you were finishing with me, I was sure you'd say yes.' He shifts his legs slightly in the bed. 'But when you didn't, when you just said you were really fucking angry with me, it gave me a tiny chink of hope – a chance that I could make things right. It was like a light switched on. I thought if I could prove I cared about you and everything you've been going through this year, you'd forgive me for being such an arse. So I rode down to Sydenham and knocked

316

on her door to ask her about your mum.'

So Fletch wasn't walking out on me – he was trying to help. I wish I'd known that. I'd still have been furious with him, but it would have saved a lot of heartache this week for both of us.

'You went to Auntie's?' I say incredulously. 'I can't imagine it was a warm welcome.'

'No, she wasn't happy about it, but I think it had been on her mind since you'd last seen her, and she agreed to talk. Nettie, I should have been there for you. I wanted to ride home and say that to you. I wanted to apologize for treating you with kid gloves when I should have been honest. I wanted to say sorry for being such an arse on the night of the Christmas Ball, and for lying to you at the Duke's Awards. I wanted to show you that I cared.' He swallows, as if his throat's aching. It could be the anaesthetic, only mine's aching, too. 'And then on my way back to you, a van derailed my plan . . .' He smiles, but I know he's wrestling with some stuff around the accident. It's exactly how his brother died. 'But I did find out one thing.'

'What?'

'It was your grandmother who ended your mum's career, Nettie. She phoned the papers.'

'What did you say?' I turn to see Miss Duke, standing in the doorway like Beatrice Stockwell in *The Drowsy Chaperone*, making her subtle entrance after everyone's accounted for. Jeez, how long has she been standing there?

Fletch repeats his last sentence. 'Nettie's mum collapsed onstage at the height of her fame. There was a big takedown piece in a couple of the papers, organized by her own mother. It finished her.'

I don't know who is more shocked, Miss Duke or me. We just

stare at each other, waiting for the other one to speak.

'But you need to see her, Nettie,' says Fletch. 'She's ready to give you the answers you've been waiting for.'

'I also have questions, Antoinette. My car will pick you up first thing,' says Miss Duke wryly and decisively.

Miss Duke leaves, again, leaving Fletch and me to process everything. Today, I performed in two live shows in front of millions of people, took down a corrupt TV producer and got back together with my boyfriend in hospital, but somehow the thought of being in a car with Miss Duke trumps them all in weirding me out . . .

After Fletch and I get over the shock of everything, we talk and talk until I fall asleep with him (on his slightly less painful side). A nurse quietly comes in at midnight to tell me that I should probably get going. I drowsily collect my things, kiss Fletch tenderly on the forehead, and leave the hospital, ordering an Uber as I go.

When I get home, Alec, Kiki, Leon and Anand are all sitting together in the living room, talking and laughing. It's good to see Leon and Alec being friends again. It's early days, but I already feel as if the dynamics of their relationship have already changed. Leon seems more relaxed around Alec, and when Leon speaks, Alec is listening – *really* listening, and replying in a positive way, not with a put-down or a remark about how he's somehow better.

We're all lounging sleepily on the sofas, tired but too wired to sleep. The conversation moves to Sam.

'I thought she was so amazing,' Kiki says with an eye-roll. 'She was the head of this big TV show, she'd had to fight really hard to get where she was, she had all these clever ideas, and I guess I just got sucked in. You tried to warn me, Nettie, but I didn't want to believe it. I wanted to believe that she had the answer to all my problems.'

'We all fell for her act,' says Leon, giving Kiki's shoulder a squeeze. 'Don't give yourself a hard time.'

'I just thought she was this badass, but she was a bully.'

Kiki's putting on a brave face, but I know she must feel so betrayed.

'We should contact See Me Now,' says Alec. 'Maybe they'll reinstate your contract now they're not being threatened by Sam.'

'Michelle already called,' said Kiki. 'Wants to talk on Monday. She was very apologetic – told me that if I was happy, they'd launch the collection as soon as possible!'

'That's great news, Kiki,' says Alec, smiling.

Kiki puts her head on me; I fold my arms around her. I'm going to make sure I'm there for her. Build her back up. Show her how much I love her.

'Anand, how are you feeling about everything?' I say. He risked everything for us. He's basically a hero.

'I feel . . . good!' he says.

'You knew, right?' I say. 'That's what you kept hinting at.'

'I knew she was doing it; I just didn't know how,' he says. 'The equipment she used was really sophisticated. I never thought I'd have the courage to bring her down.'

'Well, you did,' says Alec.

'Yeah, you were brilliant,' says Kiki enthusiastically.

Anand smiles bashfully. 'Oh, and guess what? After the show, I was feeling brave, so I asked my flatmate out. I didn't even think about it; I just *went for it* – obviously with the obligatory "no worries if not, don't even know if you're into guys lol" . . . and he said yes!'

We cheer.

'That's wonderful, Anand,' I say. 'I'm so happy it worked out for you.'

'Me too,' he says, smiling.

I'm so happy for Anand. Today has been exhausting, exhilarating and quite, quite bizarre, with some shocking revelations. It feels grounding to have some good news at last, and I go to bed feeling grateful for that.

CHAPTER 27

My grandmother comes to the door in her dressing gown. She doesn't seem surprised to see me; her face registers no emotion whatsoever. But when she sees Miss Duke behind me, she draws herself up haughtily.

'Come in,' she says.

No *Hello*; no *How are you, child of my child?* Anger prickles my face until it feels strange, like it doesn't belong to me.

I don't wait. 'You betrayed her. You ruined Mum's life. Why am I even surprised?'

'He told you, then,' says Auntie. 'Took his time.'

Miss Duke and I follow her through to the kitchen.

'After he left here, he had a motorcycle accident,' I say.

'I'm sorry to hear that,' she says.

'Sorry?' I say. 'You've never been sorry about anything in your life. You drove Mum away—'

'You know nothing.' She sits down at the table.

Miss Duke also sits down, uninvited. I stay standing.

'I gave everything to Anastasia,' says Auntie. 'Championed her talent, supported her career—'

'You never supported her,' says Miss Duke quietly. 'The ballet always came first with you, not your daughter's welfare. That's part of the reason she was so messed up. And when she started to become an "embarrassment", you ended her career.'

'Is that what you think?' she says, her voice wrung with

unexpected emotion. 'I was saving her. I was saving *you*, Antoinette.'

'What are you talking about?' I say. 'No more riddles! I need the truth.'

'Sit down, Antoinette. Sit!'

Surprised by her tone, I obey, and wait for her to explain.

'Ana had been ill. She lived the party lifestyle – at first I thought it was just that, but then I realized it was more. I'd go to her house and discover piles of gin bottles by the back door. She was drinking all night – in the morning, too. And the drugs. She always denied it, but it was plain she had a problem. Oh, I know these things happen – I wasn't born yesterday; I'm well aware of what goes on at those showbiz bashes – but the number of times I'd find white powder strewn over the coffee table, endless pills left lying around . . .' She takes a breath to steady her voice.

I remind myself to breathe too.

'Soon, her behaviour started to change,' Auntie continues. 'She was anxious; she cried a lot, sometimes for hours; she started missing work; she wouldn't wake in the mornings. I would have to go to her flat and physically get her out of bed. Every day I was afraid I'd find her cold.

'I used to take her laundry when she was out, and bring it back clean and ironed. The state of the place in those last few weeks . . . She never even knew I was helping her. Then one evening I caught her as she was leaving. She was wobbling on her feet and only just caught the doorframe in time to avoid a fall. I tried to get her to stay home, but she refused.'

Miss Duke shifts in her chair and glances at me.

Auntie continues. 'We argued – both said some horrible things. I told her she was a disgrace, said I was ashamed of her.

She accused me of being uncaring. Said I'd never loved her. Told me she never wanted to see me again. When she left, I didn't stop her. I stayed for a while to clean up after her for the last time and then the phone rang.

'It was the doctor. Said he had her results. I immediately thought of her father, with his liver, and the illness Ana had gone through when she was younger . . . I didn't think twice about pretending to be her.

'"*Congratulations, Miss Delaney-Richardson – you're pregnant.*" My addict daughter, pregnant. What could I do? Presumably Ana had some suspicion that she might've been pregnant, or she wouldn't have gone to the doctor. So, if she knew, and she still couldn't stop . . .'

'She didn't know,' says Miss Duke. 'She had no idea.'

'You can't know that. None of us can,' says Auntie. 'I had to act. I contacted an old friend of mine who wrote for *The Times* and told him to do his worst. Anything he could to stop her. Lose her the job, the friends, everything. A takedown piece. When I got home, there was a message on my answerphone that Ana had collapsed and was in intensive care. I was distraught—'

Her voice actually catches. It's strange to see her so emotional. I feel awkward, like I want to comfort her but can't because of the barrier she's put between us.

'As planned, the piece was published, validated by her onstage collapse. The company she was working for put her in rehab and said they were "supporting Anastasia and optimistic for her return", but we all knew it was over. No one would touch her after that. I tried to go to see her in rehab, but she had me thrown out. We didn't speak to each other again. I was too proud, and she was too angry.'

She stops talking. The hum of the refrigerator seems suddenly loud against the awkward silence. I pick up a vase that's sitting on the table, then put it back again. Miss Duke sits calmly, looking at my grandmother.

'Why didn't you try harder?' I ask. 'You lost your daughter because you were too proud to make the first move?'

'Our relationship was always strained. Your mother blamed me for her father's death, said I drove him to drink. I've never claimed to be perfect, Antoinette – I have my faults, but Anastasia was stubborn, too. We didn't speak until days before she died.'

'Did you tell her what you did?'

She looks as if she's weighing up whether to tell me. 'I did. She was angry. Said she'd ruined a friendship over it. But I think she understood now that she had her own child. She'd have done anything to protect you.'

'Do you know who my father is?' I say, out of the blue. I don't even think about it before the words tumble out of my mouth. Miss Duke looks at me curiously.

'No,' Auntie says shortly. 'It could have been anyone. I doubt she even knew.'

Miss Duke and I get back in her ridiculous Bentley. My head's spinning. Mum never told me what happened with Auntie before she died. I only knew they'd seen each other in the hospital. As much as I dislike my grandmother, I'm glad they had a chance to clear the air.

'All those years wasted,' says Miss Duke, mainly to herself. 'I'm sorry you were alone with her in the end. It must have been difficult for you both.' She puts her hand on my arm.

I'm not sure now is the time to mention that I stole the

contents of an envelope marked 'Private and Confidential' from her old desk, but I need to ask her about it. I uncross my legs and look her in the eyes, hoping to seem confident and not at all like a liar. 'I found a photo when I was . . . going through some of Mum's old belongings. Of her . . . with your husband.'

She knows the photo I mean. I can see it in her face. She takes a breath in to speak, then changes her mind. It looks as if she's struggling to find the right words. I wait while she composes herself.

'Ana always maintained that nothing happened between her and Nick, despite there being evidence to the contrary,' she says. 'The trouble is, she was not herself in those days. She was high, or drunk, or both – so much so that she would act out of character. She would frequently black out.'

'So why did you stop talking?' I ask.

She gives me a wry smile. 'She was convinced I'd called the papers on her as revenge. That it was actually your grandmother is as surprising to me as it is to you.' She takes a compact out of her bag and powders her nose like a Fifties movie star. I didn't even know people still did that. 'Ana and I met up before the end, when she started having chemo, before your grandmother had confessed. We made our peace.'

I had no idea they'd seen each other. 'After everything that happened between you? How?'

'We just agreed to believe each other. Should have done it years ago. Life is short, a fact of which I know you are painfully aware.' She puts her compact back in her tiny handbag and turns to face me. 'Ana asked me to look out for you if our paths ever crossed. She loved you very much, Antoinette. I think she would have told you everything, one day. She just ran out of time. I'm sorry you lost her.'

Finally I've got the answers I've been looking for, but the truth is more painful than I could have imagined. Everything that Mum went through – I wish I could have been there for her. She must've felt so alone.

But then I remember something she used to say to me:

You're my best dance, Nettie.

I never doubted her when she said that. And even now I know all the secrets and lies, I still believe it. Becoming pregnant with me was a turning point in her life, and I think she *was* ready to leave it all behind. She *chose* her life with me, and that means everything.

I take a deep breath. 'I'm sorry you lost her, too.'

CHAPTER 28

The cheer as Fletch goes up to collect his degree nearly splits my head open. Rosemary grips my knee; I pass her a tissue. It takes him a while to get down the stairs; he's out of his cast, but still a little wobbly on his feet. Fletch poses for the photographer with Miss Duke, Michael, and the guest speakers. His hand is healing well; he's having physio every day now, and they're sure he'll make a full recovery.

Luca's up next. Fletch grins back at him as he shakes hands with Michael. Their friendship is as strong as it ever was – probably stronger now after they actually sat down and did some real talking. It's weird to think they were ever fighting.

Fletch joins Bob, Rosemary and me after the ceremony, when the college ground floor is full of students and parents and teachers. Bob pulls him in for a hug.

'Well done.' He pulls away to look at his son, holding him by the shoulders.

'We're so proud of you,' says Rosemary.

'I'm proud of you, too,' I say, standing on tiptoes to kiss his cheek.

'Fletch!' Michael's clear voice cuts through the crowd. He dodges around several families to reach us.

'Hi, Michael,' says Fletch. 'Enjoy the ceremony?'

'It's the *best*,' says Michael. 'All my babies, achieving their dreams, flying the nest. I'm having all the emotions today.

Listen, have you been into the office?'

'No. Why?'

'We've had a call from David Hirst's office. *Better Spent* is transferring to the West End next year – and they want you to be MD!'

Fletch looks stunned. 'I thought they'd have got someone else, after what happened.'

'They did, but whoever they got wasn't a patch on you. They've sent the contract through – it's waiting for you to sign. Congratulations, buddy. Our first ever MD, straight out of college.' He shakes Fletch's hand warmly.

'Not assistant MD?' says Fletch, in a daze.

'Nope,' says Michael. 'Oliver and West want you in charge. They said it wouldn't have been the success it was without your input, and they're keen to continue their working relationship with you.'

'Wow,' says Fletch. 'I can't believe it.'

Rosemary squeals. 'We're thrilled for you!'

'Thanks, Mum,' says Fletch. 'Wow . . . Hey, does anyone mind if I just nip to the office? I need to see that the contract actually exists!'

Fletch ducks into the crowd.

'Nettie, could I borrow you for a second?' says Michael. 'I wanted to give you something.'

'Er, sure.'

I follow him into Studio One, which is quieter. He hands me a small white envelope. 'I found this while I was going through some things at home. I thought you should have it.'

'Thanks.' I open it. It's a photograph of Mum and Michael. Mum must be in her twenties; Michael a little older. Mum's wearing her vintage Chanel jacket, flared hipster jeans and some strange square-toed pink shoes with a block heel. Michael's got one hand around Mum's waist, the other holding a glass of champagne. Mum's got a drink and a cigarette in the same hand and is blowing out smoke towards the camera as she leans into him.

'This is gorgeous, Michael. Thank you.'

'Hard to believe I once didn't have grey hair,' says Michael over my shoulder. He's laughing. 'I think that was at the launch party of Darcey Bussell's autobiography. Although we went to lots of these things, so I can't be sure. I think Jerry took the photo.'

Why is that name so familiar?

'Who's Jerry?'

'My partner,' says Michael. 'You might have seen him at last year's Summer Showcase. Although from what I remember, you were quite preoccupied . . .'

'I can't believe Mum smoked,' I say, turning the photo over. There's writing on the back. '*Ana and Bunny 4 ever* . . . Bunny – is that you?'

He smiles fondly. 'Yes, I was always Bunny to her. It was a joke about my awful dancing. She and Jerry used to rib me terribly.'

My brain connects the dots.

'"B" for *Bunny*,' I say. When Michael looks at me curiously, I add, 'You signed your letters to her "B". I found some of them earlier this year. I wanted to ask you about Mum, but . . .'

'But I would never let you.' He sighs. 'The past was painful, Nettie. For all of us. The truth is, I loved your mother with every piece of my soul, and it ripped my heart out when she left.'

I don't know whether he's talking about when Mum cut all ties to her former life, or when she died. Maybe both. Seeing his eyes glass over makes mine well up, my own grief reflected in his.

'I'm sorry,' he says.

'It's OK,' I say. 'I get it.'

'Let's do a thing over the summer,' he says. 'Bring Fletch, come over – I'll cook – and I'll dig out all my old pictures of your mum and tell you everything I can remember. We'll have a ball. What do you say?'

'Thanks, Michael,' I say, smiling. 'That would be lovely.'

I hug him and leave the studio. As I work my way across the crowded foyer, I spy Alec and Leon laughing in a corner. I wave at them and go through to the office, where Miss Paige is handing Fletch his contract with a smile (no, really). She pats him fondly on the shoulder and makes a big show of taking some files next door, but really I think it's because she's trying not to let us see her being emotional.

'It's real,' says Fletch, staring at the document in awe. 'I really get to do this.'

I squeeze him around the waist. 'You're amazing.'

'Hey,' he says, 'I can definitely ask David Hirst about your mum now. I guess I'll be spending a lot of time with him.'

'Yeah, maybe don't do that,' I say.

He looks at me, surprised.

'There's the *tiniest* possibility that he might be my dad.'

'*Oh*,' he says. 'Yes, I see how that could complicate things.' He grins and kisses me softly.

Kiki bounds into the office. 'Ew, stop snogging.'

I laugh. How is it possible that a few weeks ago, everything was just awful, and now I feel so light and happy? My relationship is better than ever, Alec and Leon are friends again, and not only has Kiki developed a new, unshakable self-love, but her dancewear line has launched and gone from strength to strength.

'Nettie, Anand just called me,' she says. 'They've started proceedings against Sam. And Anand's been promoted!'

'That's brilliant news! I'm so pleased for him.'

Kiki grins. 'We'll tear this business down, one TV producer at a time,' she says. 'Hey, guess what? Dan Coombes messaged me. He's choreographing the new series of *Search for a Star* this summer and wants me to be one of his dancers!'

'Omigod, Kiki! That's amazing!' I squeal, grabbing her arms. We jump up and down together like kids at a birthday party. 'You got a job!'

'That's brilliant news, Kiki,' says Fletch.

'I know – I'm so happy,' she says. 'He said he'd been really impressed with my work in class over the last few weeks. They're filming at ITV, so I'll be in the West End a lot. Leon and I are going to keep the flat over the summer.'

'That means I get to see more of you,' I say. 'Even better.'

Alec and Leon appear.

'Kiki, I've booked dinner at Sophie's later to celebrate,' says Leon.

'Amazing,' she says. 'Hey, it's on me.'

Luca pops his head around the door. 'Hey – some of the third-year musos are playing in Studio Three. Full-on big band. I'm on trumpet. Everyone's in there. It's a thing. Are you coming, or what?'

'I'm all over this,' says Fletch.

'Wait – for dancing?' I say.

Fletch grins. 'Of course. The question is, are you ready for my moves?'

Kiki looks at him curiously and says with a smile, 'I don't think I've ever seen you on the dance floor. Sure you're up to it?'

'Always,' he says. He holds up his injured hand. 'I can't join them playing, so I might as well throw some shapes. Anyway,' he adds, linking arms with both of us, 'if I've learned one thing this year, it's that life's too short not to dance.'

ABOUT THE AUTHOR

Vanessa Jones was born and raised in Kent. After training at Laine Theatre Arts, she went on to be a Musical Theatre actor in West End shows, including *Sister Act*, *Grease*, *Guys and Dolls*, *Annie Get Your Gun* and *Mary Poppins*, where she met (and married!) a fellow chimney sweep. She now lives in East Sussex with her sweep and their two children. *SING Like No One's Listening* was her first YA novel.

ACKNOWLEDGEMENTS

Firstly, to my husband Howard: thank you for supporting me, for being my cheerleader, for scraping me off the floor at midnight when I was exhausted, for home schooling the children when I was on a deadline, for making me laugh and for the love and kindness you show me every day, which I am so grateful for.

To the brilliant people at Macmillan Children's: thank you so much for continuing to champion Nettie's story. I'm so happy I got to carry on her adventure with you.

To Rachel Vale: for creating not one, but two tremendous covers – they bring the excitement of the theatre world to life in vivid, glorious colour. I couldn't love them more!

To Amber Ivatt and Cheyney Smith: thank you for letting the world know about this book in ever-creative, fun and innovative ways – it's been brilliant to work with such a lovely team and I'm very grateful for everything you do.

To Sue Mason and Tracey Ridgewell: thank you for setting the book. To Gift Ajimokun: thank you for your insight and help. To Vron Lyons: the *hugest* thanks for sorting out the book's timeline (which was a complete mess), for gently reminding me that people can't be in two places at once and for standing firm that it takes more than two minutes to travel anywhere in London.

Thank you to the wonderful George Lester who was there for the start of this book's journey – I am so happy we got to work together again, even if it was just for a little bit!

Huge love and thanks to my writing group: Eleanor Prescott, Emilie Di Mario, Hannah Drennan, Kate Potter, Clair Goble and Karl Lawrence Myers. Our Zoom sessions have kept me going, and your cheerful help and suggestions have been so important to Nettie's journey. To Karl, thank you for regularly talking through the themes of the book with me, for helping me out of plot tight spots, for your infinite patience and sense of humour and generosity.

To Jane Willis, my brilliant agent: thank you for your support and advice, for always having my back and for helping me to grow as a writer. I am so excited for our new adventures together.

Thank you to my fantastic students in the Company for answering *the* most random questions (as ever) and to Class W, for their excellent ideas and help with one particular character's backstory. To the whole of my theatre school, thank you for inspiring me every day. I am so proud of you all.

To Lucy Dawson, thank you for always knowing what to do. To Annabelle Mannix, huge thanks for your calm and practical advice. To Stephen Mear, thank you for helping me find the right showbiz person to ask!

And finally, to my editor, Simran Kaur Sandhu. This book would not be the book it is without your skill, your talent and your many clever and insightful ideas. You helped me see the way through everything and find the *real* story at the heart of it. You helped me work out what I could lose (there was a *lot*, right?). It's not an exaggeration to say that I am in awe of you. Not only are you brilliant, Sim, but working with you has been so much fun. Thank you.

AUTHOR'S NOTE

If you've been affected by any of the issues raised in this book, you can find help at any of the below organisations. Please know that there is help out there: you're not alone.

Beat

Beat is a registered charity in England and Wales. It helps people with eating disorders. Their confidential helpline encourages and empowers people to get help quickly. They also have a video based, free peer support group. More information on this can be found at www.beateatingdisorders.org.uk

Help for young people

The Beat Youthline is open to anyone under 18.
Youthline: 0808 801 0711
Email: fyp@beateatingdisorders.org.uk

Help for adults

The Beat Adult Helpline is open to anyone over 18. Parents, teachers or any concerned adults should call the adult helpline.
Helpline: 0808 801 0677
Email: help@beateatingdisorders.org.uk

Childline

Childline is a charity for children and young people with many resources on topics including bullying, abuse, safety and the law; you and your body; friends, relationships and sex; home and families; and school, college and work.

It's also a free, private and confidential service where you can talk about anything. You can contact them by phone any time of day. Calls are free and do not show up on the phone bill. You can also contact Childline via online chat, SignVideo or email.

Call free on 0800 1111

Text the word 'SHOUT' to 85258 to start a conversation with a trained Shout Volunteer, who will text you back and forth, sharing only what you feel comfortable with.

Find details on how to email Childline and access their free resources at www.childline.org.uk

The Mix

The Mix is a charity providing essential support to under 25s. Along with many free resources about issues affecting young people, they offer a private, confidential helpline if you need support.

Call free on 0808 808 4994

For online chat go to www.themix.org.uk and follow the links

Text THEMIX to 85258

Grief Encounter

Grief Encounter's mission is to give every child and young person access to the best possible support following the death of someone close.

They work closely with individuals, families, schools and professionals to offer a way through the anxiety, fear and isolation so often caused by grief.

Call free grieftalk helpline open Mon-Fri, 9am-9pm: 0808 802 0111
Live chat: grieftalk@griefencounter.org.uk